ASTEROIDS
Bridge to Nowhere

Mike McCoy

ISBN: 978-1-7336307-2-6

Ingram Spark Paperback Version

Second Edition
Published by Blaster Tech in the United States of America

First published April 2019 with the subtitle; Escape from the Arcadians
Second edition published September 2019 with subtitle; Bridge to Nowhere
Minor edits and typos fixed January 2022.

Blaster Tech
Cerritos, CA. 90703

Cover Art by Lance Buckley

Acknowledgements

I'd like to thank Trinity Mak, who, at thirteen years of age, read an early half written draft of *Asteroids*. When asked if she liked it, she simply said, "Yes." She didn't offer much feedback, but her excitement at reading new pages encouraged me to keep writing. I kept feeding her pages, and she kept reading until the story was complete.

I did my best to include real science and research in ASTEROIDS. I was able to do this with the help of several experts.

A special thanks to Dr. Joe Nuth of the Goddard Flight Center who "fixed" the premise of how asteroids could rain down on Earth and gave ASTEROIDS a plausible cause.

I read all 166 pages of "An innovative Solution to NASA's NEO Impact Threat Mitigation Grand Challenge and Flight Validation Mission Architecture Development." Dr. Bong Wie of Iowa State University's Asteroid Deflection Research Center helped with the Hypervelocity Asteroid Intercept Vehicle, which I named Harpoon.

Jim W6LG taught me a few things about ham radio and using CW. Check Jim's YouTube channel at YouTube/JimW6LG. I'd also like to thank Purdue University for making their "Impact Earth" tool available to the public. This allowed me to create accurate impact craters and descriptions of meteor explosions.

I'd like to thank my editors, Jim Spivey, and Lori Criswell-Baer. Jim was as much an English teacher as an editor and helped me focus on the story. Lori's edits helped say things I meant, but couldn't find the right words.

I also thank my early readers, Jim Criswell and his eagle eyes that caught my typos, Rachelle Braiker, Alfred Bantug, Gregg Johnson, and others who provided motivation, essential feedback and suggestions that made *Asteroids* a better story.

Contents

Everything works great... until it doesn't.

~~~

Jim Criswell

Prologue

Space. Our solar system. The sun that wakes us each morning
and eight planets locked in orbit around that glowing orb. All
spinning and moving together for billions of years through space.
Pluto, Haumea, Sedna and one trillion other objects large and small,
composed of rock, metal, and ice orbit in the Kuiper belt, rotating in
the same direction as the eight planets all moving together through
space.

The heliosphere is a tear-shaped bubble of solar wind that
envelopes the total mass of our inner and outer solar system as it
moves through space. This bubble of planets, moons, comets, and
asteroids travels at the speed of five hundred thousand miles per
hour in an orbit around our Milky Way galaxy. A single transit
taking over two hundred million years.

This orchestrated masterpiece of objects has moved and rotated
in observable, predictable patterns for untold millennia, until one
day when a young scientist saw something he didn't quite
understand. He observed something unpredictable. He checked
again and as he adjusted his glasses; he spotted an old newspaper
article lying on his desk:

**Scientists have claimed that a giant meteorite that exploded
in the Earth's atmosphere may have triggered the extinction of
ice age animals such as woolly mammoths.**

Researchers found evidence that a large meteorite broke apart in
the atmosphere around 12,800 years ago; around the time when
mammoths died out. By studying deposits at eighteen archaeological
sites around the world, these researchers found tiny spheres of
carbon they say are characteristic of multiple impacts and midair
explosions from meteorite fragments. They concluded the spheres
were formed by the melting of sediment at temperatures of over
2,200 degrees Celsius, caused by the heat and shock waves created
by an "extraterrestrial object" passing through the atmosphere.
Their study, which is published in the journal Proceedings of the
National Academy of Sciences, estimates that ten million tons of
these "spherules" were thrown over an area of more than nineteen
million square miles by meteorite fragmentation.

Besides large animals dying out around the time of the impact, scientists also claim that there is evidence for major human cultural changes. Professor Kenneth Tankersley, an anthropologist and geologist at the University of Cincinnati, who took part in the study, said the changes appeared to have happened "within a lifetime."

"This likely caused climate change and forced this scenario. You can move, downsize, or you can go extinct. Humans at the time were just as resourceful and intelligent as we are today. With mammoth off the dinner table, humans were forced to adapt, which they did to great success. It's a reminder of how fragile we are. Imagine an explosion that happened today that went across four continents.

"The human species would go on. But it would be different. It would be a game changer."

Published in The Telegraph May 21, 2013

The young scientist was well aware that asteroids have impacted Earth many times throughout history, sometimes with catastrophic consequences, but what he observed was not a single asteroid. His jaw clenched. *Panic is not an appropriate response*, he rebuked himself. He adjusted his black-rimmed glasses again and straightened the collar of his white button-down shirt. He must verify his observation. If confirmed, he had bad news for planet Earth. Who could he tell? How does one prepare for the end of the world?

Part One–The Bliss Protocol

Chapter 1: Frog Giggin'

Near Future: Briarcliffe Acres—Myrtle Beach, South Carolina USA

Early Sunday Morning

Sander lies in his bed, listening in the dark. Silence. His parents are asleep. He looks to his younger brother's bed across the room. Heavy breathing. *Good, the little brat's asleep.* Sander checks the time: 1:00 a.m. He needs to get moving. His best friend, Brody, will be down the street.

Sander slides out of bed and pulls on the clothes he'd tossed to the floor earlier. The boy's bedroom features a window at a height of five feet. Sander had removed the window screen a few months earlier and hid it behind the bushes in the backyard.

Sander also moved his old toy box to rest beneath the window, creating a perfect step. Now the window is waist height; easy for him to get out. It's a six-foot jump from the window to the grass, a perfect way to sneak out of the house.

He's snuck out many weekend nights to meet up with Brody and other friends to hang out or go frog giggin' in the South Carolina wetlands. After slipping on his shoes, he steps up on the wooden toy box and slides the window open.

"Where are you going?" The voice of his younger brother, Colton, breaks the night's silence. The sound startles Sander. He's snuck out and back many times without waking Colton.

"Shush. You'll wake up Mom and Dad," Sander says in a hushed tone.

"Going out on a date with your boyfriend, Brody?" asks Colton.

Sander responds to Colton's comment by stepping from the toy box to his brother's bed, then dropping to his knees, straddling his brother's body. He lowers his fist to the center of Colton's chest. "One punch, brat. One hard punch, right here, and your heart will stop beating. You'll be dead. Good riddance!" Sander presses his knuckled fist hard into Colton's chest, knowing it's painful.

Colton thrusts his hips, attempting to buck his brother off, causing the headboard of the bed to knock against the wall with a loud *thunk*. Both boys freeze. They listen for parents awakened by the noise. Colton whispers, "Let me go with you."

Sander grinds his fist into Colton's chest once more for good measure, before rising and stepping back to the toy box. "Find your own friends, wimp. We don't want you tagging along," argues Sander.

"I won't bother you guys. Come on. Dad said I should get out of the house more," Colton pleads.

"Yeah, he said you should make your own friends, not hang out with mine," Sander replies, as he slides the window open wide enough to scramble through.

"I'll tell Mom you've been sneaking out."

"You tell Mom and I'll kill you, you friggin' little brat. God, why couldn't I have been an only child?"

"Let me go with you and I won't tell."

"All right. Shit! Don't make any noise and stay away from me."

Colton throws back his blankets to reveal he's dressed and ready for adventure. The boys then crawl out the window and jump to the grass.

Sanders' friend Brody waits down the street. Brody is a fifteen-year-old boy, tall and thin, with unruly dark hair and a face full of acne.

Brody spots the boys approaching. "Hey, Sander. I almost gave up on ya. What? You brought the little Colt? I thought he's afraid of the dark."

"He begged me to bring him along."

"Hey, Colt. Better watch out, the swamp monster might get you!"

"Yeah, let's feed him to the swamp monster, or dump him into the pond and frog gig him," exclaims Sander as the three boys walk along the street, heading toward the wetlands of scattered ponds and tall grass.

"Ah, knock it off, guys," Colton replies. "I'm not afraid. In the wetlands, it's the coyotes you need to worry about. Didn't you hear on the news? They found two teenagers in the wetlands last week. Their bodies all chewed up by coyotes. It was a bloody mess."

"Coyotes! We've never seen coyotes out here, have we, Sander?" Brody asks.

"Nah, Colton's making it up. I don't think we have coyotes on the Carolina coast," Sander says.

The boys walk along a dirt trail that winds through tall grass leading into the wetlands. "If you listen, you might hear a coyote howl in the distance," Colton whispers in his creepiest voice.

"Shut up, Colton! You won't scare us," Sander says, as he picks up his pace to walk abreast of Brody. Colton walks behind the older boys, then pulls his shirt over his mouth and lets out a soft howl, trying to make it sound like the howl is coming from a distance.

"Colton, knock it off. I know that was you. I should have tied you to your bed and gagged you, so you can't squeal to Mom." Then Sander hears another howl. He's startled and stops for a moment to listen.

Brody tries to keep his composure, but when Sander looks at him, he can't contain himself and breaks into a giggle. Colton howls again. Sander smiles, then makes a loud exaggerated howl. The boys walk through the wetlands howling in the night.

After several howls, the boys walk through the thicket of trees that ring their favorite frog gigging pond where the sound of croaking frogs replaces the sound of howling boys. Brody goes to a nearby tree to retrieve the frog gigging sticks he and Sander had prepared earlier. They'd cut long thin branches, stripped them of leaves, and sharpened one end to make six-foot-long spears. Brody hands a spear to Sander. "We only have two spears, so you have to watch our deadly attacks," Sander says to Colton as he holds his spear like a warrior.

Colton doesn't look disappointed.

"Don't worry. If I get tired, I'll let you use my spear," says Brody.

Sander walks through the tall grass to the edge of the pond, holding his spear at the ready. He listens and looks for nearby frogs, then jabs his spear into the weeds at the pond's edge, making a sound. "Hi-ya!" He extracts the spear from the weeds. No frog.

Brody tiptoes along the edge of the pond, looking for a good spot to mount his attack. He steps closer to the edge. Water seeps into his shoes. He sees a frog, raises his spear, and thrusts. The frog

6

jumps just in time to miss certain skewering. "Damn it! I missed," cries Brody. Sander and Brody search for their next quarry.

Colton quickly loses interest in the frog-spearing expedition. He studies the sky. It's a clear moonless night, allowing the stars to shine brighter. He can make out some constellations he learned about at scout camp. As he gazes at the stars, a bright light appears in the eastern sky over the Atlantic. Growing bigger and brighter, the light moves fast toward the shore, heading directly over wetlands.

"Hey guys, look at the sky," Colton yells. "It's a shooting star."

Brody and Sander look up, spears in hand. The object becomes blindingly bright before it explodes in the sky. The boys cover their eyes, shielding them from the sudden brightness. They see the explosion first. The sound comes later.

Brody jumps and hollers, "Wow, did you see that? It blew up!"

"Dang, that was awesome! Maybe it's an alien spaceship crashing to Earth," exclaims Sander.

Seconds after the explosion, a strange *sphit, sphit, sphit* sound races past the boys, sending ripples across the calm pond, tearing leaves off trees, and causing some branches to fall. The boys stand quiet and still. A dog barks in the distance.

Twenty seconds after the explosion, a tremendous hot wind knocks the boys over. The wind passes and all is calm. Sander attempts to stand. He gets up on one knee.

Colton, laying in the mud, looks to his brother and sees several blood spots staining Sander's shirt. "You're bleeding."

Sander looks at his shirt and notices the blood spots. "I don't feel anything." Sander looks at Colton. Colton has several spots of blood on his shirt, and they're growing larger.

"You're the one bleeding, don't blame me." Sander looks over to Brody, who's lying in the mud. He isn't moving.

Colton struggles to move. He tries to get out of the muddy patch he fell in, but he can't move his body. He whimpers, "I'm telling Mom." Those are Colton's last words. He lies quiet and still at the muddy edge of the pond. The blood spots on his shirt swell, growing into one big blood stain.

Sander feels warm blood run over his night-chilled skin. The blood is his. He tries again to stand. With great effort, he gets to his feet and stumbles over to Brody. In the dim light, he can see Brody's face. There's a black hole where his friend's nose was. Brody is dead.

Sander turns and takes a few steps up the trail, then slumps to his knees before toppling over onto his side. He lies on the muddy trail breathing in halting gasps. He doesn't move or cry out. Sander's eyes are open. He observes the wetland grass and watches a small bug climb up a stalk. "Damn, I left the bedroom window open." He exhales. Sander is dead.

CTBTO Monitoring Station

The Comprehensive Nuclear-Test-Ban Treaty Organization (CTBTO) has a network of forty-five infrasound stations designed to track atomic blasts across the planet. The strange thing is, beginning in the year 2000, they intercepted strange sounds that were not atmospheric atomic blasts. Through the year 2030, the infrasound system had catalogued one hundred eighty-six major explosions on Earth. A-bombs didn't cause any of the explosions. They were all the result of asteroid strikes.

The CTBTO dug into the reports. The asteroid events ranged in energy from one to six hundred kilotons. By comparison, the bomb that destroyed the Japanese city of Hiroshima was a fifteen-kiloton device. Fortunately, most of these space rocks disintegrated high in the atmosphere and caused few problems on the ground. Some events people will have heard about, such as the twenty-meter-wide object that ripped across the sky above the Russian city of Chelyabinsk in 2013 or the forty-meter-wide asteroid that lit up the skies over Buffalo, New York on a winter day in 2024. But many of the asteroid strikes on Earth went unseen and unreported because they occurred over oceans.

The CTBTO has monitored atmospheric asteroid impacts since 2013. What they don't know is another government agency is also monitoring the feed. And that agency does more than listen.

Early Sunday morning, the CTBTO detected an atmospheric asteroid explosion over the South Carolina wetlands.

A remote monitoring station managed by an obscure government agency also detects the explosion. Because the impact is over a populated region, a surveillance satellite outfitted with cameras and infrared imaging scans the impact area to determine if there is any damage.

A young woman sits in a dark room. Her young face glows from the light of several screens arrayed before her as she views the satellite footage in real time. She wears a blue tunic, and she wears her long hair pulled back. She is professional and stoic as she surveys the impact site. Three heat signatures appear on a screen. She presses an icon and reports. "We have three down at North thirty-three degrees, forty-seven minutes, eleven point three nine seconds by West seventy-eight degrees, forty-four minutes, fifty-nine seconds."

There is silence for a moment, then a monotone voice replies, "Confirmed. Dispatching."

Before Daylight–Wetlands near Myrtle Beach, SC

Fog lingers lazily over the silent wetland pond. A team of four men dressed in flat-gray, digitally generated camouflaged suits work efficiently and nearly invisibly in the predawn light.

The four men do not work to eradicate the scene. The dead are dead. No one can change that, but they can control the perception of the cause of death. Brody's body is already stiffening. Rigor mortis is setting in. All the easier to stand him up. One-man squats down and struggles to keep Brody standing while another man positions a shotgun in the dead boy's hands, pointing the barrel at his face.

The team's leader, a tall, muscular man with a bald head, receives a call on his VUE lens. He views a stout, Caucasian man wearing a white business shirt and thick, black-framed glasses. The chubby man speaks. "Kobalt, is the site under control?"

The team leader, dressed in the same gray camouflage as his team, wears no markings to indicate rank or military affiliation, yet his physique and the way he moves conveys that he is military or ex-military. He speaks, with a deep raspy tone. "We're almost finished."

The shotgun blasts. A mist composed of pulverized blood, brain and bone fills the air. The kneeling man holding Brody allows the teenage body to jolt backward. Brody's body falls stiffly in the grassy mud. The frogs are silent, watching.

The white man displayed in the VUE lens speaks. "The gun shots will be reported to the police. Local news will report an accidental shooting followed by suicide. A late-night teenage adventure gone wrong. Another episode of an illegal gun used by juveniles."

Kobalt nods. With hand gestures, he directs his men to sweep the ground to cover their footprints. He looks in his VUE lens to continue his report. "Understood, sir. That's what local law enforcement will find when they arrive to investigate the scene."

The white man with the black frame glasses gives an approving nod. "Tragic for the families. What happened is out of our control. We can only control the perception."

Kobalt and his team move through the grass of the wetlands, sweeping the trail of their boot prints while leaving the imprints of the boys' shoes, leading the way for investigators to discover the gory scene.

Kobalt speaks softly but with a force picked up through the microphone of his VUE lens. "We can't keep this up. My team is exhausted. The frequency of the events is increasing. We've been chasing these things around the globe. How long do you think can we keep going like this?"

The man in the VUE replies, "Kobalt, the time is near. We have controlled the news and information to keep the masses peaceful. We have worked ceaselessly to keep them unaware of what's coming, and we have been supremely successful. Even the highest levels of government around the world are oblivious to what's about to happen. It's almost time. Once you have secured the scene, bring your men and join us in the city."

After the sun rose on the wetlands that morning, police investigators and the coroner came to the desired conclusion. There is no news about the threat of asteroids impacting Earth killing teenage boys.

Later that morning, the portly man dressed in the white button-down shirt and black rim glasses watches a video stream from the Myrtle Beach news. He watches a young female reporter recount the story:

A sonic boom woke residents of Myrtle Beach early this morning. There are reports of shattered nerves and broken windows, but no injuries. Authorities attribute the event to supersonic aircraft flying out of nearby Shaw Air Force Base. The Air Force has not responded to inquiries. In other news, local police report that three boys were found dead this morning. Authorities believe the boys were playing with an old, outlawed shotgun they found in the wetlands. Police are calling this a terrible accident. They believe one boy fired a shot, striking his two friends. The boy with the gun then took his own life. It's a sad day for our community. We send our condolences to the boys' families.

The report moves on to an interview with the chief of police, who warns citizens not to pick up or use illegal firearms.

The news is controlled.

Control. This is the objective of the man who observes. He watches the screens displayed in his VUE, satisfied with the outcome of this event.

Chapter 2: Class Dismissed

Monday Afternoon

Assistant Professor Rick Munday checks his e-mail for the fourth time since lunch. The National Science Foundation will announce grant funding awards this week. Six months earlier, Rick had submitted a grant proposal entitled *Disturbance Beyond the Kuiper Belt: Potential Risks to Planet Earth*. Rick hopes for news of his grant approval.

His office is a jumbled mess. Stacks of books and science journals clutter the floor. Rick has plastered the walls with drawings of planets, charts, and a map of the pockmarked dark side of the moon. A diagram of the solar system covers one wall. It's marked with notes in various colors. The diagram displays the solar system with the asteroid belt hovering between the orbits of Mars and Jupiter. He has scribbled notes along the edges of the map marking the Kuiper belt, an area that lies beyond the acknowledged eight planets of our solar system.

In recent years, funds for space science have all but dried up. Although the government has slashed budgets, there's still funding out there for the odd project or study that gains attention of the right people. Rick hopes his proposal will get the attention it deserves.

His office door, blocked by a stack of science journals, opens just enough to allow the head of a thin, scraggly bearded teaching assistant to poke through. "Professor Heinrich won't be in today. He wants you to take the three-p.m. lecture."

"OK," says Munday, still looking at his computer screen as if he expects news of his grant to appear.

"The professor said stick with the syllabus and the assigned subject matter, or you will never give a lecture at this institution again! His words, not mine. I like your lectures. Fascinating shit." The door closes.

"Oh yeah, thanks," Munday says to the closed office door.

Rick touches his Smart-Band to call his wife. "Hey, hon, the three-p.m. lecture just got dumped on me. I'll be home later than expected."

"Doesn't that professor ever teach a class?" asks his wife, Courtney.

"He must be at some luncheon cozying up to alumni donors. I don't mind, the department needs funding, and the lectures give me a chance to hash out my theories. It's different when you hear yourself say things out loud," says Rick.

"You'll still make it to the picnic dinner, won't you?" asks Courtney.

"Wouldn't miss it."

"Uncle Rob called. He's coming with us."

"Great. He needs to get out of that old house more often. I feel bad. I haven't visited him for months."

Rick Munday loves his wife and family. It's the type of love rarely seen between a husband and wife. He focuses on his family, doing his best to make it to every dinner, soccer practice and baseball game. While he's succeeded in family life, his career has suffered.

Assistant Professor of Astrophysics, Dr. Rick Munday struggles to get papers published and grants funded. Without grants, Rick lives on a meager assistant professor's salary. Grant approval would mean more money for himself and the funds to hire a team of astrophysicists to conduct research and publish the results, which leads to additional funding. Providing for his family has been a challenge.

Rick checks his Smart-Band: 2:30 p.m. He'd better get going or he'll be late for the lecture. If he's late, Dr. Heinrich will be mad. Rick checks the department's cloud server and locates the lecture presentation and notes. He puts a copy in his personal folder. Seconds later, his band beeps, acknowledging the file transfer.

The lecture notes and slides for *The Evolving Universe*, a class designed for freshmen students covering basic astronomy. They are the same notes and slides Dr. Heinrich has used for the past decade, with few changes even though science has advanced. It's one of the many things that frustrates Rick about working for Dr. Heinrich.

Rick pulls his computer monitor out of its cradle, rolls up the flexible monitor, and pushes it into a fabric tube on the side of his backpack. He pulls the office door open enough to slide out and walks to the auditorium.

A second monitor in Rick's office runs a screen saver displaying the old arcade game, Asteroids. A black screen fills with odd-shaped blocks representing asteroids floating around the screen. The asteroids crash into one another, breaking into smaller rocks. A small triangular spaceship appears on the screen beeping, shooting, and blowing up asteroids, making space for the little spaceship to survive.

The TV volume is loud, competing with the noise of the construction project in the kitchen. The reality series, *Doomsday Daredevils,* is playing. This episode features a man in Nebraska building a personal submarine because he is sure God told him to do so. The host of the show asks the Nebraska fellow why God told him to build a submarine, and the man says he doesn't know. He's just supposed to do it. The interviewer asks, "Did God say it's because of climate change? Does he expect melting polar ice caps to raise sea levels enough to put the state of Nebraska in the middle of a new ocean?" The man says God doesn't need to give a reason. The man continues to work on his oddly shaped submarine.

"Crackpot," an old man yells at the TV, waving a power drill in the air. "Everyone knows the Arctic ice cap is floating on the ocean, so if it melts, big deal. Did your glass of Coke overflow when the ice melted? They'll put any idiot on TV these days." The old man grabs a wrench and tightens a bolt.

He barely hears the phone ring over the sound of the TV. The phone doesn't ring much unless it's a political party calling under the premise of a survey but is soliciting donations, telemarketers selling home fuel cell generators or, on a rare occasion, a call from his nephew, Rick.

The old man picks up the phone. "I don't vote. I don't donate money, and I already have a fuel cell generator. So, you better state your case pronto or I'll hang up faster than you can say, there's life on Mars."

"There's life on Mars. Beat you," says the voice on the other side of the call.

"Ricky-boy, is that you?"

"Yes, it's me Uncle Rob. Turn down the TV. I only have time for a quick call."

"Oh, hold on." Uncle Rob reaches for the remote to mute the TV. The doomsday show is now featuring a man building a Gatling gun. "Idiot!"

"What?" asks Rick.

"Not you, Ricky-boy. The other idiot on the TV."

"Courtney said you'll join us for the picnic dinner."

"She said you're going to Mount Wilson. I haven't been up there in years."

"I'm glad you're coming. I've loved it up there, ever since you first took me."

"There's a new meteor shower. It's supposed to be a good one. Looks like it will be a clear night for viewing the skies." Uncle Rob puts down the wrench, pausing for a moment. "And hey, Ricky-boy, there's something I'd like to discuss with you about the—" Rick cuts him off.

"Sure, OK. We'll be at your place early this evening. I'm about to give a lecture. See you in a few hours."

"Oh, giving a lecture, are you? When I taught at the community college, I didn't cut those kids any slack just because it was a community college."

"Uncle Rob, Sorry. I've got to go."

Uncle Rob starts a familiar rant, not realizing the call has already ended. "It's not my fault the establishment at those institutions wouldn't accept my new ideas. Rick? Ricky-boy? You there? Uh, must have lost the signal." Rob says as he shakes the phone, then the TV once again captures his attention.

The doomsday builder with the Gatling gun is test firing. His targets are four mannequins in a various state of undress, propped against a four-by-eight-foot slab of plywood. The Gatling gun rips the dummies apart; arms and legs flying in the air, cutting the plywood in half with a torrent of bullets. Uncle Rob picks up his wrench and shakes it at the TV. "Idiot."

Rob is a tall, grumpy, potbellied seventy-year-old who wears thick glasses and has a healthy shock of unkempt white hair, giving him the look of a mad scientist. In a way, he is a mad scientist. He's been mad for forty years. Mad because, as a young researcher at

Penn State, a younger misunderstood Robert Munday was shunned for pushing new ideas in astrophysics. His department head had refused to publish his research.

Rob had criticized the institution. They had implied that one succeeds only if you promote the ideas ascribed by the scientific establishment. If you don't agree to take their line of thought, you get pushed out. In the academic world, if you don't have support from your department head and you don't publish, you perish.

Rob had fought the system for a few years, but the realities of life and the need to make a living won out. He soon found himself teaching astronomy and physics at Pasadena City College.

Rick stands behind a podium on a stage at the front of the auditorium. Many freshmen classes meet in large auditoriums, where hundreds of students at a time are indoctrinated into the collegiate mindset.

Rick brings his band close to his mouth and speaks, "Cloud, broadcast, The Evolving Universe, lecture three." The projector then beams a presentation entitled *The Evolving Universe (Ay 1), Lecture Three*, on the screen behind Rick. Students stream in, filling the seats.

There's a type of brainwashing conducted in the halls of higher learning; professors tell students they will have better opportunities and will benefit from the knowledge imparted to them; they are the elite of society. It happens even in classes as mundane as, *The Evolving Universe*. Heinrich has scripts, such as these, written into the lecture notes that Rick reviews on the presenter's screen built into the podium. "What bullshit," he says to himself as he scrolls through the slides.

Students are entering the lecture hall. Four young female students and one male student take seats in the front row.

Three o'clock. Rick steps in front of the podium. Although in his mid-thirties, Rick is still handsome. He is tall and fit with a runner's build and a healthy head of dirty blond hair. Rick looks out at the auditorium. Two of the young women in the front row smile at him. Another tilts her head, looking up at Rick, running her hand through her hair. The male student grins, staring up at Rick adoringly. He starts the lecture even though students are still finding their seats.

"I'm Assistant Professor Munday. Today is lecture three. I hope to impart to you the knowledge and wisdom learned over the millennia by men who invested their lives studying the great beyond. Through study of our solar system, our galaxy, and the universe, we hope to learn how and why we exist. Because you are attending this university, you have the privilege of learning what others never will. Your career may not end up being in astronomy or astrophysics, like mine, but you will gain knowledge most people will never be exposed to. You will..." Rick pauses, scanning the lecture notes. Half under his breath, he utters, "OK, enough bullshit. Let's get to the lecture." Rick's comment is met with hoots, howls, and whistles from the students.

"Lecture Three," Rick says, as he swipes his hand over the presenter's screen. The projector beams an image of our solar system. "In previous lectures, we learned the solar system comprises the sun, with eight planets in orbit around the sun. You should know the planet's names from your lecture notes. The orbits of the planets are elliptical, like stretched out circles, in a nearly flat disc called the ecliptic plane. However, there are more objects in our solar system than the sun and these eight planets."

Rick swipes his hand to load the next slide. "In this slide, we see the asteroid belt lies in the area or space—ha, ha—between Mars and Jupiter," Rick read.

He almost laughs out loud. The bad jokes, even the "ha, ha" are in the lecture notes. Rick's patience is wearing thin.

Trying his best to be a good assistant professor, Rick continues reading the lecture notes. "Beyond Neptune, there is an area, or disc of asteroids, called the Kuiper Belt. Some of these objects are in strange, unstable orbits and can get bumped out of orbit; thus, the Kuiper Belt is believed to be the source of comets." Rick stops. He looks out at the students. The ones who aren't reading on their VUEs or sleeping look bored.

Rick claps his hands. No reaction from the students. Rick hates seeing bored students. How can they learn anything if they're bored or sleeping?

Rick jumps ahead in the lecture, swiping to a new slide in the presentation. It displays an animation of the solar system in motion on the large screen behind him.

"Hey, class! Hey, wake up... Look up here!" Many students shift in their seats. "Watch the animation behind me. Does this look correct? Hold up your hand if you believe this is how our solar system is moving in space," Rick says, putting additional emphasis on the word *space*.

A few hands shoot up. Slowly, hands rise. One young lady lifts her hand only halfway up. Maybe she's hoping to be only half wrong.

"All right, most of you believe what we are seeing is correct. What else should I expect? This is what they taught you to believe. You can put your hands down. And young lady—yes, you on the right—you can put it all the way down. I will give fifty extra credit points to anyone who can tell me what's wrong with this animation."

Rick pauses, looking out at the students. He shades his eyes from the stage lights, so he can see the dark upper rows of the auditorium. "No one? No brave soul? Nobody with an original thought?" He waits a moment longer, but none of the students move. "It's not a trick. You won't lose fifty points if your answer is wrong. Anyone?" No hands are raised, not even halfway.

Rick lifts his band to a few inches from his mouth. The band's display illuminates. Rick speaks. "Cloud, broadcast heliocentric model." The projector beams a new animation that shows the solar system not sitting still in space with the planets rotating around the sun, but the sun and planets, the entire solar system, moving through space with the planets rotating in their imperfect orbits around and behind the sun, with the heliosphere at the leading edge looking like a force field for the solar system as it moves through space.

"Wow! Whoa, cool!" The student's express excitement.

Rick's energy soars. It's always more interesting to teach when students are engaged or at least awake. Now, he has their attention. Maybe he can teach them something. Screw the lecture notes.

"The solar system is not just a bundle of spinning planets sitting at some stationary place in the Milky Way galaxy. No, not at all. Our solar system is moving through space at a speed of four hundred eighty-six thousand miles per hour, traveling in an orbit around the center of the Milky Way galaxy, our home galaxy. Even though we are ripping through space at almost five hundred thousand miles per hour, it takes our solar system over two hundred thirty million years to complete a galactic orbit. The last time the sun was at this exact spot in its galactic orbit, dinosaurs ruled the Earth. I don't want to scare any of you, but for that same fifty extra credit points, does anyone know what wiped out the dinosaurs?"

"Hands? Any hands? Come on." Rick tries to encourage participation. The young lady who lifted her hand halfway up earlier fully extends her arm. "Yes, young lady on my right," Rick points into the auditorium.

The young student shouts, "A huge asteroid hit Earth. Dust clouds blocked the sun, and the dinosaurs died off. They became extinct."

"Ding, ding, ding. Fifty bonus points for the young lady in the fourth row. Excellent, yes, that is the prevailing theory. I believe it could have been more than one huge asteroid. It might have been several."

The animation continues playing on the large screen showing the solar system on its path around the center of the Milky Way.

"Unfortunately, your text-books are based on science twenty to thirty years old. Things have been tough for the advancement of science because of the wars and budget cuts. The government has shut down most of the space observatories for lack of funds. However, just a few years ago, we had access to amazing telescopes and space probes. We have discovered many things about our universe that haven't made it into your textbooks. But I guess I'd better get back to the lecture as written or you'll all flunk the test!" A young man in the second row raises his hand. "Question from the front. Shoot."

"If our solar system is in the same area when the dinosaurs went extinct, couldn't the same thing happen to us?" asks the student.

Rick raises his arm to shade his eyes so he can see the young. Rick's band illuminates. "That is one of the *worst-case scenarios* that experts have kicked around. But the dinosaurs lived for over 160 million years and existed until 65 million years ago, so we aren't in the bombardment location."

Rick's Smart-Band displays *Worst-Case Scenarios*. The animation on the auditorium's large screen changes without Rick noticing.

"OK, let's get back to the subject, or Dr. Heinrich will cause my extinction." Rick again reads from the lecture notes. "The largest objects in the asteroid belt are Ceres and Vesta." The students are all paying rapt attention. Their eyes are glued to the screen. Rick believes he's making an impact.

The first scenario shows volcanoes erupting all over the planet, in Hawaii, South America, Indonesia, Iceland, and Italy, causing horrific destruction as they blast volcanic ash high into the atmosphere. Then the massive caldera, that is Yellowstone National Park, explodes in a super-eruption hurling millions of pounds of ash into the upper atmosphere, blotting out the sun and causing a volcanic winter. Earth temperatures plunge, killing off most plant, animal, and human life.

The next scenario shows the solar system in its orbit around the galaxy encountering a dense cloud. Hidden in the cloud is an area crowded with asteroids and enormous ice balls. The solar system gets bombarded by asteroids and comets. The planets look like they are in a pinball machine, being hit repeatedly by space rocks. A series of asteroids impact the surface of Mars, causing some boys to shout "Whoa" or "Yes," excited to see Mars' demise. Rocks pummel the Earth and moon with a multitude of bombardments. Asteroids crush the moon to bits and Earth breaks into large fiery chunks, spinning through space.

The final scenario entitled *Likely Someday* displays a not-too-distant yet massive star collapsing into a supernova, sending an intense gamma-ray burst at Earth. Earth roasts as if it were inside a microwave oven. The atmosphere slowly burns away. There is a worldwide drought. Crops fail. Animals die. The screen displays starving children eating handfuls of maggots from the carcass of a dead cow.

Girls in the front row gag. The boy acts like he's about to vomit and runs out of the auditorium and the girls chase after him. Other students take this as an excuse to leave class and move for the exits. Rick turns to look at the screen behind him, as Earth's oceans boil. The video cuts to emaciated animals dying on barren cracked dirt. "Oh shit. Cloud, stop broadcasting," Rick shouts to his band. "Stop, stop, stop!"

He turns to the students leaving the auditorium. "Come back! Nothing will happen!" Then he says to himself, "Well, there is a low probability," then louder, "But not likely!"

Rick tries once more to stop the students. "Class isn't over," he yells, as he packs his things, and the last students leave the auditorium. He mumbles to himself, "This will not go over well with Dr. Heinrich."

The teaching assistant who notified Rick of the lecture walks up to the podium. "Like I said, I love your lectures. So cool." The teaching assistant goes out a side door.

Rick looks out at an empty auditorium. "I'm gonna need that grant."

Chapter 3: Uncle Rob

Rick enters the kitchen of his rented Pasadena bungalow as his wife, Courtney, loads food packets into a picnic cooler. "This looks great. We'll have a feast tonight."

"You're home early. I thought you had the 3:00 p.m. lecture."

"They got out early. I guess you could say I sent them out screaming."

"Well, I hope they were screaming with joy," Courtney says.

"You could say they are happy to be alive."

Courtney holds up a piece of mail. "This came today. The lease is up next month, and the rent is increasing."

"They're raising the rent, again? I'm counting on getting that grant. Don't worry. We'll have extra money coming in, and Dr. Heinrich won't complain about funding."

"We could use some good news for a change."

"Let's put the worries of this meager planet aside. We have a picnic tonight. Don't we have two kids? Where might they be found?"

"Hiding in their rooms. They do that a lot, nowadays," says Courtney.

Rick sallies down the hallway to the kids' rooms, opens their doors, and announces, "Come out, children. I am here to save you! We are about to explore the outdoors, eat food, view space and the worlds beyond. Escape ye from these cells you call rooms. Go forth and see the world!"

Rick checks the rooms of his twelve-year-old twins. They are both using VUE lens. Ethan, his son, is unmoved as he plays a game, while his daughter Alyssa lies on her bed video messaging with friends. She talks as she touches points in midair, interacting with objects in a virtual environment where her friends are meeting. She is oblivious to her father and his antics. "Your outfit is the best, Charnel. It's so cute," Alyssa says.

Rick walks into Alyssa's room. He sneaks up behind her and removes her VUE lens. Alyssa looks up with annoyance at her father. "Hey, I'm with my friends," she says, grabbing for the lens.

"Hello, little girl, it's your father. Look, you might recognize me." Rick says.

Alyssa ignores her father. "I can't wait to see you at the fashion show," Alyssa calls out to the lens, hoping her friends can hear.

"Let's go, Alyssa. We have a family night planned, so move it." Rick walks backward, holding out the VUE lens, encouraging his daughter to follow.

Alyssa grabs the lens and puts it on. "Sorry Charnel, I've got to go. Maybe my dad will drive me to the fashion show. I'd love to see you on the catwalk," she says, then removes the VUE with a sneer before walking out of the room to join her mother in the kitchen.

"One down; one to go," Rick says to himself as he walks into Ethan's room. Ethan stands in the middle of his bedroom, wearing his VUE lens and moving his hands in jabbing motions.

Rick stands at Ethan's side and swipes his hand in an upward motion in front of the lens. The wrap around glass of the VUE changes from black to transparent.

"Hey, Dad, I can't see," Ethan shouts.

"Looks like you can see me just fine." The sound of a gunshot and a thump come through the VUE's audio. "Oops, you're dead! Sorry kiddo, time to go."

"Oh man, you're gonna get my whole platoon killed."

"Looks like you're good at that game," says Rick.

"I'd be better if we had a glide pad. I can't move the way I'm supposed to without one. Christopher and Allie have a glide pad. If we had one, you could use it too, Dad."

Rick pulls the VUE from Ethan's face. "Well, we can't afford that right now. Maybe, if I get my grant approved, we can enhance your game play around Christmas time. But there's more to life than VUE games. We are going to Uncle Rob's and having a picnic dinner up at Mount Wilson. There's a big meteor shower tonight. It's supposed to be brilliant, so let's get moving."

"Meteor shower! Cool. That's only kind of shower I like!" exclaims Ethan. He grabs his Orion StarBlast telescope and follows his dad out of the room.

23

When the AutoCar arrives, Courtney and Alyssa load it with the food cooler and blankets. Rick grabs his—well, the university's—Celestron CGE Pro HD 1600 computerized and motorized telescope. Rick had borrowed the telescope from the department a few months earlier. He figures he'll keep on borrowing it until someone else asks for it.

Rick sits in the driver's seat and touches the start button. His band syncs with the AutoCar. Rick speaks, "Uncle Rob's house." The AutoCar scans Rick's contacts, displays the mapped route, and starts driving.

Rick's parents died in a traffic accident when he was thirteen. After the funeral, Rick went to live with Uncle Rob. Life with Rob was active. He enrolled Rick in an endless list of activities, from swimming and karate to Boy Scouts and flying lessons. It was Rob who inspired and cultivated Rick's passion to study the universe. A passion they share.

Over the years, Rick and Uncle Rob grew close. Other than Courtney and the kids, Rob is Rick's only family. He lives nearby, in Altadena, in the foothills of Eaton Canyon. It isn't a long drive. When Rick sees the old house, he wonders why he hasn't been to visit.

Junk clutters the long driveway. Rick engages the AutoCar's manual steering to navigate the narrow path. A huge fiberglass tank lies on one side of the drive. Farther up the drive is a metal tank with a big hole cut on one side. Rusted pipes cemented in dried mud line the edge of the drive. Next to the house is a tall metal garage with large sliding doors, and next to that is an old cement mixer and bags of cement. Some bags are open, spilling cement powder onto the grass. Alongside the house boxes marked INSULATING FOAM MIX litter the ground.

Rick stops the car at the front of the house, and the kids jump out. Courtney yells, "Be careful and don't touch anything," as she surveys the deteriorating condition of the old house.

Rick and Courtney walk to the front door. "The old place could use some paint," Rick comments.

"Just paint?" Courtney asks. Courtney then spots the kids climbing on a rusted-out machine. "Get away from that... that thing. Come inside the house."

The TV blares with the sound of a news stream: *The Four Wars continue, with Russia and China announcing an agreement to strengthen their alliance, as China advances on Chad and Russia strengthens its hold on New Persia. In the United States, President Anderson announces further cuts to NASA, the FDA, and other non-essential departments, allowing additional funding to support our allies. In other news...*

Rob sits at the kitchen table futzing with an electronic gadget. As Rick enters the house, he calls out, "Rob!"

The kids sprint past Rick and Courtney to greet their great-uncle with hugs. Rob hugs the kids. He looks for the TV remote, finding it under a stack of papers, and points it at the big TV.

"Let me turn this thing down. I didn't hear you come in. I don't watch it. Just like the noise; keeps my brain awake. Ha-ha!" Rob mutes the volume, then gives Courtney a big hug, followed by a hug for Rick.

Rick looks around the room. The living room and kitchen look like a workshop. "Looks like you've been keeping yourself busy. Sorry, we haven't made it over for a while," Rick says as he surveys the unorganized clutter.

"You know me. I love to tinker. I always have this project, or that, going on. It would be better if I finished one before starting the next," Rob says as he walks around the room, moving parts and boxes to make space.

Courtney grabs Rick's arm, pulling him close. "Honey. You know I love Rob. But I think he's gone off the edge with all the junk he's bought for his projects. It was bad enough when he bought that old cave a few years back. Don't you worry about him here, all alone?"

"I know. I should check on him more often. I'll talk with him," Rick says.

Ethan spots a diagram tacked to the kitchen wall. Pointing at the drawing, he asks, "Uncle Rob, is this your cave fort? It looks like a long submarine."

"It's my cave fort, if you want to call it that. I call it Munday's Hideaway, or I hope it will be someday. When, or if, the shit hits the fan, we'll need a safe place to ride out the shit storm, kiddo." The kids giggle at the use of a four-letter word used twice in a single sentence.

Rob catches himself. "Oops, kids in the room, excuse my French. How old are you two now, anyway?" Rob asks.

"We're twelve!" shouts Alyssa.

"Almost twelve and a half," adds Ethan.

"Oh, I bet you learned all those bad words already. Sixth grade camp, right?" asks Uncle Rob.

"Yup," the kids reply in unison.

"But we don't say them out loud," Alyssa whispers to her great-uncle.

"At least not when they're around," Ethan says, motioning toward his parents.

Rick checks the diagram on the wall and discovers it isn't a single drawing, but several pages of blueprints and schematics detailing an extensive build-out of the cave fort.

"Rob, this is amazing. Are you planning to do all this in the mine?" asks Rick as he studies the drawings. "You have a galley with a pantry, sleeping quarters, a main gallery with a large living room, and what's this? A water filtration system on a lower level? There's a lower level?"

"Planning, just planning." Rob looks over his shoulder and smiles at Courtney.

"I guess we should call it Munday's Folly instead of Munday's Hideaway." Rob turns to Rick and lowers his voice so only Rick can hear. "However, it's designed to support a family completely self-sustained for several years. If we ever need it, that is."

Rick flips through pages of drawings. "Look here, I missed the garden and the farm."

Ethan laughs in astonishment. "A farm, in a cave?"

Uncle Rob replies with a smile and a wink.

"If we lived in there, can we have bacon and eggs, Uncle Rob? Can we?"

"You betcha. We'll have pigs and chickens on the farm, so you can have bacon and eggs every morning if you like, boy-o."

"I think we have a picnic planned, don't we?" asks Courtney.

"Yes, we do! Let's get moving," Rick replies.

"Ethan, would you grab my telescope there by the door on your way out?" asks Rob.

As they walk across the cluttered yard to the AutoCar, Rick chats with Rob. "I'm sorry I haven't visited for a while, or I would have—"

"You would have what? Stopped me? I know you and Courtney don't approve. That's why I didn't tell you about my work on the mine. But wait and see. We'll put it to good use someday."

"Wait, you mean you're really building out the mine?"

"Oh damn. I shouldn't oughta said anything, but yes, it's almost finished, Ricky Boy. Keep it between us for now, will ya?"

"But, Rob, those plans. The designs. It must cost a fortune. How can you pay for it all?"

Rob nods at the old house. "I mortgaged it to the hilt, that's how!" He slaps Rick on the back with a hearty laugh. "Either the world goes to crap, and the Hideaway comes in real handy, or I die broke with an amazing house built under a mountain of solid granite."

Rick is beside himself. He loves his uncle and would hate to stifle the dream that keeps him alive. But Courtney could be right. Maybe it's time for old Rob to move into a place where he won't be alone. He decides to not tell his wife anything for now.

Chapter 4: Flying Blind

Monday Evening

Curtis Ross sits slouched at his desk. His hefty size makes the large executive chair look small. His desk is twelve feet long and runs along the wall of what was once the dining room of his house.

Mounted on the wall above the desk is a wireless, 8K thin-screen monitor, twelve feet wide by seven feet high and two millimeters thick. The flexible monitor is paper thin. The screen displays several windows. One window displays an image of the solar system, another the asteroid belt. A third one shows a list of all known asteroids, while others display e-mail, YouTube streams and a video chat room. On the wall behind Curtis is another wall-sized thin-screen streaming multiple news channels with the audio muted.

Curtis chews on a piece of pizza and sips cola from a Giant Gulp cup while video chatting with his boyhood friend, Jin Goldberg, and Jin's girlfriend, Becky.

Jin is a Korean, Jewish blend, with light brown skin and curly black hair. The multi-cultural mix of genes created a very intelligent, handsome, young man with a stout build. "You got another one logged and verified by the MPC?" asks Jin.

Curtis sits proudly, pulling his t-shirt, emblazoned with the words, *I need my Space,* to cover his exposed belly fat, then brushes at his unruly bangs covering his eyes. "It's in process. They need to verify it's actually a new find and compute the orbit before entering it into the database. They will include it in a future newsletter and post it on the MPC website if all goes well," Curtis explains.

"Cool, Curtman. You'll have another asteroid find on the list of discoverers. You're a real space explorer documented for the rest of history," Jin says.

"Wait. Jin, the MP what?" asks Becky.

"The MPC—or more precisely, the Minor Planet Center—is the only place in the world responsible for keeping track of all minor planets, comets, and asteroids in our solar system. Anybody who spots and tracks an object can report it to the MPC to help build the database of what's out there. Curtis found a new, never discovered asteroid, and the MPC will publish his find. It's his fourth asteroid discovery."

"That is really cool," Becky says, picking up on Jin's enthusiasm. "So, do you get to name it?"

Curtis sucks hard on his straw, siphoning the cold soda into his gullet. "I get first dibs on picking a name, but they have to approve it."

"Will you name it after yourself?" asks Becky.

"Nah, I'll probably continue on the theme of the first three," Curtis says.

"What did you name the first three?"

Curtis plays with the straw of his Gulp cup. "Gintoki, Natsu, and Luffy. For this one, I'm thinking either Yusuke or Goku. I can't decide. I'd only name one after me if it smashes into a planet or something."

"I wouldn't know if those are names of Japanese emperors or sushi dishes," Becky replies.

"They're names of Anime characters. Anime, you know, Japanese comic books." Jin states, slyly.

Curtis sets his Gulp cup on the desk. "Jin knows they're called Manga, not comic books. He's just trying to start a fight. I don't think I need to worry about naming the asteroid for a while. I'm still waiting for the MPC to publish an asteroid I discovered last year. The government cut their staff by fifty percent, so it's taking forever."

"Yeah, they went from an entire team of six people, down to three. Can you imagine? There are millions of asteroids out there, any of which, if it hit Earth, could wipe out a town or erase a huge city. Not to mention an impact could cause a five-year impact winter or worse. Talk about global cooling! Our government, in their wisdom, gave the responsibility to six whole people and then cut it to three! NASA and the MPC have mapped only twenty thousand of the potentially hazardous asteroids. They're tracking the largest Near-Earth Objects, or NEOs. The Earth destroyers. The ones larger than a kilometer across. That's an asteroid three thousand two hundred eighty feet wide," Jin explains.

"The dinosaur killers," says Curtis. He makes an explosive sound, picks up a plastic toy dog from his desk, and throws it in the air while making a louder explosive noise. "Ka-boom! That dinosaur doggie is toast." The plastic toy dog flies across the room to a bookshelf, knocking over a display of Anime characters.

Becky looks concerned. "What about the other million asteroids? Who's searching for them? Isn't NASA or somebody trying to discover the orbits of all those, those rocks that could smash into us?"

Curtis stuffs a piece of mega-meat pizza into his mouth. Chewing and talking with a full mouth, "You're looking at 'em, sweetheart. These days it's us and others like us who are doing most of the searching. NASA ran several programs after the turn of the century. They found and tracked over seven hundred thousand asteroids. That was until NASA got their budget whacked to support the Four Wars. It will be some backyard astronomer, or a high school astronomy club that spots the big one. I just hope we detect it early enough to give NASA and the government time to find a solution. NASA discovered many of the asteroid near misses just days before they flew by, and sometimes not until days after. Complete surprises. Most of these asteroids are dark and too small to reflect much light, so they're tough to spot and track until they're close."

Jin adds to Curtis's explanation. "The real problem is that less than 10 percent of asteroids ranging from five hundred to a thousand feet in diameter have been identified and tracked, and only one percent of asteroids two hundred feet in diameter are being tracked. These aren't dinosaur killers but, if one lands in your backyard, you and the neighbors in the next town will have a crappy day. So, it's up to us to find these asteroids and track their orbits. People need to know what's out there and what might come at us so we can help protect mankind."

"We are Space Guard!" Curtis proclaims.

"You can't use that name," says Jin. "It's overused, and we can't guard anything. How about Sky Snoopers?"

"That's dumb. You were never good at coming up with names," counters Curtis.

"How about Comet Chasers or Sky Scanners?" Becky suggests.

"Becky, leave this to us professionals," says Curtis, waving his Giant Gulp cup.

A new video window opens in the chat room. "Speaking of professionals, glad I can be of service."

"Marcus. How's it going, man?" asks Curtis. Marcus looks like the stereotypical Aussie with uncombed blond hair, tanned skin, and a broad smile.

"Great mate. How you going? And who is this beauty we have in the room tonight? Not speaking of you, mate. Sorry."

"This is Jin's new—wait, correction—first ever girlfriend, Becky. Say hi, Becky. This is Marcus. He's from Australia."

Becky gives a slow wave. "Hi."

Curtis views Becky's image. She looks like a tomboy clothed in a denim shirt with no jewelry or make-up. She wears her long, dark hair pulled back with her face hiding behind large, framed glasses.

"Now I understand why Jin's been getting in shape. All the jogging and push-ups. Guess we can't call you 'Box' any longer."

Jin's face turns red. "Curtis, you know how I feel about that name. Why would you? Shit! Nice friend."

Curtis looks at the angry image of his lifelong friend but says nothing.

Becky looks confused. "Why would they call you 'Box'?"

"It's a mean childhood nickname. Never mind. I'll tell you later."

"Guess that's a touchy subject. Nice to meet ya, Becky. Moving on with the business of the day. Curtis, did you get that scan from Pan-Starrs for me?" asks Marcus.

"No, I can't get any time on the scope. It's off-line," says Curtis.

"How about Klet?"

"Nope, shut down. Budget cuts," says Curtis.

"Siding Springs?"

"Restricted hours."

Marcus goes down the list of resources from memory, hoping to find an active scope they can log into for some viewing time.

"How about Catalina Sky Survey?" suggests Jin.

"Come on. You know it's been down for months."

"How about Neat or Space Watch?" asks Marcus, checking off the last two on the list in his head.

"Both down. Every telescope that has allowed public access for the past decade is down for repairs or shut down because of budget cuts. I heard they defunded the Department of Astronomy for Public Access. It's as if someone shut down our eyes on the sky on purpose. I don't get it."

"We're flying blind. Earth orbiting the sun. The solar system orbiting the Milky Way, and we can't even watch where we're going. It's scary!" Jin exclaims.

"It's not as if you're driving this planet through the solar system, Jin. The Earth and solar system have been orbiting the galaxy for billions of years just fine without our help," says Becky.

Becky's comment makes Curtis irate. He slams down his Giant Gulp cup. "Sure, Earth has been just fine. No problems at all, at least during humans' short-term memory. What about the meteor crater in Arizona? That crater is three quarters of a mile in diameter. Oh, and how about the Vredefort crater in South Africa? The original crater was two hundred miles across. We should not forget the Sudbury crater in Ontario, now called the Sudbury basin. It's thirty-nine miles wide, nineteen miles long, and nine miles deep! It happened two billion years ago, but it was a big one! Then there is the Chicxulub crater in the Yucatan. The crater is 110 miles in diameter and twelve miles deep. That one hit us sixty-six million years ago; The dinosaur killer. In 1908, in Tunguska, Russia, there was an aerial meteor explosion. It destroyed everything eight hundred miles from the center of the blast. Lucky for mankind, it was all forest. Imagine if the meteor stayed aloft for a few seconds longer and exploded over London or Paris. It would have annihilated those cities. Ever look at the moon? Looks like it took a few thousand hits, doesn't it? It's been a long time since Earth has had a major hit. But what if our time is up?" Curtis ends his tirade, picks up his Giant Gulp with authority, and sucks hard on the straw.

"OK, Curtis. You made your point. Take it easy on her. She's still learning." Jin scolds.

"Wow, look at Curtis get overheated," says Marcus.

"It's OK. Curtis made some good points. So, Earth isn't exactly safe. But you said they shut all the telescopes down, so what do we do?" asks Becky.

"It's simple. We do what astronomers have always done. Break out our personal telescopes, find the highest spot we can, and search the skies. We don't need government or university funded telescopes. They are bigger, but we can still discover asteroids. Curtis discovered four already. You never know it could be an amateur astronomer like you, me, or Curtis who makes the next big discovery."

"That sounds great, Jin. Can I go with you guys? It would be great to meet Curtis in the real if you don't mind," says Becky.

"Ah, I think I'm gonna be busy whenever you meet up," says Curtis.

"Becky, Curtis lives in Henderson, Nevada near Las Vegas, where we grew up, and Marcus lives in Perth. Curtis and his dad got me interested in science and astronomy. Lifelong buds, isn't that right, Curtis?" Jin explains.

"Yup, lifelong." Curtis sucks on the Giant Gulp straw, but he's drained the cup, and it makes a loud gurgling sound.

"Becky, I'll message you. We'll set a time. I'll take you to my favorite viewing site," Jin says.

"OK, you lovebirds have fun. Let me know if you spot anything," says Curtis.

"Guess this is my cue to sign off. I'll chat you up later, Curtis," Marcus says as his stream goes dark.

"Bye." Becky drops her side of the stream.

"Later, Curtman." Jin says as screen goes dark.

Curtis, in his comfy oversized chair, flicks a finger in the air and the entire wall-sized thin screen changes to the startup icon of his Celestron GXE 8K Super Star Tracker. The fourteen-inch telescope mounted on the rooftop patio of the house is controllable from his desk.

"Going outside is so overrated."

Chapter 5: Turbulence

Monday Evening

The AutoCar drives along the Angeles Crest Highway through the San Gabriel Mountains, northeast of Los Angeles, then turns on Red Box Road to wind its way up Mount Wilson.

Rick gazes out the window of the AutoCar as it cruises past the rocky terrain. His mind wanders back to the college party where he first met Courtney.

Rick rarely went to parties, but midterms were over, and his friends Karl and Steven insisted he should get out and socialize. The party was at the house of a graduate student. Rick, Karl, and Steven filled plastic cups with beer from the keg, then settled in a corner of the living room as the house filled with people.

The conversation between Karl and Steven was going hot and heavy. "*Explorer 2* is the next big leap for mankind in space. You can launch as many space telescopes as you like, but nothing compares to human observation," stated Karl.

Karl was six feet two with a trim build and bushy reddish-brown hair. He always wore a sport jacket with a kerchief tucked in the pocket, even to class, and he always had what looked like a three-day growth of beard. The sport jacket made Karl look dashing and intelligent. At least Rick thought so. He wondered how Karl's beard never got longer since it seemed he never shaved and he never combed his hair. Karl wore glasses to complete his sophisticated look.

Steven was just under six feet, but was so thin he looked taller. He had a narrow face and a sharp nose under long black hair. Steven always wore t-shirts printed with statements like; *Never trust an Atom; they make up everything.*

"Can you imagine being a volunteer on that spacecraft traveling through the solar system knowing you will never see Earth or your loved ones again?" asked Rick.

"Yeah, kind of weird if you think about it; drift through space until you die," said Steven.

"Get over it. We're all gonna die, dimwit. Why not do it for the future of humankind? Soldiers sacrifice their lives every day," Karl opined.

The *Explorer 2* program was to fly to Jupiter, then use gravity assist to slingshot the ship and its occupants to the far reaches of the solar system, never to return to Earth. The crew would be civilian volunteers. Volunteers must be under twenty-five years of age and go through a three-month training program before the launch date.

When thousands across America volunteered, TV producer Kurt Burnette created a reality show called *Launch Quest* to select the volunteers. Each week, the contestants underwent a variety of mental and physical challenges. The program captivated America.

"Next week are the semifinals. They will go from twenty-four contestants down to twelve semi-finalists before selecting the final six who will ride off into history," explained Karl.

"I like the kid from Texas. I think he'll make it to the finals," said Steven.

"You're a nimrod. I knew you were rooting for that kid. He's only sixteen and doesn't have the intelligence or the education," Karl insisted.

"He's doing better than the college graduate from Georgetown who got kicked off last week," Steven argued.

"Well, there won't be any cows to milk in space, so the Texas boy has got to go," Karl replied with finality.

"Wow, settle down. It's just a TV show. The kid from Texas is smart enough, but he's so young. My god, can you imagine him spending the rest of his life in space?" Rick asked.

"It's not just a TV show, dick weed. This is a critical space mission. It's no place for a teat sucking kid," said Karl.

"Hey, at least he'll outlive all the others on the trip," said Steven.

Rick was finishing his third beer and considering whether he should dare to have a fourth, when he looked across the room and saw a group of girls enter the house. The girls were smiling and chatting as they looked around the room. Rick's attention focused on the blonde in the center of the group. She seemed to glow. Her smile was radiant. Her hair and face perfect. He didn't realize he was staring, but maybe it was his stare that brought her eyes to his. Their mutual gaze locked as if a laser beam connected them. Rick stared his dumb stare. He didn't acknowledge her, wave, or nod his head. Her beauty absorbed him as the feelings of anticipation, need and desire surged through his body.

She smiled, giving a shy turn of her shoulders. Rick hesitated for a moment, trying to compose himself. He smiled back, felt awkward, and then smiled again.

"Okay, maybe the kid from Texas has a chance, but what about Sandra, the cute girl from Tennessee? She killed it in the obstacle course. She is better than most of the guys and she's smart, too!" said Karl.

Rick snapped out of his trance. "Guys, do you see the blonde across the room?" The guys scanned the room to find the girl Rick was talking about. "The one in the yellow skirt, over there. She's the future mother of my children."

"Back off butt-face, I saw her first. She's out of your league," scoffed Karl.

"I like the short brunette next to her," said Steven.

"Sure, cut her hair short, put her in some Levi's, and she'd look just like your little Texas boy. I think Stevens queer," teased Karl.

Steven stood frozen with a quirky pout.

"Lay off, Karl," said Rick.

"I'm just playing. Don't get your nuts in a bunch."

Rick stared again. Somehow, this moment was meant to be. It was déjà vu without ever having seen it before. "No, guys. I mean it. That's the woman I will marry."

"Just remember I saw her first numb-nuts. I could make my move, but I'll let you get rejected first," said Karl.

Steven chimed in. "You might want to let her know she'll be the mother of your children in case she has other plans."

With that, Rick mustered his courage and walked across the room. Unlike his friends, he had talked to a girl before and had some idea of what he was getting into. In fact, he looked forward to it. He walked to the blonde and stuck out his hand to shake hers as if he were greeting someone at a business meeting. The girl hesitated, then looked down at Rick's hand. She wasn't prepared to shake hands, but she put her hand in his. Rick savored her warm, soft skin and instead of shaking hands, he just held her. They stood palm in palm.

"Ah, hi. I'm Rick. Rick Munday. I know we've just met, but I wonder if you would like to have dinner or a coffee sometime?" Rick was smart enough not to say; Hi, I know we've never met, but you will be the mother of my children.

The blonde looked at Rick and then across the room at his friends. Steven saw the girl look over at them and gave her a silly wave. Karl gave a thumbs-up.

"Is that the pickup line you use on all the girls?" the blonde asked.

"Pickup line? I didn't know it was a... No... I mean," Rick stammered, trying to recover. "Was that a pickup line?"

"It sounded like a pickup line to me. We haven't met. You said your name was Rick, but you haven't asked my name." She smiled and let her eyelids flutter.

"Oh, sorry. I'm Rick. Oh God. I already said that. What's your name?"

"I'm Courtney Greene. It's nice to meet you." Courtney smiled again and gave the slightest curtsy.

"It's nice to meet you," Rick answered. His heartbeat raced. His face flushed as they continued to stand, palm in palm. Rick's palm was getting sweaty. He tried to get control of himself and the situation. "So, now we've met, would you like to meet for coffee sometime?"

Courtney laughed. "You must really like coffee. We're here now. Why don't you introduce me to your friends?" Courtney removed her hand from his and motioned over to Karl and Steven, who were deep in debate, oblivious to the party around them.

"Oh no. That would ruin everything. I mean, those guys are just, ah..." Rick was stammering again.

"Your friends?"

"Yes, but maybe another time. You know, I heard this house has a big backyard, and it's dark. There might be some stars out. Do you like stars?"

"I guess I like stars. I never think about them much. Do you like stars?"

"I do. They're fascinating. There's so much to learn and discover, so much we don't know or understand about our own solar system, not to mention the galaxy we inhabit."

"Wow, are you a rocket scientist or something? Joaney said some guys at this party would be from Cal Tech."

"No, not a rocket scientist. I'm studying astrophysics." Rick looked over at his buddies, who had sucked two other guys into their discussion. "So are they. But let's go outside." He then held out his hand to Courtney, not for a handshake, but to guide his future wife outside to discover the heavens.

That was how they met, and it was love at first sight for both. Rick loved Courtney completely. From that first night, he was totally committed and fully in love. This was his woman, who would soon be his wife. It was their third date before he dared tell her he had decided to marry her before they introduced themselves.

Rick opens his eyes as the AutoCar enters the parking lot at the top of Mount Wilson. He observes the building housing the sixty-inch Hale telescope which once had been available for public use by astronomy clubs and school field trips. These days, the observatory is locked.

The family sets out their picnic gear and telescopes at a table on the far edge of the grassy field. Uncle Rob orients the telescopes to prepare for viewing as Courtney looks to the darkening sky. "We'd better eat before we lose the light."

Ethan tears into the food containers. "Ethan's hogging the food," Alyssa complains.

"He's a growing boy," Uncle Rob says, nudging a food container toward Ethan.

"There's plenty for everyone, sweetheart," Courtney says, handing a food container to Alyssa.

Rick eats as he gazes at the sky. "This is a new meteor shower. We believe it's the result of a small rubble pile of asteroids, like gravel in the sky. There will be lots of shooting stars tonight."

After the meal, Rick stands next to his uncle, and they survey the sky. "Did they name this one yet?" asks Rob.

"I don't think so. This event is a complete surprise, discovered by an amateur. If JPL hadn't been shut down, they'd be working to track its orbit. If it is orbiting, then the last time this clump of rocks passed near Earth was hundreds or even thousands of years ago. More likely, this rubble pile is a new visitor to our part of solar system," says Rick.

"Where do shooting stars come from anyway?" asks Ethan.

Uncle Rob provides the answer. "Meteor showers are generally composed of dust, ice particles and small rocks; remnants of comet tails as they speed past our planet."

"Dad, your office is full of Astro guys. Why didn't you see this one coming?"

"Most of the telescopes our team uses are down thanks to the Four Wars and budget cuts. This one is likely scattered debris, made up of hundreds or thousands of small rocks that don't reflect much light, making them nearly impossible to spot until they're close to Earth. That is, if anyone's looking."

"And when the rocks get close to Earth, they shoot across the sky!" Ethan sweeps his hand over his head while making a zooming sound.

"As space rocks get pulled into Earth's atmosphere, the resistance causes them to become super-heated. They break into smaller bits in a bright flash that streaks across the dark sky. Shooting stars! Most pieces burn up or explode high in the atmosphere, but occasionally larger meteors impact Earth's surface or explode in the lower atmosphere before impact," Rob answered.

Ethan stands next to his great-uncle. "I thought you knew all this stuff already, kiddo," says Uncle Rob.

"I do, but I just like to hear it again. Hey, Dad, if nobody sees a meteor shower, did it happen?"

Uncle Rob chuckles.

Rick looks down at his son. "Is that your version of, if a tree falls in the woods when no one's there, does it make a sound?"

"Yup, the space version!"

"Good one, son! How about this; Does it have to be dark for there to be shooting stars?"

"How else could we see them?" Uncle Rob asks.

Ethan shrugs his shoulders.

Rick answers his own question. "Meteors don't know if it's day or night. They come into our atmosphere whenever gravity pulls them in. If the meteor is big enough, you can see it in daylight. It's called a daytime fireball."

A series of flashes shoot across the northern sky. "It's getting started," says Uncle Rob. "How about we put these telescopes to work? We should be able to capture some great photos tonight."

"Dad, can I use the CGE Pro and Oculus X? I love the way it lets me see the stars. It's like I can reach out and touch them. Please, Dad, *please*," Ethan begs.

Rick had looked forward to using the Oculus tonight, but he's happy Ethan is interested in astronomy. There will be plenty of time later in the evening for Rick to get some time with Oculus.

"All right, let's get this on you," Rick says as he fits the headset on Ethan, tightening the head strap.

Once Ethan is ready, he says the command, "Oculus ON!" The Oculus logo appears in the display. Ethan watches the boot-up screen. Motors on the telescope whine as it runs diagnostic checks and searches the sky to discover where in the world it is. The display switches to the telescope oriented on the moon.

The system tracks hand and head movements. Ethan moves his hands to zoom out. "Good evening, Mr. Man in the Moon." He then turns his head, viewing the starry night. The telescope moves in sync with Ethan's head movements.

After a few minutes of zooming in and out, looking at space, Ethan asks, "Dad, can you load the star map into the scope?"

"Still need a cheat sheet, boy?" Uncle Rob chides.

Ethan moves his head toward Uncle Rob's voice. The telescope follows Ethan's head movement. The large display covers most of the boy's face. He nods his head up and down — "Uh huh"— causing the telescope to do the same. The motors whine in sync with Ethan's head.

Rick turns to Rob. "He likes to use the star map so he can line things up."

"Yeah, like I said, a cheat sheet."

Rick lifts his band to his mouth. "Load Star Map, Northern Hemisphere to scope number one." The band beeps in recognition and the star map loads into the scope. The star map creates an overlay of the known celestial objects in the scope and displays them in the Oculus.

Uncle Rob watches the fireworks in the sky. "Most astronomers over the past decades have focused on looking farther and farther away. It frustrates me. They love pushing images of billions of stars and cloud nebula out to the public, at least when Hubble, Kepler, and the Webb space telescopes were functioning. Those formations are thousands of light years away."

"It didn't help when Hubble dropped out of orbit and crashed to Earth. Talk about bad PR for the space industry, but images of deep space look so much better than a bunch of rocks in the asteroid belt. They titillate the public's imagination to keep the funds coming in."

Ethan giggles.

"What's so funny, boy?" asks Uncle Rob.

"Dad just said tit." Ethan giggles again.

"Yes, he did. Ricky boy, what are you teaching this boy of yours?"

Ethan steps to stand between his father and Uncle Rob. The boy focuses on his view of space. He seems to have forgotten his head is attached to his body, feeling as if he is soaring through space. A meteor shoots across the sky in a brilliant bright streak. Ethan follows the fast-moving streak with his head. "Whoa." His body follows, tipping over, falling into his father. Rick pushes Ethan to a standing position. Ethan keeps the Oculus directed into space.

"What I am trying to teach him, if he'd keep his mind out of the gutter, is that patient study and exploration is important. We might discover something someday that impacts humankind," Rick says in a fatherly tone. "Rob, you know I agree with you. Exploring space in our own neighborhood is more important than trying to study the entire universe."

Another meteor streaks through the sky, sending Ethan off balance. This time, he falls into Uncle Rob. Rob nudges the boy to a standing position. The men barely notice the teeter-tottering child. "I hope to hear news about my grant proposal any day now. I need this grant. At this point in my career, I should conduct my own research and publish my work. The grant isn't just important for my career. It will provide for the family."

"Ricky boy. The wars set lots of people back. Heck, The Four Wars set the world back. You served and came back to us. Things are getting better. The fact they're even issuing grants again is a good sign. Better times are ahead, boy. You'll see."

"I think you'll like the ideas I've been pursuing," says Rick. "What ideas?"

"There has been an increase in the number of new asteroids and comets observed in our solar system. I studied your paper on the cycle of asteroid bombardment. Based on my observations, I've built new computer models and come up with a hypothesis for the cause. It's very interesting. But I need the grant, so I have the funds to learn more."

Rob scoffs. "My paper? I thought you wanted funding. My theory got me booted down to the city college. I hope your ideas are better received than mine."

A dazzling light streaks across the sky. It moves slower and goes farther than the other shooting stars, making it easy to follow. Rick looks over at the women in his life, sitting together on the picnic bench.

"Hey, girls, look. Don't miss this one." Courtney and Alyssa look at the sky.

Ethan leans back, back, back to watch the full progression of the shooting star as it streaks from one side of the sky to the other until he falls flat on his back in the grass. "Oomph. That was cool!" Ethan makes no attempt to get up. He just lies on the ground.

Uncle Rob looks down at the boy. "You've got a strange one there, Rick. Gonna have to watch this one."

Rick looks down at his son. "Should be safer down there. Rick looks to the sky and adds, "There's been an increase in comet discoveries the past few years, not to mention an increase in atmospheric meteor activity. Just look at the sky tonight. We have a new meteor shower going off like gangbusters, and nobody saw it coming. The government defunded all the space and ground-based telescopes, so we can't see what's going on. I dug up all the old research on increased asteroid activity caused by the solar system moving through the galactic plane, but the timing is off. Something else is causing turbulence in the inner solar system."

"Turbulence? What sort of turbulence are you talking about?" asks Rob.

"You theorized the solar system periodically moves through dust clouds containing rockier masses, which causes a higher frequency of asteroid impacts. I think you could be right. But this is something different. I believe a disturbance in the Kuiper belt sent objects to the inner solar system."

"Earth has suffered from several asteroid bombardments in the past. I was trying to explain the cause of those periodic impacts," Rob clarifies.

"I know. If I can get my grant funded, I'll have the time and resources to confirm what I think is happening. I just hope, if I'm right, there's time to warn people," Rick laments.

"Well, there you go! Maybe now you'll understand why I'm building the Hideaway. Call me crazy, but if Earth ever enters a phase of increased asteroid impacts, I want to have a safe place for us all."

"Uncle Rob, you don't hear me calling you crazy. I wish you would have come to me for help."

"Nah, you've got the kids and Courtney to take care of."

While Uncle Rob and Rick are deep in their discussion, Ethan lies on his back, observing space. The asteroid belt fascinates Ethan. He uses voice command to bring up an overlay that directs Oculus to zoom in on his favorite dwarf planet. "Star map, load Ceres."

A graphic overlay appears, showing where Ceres is in space. "Oculus, zoom to Ceres." The motors on the telescope whir. The telescope moves to target Ceres, zooming in on the dwarf planet in seconds. Ethan likes to zoom close enough to view the twin white spots on Ceres. As the telescope zooms in, the graphic overlay dissolves. Once the overlay disappears, the image of Ceres replaces the overlay, but Ethan notices something strange as the telescope zooms in. "What was that?"

Ethan motions for the telescope to zoom away from Ceres so he can examine the space beyond the largest object in the asteroid belt. He sees nothing unusual. He zooms out further. Nothing.

"Star map, zoom to Ceres." The motors of the telescope go through their gyrations. Ethan watches carefully as the telescope targets the dwarf planet. Just before the journey is complete and the graphic overlay dissolves, he spots several rocky bodies beyond Ceres.

Ethan pulls on his father's pant leg. "Dad, how do new asteroids join the asteroid belt?"

Rick and Uncle Rob look at the boy lying on the ground. "New asteroids don't join the asteroid belt. The asteroid belt has had the same configuration for millions of years," answers Rob.

"Did you break the Oculus? That's an expensive bit of kit we don't own," Rick admonishes.

"I don't think it's broken. I'm not sure, but I think I saw a bunch of asteroids that weren't there before."

Rick pulls the Oculus off Ethan's head, ignores the straps, and fits it to his face. The view is of Ceres and open space with faint stars in the distance.

"I could only spot them as the scope zoomed toward Ceres."

Rick uses hand gestures to zoom out, then speaks. "Star map, load Ceres" The graphic overlay appears and the scope zooms to Ceres. Just as the overlay fades away, he spots a cluster of almost invisible objects beyond Ceres. "Huh." He gestures to zoom away from Ceres.

"What is it?" inquires Uncle Rob.

"Did you see them?" asks Ethan.

"I'm not sure," Rick says as he pulls Oculus from his face. He punches in the coordinates for Ceres on the control screen, slows the zoom rate, and disables the graphic overlay. The motor's hum as the scope moves to focus on Ceres. Rick looks through the Oculus. "They have very low reflectivity, but it looks like a field of rocky debris is moving through the asteroid belt." Rick pulls the Oculus away from his eyes.

Ethan looks up at his father. "So, you do see them."

"Is that your turbulence?" Rob asks.

"It shouldn't be starting yet. I need to check the data, but one of my models predicts—"

Rob interrupts Rick. "I think I need to buy those chickens for the Hideaway, sooner rather than later."

Ethan is relieved he's not in trouble. "Don't forget the bacon!"

Chapter 6: Homeland Security

Georgia Branch Office–Tuesday Morning

A sign on the office wall reads:
HOMELAND SECURITY
SCIENCE AND TECHNOLOGY SPECIAL PROGRAMS DIVISION
RISK SCIENCES BRANCH

The Risk Sciences Branch's purpose is vague. The people who work there and the work they do are also ambiguous. Employees don't talk about their work with other employees. There are departments and sub-departments within the branch office. Employees work as directed by their manager or director. Somehow, each department's effort filters up to an unknown overall goal of the branch, but few—if any—know what that goal is.

Management ordered Jim Sweeney to search for communications related to space studies, space research, or any new studies involving space and astronomy. He enters several keywords into the Homeland Security Information System (HSIS). Jim knows HSIS relates to some intelligence-gathering system but doesn't know much more about it and doesn't care to know.

Jim is proud of the position he holds and hopes to continue advancing his career in government service. He likes the salary and benefits; not to mention the prestige of his title: Senior Analyst. Jim has no reason to question anything or do more than what management requests unless it helps advance his career.

Jim fumbles around as he enters random words and phrases as search parameters in the HSIS query system. He has already tried typical word searches such as *rockets, studies, astrophysics, spaceship, and stars.* Frustrated with a lack of results, he enters nonsensical words and phrases such as *give me a clue, help me do my job, I don't want to be a failure,* and *grant my space wish.* He is about to enter *how I get a raise* as a query when the system gets a hit on the word combination *grant* and *space.*

45

HSIS then retrieves a grant proposal sent to the National Science Foundation. This excites him. Something worked. He pulls up the grant proposal and reviews the document. He has something positive for his department manager: an accomplishment!

Jim prints the grant proposal and takes it to the office of Francis Wright, director of the Risk Sciences Branch.

Jim knocks and enters the office. "Mrs. Wright?"

"Sweeney? What is it?"

"I got a hit on space research. It's a grant proposal of some sort," Jim says, holding out the papers.

"Bring it here."

Jim steps to the stern woman's desk. "It's a positive result. I found it. I'm sure it's helpful."

She reaches out for the papers. Once in her hand, she gives them a quick once-over, then looks at Jim. "Anything else?"

"No, ma'am. You will enter a positive note in my file, won't you?"

"You're dismissed." Jim leaves the office less excited than when he entered. "Close the door on your way out." Jim closes the door, hoping what he found will help advance his career.

Francis Wright reads the management summary of the grant proposal, then the conclusion. She knows this is all you need to read. Everything in between is statistics, charts, and fluff. No need to waste time.

Francis speaks to her VUE lens. "Director Johnson." She is instantly in a video call with the Director of Science and Technology Special Programs Division, Risk Assessment Branch.

"Director Wright." Director Johnson is in his mid-fifties but looks older, overweight, and bald. "You have something new?"

"Yes, something popped up this morning. A grant proposal. The topic is interesting. A Professor Munday from Cal Tech wants to study potential risks to Earth from asteroids."

"Asteroids. A curious topic. I thought we already gathered the best and brightest on that subject," says Director Johnson.

"We missed Munday. His theory and models are focused and unique. Is there time?"

"Not much. Maybe we can fit him in the last group. He's at Cal Tech, in Los Angeles?"

"Pasadena," Mrs. Wright corrects.

"You are aware the Director of DHS has requested all scientists in this field of study attend the seminars we've been conducting. You should have found everyone by now."

"I don't know how we missed Dr. Munday, but his work is pertinent. We should schedule him for the seminar tomorrow."

"Agreed. Send me his contact information. We'll send an invitation and plane tickets."

"Yes sir," Wright replies. "I'm pleased my team has contributed to the department's success."

"I hope you found them all. Tomorrow is the last seminar," chides Director Johnson.

"We will run another search, but I believe Munday is the last one."

"Good. Excellent work."

"The final seminar will be exceptional with the scientists we've lined up to present," adds Wright, pleased with herself.

"It should prove interesting. Anything else?" asks Johnson.

"No Director." Wright's VUE lens goes blank.

Director Johnson makes a call. A portly white man wearing a white button-down business shirt and black-framed glasses sitting in a nondescript government office answers the call. "What is it, Johnson?"

Director Johnson doesn't know who the portly man is. The office of director of Homeland Security instructed him to contact this man when they find a scientist or researcher.

"We've located another researcher. He's from Cal Tech, Dr. Richard Munday. He submitted a grant proposal. Director Wright reviewed the proposal and believes Dr. Munday has an interesting theory. Something about asteroids, and risks to Earth," explains Johnson.

"Cal Tech? We've already seen several presentations from the Cal Tech staff, including the department head, Professor Heinrich. He was not impressive, but they have a talented group of researchers.

How did you miss this one? Bring him in. There better not be anyone else you've missed," says the portly man.

"Director Wright assures me he is the last one. With your agreement, I will have an invitation and plane ticket sent," Johnson says.

"Agreed. We will make room in the presentation schedule." The call ends.

Chapter 7: The invitation

Tuesday–Pasadena

Rick wakes early. The previous night's meteor shower was magnificent. Thousands of shooting stars lit up the night sky. Rick wishes he still had access to the EELT (European Extremely Large Telescope Array) in the Atacama Desert of northern Chile. He'd like to get a better look at that group of asteroids and find out where they're headed.

He didn't sleep well. Questions tormented his dreams. Should he alert his colleagues? Should he check again before calling an alert? He would hate to look stupid, jumping to conclusions.

Rick stands by the bed, watching Courtney curled in blankets, sleeping. He considers crawling back in bed to snuggle with her, but lets her dream.

Instead, he works on his VUE lens looking for news of new asteroid discoveries. There is nothing. No news. No warnings. All is quiet. Everything is fine. But Rick feels that something is off.

He checks his e-mail scanning through newsletters, promotions from retailers—and an e-mail from Homeland Security. The e-mail is not just from Homeland Security, but from the Assistant Director of the Science and Technology Special Programs Division.

> Dr. Munday,
>
> The National Science Foundation forwarded your grant proposal to Homeland Security and our research department brought to my attention. I believe the subject of your submission is very intriguing.
>
> The Science and Technology Division has a seminar scheduled for tomorrow.
>
> A key speaker has cancelled at the last moment. I hope you can fill this important slot in the schedule. I apologize

for the short notice, but I believe the seminar participants will be very interested in learning about your area of study.

Prepare to give your presentation to an audience of your peers. Please confirm your willingness to take part in this exciting seminar. Since this is a last-minute request, we will send you an electronic flight ticket and hotel accommodations (see vouchers attached).

Sincerely,

Jordan Musgrove, Ph.D.
Assistant Director of Science and Technology
Special Programs Division

A window pops up at the top of the e-mail asking Rick to confirm receipt. Rick clicks ACCEPT.

Rick then reviews the e-mail attachments. The plane ticket is from Los Angeles to Dulles International Airport in Washington, DC, and he's booked for the evening flight.

Rick reads the e-mail a second and third time. It doesn't say they approved his grant, but they want him to present at the seminar. What an opportunity! In this environment of budget cuts and cutbacks, the government sent a plane ticket and hotel voucher.

Rick doesn't care if he's a fill-in or a last-minute replacement. Someone read his proposal, was interested, and forwarded it to Homeland's Science and Technology Division. This could be the opportunity of a lifetime.

His band vibrates. He doesn't recognize the caller, but he answers. "Hello?"

"Dr. Richard Munday?" asks a voice.

"Yes."

"This is Darby Caledero. I work in the office of the Director of Homeland Security Science and Technology Division. I received notification you read the e-mail sent to you."

"Yes, I did. It's quite a shock. I mean a privilege to be invited."

"Then we will expect you in Washington in the morning?"

"Yes, well... I'd like to discuss it with my wife. This is so sudden. Can I call you back?"

"Time is of the essence, Dr. Munday. We must fill the schedule. If you do not confirm participation, we will initiate other contingencies. I'm sure you understand."

"Hang on a minute. I am pleased to be invited. I want to accept. It's just — I owe my wife the courtesy of letting her know, before I run off to Washington, DC. If you're married, you'll understand. I'll call back or e-mail."

"One hour. We'll hold your spot for one hour, Dr. Munday."

"I never knew the government to be so efficient. I'll call back soon."

"One hour, Dr. Munday." The call ends.

The portly man listens in on the call. If Munday does not come to Washington, DC, then he'll send a visitor to Dr. Munday. Information must be controlled. Dr. Munday cannot be out in public, available to speak with the press.

The man touches the air in front of his glasses. "Captain Kobalt."

"Here."

"The colonel may have one more mission for you. Stand at the ready if we need you."

"As always."

Rick runs to the bedroom, launching himself on the bed, where he left his wife dreaming. He hugs her. He clutches her tightly, rolling around in bed, her body with his. She wakes sweetly. Some wives would not be torn from their dreams so calmly, but Courtney love's Rick's playful nature. She rolls with him. They roll across the bed until they lie face-to-face. He kisses her. She kisses him back. Her eyes, freshly woken, are bright. Her skin soft and glowing in the morning light. "I have news."

"What news do you bring, my prince?"

"My presence has been requested at a seminar in Washington, DC, where I am to give a presentation to members of the Science and Technology Division."

"That's wonderful. I am so proud of you! I knew they would recognize you for your hard work. When is the seminar?"

"Tomorrow. I fly at ten tonight!"

"Tonight?"

"They sent plane tickets and a hotel voucher. Everything's arranged. A man even called to confirm it. I told him I want to discuss it with you."

"You were hoping for news on your grant, but I didn't expect this."

"I know. This is unusual, but I'm excited. The letter said another speaker canceled, and they need to fill the spot."

"Maybe your grant is being approved, and someone recommended you."

"It would give me exposure in the scientific community. I guess that can't hurt. So, you think I should accept?"

"Someone read my brilliant husband's grant proposal, invited him to present at a seminar full of leading scientists, and they're paying for the trip. How can you say no?"

"I'll call to confirm, and I'd better call Professor Heinrich to share the good news."

"This should impress him."

"I hope so. This is good news for the entire department. It's about time I gave him something to be happy about."

Rick calls Darby Caledero. "Dr. Munday. I'm pleased to hear from you. Tick-Tock. Can I include you in tomorrow's program?"

"Yes, count me in."

"I have confirmed you for the eleven-a.m. slot. You will have time to rest and get something to eat at your hotel. A car will pick you up at ten tomorrow."

Rick straightens in his chair, feeling important. "Wow, you sure are well organized."

"Have a good flight, Dr. Munday." The call ends.

Rick stands proudly. Dr. Richard Munday is flying to Washington, DC, to present his theory to members of the Science and Technology Division.

Rick calls Professor Heinrich. A recording plays. The professor is out of town on business without access to e-mail.

The portly man smiles. *It will be good to have you with us, Dr. Munday. Much better for you than the alternative.*

He touches the air in front of his glasses. "Kobalt."

"At the ready."

"No need. Stand down."

Kobalt grunts. The call ends.

Rick is excited as he leaves home for the Cal Tech lab with an edge of confidence later that morning. He had hoped to share the news with his colleagues, but when he arrived at the lab, he found it very quiet.

Rick works in his office, double-checking his simulations and makes last-minute edits to his presentation. There is no lecture today. If there was, he'd dump it on a graduate student. He blocks out his calendar for the rest of the week.

Rick watches an animated model of the solar system as it orbits the Milky Way galaxy. It travels in a bobbing and weaving motion above and below the galactic plane, gliding through clouds and passing rocky bodies. He created the animation and watched it hundreds of times. He thinks about the nonreflective group of asteroids moving through the asteroid belt and whispers, "Turbulence?"

Chapter 8: Perth

It's 8:17 a.m., Wednesday morning in Perth, Australia. Marcus Conley and several others are sitting at a conference table, listening to a beautiful young woman giving a sales presentation on the new Armadyne automated production line. A man, the young woman's sales manager, stands at a distance, ready to assist if needed.

"The Armadyne X-54 factory in a box allows you to produce over one hundred unique products on a high-mix, low volume, production line based on the product templates installed. The patented Armadyne rapid liquid printing system extracts production ready components, which move through the assembly line and exit as final products, ready to ship to your customers."

Marcus is familiar with the production line. He's read the website, watched the videos, and studied the product data sheets. As the company's senior mechanical engineer, he'll get involved if his boss invests in the system.

"As you know, the Four Wars continue to rage around the world, disrupting shipping lanes, impacting international trade. We've all suffered from shortages and rationed items. Entrepreneurs in America who invested in Armadyne automated production lines are the bright spot of the US economy. Australian businesses are eager to get in on this new economic boom, as I'm sure you are."

The young woman is smart and attractive. Marcus thinks her boss is a bore. Marcus stares out the large conference room window at the Perth city skyline in the distance.

"The X-54 allows you to produce products locally, streamlining your supply chain, slashing lead times and cutting transportation costs—" She pauses as if she's evaluating her chances for a successful sale.

"You may recognize Armadyne for our food actualizers, but Armadyne produces much more than your next tasty meal. Today, Armadyne provides a wide range of products from autonomous personal assistants; I guess people call them noms these days to automated production lines and defense products to support our country and our allies in the Four Wars."

Marcus has shifted his gaze to the young woman, but a bright light in the sky pulls his attention back to the large window. Bright light fills the conference room as a fiery hot meteor falls through the atmosphere. The young saleswoman shrieks. The meteor is heading toward the city of Perth. Everyone in the conference room gathers at the window, shielding their eyes, trying to witness the sight.

The space rock explodes above the city in a brilliant flash. The only sounds are the words "ooh," "ah," "wow," and "amazing," as those in the room react to the aerial blast. The brightness fades and eyes adjust to normal light.

"Everybody; get down against the wall and away from the windows!" Marcus calls out as he crouches against the wall.

"Show's over. We have a couple more slides in the presentation, unless you're ready to move ahead," says the sales manager, as he walks to the front of the conference room.

"It's not over. Get down!" Marcus calls out.

The sales manager steps to the saleswoman. "Let me help you up," he says as he pulls the young lady to her feet. Then he whispers in her ear, "Great job, Cara. You're about to close your biggest deal yet."

Other people in the room stand. Marcus implores, "Get down. Shockwave—"

Marcus tucks his head low and hugs the wall. The conference room window bursts into a thousand shards of glass from a blast of wind moving hundreds of miles per hour. It feels as if the air is being sucked from the room. The wind is burning hot. His skin burns. He doesn't dare breathe. The bodies of the salespeople fly through the collapsing conference room wall and the wind flips the heavy conference table through the air. Then, for a moment, all is calm. BOOM! A loud sonic boom rattles the swaying building. The sound of alarms, moans of pain and crying follow. The only people he can see are three co-workers who followed his instruction and crouched at the wall.

Marcus stands and looks out the opening in the office wall, which was once a window. The meteor explosion has left the city scape broken. Buildings are burning. Sirens echo in the distance and smoke darkens the skyline.

Marcus staggers through the building, pushing furniture and chairs aside, as he moves to the stairwell of the three-story building. The only thing he can think of is his wife, who works in the main business district.

Chapter 9: ARC

Tuesday Evening–White House Oval Office

A small group meets for a late evening meeting in the Oval Office. President Jon Anderson, briefed on the topic earlier, asked his chief of staff to review the details one more time. The meeting includes key insiders: the president; Chief of Staff Russell Thompson; National Security Adviser Colonel Cruikshank; Chairman of the Joint Chiefs of Staff General Mahon and a portly white man who is busy checking messages on his band.

"Colonel Cruikshank, once we're underground, we will receive constant updates with casualty and damage reports. Is that right?"

The old colonel sits in a chair next to the president's desk. Colonel Cruikshank is old, yet looks sturdy and mentally sharp. His face is narrow, wrinkled, and war-withered, with thinning brown hair.

The colonel is a famous war hero who nearly lost his right leg in the war for New Persia while leading his troops to victory against overwhelming odds. The injury left a single taut strip of thigh muscle in his leg. Doctors wanted to amputate the limb, but the colonel refused. After a long painful recovery, he walks with the use of a cane.

The portly man has assisted the colonel since the old war hero entered government service; first serving as the Secretary of Defense, then as Chief of Staff in the previous administration, and now as the National Security Advisor. Many people around Capitol Hill believe the colonel has too much influence over the president and others in government.

The colonel wears a black tunic with gold trim: the uniform of a military leader, but it's not a uniform of the US military. He holds a shiny black cane across his lap. The cane is elegant. It has a gold tip and an ornate gold handle in the shape of a fierce-looking bald eagle. He speaks with a raspy voice.

Mike McCoy

"Mr. President, our command center will have open lines of communication with constant updates. You will have red-phone contact with world leaders to coordinate recovery efforts once the storm begins." The colonel coughs, clearing his throat before continuing. "We will block communications for team members and general staff. This is a security issue. I trust all is clear. We have covered it before, Jon," he says, addressing the president.

The president has a distant look in his eyes. After the colonel stops speaking, seconds pass before the president responds, speaking to no one in particular. "Very well."

The president looks at the portly man. "You there, Professor, you're sure this threat is real? This event you've spoken of will really happen. It's not like your prediction last year. What was the name of that asteroid, Colossus?"

The portly man sits on a sofa in front of the president's desk. "My name is Zsoldos, sir. Just Zsoldos. We are quite sure of the coming event. It will not be a near miss. As I have said, we miscalculated the orbital trajectory of Colossus. There was a miscommunication in the data received from the now-defunct European Space Agency. A simple error. This event is not a single asteroid. The current threat includes thousands of asteroids and comets. The best-case scenario, based on our computer simulations, is a massive worldwide bombardment."

The simple error Zsoldos speaks about caused President Anderson to make a somber announcement broadcast on all the streaming networks. His message warned of an eminent impact and a worldwide disaster. The announcement sent all developed nations of the world into chaos. Panic followed the news. People flooded stores to stock up on food and water. There was looting, murder, and hysteria. News media convinced people they would be safer in the countryside, so everyone fled the cities, jamming freeways. It was total mayhem and madness. After a week of pandemonium, Colossus passed Earth at twenty thousand miles. Very close in space distances, but Earth was safe.

Scientists proclaimed Earth was out of danger from Colossus for at least two hundred years. Panic subsided. Shopkeepers repaired broken windows, restocked shelves, and submitted insurance claims for the damage. Life went back to normal.

But a select group in power decided they would not—could not—be so transparent with critical information in the future. They understood, when faced with an unpreventable disaster, providing advance warning might cause as much damage as the disaster itself. This group inside the US Government developed the "Bliss Protocol," as in *ignorance is bliss*. The less people know, the easier they will be to control.

The president looks to General Mahon, who sits on a second couch facing Zsoldos. "General, how do you plan to control the population on the surface if this situation becomes a reality?"

The general stands and steps behind the couch. "Mr. President, as soon as we have confirmation, we'll pull the trigger, so to speak, on the homeland defense forces. Military personnel will enforce martial law. All government employees, from local police to homeland security and FEMA, will secure and control the civilian population. We've equipped every department with weapons, riot gear, millions of rounds of ammunition, and—"

Alarms, buzzers, and ringtones go off, interrupting the general. Everyone in the room receives a call, alert, or alarm. Colonel Cruikshank receives a call in his ear dot. Chief of Staff Thompson touches his VUE to check the message, while Zsoldos attends to his band and VUE glasses, dictating messages and reading responses.

Colonel Cruikshank whispers. "Perth, Australia? When? How much damage? Get me an update as soon as you can. A meteor? You're positive? Keep me posted."

Everyone in the room reads messages and talks in hushed tones. The only person not engaged is the president, who sits dumbfounded at his desk, wondering what's going on. General Mahon looks to the colonel. The colonel's eyes are fiery and alive as they lock on the general's, whose eyes reveal panic seeking guidance.

The colonel feels alive and excited but exudes calm. He speaks confidently. "Initiate Bliss Protocol."

The general nods agreement and makes a call to his staff. "Initiate Bliss Protocol. Worldwide basis. Nothing gets out of Australia. That's right, total information lockdown. Now!" The general waves over his band to end the call, then gives a confirming nod to the colonel.

The president is not known for his patience. "Why are you initiating Bliss? What in high heavens is going on? Stop what you're doing. Talk to me, damn it!"

The colonel speaks first. "Mr. President, a meteor has hit the city of Perth. We have reports of widespread destruction. Fires are raging in the city center. There is a massive loss of life."

The president leans back in his executive chair with a sigh. "Cruikshank, why are you initiating Bliss? Perth is outside of the US; we've never used Bliss before. It's not an international protocol. We developed Bliss for domestic use. Let the Australians handle this themselves. If they need assistance, we can send support, but this is not in our bailiwick."

"Mr. President, there was the Chilean situation, you'll remember, a couple of months ago. We implemented a form of the Bliss protocol for that disaster."

The president looks angry and flustered. "We did not initiate any form of Bliss for the Chilean earthquake. The news of the earthquake and resulting tsunami streamed on the networks continuously for weeks."

Thompson steps to the couch where Zsoldos sits, leans down, and whispers in his ear. "We didn't fully brief the president on all aspects of the Chilean situation."

Zsoldos eyes Cruikshank before speaking. "Mr. President, I am sure you remember that the Chilean incident was not an earthquake. That was the cover story."

The colonel gives Zsoldos a slight nod. He leans on his cane to stand and steps behind the president, then rests a hand on his shoulder. "Jon, I'm sure you recall when a meteor impacted the Pacific Ocean off the coast of Chile. We generated reports of a severe earthquake. We let the news agencies run with it. They were very effective, I might add. You decided on that plan in this room. I'm sure you remember what really happened in Chile."

The president looks frustrated. Zsoldos can see that the president is struggling to recall his memories.

The president sits erect to look confident. "I remember exactly what we decided. The news agencies did a splendid job spreading the story line we wanted them to circulate. Splendid job. An interesting adaptation of the Bliss Protocol. We should do the same for Perth. We don't want people thinking our cities can be destroyed by a... what was it, Professor? What was it in Perth?"

"It was a meteor, Mr. President. My staff is working to gather data on the incoming trajectory, dimensions, and mass. I should have an update soon."

The president's eyes darken with sadness. He works hard to keep his presidential composure, but it's difficult under the circumstances. "A meteor. How terrible. What will we tell the press?" The president looks to Russell, who is writing notes on the projected screen of his band.

Russell looks to the colonel, then to the president. "A daytime fireball in the sky?"

Cruikshank lifts his cane and taps it on the carpet. "Daytime fireball it is. Get the press on it. Stop all other communications."

Cruikshank then defers to the president. "Only if you agree, Jon."

President Anderson hesitates a moment, then asks, "Professor, is that a real thing? A daytime—?"

"A daytime fireball is a real thing. They are more common than you might think."

"Obviously so," says the president.

President Anderson sits silent for a moment before speaking again. "This is really happening. America, and much of the world as we know it, destroyed. Fiery blasts from the sky will extinguish the American dream." The president appears very despondent.

The colonel responds. "Yes, sir. The America we know, and love will most likely cease to exist, but we have prepared."

He turns to Thompson. The colonel and the chief of staff have discussed this matter several times. They've tried to convince Anderson to sign the ARC amendment, but the president continues to delay. Thompson moves to the president's desk. "As we discussed, Congress and the states have ratified the ARC amendment. It's just awaiting your signature."

ARC, or the American Republic Corporation amendment, if signed, will eradicate the US Constitution, and replace the Republic that is the United States of America with a corporate republic. The proposal is to create a new republic, run like a business, instead of suffering through the political gridlock of the present system. The new republic will function under a small controlling body, with the goal of encouraging budget restraint, business and personal growth, individual independence, and job creation with a governing body known as the council. The Arcadian Council.

President Anderson fumes. "You're pressuring me on this issue again. I have not signed the amendment into law because… well, because I don't want to sign it. Do you want my legacy to be the president who killed the American dream?"

Thompson tries to console the president. "You may not get the choice. If things go as predicted, we will need an orderly transition to a new system. If not, we will have chaos, sir."

The president huffs. "I need more time. I did not expect to be the last American president. This is not a decision one should rush."

"I understand, sir, but there isn't much time."

The president stands and stares out the window at the south lawn. He gazes into the dark, cloudless sky. No asteroids are falling. It's a clear starlit sky. The president turns to the others in the room. "So many sour topics this evening, gentleman."

The president walks around his desk and points at Zsoldos. "You there, Professor." Zsoldos pauses from reading messages. "You're sure this threat is real. It will really happen. It's not like that prediction of yours last year, of that Colossus thing, is it?" the president asks.

Zsoldos' jaw drops. Thompson rushes to the president's side. All eyes in the room are on Anderson. Russell grabs Anderson's shoulders from behind and directs him back to his chair. "We just covered that topic, sir. Please have a seat," Russell says calmly.

Once seated, the president looks, one by one, at the key advisers in the room. "Well, since we have covered that topic, is there anything else to discuss? If not, I believe I have a full calendar. You are all dismissed."

General Mahon makes his way out of the Oval Office. The colonel doesn't move as fast. It takes some time and effort getting to his feet. He relies on his cane and the back of a chair for support to stand erect. "I'm moving slowly this evening, Jon. I believe I could benefit from some time in the spa. Would you like to join me?"

Thompson agrees. "Mr. President, this was the last meeting on today's calendar. I think a visit to the spa is a splendid idea. It will give you a chance to clear your mind."

"Yes, I do feel muddled," Anderson concurs. "It must be all this bad news. The poor people in Chile. An earthquake, and a tsunami to boot. What a terrible thing."

Chapter 10: Straight Up

Pastor Keith Wardlow is on the stage in front of his Tuesday evening Bible study group. The Pastor is agitated. He paces back and forth, working to gather his words. He's holding a book in his hand, and it's not the Good Book. Pastor Keith is a lanky, fifty-four-year-old, white Mid-Westerner. His face is wrinkling and showing his years. He wears Levis and cowboy boots. His plaid flannel shirt is untucked. He dresses this way even for Sunday service.

The people of Burwell, Nebraska, are regular working folk. So is their pastor. The most striking thing about Pastor Keith is his Jesus' hair, as some people call it. He knows his long hair, once dark brown, now almost pure white, might be offensive to some, so he wears it in a ponytail. Pastor Keith grew up in this town with these people. He has been a man of God since he was a teenager.

"It's come to my attention several members of our church have been reading this book." He holds up the book *Straight Up: Ten Ways for Christians to Prepare for the Rapture*. Pastor Keith wants to say, "How can you people be reading such crap?" but he bites his tongue. Several of the Bible study group of thirty souls nod their heads in confirmation. Pastor Keith shakes the book at his congregates. "Some of my lambs have strayed. God spoke to my heart. He said, Gather the stray lambs of your flock. They are in danger! A-men!"

He looks at the cover of the book. "I know books like these are written by well-intended Christians. A famous pastor, out in California, wrote this one. But I tell you. The Devil got hold of that man's mind. People let me ask you. Do you know what's wrong with this book?"

There are murmurs among the congregation until an older woman named Beatrice shouts, "Tell us, Pastor."

"Bless you, Bea. Books like this cause people to be nervous and afraid." Keith studies the book, turning it over in his hands. "Not to mention, it's an actual printed book! With the book tax, these things cost a fortune. But I'm not here to mind your pocket. No, ma'am!"

He holds the book over his head. "The problem with books like this: they ask you to focus on things we can't know and cannot control. What good comes from studying signs, warning of the end times, or predicting when the Rapture will occur? Will knowing such a thing help you prepare? Will it help you live your life better? I say no!"

Pastor Keith points to the crowd. "And Frank Brown, if you spent more time taking care of your wife instead of building that submarine. I can't imagine what got into you, thinking the Earth will flood and a submarine will save you in the middle of Nebraska." The study group laughs. Frank sits in his pew, arms folded, wearing a tight, grim face.

It was quite an event when the TV show, *Doomsday Daredevils,* came to film Frank and his submarine. The show's host seemed serious during the filming, but when the episode aired, Frank appeared ridiculous and crazy.

Pastor Keith continues, picking up his Bible. "Frank, if you just read the good book instead of reading books like this rapture nonsense, you'd know God promised there will be no other floods."

"I didn't buy any stupid rapture book, Keith." Frank looks to his wife, Debbie. "God spoke to me, just like he does in the Bible. Laugh if you like. I never said the Earth will flood. I didn't question God, and I don't have to sit here and take your crap." He stands and holds his hand out to his wife. "Come on, Debbie doll. We're leaving," he says. Debbie stands, stepping sideways between the pews to the aisle. Frank and Debbie walk out of the small church. A copy of the rapture book is on the pew where Debbie sat.

Pastor Keith waits for Frank and Debbie to leave before continuing. "Frank and Debbie are our friends. Most of us have known them our whole lives. I'll have to apologize to Frank, and I will do that. Wandering from the word causes trouble and confusion. We must focus on the word."

Keith gauges his flock. Are they upset about the episode with Frank? He doesn't sense any tension, so he continues. "Well, just so happens, tonight is Bible study. We're here to learn and study the word."

Keith sits on the edge of the stage, looking through his notes. "The Book of Revelation tells us mankind will go through a terrible time of tribulation. Who wouldn't want to avoid this time of death and misery if you can escape it? The idea of a pre-tribulation rapture, however, is not biblical. The rapture concept was created and promoted in the early nineteenth century and is a myth. This lie was repeated, written about, and promoted to the point most Christians don't question where the idea came from, or if it's biblical. The word *rapture* isn't in the Bible. It's a made-up word; a bad translation."

Keith now has their attention. "Books like this scare good Christians, like y'all here, into believing you aren't good enough, or righteous enough, to be saved. They say you need to be more than a good Christian to be saved. This is false teaching by false prophets, as Jesus warned."

The old woman, Beatrice, asks, "If there is no rapture, when will we be taken up to be with Jesus?"

"Yes, when?" asks another voice in the crowd.

Pastor Keith sets his notes beside him on the stage and stands. "Concerning that day and hour, no one knows, not even the angels of heaven, nor the Son, but the Father only. That is Matthew 24, verse 36."

Pastor Keith watches the congregation's reaction. He doesn't want them to lose hope.

"We must wait until the end of tribulation. We must wait for the second coming of Christ, and that does not happen until after great tribulations. So, when will Jesus take us up with him? In John 6, verse 40, Jesus tells us. And this is the will of him who sent me... that everyone who sees the son and believes on him may have eternal life, and I will raise him up on the last day. So, we must all be patient in our faith until that last day, when Christ returns."

Pastor Keith walks to his pulpit and again picks up the rapture book. "So, you don't need this book. You need not follow silly rules written by false prophets scaring you into spending your hard-earned money."

Beatrice takes the rapture book out of her purse, stands, and tosses it in the aisle. "Thank you, Pastor Keith. I don't need this book. I was led astray, Lord forgive me." The woman sits down, repentant.

One man tosses his rapture book in the aisle, then asks. "But what about the signs? The signs show the end times are near. I've heard said the Four Wars are the four horsemen. What do you say about that, pastor?"

Pastor Keith waves his hand in a downward motion, signaling the man to sit down. "Douglas, we don't need a list of signs. If we read the Book of Revelation, we can see what will happen. There is nothing to interpret. Revelation 6, verse 13. And the stars of Heaven fell unto Earth, even as a fig tree casts her untimely figs when she is shaken of a mighty wind. This is the start of tribulation. So, when the stars in heaven fall on Earth, that will be the sign you can believe."

Keith wants to wrap things up. "Since this is a very interesting topic, let's all read Matthew 24 and Revelation. Get through as much of it as you can—Revelation can be a tough one. We don't spend enough time on that book, which has become clear tonight."

Pastor Keith concludes the Bible study with a prayer, followed by handshakes and hugs. Later, he gathers the rapture books from the floor and tosses them in the trash bin.

Chapter 11: Departure

Ethan and Alyssa are in the living room, each glued to their VUE lens. The TV is on, but no one's watching. Rick uses a voice command to change the stream to the evening news. The kids notice the change in audio and express their disgust. "Anything but the news, Dad," cries Ethan.

"You can switch it to your show when I'm out the door. You're not watching, anyway."

Courtney is in the kitchen, giving last-minute instructions to the teenage neighbor girl who will babysit while she rides with Rick to the airport. Rick could take the AutoCar by himself, but Courtney wants to see him off.

Courtney walks to the living room with the teenaged girl, Vanessa, in tow. "Ethan, Alyssa, this is Vanessa. She will stay with you tonight. Your bedtime is nine o'clock, no later. It's a school night. While I'm out, Vanessa is the boss!"

"Mom, we don't need a babysitter. We're twelve already. We're not babies," Ethan complains.

"If my friends find out I had a babysitter, I'll die of embarrassment," says Alyssa.

Rick hears the complaints and steps in. "Vanessa is not a babysitter. She's a security guard. Here to keep a guard on your behavior. If she reports to your mother, you were no problem, that you finished your homework and got to bed on time, then maybe you will earn our trust to let you stay home by yourselves next time."

"Ah geez," say both kids.

"Deal?" asks Rick.

"Deal," says Ethan.

"Deal," says Alyssa, reluctantly.

"OK, get over here and give me a hug," Rick says as he gives his twins a goodbye hug.

"We'd better go if you want to catch your plane," says Courtney.

"Don't forget to buy me a souvenir," Alyssa says, waving goodbye.

"Me too," shouts Ethan.

"We're off." With that, Rick and Courtney head out the door. They ride away while the kids and Vanessa wave.

Ethan and Alyssa settle in the living room. The evening news streams on the TV. Ethan is about to tell the TV to switch to the previous channel when he notices a news ticker scroll across the bottom of the screen: "Meteor explodes over Perth, Australia." The word *meteor* catches Ethan's eye.

The ticker continues to crawl along the bottom of the screen. "Damage to the city is widespread—" The news ticker stops and the news cuts to a commercial.

Ethan watches in shock. "Dad, you've got to see this!" he calls out, then remembers his father has already left. News of a meteor exploding would intrigue his dad.

Ethan hates watching news streams, but he sits waiting for more news on Perth. An hour later, there is a brief mention of a daytime fireball over Perth, with no mention of damage to the city. The report only states a daytime fireball flew over Perth. There are no further details. "Huh, must be nothing," Ethan says to himself.

Mike McCoy

Chapter 12: Sky Storm

Tuesday Night–Denver, Colorado

Jin and Becky planned to meet at Red Rocks Park and Amphitheater outside of Denver. Jin offered to pick up Becky and drive her, but she insisted on driving herself.

Becky thinks of herself as practical and organized. She's always shunned girly things. As a child, she was more interested in math, science, and a good book. She shunned Barbie dolls and dresses. If she was ever near the color pink, she would involuntarily convulse.

She is most comfortable in baggy Levis and an unbuttoned flannel shirt over a T-shirt. You might see her wearing a bracelet or necklace, but nothing flashy or bright. Becky isn't an athlete, but under her baggy clothes, she has a nice body. She doesn't wear makeup and wears her hair pulled back in a loose ponytail, because it's the easiest thing to do. Becky likes her long hair.

Tonight, even after dating for two months, Becky finds herself nervous, as the womanly behaviors she has avoided for most of her life sneak up on her. She prepared a picnic dinner of tuna sandwiches, celery and carrot sticks, chips, and bottled water. She hopes this is enough. What does one pack for watching a meteor shower? She loaded it all into a small cooler. As an afterthought, she had tossed a blanket in the back seat of her car before driving off to Red Rocks Park.

Becky isn't just Jin's first girlfriend. Becky is the first girl Jin has ever dated. After high school, Jin left Las Vegas for the University of Denver on a full scholarship. He lived in the dorms, but not a co-ed one. He lived in the guy's only dorm for engineering and math students. The University of Denver is a party school. Someone should have told Jin. He filled his time with math, computer engineering, and the robotics club. Jin built robots. He didn't party.

Jin picked up astronomy as a hobby, growing up with Curtis and Curtis's father, Walter. Jin's parents never married. His father was out of the picture before he was born. Jin's mom worked nights at a casino and slept during the day. Jin spent most of his time at Curtis's house. It was the closest thing he knew to having a real family. Jin graduated university with degrees in mathematics and computer engineering and earned a master's degree in computer science before beginning a career in his new hometown of Denver.

Jin likes girls, or at least the idea of having a girlfriend, but he'd never tried to find one. He was busy with work, astronomy, or video games.

Jin and Curtis spend their spare time logging in to telescopes through DAPA (NASA's Department of Astronomy for Public Access) searching for asteroids, and they stay in touch with a network of astronomy enthusiasts around the world through online forums and ham radio.

It was a typical night on an astronomy forum. Jin provided an answer to some guy's basic question, then out of the blue, he got a private message from a girl! She'd liked the response he gave to the guy's simple question. Jin checked the girls' profile. He noticed she has a degree in mechatronic systems.

"Huh, mechatronic systems, that could be a conversation starter," Jin had said to himself. Jin replied to the private message: "thx." That was how his relationship with Becky had started.

Jin might be new to dating, but he could not have selected a more exquisite site for a date. Red Rocks Amphitheater is built around a geologic masterpiece; a natural amphitheater that consists of two three-hundred-foot monoliths—Ship Rock and Creation Rock—that provide acoustic perfection for any performance. The site has been used since the early 1900s for concerts and has developed into a world-class concert venue. The concert venue, the scenic hiking trails with real dinosaur tracks in the rocks, and the landscape of the park are beautiful and awe-inspiring.

Becky and Jin had planned to meet at the picnic shelter parking lot, north of the amphitheater, away from the lights. The scenery is spectacular. From this location, you look down the hill to see the "Ship Rock" monolith of the amphitheater. Jin arrives first. His drive from Denver is shorter than the drive from Boulder. The sky is clear, with only a few wispy clouds in the distance. Jin throws his knapsack, packed with gear, over his shoulder, and walks to "his" picnic table.

When Jin returns to his truck, he sees Becky arrive. He rushes to her car and opens the door for her.

"I brought food," she says, motioning to the cooler in her back seat. "It's not much."

"I'll grab that for you," he says. He takes the cooler from the back seat. "I have my usual spot saved for us. It's just up the trail." Becky grabs the blanket and follows.

Once at the table, Jin sets up the Alcor OMEA–All-Sky Camera and unrolls a viewing monitor. The monitor's built-in stand pops out as he sets it on the picnic table. Darkness is settling in, and the sky becomes dotted with glimmering sparkles. Becky sets the food out while Jin aligns the sky cam.

"I can't believe I haven't brought you here before. It's my favorite spot," says Jin.

The table is lit only by the glow of the monitor, but Jin can see Becky well enough. He catches himself staring at her, examining her every detail.

"It's a beautiful location," Becky says as she hands a sandwich to Jin. They sit side by side on the picnic bench, eating tuna sandwiches and carrot sticks under the starry sky. Music from a concert in the amphitheater plays in the background.

"Red Rocks Park is almost the perfect viewing site. The elevation is sixty-five hundred feet and we're far from city lights," says Jin. The darkening sky fills with an amazing array of stars. "Look," Jin says, pointing at the sky. "See the long dusty cluster of space clouds? That's the Milky Way."

"It's beautiful. Do you think we'll discover a new asteroid tonight?" Becky asks.

"It might be difficult tonight, but it should be special. There's a new meteor shower, and it's supposed to be spectacular."

"What makes this meteor shower special?"

"Just that it's new. NASA tracks comets as they orbit around the sun. We typically have a few years' notice before Earth passes through the debris field, which creates a meteor shower. But this one just appeared out of nowhere. An amateur astronomer discovered it two weeks ago. We aren't even sure it's from a comet. This meteor shower has been going off for the past few nights. Tonight, it's predicted to be at maximum activity. But nobody knows. It could be a complete dud, a wasted night," explains Jin.

Becky leans into Jin, nudging him. "I don't think it's a wasted night." she says.

Jin is slow to catch on. "Oh no, I didn't... I mean with you, it's a special night no matter what happens."

They laugh as a shooting star races across the sky. "Look there. They just named this meteor shower today. They're calling it Bootes P2604 because it radiates from the constellation Bootes, also known as the protector of the Bear or Ursa Major. All the shooting stars should start in that area tonight." Jin points to the north sky.

"I'm getting a chill. Can you grab the blanket?" Becky asks.

Jin scoots close as he lays the blanket over Becky's shoulders and wraps the other end over his. As he fumbles with the blanket, Becky finds his free hand, touching her hand to his. Jin responds by clutching her hand. Her skin is cold but warms with his touch.

Five bright lights streak across the sky. Then six more blaze the night sky, followed by a dozen brighter streaks in rapid succession.

Becky squeezes Jin's hand. "Are there always so many?"

"This is unusual, but there have been events known as meteor outbursts or meteor storms that produce over one thousand meteors per hour. If it stays this active, we could be in for a great show." Jin releases his hand from Becky's. "Hold on a sec."

He adjusts the sky camera and sends the stream to a server he shares with Curtis. Curtis will see what Jin and Becky are viewing in real time.

Jin sits back, adjusts the blanket, and feels around for Becky's hand. "All set. The first great meteor storm recorded in modern times was the Leonids, back in November 1833. They observed up to two hundred thousand meteors in a single hour. It was a short but a brilliant show," Jin explains.

"I can't wait. How can we even count them all if it's a real meteor storm?" asks Becky.

"I don't know. Maybe Curtis will count them," Jin chuckles. The sky explodes with bursts of streaming light.

"Ooh, wow," Becky exclaims. "That must have been twenty shooting stars, right there. This is great!"

The intensity and frequency increase dramatically. The shooting stars come like waves across the sky. "I've never seen anything like this," says Jin, as Becky wraps her free hand over their joined hands. Jin turns to see her face lit by the glow of the monitor.

Becky moves her mouth close to Jin's ear. She whispers. "This is really special. Thanks for inviting me." Jin turns his head so his lips can meet hers. She leans in. He leans in. Their lips are about to touch.

The theme from *Star Wars* plays loud, and Curtis's image appears on the screen. Becky jumps when she hears the music.

"Dude, are you seeing this? It's like the sky's exploding." Curtis smiles as he watches Jin and Becky's startled reaction. "Oh hey, dude and ah... dude-ette. Sorry if I interrupted anything," Curtis says as he leans forward, his face growing larger on the screen.

Jin moves away from Becky. "Hey, Curtis. Are you picking up the stream? It's going gangbusters."

"Yeah, it looked like things were about to get seriously active. I guess I saved the day," Curtis says.

Becky looks perturbed. "Hi, Curtis." She drags out his name in a low tone along with a slow, dispassionate wave now that her hands are free.

"What's up, Curtis?" Jin asks.

"We could have a record-breaking meteor shower. I've been trying to focus in on the particle cloud. Normally, everything is too small to see, just ice particles and grains of sand or dust balls, but I swear I can see some incoming. This stuff is made of larger chunks breaking up in the atmosphere."

Jin scoffs. "You can't see space dust, Curtis. This is a big event, but you're getting over-excited."

"Don't believe me? Check this out. A guy in Maine shot this with his fourteen-inch Galaxy Viewer."

An image appears on Jin's monitor, showing what looks like clumps of gravel clinging loosely together in space. "That was taken an hour ago, and check this." Another image appears with a wider-angle showing hundreds of small rocky masses. "These were about a hundred thousand miles out two hours ago. I bet we're running right into this rocky road," says Curtis.

The sky above Jin and Becky continues to light up with streaks of meteors rocketing across the horizon. "Should we be concerned for our safety?" Becky asks.

"No, they'll burn up in the atmosphere," answers Jin. "They would have to be a lot larger to hit Earth and cause damage."

"Some of this stuff is pretty big for a dust storm. If we can see asteroids a hundred thousand miles out, they must be at least several meters in diameter," Curtis rebuts.

Another burst of shooting stars ignites the sky. Jin and Becky watch the fireworks above. Curtis can't take the silence. "Did you hear about Perth? There was a daytime fireball today."

"What happened in Perth?" Becky asks.

"It was on the news stream a few hours ago. There was fireball that lit up the sky over Perth this morning," Curtis explains.

"Daytime fireballs aren't that uncommon," says Jin.

"But what's weird is they announced it like it was a major headline, then they never followed up with any details. I scanned the web. There isn't any additional news about the meteor," Curtis says.

"Maybe there isn't anything more to the story. Fireball in the sky. It's over, get on with your day," says Becky.

Curtis shakes his finger at the screen. "No way, kiddos. I'm telling you something weird is going on. All the government-funded scopes are down. There's a huge daytime fireball in the sky over Perth and no news about it. I tell you; something is going on. It's a cover-up," Curtis hypothesizes.

"Curtis, this is like a couple months ago. Some guy posted a message in the forums claiming a meteor caused the Chilean earthquake and tsunami. You got so excited."

"That's right. They deleted his post, and nobody heard from the guy again. It was a government cover-up. I'm telling you," Curtis says.

"How is a deleted post a government cover-up?" asks Becky.

"How about this? We have the biggest meteor storm in recent history. We have fireballs over Perth, and nobody is reporting it. All the telescopes are down. It's a government conspiracy. I'm telling you."

"Curtis, you're starting to scare me. I hoped to enjoy the evening," Becky says, giving Jin a slight nudge.

"Something big is about to happen. I know it," Curtis says.

The silent fireworks in the sky erupt with a sonic boom and hundreds of flashes stream across the sky. Then a second sonic boom, followed by a third boom in rapid succession. Becky clutches Jin.

Curtis cheers. "Whoa, ha-ha, you hear that. I told you! This isn't a meteor storm; it's a sky storm! The whole frickin' sky is exploding. This is so fuckin' cool. Becky, you picked the right night to get some fireworks. Maybe not the kind you planned, but whoa." Three more sonic booms shock the night sky as Curtis whoops and cheers.

Jin throws the blanket off, pulls Becky up, and gathers their things. "Curtis, it might sound great where you are, but those sonic booms are a too close for comfort. We're gonna clear out of here."

"You're gonna let a little rumble in the sky get you upset? Settle down. It's just a frickin' sky storm!" exclaims Curtis.

"Thanks for your concern, Curtis. I don't think you'd find it funny if a sky storm landed in your front yard," Becky scolds, as she folds the blanket and stuffs food containers into the cooler.

Jin rolls up the monitor. It's still glowing with Curtis's image as Jin stuffs it in his bag. "Hey, where are you going?" the rolled-up face asks.

"Talk to you later, Curtis. The show's over," Jin says as he motions over his band and ends the call.

Jin and Becky hurry down the trail to their cars. Jin helps Becky load the cooler and blanket. When he closes the back door of her car, they are standing face-to-face. Becky reaches for his hand. "He's right, you know. Sonic booms can be generated from meteors as small as a baseball. They won't cause any damage."

Becky pulls the big lug to her. Jin finds himself inches from Becky's face. He doesn't hesitate. He presses his lips to hers. She moves her lips with his as he hugs her. He kisses her deeply and passionately. Becky returns the passion. They kiss until another sonic boom erupts in the sky. They separate. Panting.

"I think I'd better make sure you make it home safe. Let's get out of here."

Becky bites her lower lip, looking up at her man. "OK."

Chapter 13: The Spa

Tuesday Night–White House

Zsoldos helps the two old men to the door of the Oval Office. The Secret Service detail takes charge once the office door is open. "The president and the colonel would like to spend time in the spa. Please assist them."

The spa is in the basement of the West Wing next to the swimming pool. The colonel had it remodeled into a modern treatment center during a previous administration. President Anderson and the colonel walk into the luxurious treatment room and sit in comfortable reclining chairs. Male attendants dressed in medical garb work to prepare customized individual treatments.

President Anderson will receive a new course of Alzheimer's therapy. The treatment involves flooding the brain with a mix of chemicals designed to dissolve amyloid and tau protein buildups, revitalizing damaged nerve cells.

Before beginning this course of treatment, the president went through a procedure to install small plug valves in his skull, hidden beneath his hair. An attendant connects tubes to the valves.

Cruikshank notes the bizarre sight; the leader of the free world, sitting with colored tubes coming out of his skull. The attendant starts the cerebral flush and fluids gush through the tubes with a pumping, sucking sound, saturating the president's brain with healing fluid.

Colonel Cruikshank is an enthusiastic devotee of a unique treatment to cure his ails. His procedure involves using blood, plasma, and stem cells from young subjects. A young person's blood replaces the blood of an older person through a process called parabiosis, resulting in mental and physical rejuvenation of the older subject. He considers it his fountain of youth.

Scientists tested the Parabiosis process on mice. The scientists found when an older mouse shared the circulatory system of a younger mouse, the stem cells and blood factors from the younger mouse rejuvenated the older mouse, effectively making the older subject young again. They've since developed new techniques for extraction and processing of young blood factors, making the complicated parabiosis transfusion process unnecessary, but the colonel trusts the traditional method. He prefers a human touch.

A door opens on the far side of the spa and a small boy, wearing only sky-blue pajama bottoms and white slippers, walks anxiously into the room. He catches a fright at the sight of the old men and freezes in place. A husky male attendant lifts the boy, carries him across the room, and straps him into a small reclining chair next to the colonel.

The boy looks to be nine or ten years of age. He is rosy-cheeked with blond hair. The boy is thin but tall for his age. The colonel looks the boy over approvingly. Two attendants extend the boy's arms and strap them to padded boards. They swab his arms with alcohol, then pierce him with needles. The boy whimpers. The male attendant connects tubes to each needle. The man attaches one tube to an IV bag of saline and the other tube fills with the boys' blood. A tear rolls down the boy's cheek.

Blood pulses from the boy into a small machine. This machine pulls blood from the boy and pumps it into the old man. One attendant swabs the old man's leg on the inside of his upper thigh and inserts a tube. Another attendant does the same to the boy. They connect these tubes to a similar pump system, but this device pulls blood from the old man and stores it in a reservoir. The reservoir ensures none of the old man's blood gets recycled through the boy during the process. The final step of the procedure is to pump the old blood into the boy.

Tears stream down the boy's face. The attendant leans down and whispers into his ear. "You are helping Colonel Cruikshank. He is a great man and you're a brave boy. You are helping the colonel and the glory of Arcadia."

The attendant pushes a lozenge between the boy's lips. It's cherry flavored. He smiles. The lozenge contains a relaxant to calm the boy during the procedure. They don't inject the drug. If injected, the drug would enter the bloodstream too quickly and travel to the old man. The attendant starts the pump. It makes a soft whirring sound. Blood surges into the old man's arm. Cruikshank feels the young, warm blood flow into his veins. His body surges with energy, forcing his eyes shut. A thin smile forms on his face as his head falls back into the spa chair. The attendant starts the second pump to evacuate old, tired blood from the colonel.

The attendants check on the president. Pumps send a mixture of drugs through the tubes, running to his head in timed sequences. The mix works to unclog the autophagy system, the body's natural brain-cleaning system, improving learning and memory. The treatment is proceeding without complications.

Besides the chemical mix, a slight electric charge runs through the scalp plugs. This electric charge assists the restoration of synaptic response, rebuilding neural connections. They call this process a sub-neural flush, but those who perform the procedure have a tough time resisting a less professional term: brain wash.

A side effect of the sub-neural flush is that the patient becomes susceptible to suggestion.

With the spa treatments underway, the attendants leave the men alone in the room. Both men relax in the reclining chairs, enjoying their treatments. The colonel turns to the president and asks, "Are you all right, Jon?"

The president nods his head. "Much better. I hate losing control. I'm the damned President of the United States. I can't be off my game."

"Everyone has a profound respect for you, sir. Don't worry, we're all getting old."

"But you're not the leader of the free world. I can't let that happen, not in public."

"Mr. President, no matter what happens over the next few weeks, you will go down in the history books as a great president. You accepted the reins of power with honor and grace when President Harmon could no longer serve. You handled the end of US involvement in the Four Wars as a true leader, and I know you will manage the coming disaster in the manner of a true and noble commander."

"Thank you, Colonel. You're a true friend. I have valued your wisdom and advice through many difficult times. I pray mankind will survive the terrible storm that is coming."

Colonel Cruikshank sinks into the recliner, reveling in the sensation of hot, young blood pumping through his body, reenergizing every fiber of his being. His brain buzzes; new neurons fire, reconnecting pathways in his brain, sending his mind racing. His ideas effuse and flow, forcing him to express his thoughts.

"Humankind will survive the asteroid storm, Jon, just as mankind survived periods of destruction many times over many millennia. Man is an inbred race of domesticated mongrels who murdered, robbed, and fucked their way to the top of the food chain. Mankind has persevered through wars, famine, disease, even the Ice Age. Only God knows what man survived before that, but we did. What does not survive devastation is human knowledge. Ask yourself and consider: What does a man know? I will tell you. Man knows what other men tell him. Myths, beliefs, religion, culture, Santa Claus, the Easter Bunny, and the nature of God are all absorbed by one's psyche from birth to death. It's all a grand phantasm created to provide social stability and a sense of purpose in an aimless world. Mankind loses knowledge, then struggles to regain what he's lost. Each new epoch develops unique cultures with new languages, myths, and religions. The problem is not the destruction. The problem is man. Stupid, hapless humans. We are our own undoing. If the world is not destroyed by an outside force, leave it man to destroy what he has built and learned for the sake of riches, war, selfish beliefs, or control of his fellow man. Man has lost knowledge and wisdom over and over again. How many centuries of thought and strife passed until the concept that all men are created equal with certain unalienable rights was written on parchment? Three centuries later and this acknowledged ideal is not yet achieved. Arcadia is the answer. The few and fortunate will survive the storms to repopulate the surface with human knowledge preserved, allowing mankind to step forward. We have mastered myth and religion. We will tell new stories written to embed pure values and beliefs. The Arcadian way will develop a new phantasm for the human psyche, resulting in a perfect society. The pinnacle of humanity is within our grasp." Cruikshank is enthralled, sweat beading on his forehead.

In his excitement, he almost forgets his purpose. Cruikshank needs the president to sign ARC before it's too late. The president's breathing has slowed. His eyes flutter: he is groggy, an effect of the sedative and sub-neural wash. This is the time he will be most susceptible to suggestion.

"Mr. President, Jon. My friend, you are a great president and leader. You will lead us into the future by signing the ARC amendment. The Arcadian Council and your leadership will bring humanity through this crisis."

As the colonel speaks, his harsh, raspy voice becomes smoother and softer. "You will be honored as a true hero. Making this monumental decision will move humankind forward. Cities will be destroyed, civilization and government as we know it be erased, yet we will preserve human knowledge." While the colonel is voicing his excitement about ARC, young stem cells and blood factors are showing their effectiveness. The once dead, gray pupils of an old man transform into the sharp blue irises of youth.

"ARC will make Arcadia the legitimate government, allowing those living in the underground cities to grow and prosper during the storm and reemerge to the surface as a stronger society. You cannot allow humanity to decay into chaos and disorder."

The president rests in his reclining chair. His eyes are glassy, and he groans in response to Cruikshank's fiery speech. Cruikshank looks at the president, hoping for confirmation. He wants assurance the president will sign the amendment.

The wrinkled face of the old colonel fills out; his skin smooths and softens as the color of youth returns. He feels growing strength. "You will sign ARC. You will sign the amendment." The colonel repeats the phrase over and over, as if chanting a mantra, hoping to ingrain the words in the president's sub-conscious. "You must sign the amendment. You will sign ARC. You will be honored as a hero. We will be the legitimate government leading humanity forward. You must sign ARC."

The attendants enter the room to check the progress of the president's therapy. The tubes connected to his scalp jump and vibrate with fluids pumping in and out as the therapy timer counts to zero.

A spa attendant rushes to the boy. His face is ashen white, and his eyes have rolled back into his head. "He isn't tolerating the blood loss. We need to hurry, or we'll lose this one." The attendant lowers the head of the boy's chair and raises his feet before turning the IV to full flow. Then he reaches to the pump and stops the flow from the boy to the colonel. The reservoir of the colonel's old blood flows into the boy. The once vibrant youth, flush with color, now has sunken cheeks and sallow skin. This boy will not bleed to death, but the blood flowing to him is nearly death itself.

"The procedure isn't finished. What's wrong with him?"

"Some boys can't tolerate this much blood loss. The saline drip helps, but can't work miracles. You don't want to lose another one, do you?"

"If it's over, get these needles out of me!" shouts the Colonel.

The neural wash timer chimes. An attendant unplugs the tubes from the president's scalp, dabbing the plugs with disinfectant, then smooths the president's hair to cover them. He then gives the president a glass of water as the recliner's motor whines, raising the chief executive to a sitting position.

The colonel stands and taps his cane twice on the tile floor. "Now that's a neat trick." He smiles and stretches, looking youthful and spry.

The attendant helps the weak boy, lifting him out of the chair and steadying him to stand, then holds the boy as he shuffles out of the spa.

The president looks at the rejuvenated colonel and remarks, "That therapy seems very effective for you. However, the poor boy appears quite spent."

The colonel watches the weak boy exit the room. "He'll snap back in no time. He's on a special diet designed for rapid recovery."

The men exit the spa in a much-improved physical and mental condition than when they entered. A Secret Service detail flanks them as they walk back to the Oval Office.

"I would like to give your therapy a try; it seems to do wonders for you. But if I suddenly looked ten or fifteen years younger, the news media would go frantic asking questions about my health," the president remarks.

When they reach the Oval Office, the colonel excuses himself. "Mr. President, it's late. I'm sure you'll want to retire. We all have full schedules tomorrow. I'll let you get some rest."

"Not so fast, Cruikshank. I'm not letting you get away yet. Come in. I have a few questions for you."

The president stands behind his desk in the Oval Office. He puts both hands on the polished wood surface, leaning over the desk in a menacing stance, staring into the crisp blue eyes of the colonel. With a strong voice, he says, "Cruikshank, I know you have been working behind my back and I don't like it one bit."

The comment catches the colonel off guard. Was the president conscious during the treatment? Had he heard what he'd said?

"Mr. President, I'm not sure what you mean."

"What I mean is, you've kept me out of the loop on some situations, and I don't like it. I know I've had some awkward moments, but you must appraise me of every issue, so I can make the proper decisions. I will not be undermined by my chief of staff, General Mahon, or you. I need you to understand that if you are to continue as my National Security Advisor."

The colonel feigns ignorance. "Mr. President, what situation do you mean?"

"You have not been forthcoming about the Chilean incident. I racked my brain during therapy. None of you consulted me about implementing Bliss or creating the cover story of an earthquake for the press. I learned this for the first time today. I am sure of it."

The neural therapy re-initialized the president's memory and personality, which includes his temper and fiery tongue.

"I apologize, Mr. President. You made the decision, it's just, at the time of that crisis, you were... how can I put this delicately? You could not remember what you decided." Cruikshank takes the chance the president is still fuzzy on the entire episode.

"Well, if that situation occurs again, I want any decisions delayed until I've had a spa treatment, then we can continue when I am..." The president pauses. "Until I am—"

The colonel interrupts. "Until you are on your best game. Understood, sir. It won't happen again."

"Right then. What was it?" the president asks.

"What was what, sir?"

"If not an earthquake. What was it? What caused the tsunami?"

The colonel gives a direct and solemn response. "An asteroid, sir. It was a large asteroid. Not an earthquake. You could imagine the panic if the truth got out."

The president is angry. He rises and paces behind his desk. "You see. I must be informed of every situation or briefed later if..." The president drags out his words as he looks into the colonel's blue eyes.

The president continues pacing. "First Chile, now Perth. The threat of this asteroid storm is imminent. I don't think we have time to waste. We must act now, allowing those living in the underground cities to grow and prosper during the asteroid storm. When it's over, we will live on the surface as a stronger society. We cannot allow our people to exist in chaos and disorder. I must sign ARC."

The colonel smiles.

The president touches a button on his desk console, alerting his chief of staff. Even though the hour is late, Russell Thompson responds instantly. "Yes, Mr. President? How can I assist you?"

"Russell, come here and bring the ARC document with you."

Russell grabs the document from his desk and rushes to the Oval Office. He moves briskly across the room to the president's desk, arranging the amendment for the president's signature. President Anderson gives the pages a quick once-over, then signs the ARC amendment. With a swift stroke of the pen, the President of the United States dissolves a republic that lasted nearly two hundred seventy years.

Once the president signs the amendment, the colonel assumes a relaxed posture, pulling his damaged leg up over his good leg. "Very good, Mr. President. You will be honored as a true hero for making this monumental decision to move humankind forward." Jon Anderson mouths the last few words as the colonel says them. The words sound so familiar.

The colonel feels a buzz in his ear and touches his ear dot to answer. "Yes, what is it? Oh, yes, that. I almost forgot. I will be there shortly," the colonel speaks cryptically. He rises and bows slightly to the president.

"Sir, I am honored to have been present for the signing of this important document; However, I must excuse myself. I have other duties to attend. Good night, sir."

The colonel stands erect and taps his cane energetically on the floor before striding valiantly out of the Oval Office.

Chapter 14: The Presentation

Wednesday Morning

The business class seat should have allowed Rick to sleep comfortably, but his excitement kept him awake most of the flight. The plane touched down in Washington, DC, at 6:30 a.m. Eastern time. As he exited the plane, he looked back at the luxurious seat. So much for government cutbacks.

Rick's bag waited for him in baggage claim. Once Rick is in range, the suitcase beeps, and wiggles, scooting ahead, leading Rick to the AutoCar zone.

The AutoCar stops at the front of his hotel. Rick sets his suitcase on the pavement. The hotel is fancy and traditional. A doorman wearing a large jacket and hat holds the hotel's grand door open, greeting Rick. It takes a moment for Rick to realize the doorman is a robot or nom, as people call them these days.

Rick's suitcase scurries across the elegant lobby to the front desk as Rick follows. Rick stands in front of a screen at the front desk. The system confirms his reservation via facial recognition and a room code appears on his band, whereupon a nom wearing a bellman's uniform appears next to him.

"Please follow me." The bellman nom moves briskly to the elevator. Rick's suitcase speeds along with the bellman, leaving Rick to catch up.

The bellman opens the hotel room and holds the door open for Rick, then sets the suitcase on a charging bench. His initial view of the large suite leaves Rick awestruck. The bellman walks through the large room, signaling lights to illuminate, and triggers the curtains to slide open while giving Rick a quick tour of the suite by pointing and uttering one-word descriptions, bedroom, desk, closet, bathroom.

The room is luxurious, decorated with fine furniture and artwork. A dining table with a flower arrangement sits in the center of the room and a couch and coffee table are arranged in front of a video wall. A desk is next to the floor-to-ceiling windows, which offer a magnificent view of the Capitol building. Off the main suite is the bedroom and a large bathroom.

When the bellman finishes, he stands at attention and speaks. "Will there be anything else, sir?"

"No. This is amazing. Thank you."

The bellman hesitates. "Very well then," the nom says before leaving the room. Rick wonders if he should have tipped the nom as the door clicks shut.

Rick walks to the large windows and marvels at the brilliant view. The city is coming to life in the early dawn light. The White House, in the distance, looks majestic.

Rick settles in and catches a couple hours of restless sleep, dreaming about his grant. He realizes getting funded is a long shot, but he'll be presenting to his peers. He must be on the right track. Times have been tough but are getting better.

The industry and economy of North America changed drastically during the Four Wars. After nuclear attacks destroyed New York and Chicago, everyone suffered. Everyone sacrificed. It wasn't just the bombed cities and the dread of world war. Products once imported from Asia and Europe became scarce. Global commerce all but ceased. Industry focused on developing technology and weapons to fight wars instead of producing products for consumption. Poverty soared. Government-issued apps doled out ration coupons. Life has improved since those darkest days.

After the US signed treaties to cease involvement in the Four Wars, the economy blossomed. Cities affected by the wars worked to recover and rebuild. The government funded the initial stages of the recovery. Entrepreneurs raced to develop innovative technologies and created automated factories to produce food and consumer products.

Companies like Armadyne produce a new generation of home appliances called actualizers. Actualizers are designed for a variety of applications. Many households now have a food actualizer to create quick meals. If you have enough money, you have a product actualizer or an Electro-Weave, a device that makes clothing from designs purchased online.

Auto-noms — autonomous, self-operating systems have replaced the restaurant and service jobs. People initially called them robots or bots, but as they became more intelligent and autonomous, they called them noms.

People of all income levels somehow afford communication devices. They might not spend money on Electro-Weaves, but everyone has a Smart-Band or VUE lens and some use both bands and lenses.

Even though the economy is looking brighter, the government continues to cut budgets. New projects go unfunded. The Four Wars continue in many parts of the world. People think the government spends too much money funding one side or maybe both sides of the conflicts to keep the wars from once again spreading to US soil. Some people claim the government fuels the wars to keep the weapons industry alive. The government denies these accusations, yet while industry and citizens pay their taxes, government coffers bleed dry.

Rick needs his grant funded. If he can achieve this goal, he'll be able to provide a comfortable life for his family. Ethan might even get the Glide Pad he's been begging for.

Rick wakes and goes for a short run. At breakfast, he sends a message to Courtney — "I'm in Washington, DC!"—along with a photo of the White House. He is ready and waiting in the lobby when an executive AutoCar arrives to drive him to the seminar.

Rick settles into the comfortable back seat of the AutoCar. As it drives through downtown DC, he realizes he doesn't know where the seminar is being held. Rick recognizes several landmarks as the car crosses a river, he assumes is the Potomac. The AutoCar enters a major highway and is soon cruising through the countryside.

Rick touches his band to give Courtney a morning call. The band flashes NO SERVICE. "That's strange." He cycles the receiver module. It still flashes NO SERVICE. It seems unusual to not have a signal in Washington, DC. Rick resolves to call his wife as soon as he finishes his presentation. He hopes to have good news. Thirty minutes later, the car pulls off the highway.

The car moves down a wooded road, then turns into a wide entry drive. A solid-looking gate opens, allowing the AutoCar to enter.

Rick is excited as he looks out the car's window, but he thinks it strange there are no signs marking the fenced-in campus.

The AutoCar slows but does not stop at the sentry station and proceeds into the complex, driving past several large buildings, most of which look unoccupied. Rick notices the parking lots are empty except for a few scattered cars. The AutoCar comes to a stop along the side of a large gray building.

This building has no windows or markings. A double door with an entry pad, an overhead light, and a domed camera are its only features. The odd location confuses Rick.

The AutoCar's door opens. Rick doesn't get out. He sits looking at the gray doors, talking to himself. "I'm… ah… I was invited to a government seminar. I'm supposed to give my presentation to…" Rick's voice trails off as he hesitates. "To an audience of my peers," he whispers. He realizes he doesn't know who else is attending this seminar or to whom he is presenting. He feels foolish.

The gray doors open and out steps a well-dressed young man who walks with a quick stride, a big smile, and thick, well-groomed hair. He carries a small tablet under his arm. Two men looking like FBI agents, dressed in dark suits, also exit the building and stand by the double doors.

The young man walks briskly to the AutoCar, extending his hand in greeting. "Dr. Munday, I presume," he says with a southern accent. "I've always wanted to say that." He smiles, laughing at himself. He tries to explain his humor. "It's as if we're in an African jungle. I've found y'all, Dr. Munday." He cackles.

Rick stares at the young man. "Yes, you found me sitting in an AutoCar, in an empty parking lot, somewhere in Maryland. Very exotic." Rick pauses. He doesn't lose it often, but he is unsure of what's happening. "I'm supposed to be attending an astrophysics seminar. What is this place? I'm here to give my presentation to an audience of my peers, not meeting somebody, you, in a parking lot at the back of some dreary building."

Unfazed, with twinkling eyes and wearing a broad smile, the young man bends down and reaches to lift his charge out of the car. "Don't you fret, Dr. Munday. That is precisely why I'm here. I will escort you to the presentation room. Now come this way. You silly." The young man's smile widens as he pulls Rick from the car.

Rick grudgingly walks with the young man through the gray doors. The two FBI-types follow a few paces behind Rick and the young man as they walk down a nondescript institutional corridor. As they walk, the young man explains what is to take place.

"You must realize, security is so important these days, you know, with the Four Wars and all that trouble in New Korea, not to mention the Cyber-wars. Me oh my! You'll be giving your presentation to some very important people. But they don't want you to know who they are unless you move forward. I'm sure you understand."

The young man speaks quickly as they continue along the dull corridor, past intersecting hallways and locked doors. He stops at a black door and applies his palm to a soft gel filled square next to the heavy-looking door. The gel forms around and accepts his hand. The door clicks open.

"In you go," says the young man with another broad smile. He then gives Rick a good ole boy slap on the back and a firm push into the room.

Rick staggers into a dark room, then turns back to look at the young man and the two FBI guys. The young man smiles once more. "Just give your presentation as if you were standing in front of a packed lecture hall." The man gestures with big arms. "You'll be fine, honey," he says with a wink.

Rick stares at the young man. As the door is closing, he asks, "What do you mean, if I move forward?" The door closes with the whisper of vacuum. A series of clicks secures the door.

Rick looks around the room. In front is a floor-to-ceiling glass wall twenty feet high. The wall stretches across the length of the room, which was about thirty feet wide, but the room was only fifteen feet deep. The glass is dark and doesn't reflect his image. It isn't a mirror. Rick is glad for that. The floor is black except for a single gray line on the floor, like an actor's mark on a stage, showing where the performer is to stand.

Lights hang from above, angled toward the mark on the floor providing shadowy illumination. Rick scans the empty room and then tries to look through the glass wall. Is he a caged animal on display? "Who is out there? What's going on? Am I supposed to just start?" Rick looks back at the door. There is no doorknob, just a gel pad on the wall. "Shit," Rick says, louder than expected.

The glass wall explodes with color and sound startling Rick. Clouds stream across a blue sky, then a rocket launches with a thunderous sound, making the glass wall vibrate. Words appear in reverse: "Welcome to the Astrophysics Science Center." A voice accompanies the video, introducing the science center and its goals. Rick stares at the video. He assumes this is an introduction for the audience sitting in front of the glass. As the voice over drones on about the science center, Rick feels a tickle in his ear, then hears a voice speaking to him as if he were wearing an earpiece.

"Dr. Munday, your presentation will begin once the introduction has finished." It's a woman's soft voice, but it sounds strange. The voice seems far off, yet it's inside his ear, or maybe inside his head. Rick rubs his ear, but the sound is undisturbed.

"Please move to your mark on the floor." Rick steps to the mark, then touches his band. Its projected screen does not appear. Rick tries to activate his band and load his presentation, but nothing works.

The voice comes back. "We have loaded your presentation to the projection system, Dr. Munday."

"My band isn't working. How did you get my presentation?"

The voice speaks again with no emotion. "I accessed your presentation from your cloud files. The slides will appear in speaker mode. They will appear in front of you in case you wish to refer to your notes. The presentation is motion controlled."

"You don't have access to my cloud files. How could you? You don't have my permission."

The opening slide of Rick's presentation appears in midair a few feet in front of him. The slide hovers just below Rick's eye level. There is no screen or display. The slide floats in space before him.

The introduction video continues to play. Rick is angry but doesn't have much time. He motions with his right hand. The slides slip by as if he were flipping pages of a book. Rick notices some mistakes. He made changes during his flight.

"This the wrong version," he says to himself. Then he speaks loudly, hoping the voice is monitoring. "I can't use this version. I made several changes. How can I load the final version?"

His ear tickles. "Cloud access in this facility is restricted."

Rick thinks for a second. "I have it stored in my band, but it isn't working here. If I could load from—" The display on his band glows.

"Latest version loaded," the voice announces.

Rick looks at his band and then looks up to the ceiling. "My band is password protected. You can't just take my files. And the file is eight hundred gigs. It can't load that fast."

The voice interrupts Rick. "Presentation loaded. You begin in nine seconds. Move to your mark."

Rick is confused and upset, but convinced his future depends on this presentation. He will find out what's happening later. As he looks down and steps to his mark, the voice comes back in his head. "Take a deep breath. Relax, Dr. Munday. You are in a large lecture hall. Teach."

The video ends. The glass wall goes black. A new voice. "Today it is our pleasure to introduce Dr. Richard Munday and his presentation entitled Disturbance beyond the Kuiper Belt - Potential risks to Planet Earth. Dr. Munday comes to us from Cal Tech. We learned of his unique theory and felt compelled to bring him to the committee's attention for consideration. I present, Dr. Richard Munday."

Lights in the floor ignite, bathing Rick in the new light. The black glass becomes semitransparent. As the introduction ends, the opening slide of Rick's presentation appears high on the glass above. Whoever is in the audience can see Rick, but Rick can't see beyond the glass. Rick expects applause, but there is silence.

Rick tries to imagine a filled lecture hall before him, but it isn't working. Standing alone, illuminated by bright lights, he peers into the glass wall then plows forward.

"Good afternoon, ladies and gentlemen. It… ah, it's a pleasure to be here. Today I would like to share my work regarding the potential dangers facing our solar system and potentially to Earth. There have been significant increases in the number of comets and asteroids in the inner solar system. This phenomenon has been difficult to study. Budget cuts have shuttered most terrestrial and space-based telescopes, but I believe something significant is happening. Before I present my theory of what could cause this increased activity, let's review some astronomy basics and past theories to set the background." Rick moves his hand and the slide changes to a video.

"As you all know, it takes about two hundred thirty million years for our solar system to complete an orbit around the Milky Way galaxy. Think of the Milky Way as a large plate lying flat. It is round and wide, but not very thick. The thickness of the plate is the galactic plane. As our solar system rotates around the Milky Way, it rises above and dips below the galactic plane many times. This up and down cycle occurs every thirty to thirty-five million years. The movement looks like a looping wave as we orbit the galaxy. Many scientists have theorized that our solar system's movement through the galactic cycle matches historic periods of asteroid bombardment. The asteroid activity we see might have proved these galactic plane theories correct except, our solar system is moving away from the galactic plane and won't likely cross it again for another ten million years. The exact date is up for debate, but we aren't even close."

Rick let the audience read the slide. When enough time elapses, he speaks again. "So, what is causing today's increased activity and is Earth at risk? We are not crossing the galactic plane, so it must be something else, something different." Rick pauses again for effect.

"So, I went looking for something different, and I believe I have found it."

Rick moves through several slides and animations, building a foundation, as he prepares to get to the heart of his theory.

"The asteroid belt lies between the orbits of Mars and Jupiter. It's a wide band of rocky objects thought to be the leftovers of early planet formation. The asteroid belt has billions and billions of space rocks in stable orbits. We have identified and explored the largest ones, and we track the orbits of thousands of these asteroids. Researchers have attributed ancient bombardments to objects from the asteroid belt; However, I do not suspect them as the cause for the recent activity. The Kuiper belt is larger and more distant—fifty times the distance Earth is from the sun, home to a trillion icy comets, millions of rocky bodies, and dwarf planets such as Pluto, Sedna, and Haumea, to name a few. The Kuiper belt moves with the solar system in a pro-grade, or counterclockwise orbit and lies within the heliosphere, so while very distant, the Kuiper belt is part of our solar system."

Rick loads a slide titled: *"Effects of a black hole transiting the outer solar system."*

"A black hole is a place in space with mass packed so densely and its gravitational pull is so strong that nothing can escape. They are the universe's vacuum cleaners, sucking up everything in their grasp. Since they pull all matter into their mass, even light, they are nearly invisible. Black holes typically stay in one place, usually residing at the center of large galaxies, like the super-massive black hole at the center of our own Milky Way. But not all black holes are stationary. Some move through space. They can move at incredible speeds, up to five million miles per hour. Can you imagine the mayhem a fast-moving black hole might cause as it jets through space, sucking up all matter in its path? I believe a black hole passed through the outer solar system moving in a retrograde, or a clockwise, orbit—which is the opposite direction of our solar system. The gravitational attraction of the black hole caused the typical pro-grade orbital velocities of comets, and other Kuiper belt objects, to slow, causing them to lose orbit and drop into the inner solar system."

Rick pulls something out of his pocket. "In my hand is a steel washer; a flat, round piece of metal with a hole in the center. It's hefty. It has some mass. I've tied a string to the washer." Rick holds the end of the string and twirls his hand.

"As I turn the string, the washer spins in a circle, an orbit." The metal washer spins at the end of the string over Rick's head.

"As long as there is enough orbital velocity, the washer remains in its orbit, but if the orbit slows, the washer will drop out of orbit. I believe this happened to a multitude of objects in the Kuiper belt," Rick says as he slows the spin of the washer, allowing it to fall to the floor.

A video of the solar system plays. The camera's view is far above the known planets and the Kuiper belt all spinning in a counterclockwise motion. A transparent disk moves through space, transiting high above the solar system. The stronger gravity of the transparent disk spinning in the opposite direction slows the rotational speed of the orbiting comets. Gravity pulls tens of thousands of objects up toward the invisible disk. The orbital rotation of another million objects slows, causing them to hang frozen in place as the disk passes above. As the invisible force moves past our solar system, objects that have lost their orbital momentum drop, falling into the inner solar system.

Some objects crash into planets. Many asteroids and comets collide during their descent toward the sun. Rick moves his arms in sync with the video, raising them as the objects rise, lifted by the incredible invisible force, then drops his hands as they fall.

"A fast-moving stellar black hole could pass beyond the Kuiper belt, unseen. A black hole doesn't give off any light. We'd never see it coming!" Rick says as he motions to load the next slide. There is no feedback, no gasps, no terrified students running out of the auditorium, just the black glass wall.

Rick tries to look through the glass for a moment before continuing. "When you hear the words black hole, most people jump to the conclusion that black holes are always massive monsters chewing up planets, solar systems, and galaxies, with all matter being dragged into its super-dense gravitational jaws. Surely, if a black hole passed near Earth, we'd be sucked into oblivion. Not necessarily. It depends on many factors; black holes come in all sizes and densities. The purpose of my grant is to conduct the research, to gather data, and to prove a black hole caused the increase in activity being observed. I hope to determine its size, density, and track the orbit of the black hole to determine the potential danger to our solar system and Earth."

Rick motions to move to the next slide. This is the crux of his theory. He hopes he has not lost his audience getting to this key point. Rick displays an image of an X-ray emitting object. It's a small blue blur in the middle of the blackness of space.

"This x-ray image, taken by the Imaging X-ray Polarimetry Explorer known as IPXE, is faint, but I believe it represents the black hole. Unfortunately, I haven't accessed IXPE for several months. If the black hole collects material as it continues to move through space, an accretion disk may form, making the black hole easier to detect. I also need to verify that objects are moving into the inner solar system and confirm that they are the source of the increased activity we have observed. We must determine the number, size, speed, and trajectory of the objects. I got some time on the European Extremely Large Telescope Array or EELT. I detected and tracked several new comets. But I need more time on the IXPE and EELT to confirm the data—"

Rick's ear tickles then he hears a gruff sounding voice. "You mean to tell us you gained access to both the IXPE and EELT?"

The question startles Rick, but he answers the question. "Why, yes? I examined—" The tickle interrupts Rick again, causing him to touch his ear.

"You don't have clearance for those systems. How did you gain access?" asks the voice.

Rick is busted. He planned to cover up his previous unauthorized use once his grant was approved. He's said too much, now he's caught. The scientific world is small. Scientists often exchange favors and information between friends and colleagues. His college friend Karl gave him an access code to IXPE.

Rick recalls the conversation.

"If I give you the code numb nuts, you've got to promise you'll cut your tongue out before revealing who gave you access. Remember, you owe me. I saw Courtney first. She's your wife only because I held back to give you a chance." Rick got the code but lost access to IXPE two weeks later when Karl died in an auto accident. Dead people don't need access to secure x-ray imaging systems.

Accessing EELT was not as easy. For that, Rick used the old-fashioned tactic of breaking and entering. One of his students was a talented computer programmer but was failing astronomy. Rick offered the student an extra credit project. All he needed to do was hack into EELT, allowing Rick complete access while leaving no trace of his activities. The student might have been horrible at astronomy, but he was great at hacking. Two days later, Rick had access to the EELT, and the student remarkably got an *A* in astronomy. That was before they shut down EELT.

Rick stands looking dumbfounded, his hopes of a grant crumbling. His ear tickles. "Your response is required, Dr. Munday."

Rick tries to laugh it off. He shrugs his shoulders and says, "Sometimes a scientist has to do whatever it takes to get data. The Europeans weren't using the EELT. They're still fighting the Four Wars. I didn't think they would mind." A painful shock in his ear causes Rick to lurch over in pain.

"Do not be flippant with me, Munday. Answer."

Rick draws himself up and looks through the dark glass wall at whoever is the voice in his head. His jaw set, his lips tight. "I must get grants to support my department and put food on my family's table. I must publish to attain tenure. I've spent years running into barriers and roadblocks trying to gain access to systems and information. When there is no other way, you find a way. I found ways. I don't care if I broke a few rules because the system is not fair. These days, the only way to make the system work is to break rules." Rick fears his career is now over. "I know I cheated. I'll go now." He turns to walk to the door, then remembers he's trapped in the room.

He hears a whispered conversation for several seconds, then the voice says, "Continue."

The response shocks Rick. He isn't sure he understands. "What?"

"Continue your presentation."

Rick moves to his mark on the floor and starts again. "One might wonder what happens when a black hold disrupts the orbits of comets." Rick's ear vibrates. "Yes, one might wonder about such a thing. Get on with it, Munday."

"As I noted earlier, the Kuiper belt lies beyond the orbit of Neptune. It includes forty thousand objects larger than sixty miles in diameter, not to mention dwarf planets and a trillion other objects. As the black hole passed beyond the Kuiper belt, it would have disrupted and slowed the orbit of the belt's objects, causing them to drop into the inner solar system. Millions of objects could have suffered this gravitational misfortune, sending a vast cascade of comets and rocky bodies to the inner solar system. As comets and Kuiper belt objects pass through the asteroid belt, they may cause a secondary wave of disruption, bringing asteroids and broken fragments along with them. Objects would impact the inner planets, and could cause a severe asteroid bombardment on Earth, lasting months or years with devastating results to the planet's inhabitants—meaning us." Rick pauses, looking at his dim reflection in the glass wall.

"Imagine if a million objects fell out of orbit. It would be a very destructive force. Only a small percentage of them need to strike Earth to create an end of the world scenario. As I stated earlier in my presentation, there have been an unusual number of new comets over the past few years, resulting in new meteor showers. We have also logged an increase in the number of asteroid flybys, near misses, and collisions with Earth." Rick takes a breath. He hopes he is getting his point across to the invisible audience beyond the glass.

Rick moves his hand, advancing to the next slide. "My research shows the potential for a storm of comets and asteroids moving through the inner solar system toward Earth. I don't know when it's coming; it may be close already. I haven't been able to gather new data for months, but I believe Earth is at great risk of multiple catastrophic collisions. We must warn people of the danger." Rick's ear then stings with enough pain to make him stop talking.

The gravelly voice is back. "You are saying Earth could experience more events like the meteor explosion that destroyed much of Perth, Australia, yesterday?"

"Perth? I didn't know."

Images of destruction appear on the glass wall. The once-beautiful seaside skyline of Perth is in ruins.

Rick stutters and steps back. "I've been traveling. I-I didn't know," Rick says.

The voice of a different man speaks. "We believe a meteor, eighty meters in diameter, exploded over the city center, destroying most of the buildings downtown, causing fires citywide. Thousands are dead. Billions in damage." Rick watches the video footage in stunned amazement. The destruction is widespread.

The gruff voice returns. "That will be all, Dr. Munday." The stage lights dim, and the glass wall goes black. Rick stands alone in the silent empty room.

Chapter 15: Moving Forward

Rick stands staring at the glass wall. "Is that it? Not even a thank you very much?" Rick asks the wall, his voice growing louder. "What do you mean, that will be all? What do you think of my theory? If the bombardment is coming, we must warn people. That will be all, Dr. Munday. That will be all?"

Rick bangs his fists on the glass as he shouts. "I was to give my presentation at a seminar to an audience of my peers! Who's out there? Do I go home now? I need to call my wife. What the hell is going on?"

The door behind him clicks and whooshes open. Rick turns to see the young man standing in the doorway. "You, again?"

"Well, well, I know it can get stuffy in the presentation room. No need to get nasty, mister—oh, Dr. Munday, I presume." The young man cackles at his own bad humor. "Come with me. You're moving forward."

The two men in dark suits flank the young man. One of them motions for Rick to exit the room. Rick isn't sure where he's going, but is more than happy to leave the presentation room.

The young man walks down the corridor, moving deeper into the facility. Rick takes a couple of quick strides to get alongside him. "What do you mean, move forward? Who was in the audience?" The young man walks cheerfully without answering. "What is your job here, anyway?" Rick asks.

"I am the guest liaison officer of the Astrophysics Science Center. I greet all the guests."

"What do you mean, move forward?"

The young man pauses and turns to Rick. The two men stand behind Rick and the young man. "Your presentation must have gone well. You're moving forward in the program. I'm sure you understand," the young man says with a quirky turn of his head, then continues walking.

"I don't understand anything. This isn't a seminar. I want to go home. Where are you taking me?"

The young man beams his friendly southern smile at Rick as he walks down the bland, institutional corridor, clutching the small tablet to his chest. "Those that move forward go in the green elevator. Those that do not move forward go in the blue elevator. I apologize, security is tight. That is all I know, Dr. Munday. Come along. Green elevator for you. You have done yourself proud today."

Rick is perturbed. This situation is unlike anything he has experienced before. The people around him don't know or aren't telling him much. He tries to change the conversation to see if he can learn anything. "Have you had many visitors giving presentations? It's just, I wonder if I have competition getting my grant approved."

The young man peeks at his tablet as they walk. "We have kept the presentation room busy the past few weeks. I believe a Dr. Heinrich, from your own Cal Tech, was here the other day. Would you consider him your competition?"

The news surprises Rick. That's why Dr. Heinrich is out. "I don't consider Doctor Heinrich competition. I consider him my boss. He's the head of my department. Is he at this facility?"

"I shouldn't speak about our other guests. It's confidential. You understand. Since you work with him, you must have seen him back at Cal Tech. He did not move forward."

Rick pauses a step. If Dr. Heinrich didn't move forward and has not returned to the lab, where could he have gone? If they control information about who moves forward, who does not, and what moving forward means, Rick wonders if they control other information.

"Terrible about what happened in Perth," Rick says causally.

"A daytime fireball shooting across the sky. It must have been a sight."

"But what about the severe damage to the city?"

"I wouldn't classify some unnerved people as severe damage, Dr. Munday."

"No, I guess not."

The young man turns down a hallway. Rick and the two men follow. At the end of the hall, Rick sees two elevator doors. Painted above one door is a blue square and above the other a green square.

Instead of an elevator call button, there is another green gel pad. The liaison officer sticks his hand into the gel. Rick isn't sure he wants to enter either of the elevators.

"I need to call my wife. She must be worried sick. I haven't been able to reach her," Rick says, trying to activate his band.

There is a *ding* and both elevator doors open. A strong hand pushes him to the elevator with the green square. Rick peeks into the blue elevator to see if there is any difference. They are both empty elevators.

"I'm sure you will have plenty of opportunities to call your wife, Dr. Munday," says the young liaison officer.

Rick stands in the elevator, facing the young man and the FBI guys. As the doors close, Rick calls out to the young man. "It was, Dr. Livingstone, I presume. Not Dr. Munday."

"What?" asks the young man, looking befuddled.

"When Stanley found Livingstone in the jungle, he said—" Rick can tell the young man does not understand what he's talking about. In anger and frustration, Rick adds, "You are dumb as a stump, aren't you?"

"Now that was uncalled for, Dr. Mund—" The elevator door closed.

Little does Rick know; The young Astrophysics Science Center guest liaison officer uses the same line on every visitor who is a doctor this or that. His job as liaison officer isn't as glamourous as it sounds. He must entertain himself.

The elevator descends rapidly. There are no numbers to show floors. There is only a green gel pad and two black keyholes where buttons should be. The elevator descends faster. Rick feels pressure build and pops his ears to equalize them as the ride down continues.

The elevator stops. The doors open.

Chapter 16: Sky Watch Command

Wednesday

The colonel ended the presentation abruptly. He and Zsoldos sit alone in the dark auditorium, watching a confused doctor Munday pound on the glass.

The portly man looks to the colonel. "Send him through?"

The colonel hesitates, then nods affirmative.

Zsoldos reaches several inches in front of his glasses, touches the air, and speaks. "Move him forward."

The men watch the door of the presentation room open and Munday led away. Rick's presentation impressed Zsoldos.

"Very remarkable. He nailed it. I worked for a year with a team of astrophysicists before I discovered the cause of the asteroid activity. He knows everything."

"He's a criminal. I want to know how he got access to IXPE and EELT and who helped him. He illegally gained access to privileged systems. I want his personal communications blocked."

Zsoldos stands, pushing himself out of the comfortable chair. "I've had his communications blocked since he left the hotel. I agree he got into systems he should not have accessed, but to put it all together, by himself, without access to our other capabilities, is brilliant. No one else has done that."

The colonel taps his cane on the cement floor slowly as he speaks. "He's a thief. He got his information illegally. I'm glad we found him. I wouldn't want him in Los Angeles talking to reporters. We should have sent him down the blue hole with the other idiots and fools. I want you to find out how he got into the EELT. I want assurances it's locked down. We can't afford to have high school hackers accessing our capabilities. Time is short, but we must contain information."

The colonel moves to the exit. Zsoldos follows. "Yes, Colonel. We will find out how he got in. You heard him say he hasn't had access for several months. I have confirmed every space mission, every space-based and terrestrial telescope accessible to schools, universities, and the public in the US and Europe are offline. We can't control every telescope and system worldwide, but we have done our best. The wars are a great distraction. Regardless, we continue to monitor and quash all related communication. It's good you moved him forward. I believe Munday will become a valuable member of our scientific team."

The colonel grumbles. "Huh, we'll see about that. He's a loose cannon. I am glad we have him under control."

The men exit the auditorium and walk a short distance to a door with a gel pad. The colonel inserts his hand, and the door slides open to an underground rail station with a single car waiting. Zsoldos and Cruikshank enter the well-appointed subway car. A tone chimes.

The colonel speaks a command. "To the White House." The doors close and the train speeds to its destination via underground rail.

"Our world is about to face the worst disaster since the dawn of mankind and we're running around interviewing criminals and crazies," Cruikshank mumbles angrily.

A screen appears, floating twelve inches in front of Zsoldos' glasses. He views the image of a young Asian woman in uniform. He touches the air to answer the video call. It's Sky Watch Commander Chen, with two team members wearing navy blue tunics.

"Sir, we have an important update. Is the colonel with you?" asks commander Chen.

"Just a moment."

Zsoldos touches the air again, making a sweeping motion. The display moves to his band, mounted on the man's forearm, which then projects a display of the video call in midair. Zsoldos pinches one corner of the projected display, stretching the screen larger.

The colonel looks at the floating display. "Chen. What is it?"

"Colonel Cruikshank, we have incoming. We have confirmed the measurements. There is a large, scattered mass of asteroids approaching Earth. It's coming in quick. We have clocked the velocity at forty-five thousand miles per hour," reports the commander.

The colonel has a look of apprehension, or is it his battle face? "It is beginning. Perth was not an anomaly. It's real. It's starting."

The Sky Watch Commander defers to a young male team member. "The main mass of asteroids hasn't arrived, but it is approaching. We are tracking a scattered mass of medium-sized asteroids, arriving ahead of the main body. We have observed scattered impacts around the world. It was one of these wayward asteroids that hit Perth. We expect to see—"

Commander Chen puts her hand on the young team member's shoulder to stop him. "Colonel, there is a large mass of asteroids heading toward Earth. It is about to be a bad day for anyone topside."

"How long until the mass enters the atmosphere?" asks the colonel.

A female team member steps up to give her report. "Colonel, we got lucky. Mars is currently aligned with Earth and the incoming asteroid field. A few days ago, we recorded over four hundred impacts per hour on the surface of Mars. The red planet may have taken the worst of the first wave."

The colonel swipes his cane at the projected display. His cane passes through the hovering image. "I didn't ask about Mars, damn it. How much time do we have to get secured in New Arcadia?"

The female team member gulps. "Excuse me, sir. At its present rate of speed, the asteroid field will penetrate our atmosphere in the next eight hours."

The colonel lifts his cane, then smacks the gold tip on the metal floor of the car, making a loud pinging sound. "Eight hours! Damn it! Do you have a projected impact path? Where is this mess going to hit first?"

"Sir, trajectory tracking shows the flow coming in over the northern hemisphere across Southern Europe and as far south as the equator. Our tracking shows that initial impacts will hit France, Spain, and North Africa before crossing the Atlantic. Impacts will begin along the eastern seaboard of the US no later than 10:00 p.m. tonight."

The colonel is excited. "What? The UK gets spared? And Russia? Those bastards get to watch while we get pummeled?"

The team female team member isn't sure how to answer the colonel. Commander Chen speaks up. "Colonel, if the UK, Russia, and China are spared from initial impacts, they have only a matter of hours to rejoice or prepare. The asteroid field is massive, coming in several waves. Asteroids will impact every part of the globe as Earth rotates. It may take weeks for the mass of asteroids and comets to pass Earth."

The subway car comes to a stop, and Zsoldos stands to exit. He holds his arm level to keep the display viewable while the men walk through the tube station. The station is large, with several rail lines ending under the White House.

"We have arrived at White House station. Set the security level to red. Signal the nuclear war drill for the cities. Send alerts advising council members and Arcadians they must move to the cities. Do it now!" the colonel orders.

The alert will advise anyone with approved access to move to the cities and restrict movement to topside. No one is getting in or out of the new cities unless approved by the colonel himself.

Later that Day–Commander Chen's Quarters

Chen sits in front of a video screen talking with a Chinese military leader. "Thank you for the update, Chen. Your information has proven invaluable. We continue to prepare."

"But General Tsoi, the African campaign and the push into Chad. It seems the Four Wars are intensifying," says Chen.

"A charade. A small sacrifice to mislead our enemies as we prepare for the grand battle and our ultimate victory after the storm. We are building an insurmountable arsenal of weapons in our underground factories," General Tsoi steps aside. The camera views rows of fierce looking tanks just off the assembly line.

"We will be on lock down soon. I won't be able to communicate again until the storm has passed," says Chen.

"Until the storms pass," says Tsoi.

Part Two–New Arcadia

Chapter 17: Burwell, Nebraska

Wednesday

Pastor Keith takes Monday off but attends the Boy Scout meeting Monday evenings. Tuesday, he prepares for Tuesday night Bible study. Wednesday is his office day. He counts the tithing from the previous Sunday and totals the giving. He pays bills and updates accounts.

Bigger churches have bookkeepers and accountants. The Living Waters Church of Burwell, Nebraska, has one full-time employee: Pastor Keith. If times are tight and tithing is below budget, the church has one full-time employee at half pay. Keith doesn't mind. He and his faithful wife, Haylee, knew what they signed up for when they started.

Keith Wardlowe is not in the preaching business for money or fame. He has no plans to write a book or start a worldwide preaching network. He is devoted to his family and the people of Burwell, Nebraska. Pastor Keith Wardlowe has his schedule, and you might say he follows it religiously, so it's no small surprise on Wednesday, after the previous night's bible study when he preached against the book, *Straight Up–Preparing for the Rapture*, he broke from his schedule to pay a visit to Frank Brown.

Burwell, Nebraska has a population of twelve hundred forty souls and is the county seat of Garfield County. In 1887, the Chicago, Burlington, and Quincy Railroad was extended to Burwell. People imagined that the railroad would bring rapid growth and prosperity to the small town. They didn't realize the railroad would continue all the way to Denver, Colorado. Burwell became a stop along the way. Few stopped.

Burwell is most famous as the host of "Nebraska's Big Rodeo," an annual event held the last weekend of July. The rest of the year, it's a small rural town in the middle of nowhere, Nebraska. It's a three-hour drive to big cities like Lincoln or Omaha and seven hours to Denver. Burwell is a town left behind by modern standards. What it lacks in the latest tech, it has preserved in tradition.

Burwell has the look of old time Americana. Livestock and the fish hatchery are the main industries. The rodeo might be the big event of the year, but people enjoy fishing, hunting, and family activities year around. Ninety-nine percent of the six hundred households are families. Being a divorced, single mother is a rarity rather than the norm. Families attend church. Young boys and girls join Scouts or 4-H. It is a friendly, wholesome environment. The remote location of the rural town, with the peaceful Calamus river flowing through it, allows their traditional lifestyle to continue keeping things the way they've been without feeling old-fashioned.

Construction of the Calmus Reservoir in 1986 tamed the Calamus River of springtime floods. The reservoir is two miles northwest of town, providing water for irrigation of local farmland, fishing, camping, and recreational activities. The reservoir is fifteen miles long and held back by the hundred-foot-tall Virginia Smith earthen dam. At the base of the dam is the fish hatchery.

Frank Brown worked at the fish hatchery for almost thirty years and has been a hard-working, loyal employee all his adult life. Frank had married his high school sweetheart, Debbie Wilcox. Their fun teenage relationship changed when Debbie learned she was pregnant. The pregnancy forced Frank and Debbie to grow up fast. They married and a few months later they welcomed their son, Thomas, into the world.

Frank's uncle worked at the fish hatchery, and with his uncle's reference, Frank was hired. Frank advanced over the years from feeding the hatchlings to Assistant Manager of Operations.

The Nebraska Game and Parks commission operates the fish hatchery. Two years ago, they hired a new manager and invested in technology to bring the facility up to date. Frank had become a fixture at the hatchery and did things a certain way. Some people said he was stubborn; others said he was too old to learn new ways. For whatever reason, Frank didn't get along with the new hatchery superintendent. After a few months of butting heads with the new boss, they agreed Frank would find other employment.

These days, Frank mows grass at the golf course. After his years at the hatchery, Frank enjoys his independence out on the course. Nobody watches his every move. Out on the course, it's just Frank on his riding mower with his thoughts. It was one day, while edging the green of the ninth hole—Frank remembers it vividly—that he received his revelation from God. There will be a flood. Frank must prepare. He should build a ship to save himself and his wife. God spoke to him, so he built his submarine.

As Keith drove, he thought about his friend and church member, Frank Brown. The Brown family has had a rough go of it the past few years. First, their only son, Thomas, died in the Sulu Sea conflict, then Frank lost his job at the hatchery. Thomas's death devastated Debbie. He was her whole life. Frank had his work at the hatchery, his hunting and fishing friends. Debbie had Thomas.

Although Debbie had a hard time adjusting to the loss of Thomas, Pastor Keith worries about Frank and his submarine-building mission. Keith had hoped once Frank saw how silly he appeared on the TV show. He would give up. Instead, the show had pushed Frank to complete the project.

Pastor Keith pulled into the Brown property. The house sits on a large lot a few miles out of town. The property is on the way to the reservoir, near the hatchery, just off Dan Road and Pebble Creek Road. Keith walks to the front door.

He figures Frank will be out back somewhere, but the neighborly thing to do is to knock on the front door, so Keith knocks. Debbie opens the door halfway. Keith can see it's dark inside the house. Debbie looks sad and depressed, but once she notices its Pastor Keith at the door, she puts on her "going to church" smile.

"Why, Pastor Keith, what a surprise. What brings you all the way out here?" Debbie asks, as she opens the door wider while smoothing out her wrinkled blouse.

Keith smiles his "I'm your neighborly preacher" smile, as polite as he can be. He knows Debbie's emotions are still close to the surface. Haylee, Keith's wife, spent many tear-filled hours counseling and consoling Debbie after Thomas's death. Keith doesn't want to get her started. He's here to see Frank.

"Well, I wanted to come out and see Frank's submarine for myself. It sounds like he's made a lot of progress," Keith says.

Debbie appears disappointed the visit isn't for her. She doesn't hesitate showing disapproval of her husband's project. "That man and his stupid ideas. I don't know what drives him to have these outlandish thoughts. He's out back. His contraption is out there, next to the shed. Go on back. I'm sure you'll hear him banging about, wasting his time and our money."

Keith is sure that Debbie's tirade is one Frank has heard many times. He gives her a polite nod before walking to the back of the house. Debbie follows for a few steps, still talking.

"He gets these crazy ideas, then uses God to justify them. I don't know how he thinks he can get away with using God as his excuse for whatever he does." Keith picks up his pace, hoping to get out of earshot.

He makes it to the back of the house just in time to see Frank's head disappear into the submarine. Keith hears noises from inside the vessel. Frank's head then pops up. He looks for something on the ground and disappears again into the submarine. Keith can't help but think Frank looks like a prairie dog popping in and out of his hole.

The submarine has a large, curved window in the front. Keith covers his brow to block the sun and peer through the windshield. Frank squats on the floor and notices something has blocked the sunlight coming into the sub. He turns, catches a fright, and jerks to pop out of his hole, this time smashing his head on the metal roof of the sub.

"Ouch, goddamn it! Who the hell is out there?" Frank cries, rubbing his head as he comes up through the sub's hatch. Frank lets loose with a string of expletives but stops when he notices the unexpected visitor is Keith: "Shit. Who the fu... frock is scaring the holy Jesus out of me? Preacher, what are you doing out here?"

"I've heard so much about your submarine project. I wanted to stop by and have a look for myself." Keith gives the submarine a once-over, patting the metal exterior. "Looks solid. How deep do you plan to go with it?"

"I'm not sure how deep I need to go, but it should be all right for thirty feet. It's meant as an all-weather vessel. I saw a show about the Coast Guard on the Oregon Coast. They have these boats that can go underwater or flip over in a storm and not sink, but they're not submarines. This ship is a hybrid like the Coast Guard one. Everybody calls it a submarine, so it stuck," Frank explains.

Frank had tried to explain this to his wife, but she never let him finish the first sentence. One of the townsfolk called the TV show, and they came out to film. The TV crew listened to Frank's explanation. They filmed and took notes and still called it a submarine.

The ship looks unique. Keith inspects the vessel, thinking he would have a tough time describing it. He can see it's easier to call it a submarine. The ship is twelve feet long, eight feet wide, and six feet high. It has a keel like a boat, but round in front instead of having a sharp V, like the bow of a boat. It's covered with a metal roof with a big round hatch like a submarine. There are two portholes along each side. The ship rests on a wooden brace. Overall, it looks like a professional job for a guy who worked at a fish hatchery most of his life.

Keith stands back, making a show of examining the craft. "It looks like you've done a real good job building it, Frank. It's a unique design. Maybe you should test it out in the reservoir."

Frank stands in the hatch with his hands on the roof. "It's not meant to go boating on the reservoir. You don't believe me, do you?"

Keith hadn't planned on how to confront Frank. "Frank, I have little experience with people who say God spoke to them, and then build an, ah…" He searches for words while motioning at the strange ship.

"I knew it. You're the same as the rest. You picked on me and had your fun last night. Everyone had a good laugh. Frank Brown and his submarine. The joke of Burwell on national TV. You might be a preacher, but you're no better than the rest, Keith."

"Frank, I apologize for last night. I didn't mean to single you out, I—."

"No experience, you say. I sit in church listening to you tell us about God talking to people every week, and how those people acted on what Gold said. Seems to me things turned out worse when they ignored what God told them to do. You stand here and ridicule me for following God's word. Why is it any different for me?"

Keith thinks for a moment. "Well, I mean personal experience. In the scriptures of the Old Testament, God was… well, that was a different time. These days, God doesn't speak to people directly. It's more of a feeling or a pull in one direction or the other, not explicit directives to build something."

Frank climbs down from his submarine. Once he's on the ground, he faces Keith. "Trust in the LORD with all thine heart; and lean not unto thine own understanding. In all thy ways acknowledge him, and he shall direct thy path." Pastor Keith is about to reply, but Frank interrupts him again. "Listen, Pastor, I know you think I'm crazy. Those TV guys had fun making me look the fool. It doesn't matter. I know what God put on my heart. Maybe I am crazy. I don't care. I'm gonna finish this thing and I'll be prepared—for what I'm not sure, but I'll be ready, just as God told me. This ship is for Debbie and me when the time is come, and that's all she wrote, Pastor."

Keith is speechless. Frank walks toward Keith's truck, and Keith follows. After a few steps, Keith finds some words. "Frank, I don't think you're crazy. I care about you and Debbie. I wanted to know if you're OK, that's all."

"Keith, we've been friends for a long time. I'm fine. I got the mowing job over to the golf course and I like it. It's decent work and gives me time to think. It's Debbie I'm worried about. She never got over losing Thomas, you know that. Maybe you could ask Haylee to look in on her again."

"I will, Frank."

"Thanks. She gets lonely out here. Some company for her would be nice." When they reach Keith's truck, Frank opens the door. An invitation to leave.

"Well, I'll get back to the office. It's my bookkeeping day," Keith says as he climbs into his pickup.

"Thank ya for taking the time to check in on us, Pastor. I do appreciate it. I'll say your goodbyes to Debbie, for ya," Frank says as he shuts the truck door. Frank turns and walks back to his submarine. Keith waits a few moments before driving back to town.

Chapter 18: Lockdown

Wednesday Late Afternoon

Russell hurries into the Oval Office unannounced. Russell expects to see the president working the phones or rehearsing a speech. He expects to see the dynamic man he has served and supported for many years. Instead, Russell finds the president staring out the window. Russell is beside himself. He respects the president, but he isn't sure how much longer he can provide political cover for the man. He will do anything to support and protect him, but Russell knows there are limits. The president can no longer make decisions on his own. Russell knows how the president thinks and what he believes. Lately, he follows his conscience to direct the president along the path he believes the president would have chosen if he were his old self.

Russell can't tell if the president is awake or sleeping with his eyes open. He thinks to himself, as he rouses the president, *the spa treatments are wearing off faster. Thank God, he's not drooling. I couldn't take that.*

Russell shakes the president. Anderson realizes Russell is standing close to him. "Ah, Thompson. What have we got on the calendar today?"

Russell steps back and stands at attention. "Sir, I'm sorry to disturb you. Vice President Baker has called a meeting in the cabinet room. He is in there now with some of your cabinet members." The president feebly tries to stand. Russell steps in to assist Anderson to his feet.

The cabinet room adjoins the Oval Office and overlooks the Rose Garden. It is the president's conference room. A large oval conference table with twenty chairs occupies the room. The president's chair sits with its back to the windows and the Rose Garden and is two inches taller than other chairs around the table.

The vice president's chair is across the table, facing the president. Brass name plates on the back of the chairs note the seating position and rank of the various cabinet members' chairs circling the large table.

Vice President Cliff Baker called the meeting. He invited only a few cabinet members, people he trusts. People he knows will support him and can influence others. Baker stands at the table in the location where the president should sit, with the president's chair pushed behind him. Vice President Baker did not invite or notify the president of the meeting.

Vice President Baker holds a copy of the ARC Amendment. Two hours earlier, the vice president and Senate Majority Leader, Mitch Campbell, received notification the president had signed the amendment late the previous night. The vice president holds the document in his hand and shakes it in anger. "This thing is a piece of crap. You know that Mitch. How did you ever let this manure get brought to a vote? How could this have passed in both the House and the Senate?"

As the majority leader of the Senate, Mitch Campbell could have refused to allow consideration of such an outlandish proposition. But midterm elections are coming up. Political games are being played.

"If I hadn't let this go forward, the media would have slammed us. The social democrats dreamed this thing up to make it look like we don't believe in our principles of small government and budget control. The media blew it out of proportion. The idea gained steam, and the states ratified the damn thing. How was I supposed to control that? This charade was to stop in the Oval Office. You said Anderson would never sign it."

"If you want to blame someone, blame former President Sanchez. He's the one who sued to uphold Article 1, Section 7, stating the president must sign every resolution that requires concurrence of both houses of Congress. Before that, the president didn't sign constitutional amendments," said Joyce Pritchett, the Secretary of State.

"Thanks to Sanchez, we lost the second amendment. Those socialists made owning guns illegal! Now Anderson has ripped the constitution to shreds," says Vice President Baker.

Senator Campbell stands to face off against the vice president. "You said Anderson would veto it the minute it hit his desk. I thought we had a consensus on this, Cliff. You said this was under control."

Vice President Baker slaps the papers on the desk, pulls in the president's chair, and sits down. Baker has not always seen eye to eye with the president on topics of the day, but the president was adamant about vetoing ARC.

"The amendment is unconstitutional. Do we have an opinion from the attorney general?" asks the Secretary of the Interior, Jerome Hargrove III.

"I'll get the attorney general looped in after this meeting. Anything he does will take months. This is a national crisis requiring immediate action. I called the brightest team I know to get things done without bickering, and here you are. How do we tackle this? We need an action plan before the media learns of this." Cliff Baker removes his cuff links and rolls up his sleeves. To people who know him, this is a sign he's ready to get down to business.

Joyce Pritchett speaks. "I agree. We need to have our talking points laid out. A change in the fundamental structure of our government will make us look weak to the rest of the world. The heads of states will swamp me with calls once this news breaks."

Cliff Baker turns to his old friend, Charles Adams. Cliff and Charles worked at the same law firm right out of law school and have been friends ever since. It was Cliff Baker who put Charles' name forward for nomination as Secretary of Homeland Security. "Charles, what have you got for me?"

"First, we put all state and local government police forces, and the National Guard, on high alert. There may be public rioting and social unrest," said the Secretary of Homeland Security.

"OK, what else?" asks Cliff Baker.

"Well, that's the easy part. How do we correct this tragic error? That's tricky. If we knew the president would do this, we could have invoked the Twenty-Fifth Amendment to have the president step down and this never would have happened. With his condition, you could have made a move much sooner, Cliff."

The cabinet members gasp. There have been rumors and whispers about the president, but no one has spoken openly that the president might have a serious health condition. Secretary Hargrove searches on the Twenty-Fifth Amendment. "So many amendments, who can remember them all," he mumbles, as he engages his VUE, tapping his query in the air.

The president bursts into the cabinet room with Russell Thompson close behind. The president, in a booming voice, asks "What is the meaning of this? You call a meeting in my cabinet room, without advising me, Baker? What's going on here?"

The president sizes up the room. There is silence. The president looks each person in the eye, moving in silence from one person to the next. Joyce Pritchett cannot hold his gaze and looks away. Hargrove smiles like an idiot. The president looks at the steely eyes of Tug Grimes, his Secretary of Defense. Tug acknowledges the president with a slight tip of his head. Senator Campbell stares back at the president with a poker face. Cliff Baker returns the gaze of the president, with eyes full of fury and rage.

Baker responds by picking up the signed copy of the ARC Amendment and shakes it at the president. "What is the meaning of this?" he shouts.

"I don't understand what you are talking about and stop yelling. I will not accept this insolence. Get out of my god-damned chair."

"It's not your chair any longer. There is no President of the United States. Hell, there isn't even a United States after what you did," says Mitch Campbell.

"What are you talking about? What I did? Damn it, Cliff. Tell me what this is all about. I have done nothing."

Baker slides the ARC Amendment across the table to the president. The president looks down, reading the title. The president reaches out, almost touching it. He seems lost in momentary thought. He looks across the table at Cliff Baker.

"I will veto this. We discussed it."

Baker has covered for the president for months. How could this have happened? It exasperates him. "Then why did you sign it?"

The president is dumbfounded. He looks at the document; he looks to Russell, then back to Cliff. "I-I didn't sign it." The president slumps into the nearest chair, looking confused.

The president looks at his vice president without focusing, then mumbles. "They will honor me as a hero. Must move humankind forward. The colonel said…" The president's voice trails off as he runs his fingers through his hair, trying to remember.

Cliff Baker can't follow what the president is saying but hears the word colonel. Hearing that name is enough to raise Cliff's blood pressure. "Cruikshank is behind this? I should have known that old bastard was up to something."

The door to the cabinet room opens. Colonel Cruikshank enters the room, followed by Zsoldos, and stands behind the president. The colonel puts his hands on the back of the chair the president sits in and smiles. He looks younger and stronger than when Cliff saw him last. A slight limp from his bad leg betrays the more youthful colonel.

"Did I hear my name used in vain?"

"Cruikshank, did you have something to do with the president signing this document?" asks Senator Mitchell.

"I had the honor of being present when the president made a courageous decision to advance our governmental system and move our society forward. If that is your question, then yes."

Cliff almost leaps across the table to strangle the colonel. "You evil bastard. You've been working behind the scenes, pulling strings, lurking in the shadows for years."

The colonel laughs at the vice president. "Mr. Baker, you are so naïve." An outburst from the president interrupts the colonel.

"Chile, not an earthquake. Asteroids. Perth destroyed. Storm coming. Must get underground." The president sputters.

The cabinet members around the table are in shock. They've never seen their president act this way. Looking around the table, their body language confirms a form of telepathic communication. The cabinet members agree.

Charles Adams is first to speak. "We must invoke the Twenty-Fifth Amendment, Section 3. The president will sign a declaration stating he cannot discharge his duties and transfer power to the vice president."

"I will advise the press the president has suffered a stroke and Vice President Baker is now acting president. There's no need to mention ARC," suggests Joyce.

Secretary Adams reaches for the amendment. He flips through the document and tears out the signed pages of the bill. "It never happened. It's over and we move on. Cliff, I mean the vice president, will be President Baker, President of the United States."

"Uh, acting President Baker," says Tug Grimes.

"Get that document drafted immediately. President Anderson still needs to sign it," says Senator Campbell.

"Let's get moving on this, posthaste," says Acting President-to-be Baker.

Russell Thompson steps out from behind the colonel. "Excuse me. I regret to inform you, but I submitted the signed original to the government archivist this morning, and they assigned the amendment an official number. ARC is the law. You're too late," he explains. The news silences the cabinet members.

The colonel taps his cane on the floor as he ambles down the length of the room. "You are all out of office and unemployed. The Arcadian Council is now the legitimate government of the land. President Anderson is the Chairman, and I am Vice Counselor," he says.

President Anderson isn't following the conversation and cannot contain his thoughts. "Look out. The sky is falling. Must get to the new cities. We will save the few and the fortunate. Watch out, a storm is coming," he says, rocking in his chair, fingering the plugs on his scalp.

The president's words assault the former vice president. Cliff looks at the smug colonel, who is pacing with his cane like an elegant peacock. "Cruikshank! What's he babbling about? New cities? A storm is coming. Is this one of your black projects? I demand to know what's going on here."

The colonel stops at the end of the table. He looks at the cabinet members with a condescending sneer. "Mr. Baker. If you'd afforded me any level of respect when you came into office, I might have considered sharing certain information with you. You may recall that I have held key positions in three previous administrations. One gains knowledge and influence through years of experience. I could have been very helpful to you. But since you and your ilk arrived in this city, you have been complete bombastic asses."

The colonel pauses. Cliff Baker is dumbstruck trying to figure out what the colonel is talking about. The colonel raps the end of his cane on the long table. "Still slow on the uptake I see, Mr. Baker.

Well, we can't all be the brightest bulb in the room, now, can we? I'm sure you will figure it out soon enough."

Cruikshank stands behind the president and puts a gentle hand on the shoulder of the CEO of Arcadia. "Sir, I think we should visit your doctor and have your medication adjusted."

The colonel looks to Russell Thompson and Zsoldos, then turns back to the cabinet members. "Well, we should be off now. You are all dismissed."

Cruikshank waves them off and helps the CEO of Arcadia from his chair. The CEO, Russell, Zsoldos, and the colonel prepare to leave the cabinet room.

The vice president and cabinet members look at each other exchanging whispers, unsure of their positions. Cliff Baker stands, yelling out to the colonel. "What are you doing? Where the hell are you going? This is not finished, you bastard!"

The colonel stops in the door frame and replies. "It is not finished, but I recommend you find a deep hole and stay there until it is. That's the most help I will give you. I am sure it's more than you would have done for me."

With that, the colonel closes the door and rejoins his group as they walk through the White House.

The colonel gives instructions to Zsoldos as they walk. "Get a message to Sky Watch Command. Tell them to move up the schedule. We are evacuating to New Arcadia. Everyone should head to the cities. They have two hours before we go on total lockdown." Zsoldos taps in the air in front of his glasses to send the message.

The colonel and Zsoldos walk side by side. Russell follows behind, helping CEO Anderson, flanked by their security detail. The colonel leans close to Zsoldos, who is tapping his fingers in the air. "Alert General Mahon. Have the Navy get all ships out to sea and hunker down for incoming."

They make their way to the spa. During the remodel of the spa, the colonel had an elevator added leading to a secret rail station far below the White House.

"Colonel, you don't want to warn them about what will happen?" Russell asks.

The colonel sets his gaze on Russell. "I would have if Baker and Senator Campbell weren't such pompous asses. I might have invited them to New Arcadia, but they would turn it into a bureaucratic monstrosity. There are plenty of underground structures in the capital. Let's see how they fare when the sky falls. Maybe they will redeem themselves." The security detail stays stationed outside the spa. The colonel's group moves to the hidden elevator.

"I hope they survive. I mean, it will be such a pity for so many to die. We could have warned them," Russell implores.

The elevator descends. "Remember why we have the Bliss Protocol? It's better to let people problem solve in the moment of emergency. It lessens the impact of human-on-human violence," Zsoldos explains.

The colonel taps his cane. "Yes, nothing like a good crisis to clear your mind. The battlefield brain is a wonderful thing; all becomes sharp and clear. Act decisively or die. Oh, I miss that feeling." The colonel shivers with excitement.

Russell's conscience is unsettled. "We could have warned the state governments or the military. We can save more people."

The colonel has heard enough of this. "The smart ones will find a way. Don't worry, Mr. Thompson, everyone will not die. General Mahon has control of the Army and Navy. Many battalions, facilities, and equipment are protected. He will manage things topside. We are saving the few and the fortunate. I don't want to hear any more on the subject. We have a mission to accomplish."

The elevator doors open on the secret White House rail station. The group enters a waiting electro-rail car ready to take them to New Arcadia.

Chapter 19: New Arcadia

Wednesday Afternoon–New Arcadia

Rick steps out of the elevator. Painted on the floor is a green square. *Well, at least it's still green.* The elevator opened on to a small subway platform. As Rick exits the elevator, a subway car arrives, and its doors open. Rick feels his ear tickle.

"Welcome, Dr. Munday. Please have a seat. It's a short ride."

The sound in his ear is strange. It isn't like hearing sounds from a headset or speaker. The sound is inside his head. Rick hesitates.

"Have a seat, Dr. Munday." Wincing pain accompanies the sound in his head.

The elevator doors close behind him. The subway is the only option. Rick steps into the car and sits. The door closes, and the car moves out of the station into a dark tunnel.

A series of back lit images are mounted on the tunnel wall. As the car leaves the station, it passes the panels at a faster and faster pace. The images flicker, becoming a blur. Soon the blur becomes animated. As the car passes, the images play out like a video stream. A speaker in the car plays upbeat music and a female voice-over is synced with the images.

"Welcome to New Arcadia. A development under the auspices of Operation Hard Shell. We've created an optimized, self-sustaining environment with an emphasis on entrepreneurship, business growth, and cultural development that allows for personal freedom, and the attainment of your full human potential."

The panels display artist concepts of a futuristic city filled with hard-working, happy people. Rick thinks it looks like Disneyland's old Tomorrowland. Rick feels cheerful, but sleepy. He yawns, then slumps to a deep sleep.

When the subway car comes to a stop, medical staff move Rick to a waiting gurney. Zsoldos watches the scene while on a video link with the doctor. "The normal course of *Rehabilitation* for this one, sir?" the doctor asks.

"I don't want him thinking he's been under for twenty years. I need him functional and ready for orientation within four hours," Zsoldos replies.

"In that case, I recommend a moderate dose. When the subject wakes, he will feel disoriented and have no memory of the life he left behind. He may think he has lost several days, while he's slept for only three hours. The effects of *Rehabilitation* will dissipate over time, but city atmosphere will help maintain compliance," the doctor explains.

Rick wakes as if startled. He's lying on a narrow bed in a white room. The floor is unpainted cement. He looks at his arms and body and finds himself dressed in a silver tunic, gray slacks, and black canvas deck shoes. He sits up on the bed, admiring the uniform. Rick tries to think, but his brain won't let him. He tries to remember how he got where he is, but his mind is blank. He doesn't notice his Smart-Band is missing.

A door opens at the far end of the room. Two young men, led by a young woman, walk briskly into the large room, stopping smartly at Rick's bedside.

"Hello," they say in unison with big smiles, and such a friendly tone, it's almost unsettling.

"Welcome to you, Richard Munday," says the young woman in a sing-songy voice and a bright smile.

They are young, sharp, and fit. The young woman is very attractive. The two young men wear VUE lens, but the young woman does not. They wear uniforms of black slacks and sky-blue tunics, with gray piping around the neck and the shoulder seams but with no insignia or rank. They each wear a kepi—small caps like the ones worn during the US Civil War. The caps have an '*A*' embroidered on the top in silver braid.

"Who are you? What is this place?" Rick asks.

One of the men answers, "We are City Guard," he says proudly. The woman touches the young man's arm as a sign to quiet him.

"We will guide you to your department orientation. Please come with us," the beautiful, young City Guard instructs.

The three guards turn and march toward the door. Rick follows. A door opens and Rick steps into a bright, enormous space, giving him a view of a magnificent city. It's bright, clean, and fresh, filled with large buildings, gardens, and trees. Several artfully designed buildings rise several stories, each one ringed with gardens of colorful flowers. The city bustles with activity.

An orange tiled floor stretches across the city. Small, raised bumps cover the six-inch by four-inch tiles. Driverless electric carts, trucks and trolleys move over the tiles without wheels, levitating a few inches off the floor, zipping across the orange road. Walking on the floor feels like cold cobblestones.

The air feels cool and smells sweet. Rick draws in a deep breath as he looks around in amazement. He's never seen a place like this. The sky is blue, but when he looks more intently, he notices it's not the sky but a curved ceiling. High above, the roof is a smooth dome painted and lit to replicate daylight.

The area under the dome looks like the main street of a small American town from the 1950s, designed to be futuristic. At the base of one building is a restaurant with sidewalk seating ringed by flower boxes. Another building has a convenience store and clothing shop. Levitating carts and trucks move past the shops. At one end of the cavernous space, the carts and trucks drive into a brightly lit tunnel.

People sit, relaxing, at the café's sidewalk tables, while others check the shops and walk from place to place. People smile, chat with one another, and wave at passersby. The city is active and friendly.

Rick hears cheerful music. He can't place the song, but it's something playful like, I've been working on the railroad or whistle while you work.

Encouraging images with slogans such as, "We work for the greater good," "You can reach your full potential," and "We are the few and the fortunate" adorn the walls of the dome on electronic billboards.

Rick stands in awe, trying to absorb the magnificence of the city. He turns to the young woman and asks, "What is this place? It looks fantastic! Are we underground?"

"We are in the experimental underground city of New Arcadia. You are among the few and the fortunate," she says cheerfully.

"Welcome to New Arcadia," says one of the young men. The other young man stands, nodding his welcome.

The young woman's eyes appear to flash around the edges of her irises. She touches a spot in the air. Rick stares into her beautiful eyes, watching the small flashes.

The woman smiles again. "VUE contact lens, made here in New Arcadia." She then turns to her male companions. "We must go. We will give Dr. Munday a short city tour before delivering him to his department for orientation."

The young trio walk a few steps to contraptions that look like floating platforms. The City Guard climb onto the devices, placing their feet into footholds, causing the platforms to wobble briefly before becoming stable.

"We are standing on robotic, self-balancing, Mag-Lev panels. We call them Maggies. The orange tiles are a unique ceramic material, allowing room temperature superconductivity. The tiles create a high-powered magnetic field across the entire city floor. Our maglevs have an opposite magnetic polarity, creating magnetic levitation. It's fun," explains the young female. The two male City Guard hover, rocking this way and that. They balance with their feet in the footholds without hanging on to anything.

The female guard's maglev is larger with a second row of footholds and handlebar for a passenger. The female City Guard signals to Rick. "You'll ride with me. Step up."

Rick hesitates, examining the maglev floating inches above the tiled floor. The woman motions to Rick. "Step up. It's easy. You have the city tour now." She holds her hand out to him. Rick reluctantly takes the young woman's hand and steps onto the platform. The panel wobbles as it compensates for the additional weight and Rick's uneven step, but quickly steadies.

The woman commands. "Maggie, city tour, central section. Go."

The Maggie moves off so fast, Rick nearly falls off. He wraps his arms around the young woman's waist as the Maggie transports them across the cavernous room. The men stand straight with arms at their sides, leaning forward, looking as if they are gliding on ice;

their firm bodies lean into each curve and turn. The group weaves in and out of traffic, crossing lanes of a road painted on the tiled floor.

Rick hangs on as they fly rapidly across the central room. The young woman speaks. Rick pulls closer to hear what she's saying. His chest touches her back. His hips press against her buttocks; only the metal handlebar handle separates them.

"This is the city's central room, the center of New Arcadia. This city, working together with our other cities, is self-sufficient. Each city produces unique products and trades with other cities. If there were ever an emergency, we can survive in our underground facilities for several years, with no outside help."

Rick hears a rumbling sound in the distance. As they come around a building, he spots three massive parallel tubes, each fifteen feet in diameter, running from the top of the dome all the way down and into the floor. The lower fifty-foot sections of the tubes are glass. Water rushes down the huge pipes like a giant, contained waterfall. It's an impressive structure. The top section of glass is wider and open, allowing a light watery mist to drift down to a park covered with green grass, tall trees, and flowers. The City Guard hovers in front of the glass tubes in a hypnotic gaze.

Rick shouts. "What is it?"

The talkative male guard hears Rick's question over the roaring sound of the water and is eager to answer. "It's part of our power system. Hydroelectricity. We can generate more than a thousand megawatts of electricity. That's equal to the output of a nuclear plant."

The female guard smiles. "We have two power stations like this in New Arcadia. They provide unlimited, safe, clean power. All our cities generate power using clean, self-sustainable methods. Isn't it wonderful?"

Rick is awestruck. "It's brilliant."

"We've also equipped the city with small modular reactors. We use nuclear power plants to supplement our power requirements. These specially sealed modules can never go haywire or meltdown, so they're much safer than nuclear power plants of the past," explains the second male guard.

The three city guards speak in unison. "We have more to show you." With a slight forward lean, they are once again flying across the tiled floor. The young woman continues her tour guide speech.

The edges around the pupils of her eyes glow. It looks as if she's staring into space instead of guiding the Maggie. Rick thinks she's reading a script.

"We have housing facilities for up to one hundred-seventy thousand here in New Arcadia. Everyone has free living quarters, a base salary, and free access to the cafeterias. We have barber shops, restaurants, and clothing shops."

The Maggie makes a sharp turn around a corner. The young woman leans into the curve. Rick leans with her as the maglev glides into a long, wide cavern glowing with a soft purple light. This cavern is tall, but narrower than the central room. There are rows and rows of multi-level gardens stacked one hundred feet high. Workers sit on trapeze seats that raise and lower to work on different levels of the garden.

"Is it a farm?" Rick asks.

"Yes, we grow all our plants and vegetables aeroponically. Everything is organic. The plants grow fifty percent faster with no fertilizer or pesticides. Just add water mixed with nutrients and voila, you've got broccoli." At the end of a long row of vegetables, the Maggie takes a sharp turn down a corridor and through a tunnel. After a short distance, they zip into another large cavern.

"This is the print and assembly room where we use 3-D printing, rapid liquid printing, and automated assembly systems to manufacture products needed for the city. In the medical department, we can actualize a new liver, kidney, or skin tissue," the young City Guard explains. The group speeds along on the Maggies. "Next stop is the Electro-Rail Station."

"Electro-Rail?" Rick asks.

"It is our high-speed rail system connecting New Arcadia with the other cities, allowing us to travel and trade goods."

They ride down a corridor until it opens onto an enormous cavern. They stop and hover next to a railing overlooking a vast rail station. Rows of clear tubes come out of a rock wall in the distance, ending at the rail platforms. There are twenty rail tubes running across the floor of the station, but only the first twelve tubes appear to be active.

The rail cars are very sleek and glisten with a silky white finish. Blue and red swooshing stripes complete look of fast rail cars. Rick

notices that there are cargo cars and passenger cars. He watches as
people step into a passenger car from a loading platform. Once the
door closes, the car advances to a transparent airlock. Pumps suck
air from the airlock, creating a vacuum. Seconds later, the rail car
launches, zooming down the tube, disappearing into the rock wall.

"Wow, it's amazing. All this built underground. Why are they
only using half of the tubes?" Rick asks.

"The other tubes are for cities planned but not completed."

"Whoever built this has ambitious plans," Rick comments.

The group speeds away from the train station. As they scoot
along a corridor, Rick notices a large room marked SURFACE
INTEGRATION STORAGE.

"What's that area?" Rick asks.

"It's storage for products and equipment we would use when
moving back to living on the surface after a nuclear disaster. They've
thought of everything for this nuclear war experiment," his guide
explains.

"Nuclear war experiment? What do you mean?" Rick asks.

The Maggies begin their return to the city center as the young
guard explains. "Operation Hard Shelter, New Arcadia and the
other cities are an experiment to learn if humans can survive a full-
scale nuclear war. With the Four Wars escalating, we must
prepare to survive the worst-case scenario. We are all volunteers
selected for this duty. We are the few and the fortunate. You'll
understand after orientation."

Rick hears a loud tone broadcast across the city.

"That is the hour tone. It's easy to lose track of time in an
underground city. We must get you to orientation." The trio of
Maggies accelerate to full speed.

The underground complex fascinates Rick. He now feels like an
expert riding the maglev. It's an exhilarating experience, riding body
to body with his young guide, absorbing her warmth. Their bodies
move in perfect sync as they lean into curves and around corners,
zigging and weaving between vehicles along the tiled roadway.

They stop in front of a building marked DEPARTMENT 17. The
girl motions for Rick to step down. The male guards stay on their
Maggies, swaying back and forth.

"You will work in this building, and across the street is your
residence." She points to a three-story building with shops on the

first floor and two levels of residences. A sign, RESIDENCE 240, marks the building.

The young guide hands Rick a plastic card. "This card has your building number, floor, and compartment number. Keep it handy in case you get lost. If you haven't noticed, everything looks the same. It's easy to get lost until you learn your way around."

"That's handy. Not much of a commute. Do I go to the office now?" Rick asks.

"Orientation first, through those doors." She points to double glass doors. Letters over the door spell out AUDITORIUM.

The male guard's wave. The talkative one calls out, "Goodbye, Dr. Munday. Hope you enjoyed the tour. We will see you around the city."

His young guide opens the glass door and enters the lobby, directing Rick to the auditorium. "You will now view an orientation video before meeting your department team. Your department manager will complete your orientation. It has been my pleasure, Dr. Munday," she says, with her never-ending smile and glowing eyes.

Rick hates to see her go. He doesn't want the tour to end. Riding on the Maggie pressed against her fit body was thrilling. He acts on impulse and gives the young girl a hug. "Thank you so much. I don't even know your name." Rick looks past the glowing edges of her pupils to peer into her sharp hazel eyes. The young woman breaks away from Rick's grasp. She straightens her tunic and stands erect. "I am City Guard," she scolds. She looks over her shoulder. The male guards are chatting as they sway on their Maggies.

"City Guard, don't get hugged, and I'm not supposed to share my name."

"I enjoyed riding with you. I hope to see you again." Rick walks across the lobby. As he opens the auditorium door, he looks back at the young beauty. When she sees Rick sneak a goodbye look, the young guard calls out softly, "Joanna. My name is Joanna."

Rick feels a tug at his heart as he steps through the auditorium door.

Chapter 20: Spherules

Wednesday Afternoon–Henderson, Nevada

Curtis sits at his desk littered with empty chip bags, candy wrappers, pizza boxes, and his Giant Gulp cup. A single desk lamp is the only light source other than light emanating from the wall-size thin screens in front of him and on the wall behind him.

Most people have a home office or a computer room. Curtis isn't most people. Curtis lives in the dining room, or what had been the dining room. The room is full of computers, monitors, his ham radio, portable electronic gadgets, figurines from *Star Trek, Star Wars,* anime, and other rare and obscure collectibles. Products from his past hobbies fill the living room. Curtis likes his stuff.

He doesn't get out much, but people like to chat with him because he's friendly and almost always available, so he has lots of friends around the world. Curtis and Jin are members of the Slooh community, a group of astronomy enthusiasts who watch the skies looking for asteroids and share what they find with other members worldwide. Curtis also uses ham radio to communicate and make new friends. Most people have forgotten that ham radio is a worldwide communication system. But ham operators have not forgotten. Curtis has a complete setup with a large antenna on the roof of his house.

This afternoon he's working at his desk editing video streamed from Jin's All-Sky cam to their server, and posting the best, most dramatic scenes of the sky storm to the Slooh forum when he hears a ringing chime. The image of Aman, his friend from India, appears on the screen.

"Hey, Aman. How's work going after that big promotion? You must go crazy managing hundreds of software engineers."

Aman speaks fast and always uses more words than necessary. "Oh my. Sometimes, it's more like herding a gaggle of geese than managing people. I've been watching your new vids. Wow, I love the name. Sky Storm! Do you have a few minutes? Sorry if it's a bad time. You can call me any seven days, twenty-four-seven. You're my bro, we're family, but if you're busy, no problem, you can reach me any seven days."

"No problem, Aman. It's the middle of the day here. But it must be late for you."

"I couldn't sleep. Maybe the job is getting to me. Your notes say Jin shot the video. Why didn't he post it?"

When Curtis attended community college, he befriended a young Indian boy named Raj. Raj was a skinny, shy boy overwhelmed by the American lifestyle. Jin was off to university, so Curtis and Raj became quick friends. It wasn't long before the two were eating pizza and going to movies together. A few months later, Raj died while taking a selfie at the edge of the Grand Canyon. Raj must have told his older brother Aman stories about his friend Curtis. When they met at the funeral, Aman treated Curtis as his family.

Curtis rummages through pizza boxes on his desk. He finds a piece a few boxes down the stack. *How had he missed this one?* He examines it. No mold. He flicks off a piece of questionable-looking Italian sausage. *Hmm, looks OK.*

"I'm posting because Jin was busy with his girlfriend last night. He's working today, anyhow." Curtis takes a bite of the pizza.

"Girl friend? Is this the girl named Becky on the forum? What's she like? Is she pretty? Is she smart, or is she smart and ugly? That is sadly too often the case. Sorry for saying."

"Ah, Becky's OK, and she's not ugly. She's smart and a quick learner, but that girl can get snappy if you say something she doesn't like."

Aman is older than Curtis. He wears large eyeglasses that slip down his long nose. His dark skin is wrinkling, and his hair is turning gray. "Girlfriends take so much time and money. It's no wonder you're picking up the slack for him."

"Me and Jin are good. No matter what, Jin is my lifelong friend. We're brothers. Nothing changes that, but the way he talks, he's found true love. Good for him. He can do the couples thing. I'm going solo."

"You go, bro. My cousin, Hapreet, he got a girlfriend and after a while we never saw him. He used to be my bro, any seven days. After he fell in love, he does what she wants. He likes what she likes.

He thinks the way she thinks. It's like his body was taken over by a virus. I don't know Hapreet, anymore."

"I hope Becky isn't a virus. I don't think Jin has anti-virus protection!"

"Anti-virus. Oh man, Curt-tis, you crack me up." Aman's laughter crackles through the screen.

"But maybe you're right. Becky made some comment about conspiracies, and Jin suggested I'm a conspiracy nut job. Where's that coming from?"

"What conspiracy were they accusing you of being nuts about?"

"My gut tells me there's something behind the increase in meteor activity. The government shuts down all the telescopes so we can't monitor the skies. It's the heaviest asteroid activity in decades, and we can't observe it properly. The forum is buzzing with new finds every day, but none of it makes the news streams. Doesn't that seem strange? Something is going on and the government is covering it up. I told Becky, I believe the Chilean earthquake was really a meteor impact, and she went all psycho-conspiracy nut on me, geez."

"I'm with you, Curt-tis. The government has been covering up asteroid impacts for decades. An asteroid impact certainly could have caused the Chilean tsunami."

"I hope I'm wrong about Chile. Either way, lots of people died. I guess it doesn't matter how. If the government is covering stuff up—" An alarm on Curtis's band sounds.

"Dang. I gotta run. Thanks for the chat, Aman. Hey, I want to catch up on those game mods we've been working on. I take longer to mod than you, but I don't have a team of software programmers working for me. Call you later."

The alarm is from his CO_2 extraction system in the garage. Curtis may not venture out of the house much, but he still needs an income. During his year and a half of junior college, he turned a hobby into a lucrative business. Marijuana has been legal in Nevada for decades. Curtis discovered a niche providing exotic, high-quality THC oil and medicinal CBD extracts. Where others provide basic THC oils, Curtis creates oil blends with unique tastes and aromas.

His flavorful, aromatically pleasing blends gained a strong following. With the money he made, he invested in a professional lab-certified, high-pressure, supercritical CO_2 extraction system. He ordered the system online and installed it in his garage.

Curtis's dining room might look like a college dorm after an all-night party, but his garage is immaculate. It looks like a high-tech clean room. The garage is deep and wide enough for three cars and has a fifteen-foot-high ceiling. The walls are bright white, and the room is lit with custom LEDs. He treated the cement floor with a glossy white industrial coating. Curtis does not allow shoes in the garage. A row of slip-on footwear sits just inside the garage door.

In the far corner of the garage, there is an enclosed room with a sign that reads COMPRESSOR ROOM–DO NOT ENTER. Next to the compressor room stands an exotic contraption: a clinical-looking configuration of steel cylinders, tubes, pipes, and wires. This is the latest APEX M7-2500 max efficiency, high pressure supercritical CO_2 extractor.

Curtis uses the device to extract pure THC oil, the chemical in marijuana that makes people high. Curtis also extracts oils from coffee, vanilla, mint, almonds, and spices. He then mixes and blends THC oils with his spice extracts to create unique blends of smoking oils and therapeutic ointment rubs.

He stores the collection of flavor extracts in a refrigerated glass enclosure with sliding doors. Hundreds of labeled jars line shelves of the temperature-controlled cooler. The cooler is lit with blue fluorescent lights that produce a soft glow. A long white table populated with lab equipment stands next to the storage cooler.

Curtis has filled the rest of the garage with his favorite and most sentimental objects. In the middle of the garage is a large leather couch facing two shiny Harley-Davidson motorcycles. These are not the fat hogs of earlier days. Instead, they are powerful fuel cell Harley's with sleek, tough designs. The masculine, forward-slanting chrome metal frames, satin-white wheels, custom painted tanks, and fenders give the perception of speed, even while the cycles are standing still.

Next to the new Harley's is an antique Indian motorcycle. It's old. It has spark plugs and runs on gasoline. The Scout was Curtis's father's pride and joy. It was a classic even when his pop was alive. Curtis's father had painstakingly restored the bike. Curtis maintains the bike in its immaculate, original state and makes sure it's always well-oiled and sparkling clean.

On the other side of the Harley's is a white Chevrolet Corvette. Beyond the sports car is a steel door in the garage wall. Curtis knows the Corvette is old. General Motors went out of business years before. The Corvette can't drive itself and doesn't have a fuel cell, but he likes it. The car is in factory new condition. Curtis likes to look at the Corvette. He's only driven it twice. Once off the dealer's lot to his house and a second time from his house to the airport and back, when he took Jin to the airport after a weekend visit.

Curtis runs to the garage to silence the alarm. He moves through the kitchen to the garage, kicking his shoes into the kitchen before stepping into a pair of slippers on the garage floor. The alarm continues to ring. Curtis rushes, almost sliding across the sleek white floor to his extraction contraption. Stopping in front of the systems touchscreen monitor, Curtis skims the readings. Pressures are excessive.

"Shit, shit, shit." Curtis frantically pushes buttons to force decompression. The pressure readings retreat from the red zone to yellow and keep dropping. "Great. I lost that batch. What's wrong? I just cleaned you. Did something get gunked up in there? Looks like you'll get torn down and swabbed out again tomorrow." Curtis pats the pressure vessel as he speaks.

Curtis leaves the slippers in the garage and goes back to his desk. He orders a pizza by reaching out to the thin screen. The pizza icon for automatic re-order of his favorite pizza appears to stretch out from the screen toward his finger. The icon makes a tone to confirm his order without him touching the screen.

Curtis checks the Slooh forum. This afternoon, communication is sparse. Only a few people are in the chat room. There aren't many new posts. All is quiet.

The ham radio emits tones. *Dit dit dah dah dah dit dit dit.* The message repeats. *Dit dit dit dah dah dah dit dit dit.* Curtis slides his chair to his ham station at the far end of his desk. Call letters come across in a series of *dit*s and *dah*s. "VK6GCX. That's Marcus' call sign. He's sending an SOS. What's he?"

Curtis grabs his Morse code key or CW key. He sends a message out in Morse: "Why using CW?"

CW is the term radio operator's use when referring to International Morse Code. *Why doesn't he just post on the forum? Something must be very wrong for him to send an SOS.*

Curtis has his notepad and pen handy to write out the words received from across the world. He could use his computer to decode incoming messages or QSO and encode his outgoing messages, but he prefers to use the CW key, and his brain to encode and decode the old-fashioned way.

Curtis sends. "What wrong?" "U OK?" Beads of sweat swell on his brow. He stares at the radio, anxiously waiting to hear tones in response. It seems like forever before the *dit*s, and *dah*s start again. He writes the words out as he hears the tones.

"Perth destroyed. News blackout. "

The message stops. The news stuns Curtis, but he feels affirmed. He shouts, "Perth destroyed! News Blackout! You are shitting me! Shit, shit, shit."

Curtis sends as fast as he can. "News report fireball only."

Curtis stops and waits until the response comes. "Wrong. City destroyed. Yesterday morning by asteroid."

Curtis keys. "Shit."

More *dit*s and *dah*s come in from Marcus. "Net is down. Radio voice channels monitored. No news out. No help. Switch 14.233. Wait, SSTV."

Marcus wants Curtis to change frequencies to receive an image. SSTV stands for Slow Scan Television; It's an old method used to send photos over ham radio. If the government is monitoring voice transmissions, this is risky. SSTV uses voice frequencies, but maybe they won't pick up an SSTV transmission.

A computer monitor connected to the ham radio transceiver comes to life. An image slowly appears.

While the image comes through, Curtis turns to his thin screen wall. Six news streams and an anime are playing with the audio muted. He has seen nothing more on Perth since the news blip mentioned a daytime fireball. A quick scan of news sites offers no updates on the fireball. If a meteor destroyed Perth, news of the disaster should occupy the streams 24/7, but there is nothing.

A few minutes later, an image appears. The picture shows city buildings destroyed. Skyscrapers have toppled. Fires burn and smoke blots out the background. Another image fills the screen; It shows a main thoroughfare with cars crashed. Bodies lie dead in the street. A third image appears on the screen. It displays three small teardrop–shaped rocks with the word "Spherules" written beneath the rocks. Two of them look like blobs of glass, the third blob is metal.

No more images come through. Curtis switches back Morse code. "Why no news?"

Don't know is the response that comes in a series of tones. Marcus spends the next minute transmitting a long message. Curtis struggles to keep up.

"Fireball low in sky. Oid exploded. Shock toppled buildings. Millions of spherules. Blast like machine gun. City burning."

Curtis comprehends the reality of death. This is worse than he imagined. He thought the government might cover up news of the fireball, but he never dreamt an explosion above Perth could cause the level of destruction he's viewing. The Australian government must be requesting help from the US and other countries. The civilized world always helps countries in times of great need.

Curtis sends: "Help will come. Hang in there."

There is no response. Curtis presses the repeat key. His last message is re-sent. No response. Time passes in silence. Curtis sends a general request for anyone on the frequency. A response comes through. "Channel Restricted. What is your call sign?" The request spooks Curtis. He switches off his transceiver and scoots his chair away from the radio.

Curtis calls Jin. He knows Jin is at work, and that the place he works requires employees to put their bands, VUEs, watches, and phones. If a person still has something, they call a phone in a locked safe before entering their workspace. Jin will not receive any calls or messages until the end of his workday, but Curtis must get a message to him.

When Curtis hears Jin's voice requesting the caller leave a message, he stops the call. He calls a second time, but when he's supposed to leave a message, he cancels the call again. Curtis knows he's overly paranoid, but he also knows the government monitors calls. Heck, Jin works for the agency that does the monitoring. Leaving voicemail is risky, but he must get a message to Jin. He has an idea.

Curtis and Jin love the old TV series Star Trek. They loved Star Trek so much; they learned to speak Klingon. During high school, Curtis, Jin, and some of their dorkier friends spoke Klingon daily. Curtis leaves a voice message for Jin—in Klingon.

Mike McCoy

Chapter 21: Awakening

Wednesday Afternoon–New Arcadia

Rick reluctantly walks into the auditorium. The room is vacant but has seating for at least two hundred people. A large screen hangs above the stage. Rick strolls down the aisle. The lights go dark. The screen lights up. Music with triumphant chords plays. A military coat of arms appears on the screen; a clamshell-shaped object, with the word *Homeland* above the clamshell, and the word *Defense* below. Stars border either side of the shell, connecting the top and bottom words.

Jon Anderson, the President of the United States, appears on the screen.

"Welcome, brave volunteers. Our country has faced many challenges. Nuclear weapons destroyed New York and Chicago, and a million souls paid the ultimate price of freedom. Faced with defeat, we fought to protect our homeland, and with great courage, we drove the conquering horde from our shores. Our men fought in Europe. We lead a coalition of allies in the creation of New Korea. Our troops fought because we believed victory would create a safer world. But the Four Wars are an inextinguishable inferno sweeping across the world. Stepping back from the flames of war has resulted in a US economy that is recovering. But America is not out of danger. Those who pursue war will use ever more devastating weapons. We must act to protect the future of humanity. To ensure the continuity of government, and the survival of mankind. The Department of Homeland Security's National Protection and Programs Directorate working together with FEMA, have developed a network of protective underground cities. We selected you to be part of a very important mission. Operation Hard Shelter's charter is to develop twenty underground cities spread across our vast nation, each one interconnected by high-velocity rail, providing shelter for three million US citizens. We now have six functioning facilities capable of housing 720,000 citizen workers, scientists, and military volunteers. Our European allies have planned similar cities to protect their populations."

A map appears on the screen while the president speaks, showing facilities across the country. Rick studies the map. It doesn't mark state borders and the names of the underground cities are strange: New Arcadia, Nod, and Edendale. He doesn't recognize the names, but the cities are located near major US cities. The one named Edendale is in Southern California.

"Volunteers, you can be very proud that we selected you for this experiment. You are the best and brightest minds chosen to propel humanity into the twenty-second century as a stronger, smarter, new society. We will build a brighter future for mankind. Our planners have designed each city to have unique manufacturing and agricultural specialties to stimulate trade between cities, generating a robust economy. I ask for your pledge to do your best. I trust in your abilities ensuring that this project will have the highest level of success. You are the few and the fortunate." The president salutes.

The orientation video moves to the next topic: The Corporate Republic.

"As we move from the developmental stage to operational cities, we are adopting a new name for our experimental society. Welcome to the city of New Arcadia. Arcadia is the model for a new society. An optimized, commercial economy with incentives, fairness, and opportunities for all. Arcadians will become an advanced human culture, free of wars and crime. Everyone has an equal chance to succeed. You are the few and the fortunate. You are Arcadians!"

A light appears on the left side of the video screen. A door has opened. Rick can see the outline of a man motioning for him to move to the door. "Hey get over here, numb-nuts."

Rick walks to the door as the presentation continues. The man greets him with a pat him on the shoulder as if he's an old friend, then pulls Rick through the door into a narrow hallway.

The man speaks under his breath to Rick. "They finally got you. I was hoping you'd remain insignificant. Then, you write something interesting. Way to go, dimwit. I should never have given you access to IPXE." The man shakes Rick and looks into his eyes. Rick smiles dumbly at the man. "You're still suffering from rehabilitation, and you've been breathing that nice city atmosphere, eh? You're unusually happy and your brains foggy, isn't it? This will straighten you out."

Ouch! Rick senses something jab his right arm.

Rick stares at the man. He has messy reddish-brown hair and several days' growth of beard. The man looks familiar. He looks silly wearing a suit jacket over his silver tunic. Rick tries to make his brain remember. There is something, some memory, but Rick can't place him. The man directs Rick down the hall and through another door, which leads to a large conference room. "I'm here to introduce you to your department," he says, louder than needed.

The conference room is bright, luxuriously carpeted, and decorated with artwork and paintings. A long credenza sits along one wall with an expensive looking vase and flower arrangement. The room looks like a modern executive suite. The man sits at a large conference table and motions Rick to sit. Only one of the leather chairs is vacant. Everyone at the table, except for two men at the far end, are wearing silver tunics like Rick's.

One man is older, but his light brown hair is thick and well groomed. He wears a black tunic that looks like a military uniform, with shoulder epaulets and an emblem on his left breast. He looks dignified and important. The second man looks ordinary wearing a plain white shirt. He's pudgy and wears thick, black-rimmed glasses.

The old man stands, holding out both hands in greeting. "Ah, Dr. Munday. We are happy to have you join us. Please have a seat."

He sits in the empty chair halfway down the table. The man from the auditorium is across from Rick. Rick looks at the people around the table. They are all staring at the new arrival.

The old man continues with his greeting. "Welcome to the Astrophysics department. I am Colonel Cruikshank. It is the work of this group that convinced the government to build cities like New Arcadia, thus ensuring our survival. You can be very proud to be part of this department, and I must say, you made it in the nick of time. What do you think of our city? I trust you enjoyed your tour."

"I enjoyed it very much. It's a fantastic city. Everyone is so nice."

"We would like you to stay here and work with us. You'd like that, wouldn't you?"

Rick tries to think of a reason he wouldn't want to stay. There is something nagging him, deep within, but he can't connect emotion to it or bring whatever it is to the surface. Rick pauses before responding.

"I guess so."

Rick's hesitation to respond seems to worry the colonel. He turns to Zsoldos, questioning him in a whisper. "You're sure he's rehabilitated?"

"Yes, I'm sure he doesn't remember a thing. You can see he is under the influence of the city's atmosphere. That may wear off in here, but it shouldn't matter."

Rick takes a deep breath. The air is not cool and sweet in this room. A wave of heat flows through his body, making his cheeks flush. The smile on his face fades. His mouth is dry. He stares forward.

The colonel continues to speak. "Under the decrees signed by the CEO, and the Arcadian council, citizens in the six cities will be the dawn of a new society. The disaster we face provides the opportunity to rebuild a better world. The storm will destroy the world mankind has created, but we will preserve knowledge and technology. We are developing new values for the human psyche. Prejudice, bigotry, and racism; the differences between people which create strife will not exist. There will be no war, no hatred of race or religion, no fighting over territories or resources. We will be of one mind. The belief system we are designing for Arcadians will establish the optimal social environment for all mankind. Out of devastation, the best of humanity will emerge."

Rick's body tingles and his head feels prickly. He looks at faces around the table. Several look familiar. Rick tries to remember who they are and how he knows them when the man from the door speaks to him.

"Hey, Dickwad, aren't you glad you made it here! An asteroid bombardment will destroy the world, but you've got a front-row seat for the birth of humanity two point oh. Welcome to the party!"

Rick feels as if a translucent veil covering his head is being pulled away.

He looks at the man with the messy hair and scraggly beard. He's sure he recognizes the man, but how can it be? "Karl, is that you? But it can't be. You, you're dead." Rick says, staring at his old college friend.

"Sorry to break the news, buddy; not dead. And it's Dr. Wetzel, if you don't mind."

"But your car crashed. You hit a tree at high speed, and your car exploded. You died."

Rick looks around the table and spots another familiar face. A woman he remembers meeting at a conference while studying for his master's degree. "You." Rick points at the woman. "You're Trudy Scales, right?" She nods with a demur smile. "You drowned in a boating accident on the Hudson River two years ago."

The people at the table remain silent. Rick is sure he recognizes others at the table but can't recall their names. "Are you all dead?"

The colonel speaks up. "Now, Dr. Munday, there is no reason to be upset. All the men and women here are renowned in their fields of study. You must understand, we conducted our project under the strictest level of secrecy. Sometimes, it was necessary to create a cover story to explain a person's disappearance from their normal work and life."

"Am I dead? Is that what you will tell people?" Rick is awakening. Memories flood his brain. He looks at his wrist. "My band is missing. I gave my presentation. I moved forward, and you hijacked me to an underground city. Oh, wait, wait. I have a wife and children. Did you tell my family I'm dead? Am I dead?"

"No, Dr. Munday. You are not dead. We could not contact your wife. There is no time. As Dr. Wetzel said, and as you so adeptly predicted in your presentation, asteroids will bombard Earth. You even impressed Zsoldos with your presentation; However, your timing was off. The event has begun. Asteroids will destroy most of the cities on Earth over the next several weeks. But not to worry. You are safe with us, in New Arcadia."

"We are the few and the fortunate. Aren't we the lucky ones?" says Karl cynically.

Rick's breathing rate increases. The flushed, tingling feeling fades, replaced by anxiety. How can he get word to his family? If what the colonel said is true, he must save his family. How will people protect themselves? Memories, mental images, and emotions surge in Ricks' brain. It's too much to absorb. He puts his head in his hands, attempting to gain control of his thoughts.

"You showed me. Perth was destroyed, but that's not what the news reported. The liaison officer… he said the news reported a fireball in the sky. Just a fireball, nothing to worry about." Rick's mind whirls. His perception is sharp and clear for the first time in this strange city. "How can there be no news about Perth being destroyed? It's impossible. It would take a massive cover-up."

Rick freezes, pointing at the old man. "You're not telling people. Cities will be destroyed, killing millions, and you are not telling people. How can you sit here, allowing people to die without warning?"

The old man chuckles as his hand massages the only remaining thigh muscle in his damaged leg. It is thick, firm, and muscled, rejuvenated from the recent spa treatment.

"Dr. Munday, your intuition does not disappoint. We have a total news lockdown on the Perth event. No one outside of Perth can know what has happened there. It would only cause unnecessary panic," the old man says.

"Thousands of asteroids will bombard Earth and you're doing nothing to warn them? People could have prepared, gathered supplies, and found shelter. You don't know how bad it will be. If you do nothing, it's murder. It's the same as murder." Rick leans on the table in shock.

Colonel Cruikshank looks at Zsoldos menacingly. "What is wrong with him?"

"The dose of rehabilitation must have been too small. He should not be acting like this. I'll get him under control." Zsoldos says.

"Dr. Munday, you need to understand. Our computer models analyzed every scenario. We have superb imagery of the NEOs. My team has been tracking thousands of objects from the Kuiper belt for years. Hundreds of thousands of objects are moving through the inner solar system, just as you described in your presentation." Zsoldos pauses for a moment. Rick is listening and appears to be calming down.

"Your presentation was excellent. Dr. Munday, to put it bluntly, your theories are correct. However, your timing for a likely event was not accurate. The first cluster of over two thousand objects, large enough to make it through the atmosphere, will soon impact Earth. There will be trillions of dollars in damage, and hundreds of millions of casualties worldwide."

Rick remembers the dark formation he saw pass behind Ceres. "You've known. You built underground cities. You've known for years this would happen, and you warned no one? The government covered this up and kept it a secret from the people?"

"Yes, we have known for years there was a high potential for a massive bombardment. We also knew we could not protect everyone, so we built cities like New Arcadia to protect as many as possible. We kept our work secret, so if you call that a government cover-up, then yes, it's true. I wish we could have done more, but there wasn't enough time or resources," explains Zsoldos.

Rick's emotions are out of control. He stands and screams at the people around the table. "Liars. You are all liars. You lied to me when you invited me to this place. You've lied to every person who lives and works here. They think this is an experiment about living through a nuclear war! Have you told them their loved ones will die? Do they know what the world will be like when this is over? You're all liars and murderers." The people at the conference table sit like sheep without reaction.

"I will not stand for this insolence," the colonel shouts, scowling at Zsoldos." Get him under control."

Zsoldos touches a spot in midair. Rick feels severe pain in his head, dropping him to his knees.

The colonel rises, pounding the table. "Stop, now Dr. Munday. We are not liars. We are not murderers. We took measures to ensure the success of this project for the greater good of our staff and volunteers. I will not tolerate any further outbursts, or—"

Rick writhes on the floor in pain but gets words out, interrupting the colonel. "Or what? You will drug me into submission?" Rick looks up at the colonel's face. It appears more wrinkled than before.

Karl speaks. "What were we supposed to do? Tell people asteroids will destroy Earth, duck, and cover. Kiss your ass goodbye? How would people have prepared for this? By killing, robbing, stealing, or digging a hole to China? If the asteroids don't get them, starvation will finish them in a few weeks."

Rick stops fighting and the pain eases. He gets up to his knees, holding his head in his hands, trying to push away the pain. Saving his family is the motivation that drives him. He cannot let them die. If he can get word to Courtney, or Uncle Rob, they can get to his uncle's hideaway.

"I need to warn my wife, my family. I can save them. Just let me call or get a message to them. You can get a message to them. I know you can. Help me and I'll stay. You can have me. Just let me warn them, then you can do whatever you want with me," Rick pleads.

The colonel speaks. "If you continue your unruly outbursts, I will have you relaxed. We tried to get word to your family, but we were unsuccessful. The president and Arcadian Council members have arrived in the cities. We have cut all communications with the surface to ensure our location is secret and secure."

Trudy Scales speaks up. "Dr. Munday, we've all left behind people we love and care about. It was a difficult decision. We made the choice to save a few instead of saving none. We did the best we could."

"You Arcadians didn't give me a choice. I was moved forward—your phrase for kidnapping. No one gave me the choice between this place or my family. I chose family. I did not volunteer."

The old man leans on his cane, watching Rick grovel. "After seeing your presentation, we could not allow you to be topside with the storm starting. We cannot have someone with your knowledge talking to the press, causing panic and confusion. We hoped that by sharing the marvel of New Arcadia, you would join us and help with the work ahead."

Rick thinks of Courtney, his children, and Uncle Rob. Can they make it to safety? He is desperate to warn them. Rick doesn't know where he will go or what he will do, but he can't stay in this room any longer. He dashes for the conference room door.

Zsoldos taps the air, confident he can subdue Munday. Rick drops to the floor squirming, holding his head in his hands, attempting to shield himself from the pain. The scientists around the table sit idly watching Rick's painful attempt to escape.

The colonel is losing his patience. "Dr. Munday. We are working to create a world without conflict, action with obedience, citizens working together in peace and harmony. Therefore, I do expect joyful cooperation. If you are not willing to comply, we have methods that will subdue you."

"Drink the colonels' Kool-Aid numb-nuts or suffer the consequences. It's the price of admission to utopia," Karl quips.

"That's enough from you, Dr. Wetzel. Zsoldos, call Captain Kobalt. It appears Dr. Munday requires permanent rehabilitation."

Rick struggles through the pain. He uses every ounce of his strength to crawl toward the door. Zsoldos taps his fingers in the air, sending a message to Kobalt. "It seems the captain and his team are busy containing another incident."

The colonel is furious. "Another incident! I will not stand for disorder as we stand on the cusp of our greatest test. Release the Buzz-Bees," the colonel orders.

A panel in the ceiling opens above the conference room table. Four round yellow balls, each with a black stripe around their center, drop into the room. The mechanisms engage, hovering above the table making a buzzing sound. One of the female scientists at the table screams. Zsoldos attempts to use his finger to line up the crosshairs in his VUE on Rick, but Rick is a moving target scrambling for the door.

Zsoldos gets the Buzz-Bees to lock on their target. They buzz, moving rapidly across the large room toward Rick just as he makes it to the door. He looks back. Four yellow-and-black flying balls are bearing down on him. He twists the handle and pulls the door open just enough to scurry through. The Buzz-Bees hover a few feet from the door and fire as Rick pushes his body through the doorway. The Buzz-Bees spin, firing six darts each. Darts stick in the door and wall as the door closes. One dart hits the bottom of Rick's shoe, sticking in the rubber sole.

The door shuts with a whoosh and a click. Rick rests against the wall. The pain in his head stops. Rick pulls out the dart to examine it. The needle is black and sharp. The rear of the dart has short, black fletching, like arrow feathers, and a small muscular bladder that pumps its venom through the needle. Rick tosses the dart aside and gets to his feet.

Inside the conference room, the colonel bangs his cane on the conference table. "How could you let him get away?"

Zsoldos drops his arm from the targeting position. "I'm not trained as a marksman. Shooting escapees is not my forte. It doesn't matter. A few minutes breathing the city atmosphere will calm him."

"I told you he's a criminal. You said he would be valuable to the department."

"He's in shock. It's all so sudden for him, poor thing. He needs some time to adjust and accept the truth; that's all," says Trudy. The woman's sweetness seems to enrage the colonel further.

"Send the Black Guard after him. I want him relaxed and in custody."

Karl stands. "Colonel, Zsoldos is right. The city's refreshed air will calm him down in no time. No need to call the black shirts. They tend to break bones. If they break him, he'll be no good to anyone. Let me find him. I'll bring him in."

"Yes, Wetzel, you were his friend. Find him and take him to Black Guard headquarters for rehabilitation. The rest of us have an imminent asteroid bombardment to prepare for."

Chapter 22: Star Treatment

Wednesday Afternoon–Pasadena, CA.

Courtney checks the clock on the food actualizer. It's afternoon and Rick has not called. He always calls to check in. Courtney knows Rick has been stressed about work. He tries not to show it, but she can tell. The grant means so much to him. She doesn't know much about Rick's proposal, but she knows it's important to him and their family.

Courtney's band chimes and a semitransparent display projects an image in the air. Seeing Uncle Rob dashes her hopes, but Courtney touches the display to accept the call. "Have you heard from our boy yet? How did the presentation go?" asks Rob.

"No, he hasn't called. I've called, but it goes directly to voice mail."

"That doesn't sound like Rick. He's good about checking in, isn't he?"

"Yes, he should have called by now."

"I bet those government boys loved his presentation and have him tied up in meetings. I'm sure he'll call as soon as he can."

"He's probably being lavished with praise, rubbing elbows with all the famous scientists and government officials while being treated to a luscious five-course dinner with fine wines and white tablecloths. Can you believe they flew him business class? He sent a message during his morning run. They had an executive AutoCar pick him up at the airport."

Rob gives a wolf whistle. "Wow! Movie star treatment. Must be nice to be a famous scientist. Guess I'll never know."

"Yes, he's getting doted over like a rock star, while I'm stuck at home trying to wrangle two wild kids."

"How are you and the kids?"

Courtney puts clean dishes in the cupboard as she speaks. "They're at school; should be home soon."

"Hang in there, sweetie. Let me know if you hear from our boy. I'm sure once he's had enough star treatment, he'll call."

Chapter 23: Delirium

Wednesday Evening–New Arcadia

Rick hurries through the dark auditorium. He needs to move before he's attacked by more flying bee-bots. He feels like his normal himself again. The shroud that clouded his mind has lifted. He pushes past the glass doors and into the city. His fresh perception of the underground empire is striking. The walls are drab, painted a dull puke green. Conduits, pipes, and tubes crawl along the walls and ceilings in all directions. The city's design is bland industrial mixed with boring institutional. The entire city looks dull everywhere, but the luxurious conference room of the silver tunics.

All the corridors look the same, with endless runs of conduit and pipes snaking on the walls and drooping from the ceiling. Ever present are the ugly, bumpy pumpkin-colored tiles. The floor is freezing cold.

Rick thinks of Ethan's comment about the hideaway being like a submarine and feels this city could be the bowels of a navy ship. Rick runs along a corridor as autonomous maglev vehicles, carts, and the occasional person riding a Maggie zip past him. He must stay close to the corridor wall and wary of traffic to avoid getting smashed.

Rick remembers the Surface Integration Storage room, full of products to prepare people for living on the surface. He decides he will get to that room, stock up on gear, make his way to the Electro-Rail Station, and catch a speed train to Los Angeles. He tries to recall the map he saw in the orientation video and thinks there's a direct route to Los Angeles or Edendale, the underground version.

Rick envisions his beautiful wife, Courtney. She must wonder where he is. Rick can't recall when they last spoke. He takes a deep breath. The air is sweet and fresh. He has renewed energy. Rick runs down a familiar-looking corridor he thinks will lead to the supply room. He feels like he can run and run. He breathes deeply.

After a few minutes, his pace slows to a walk. The urgency to get to where he is going grows less intense. Rick wanders through corridors in search of the Surface Integration room, but he can't find it. He looks at his wrist to check his band, then remembers they took it from him.

Rick walks down a dark, narrow hallway. The painted cement floor is warmer than the orange tiles. He hears a scuffle further down the hallway and a man shouting. Rick spots an open door ahead. The sound is from the room behind the door. Rick creeps to the door, then peers in.

A man in a navy-blue tunic struggles with men in black tunics. "Let me out. This isn't a nuclear war experiment. I didn't sign up for this." The man fights and kicks the men in black tunics. The men in black look like military men. They wear black caps, utility belts, dark-shaded wrap around VUE lenses and they have strange-looking silver rings hanging under their noses.

Two men wearing black fight with the raging man. One of them howls when the man yanks his nose ring and tosses it. The metal ring clinks along the floor, landing a few feet from Rick.

The black tunic yells, "Ow! He pulled my D-Nox." The black tunic panics for a moment, wipes blood from his nose, then forces the man to the floor with increased fury. The two black tunics get the man down to his knees but struggle to get him prone on the floor. Rick looks at the metal nose ring. The ends that insert into the nostrils are flesh-colored and are wiggling.

A third black tunic holds a gun. He tries to aim, but the blue tunic keeps flailing his arms, fighting the guards. He moves the gun, trying to aim but can't get a clean shot.

A large, strong-looking military man, also wearing a black tunic, stands to the side of the fray. He has a silver nose ring but doesn't wear a black cap. His head is bald. Rick assumes that the large man is the leader because he's barking orders. "Pin him to the floor and relax him!"

The struggling man continues to rant. "The Black Guard cannot stop me or the others who will tell the truth! You lied to us! Fucking liars!"

The Black Guard leader steps forward and hits the struggling man with a fierce punch to his head. Rick hears the crunching sound of bones breaking. The man slumps unconscious. When the Black

Guard release him, the body falls forward with a heavy face-plant to the cement floor. The Black Guard with the gun aims anxiously and shoots the unconscious man with a dart, though it's obvious the prostrate body no longer requires relaxing.

The guard who lost his nose ring walks to the doorway, searching for it. Rick steps back into the darkness of the hallway.

"Get this garbage out of here," orders the Black Guard leader.

The other Black Guard, who struggled with the unconscious man, looks at his leader with excitement and admiration. "Yes, sir. That was great, Captain Kobalt." He then helps drag the body into the dark recesses of the utopian city.

The Black Guard leader touches the air to answer a call. The edges of his eyes twinkle. "Colonel, we had a mental disturbance. A blue shirt. It's under control."

The colonel's voice is brusque. "Episodes like this cannot be allowed. Control must be maintained. Our citizens will soon learn of the real disaster and realize that New Arcadia is not an experiment. We have spared them death. They are the few and the fortunate. They must be grateful. Non-compliance will be dealt with swiftly. There will be no panic. Do you understand?"

"Yes sir. This was a singular episode. The problem is solved."

"Stress levels will increase. We will raise city atmosphere levels. We must maintain control."

Kobalt grunts a "Yes, sir." The call ends.

The colonel is in the elegant conference room. He ends the call and notices the scientists around the table are staring at him. They had listened to his call. They don't move. The colonel taps his cane on the edge of the table—*smack, smack* — and observes the group.

"We can't have our team members upset about a billion dead people on the surface. It is Earth's destiny. There is nothing we can do." The colonel pauses. No one stirs.

"We *are* saving the world, at least as much of it as we can. Six cities full of talented people. You saved them. I will do whatever it takes to survive this crisis and create the highest level of human civilization the world has ever seen. That is our mission." The colonel walks to the conference room door, giving a last order before exiting. "Sound general quarters. I will monitor from my office."

Once in his office, he calls Kobalt. "We have another situation. We have a silver tunic wandering about the city: Dr. Munday, the last arrival. I've sent his profile to you. He is a disturbed criminal. I subdued him with an earwig in the conference room, but he escaped into the city. He doesn't have a band, so you can't track him. The city atmosphere should calm him, but keep an eye open. I won't stand for more trouble."

Rick makes his way along a busy corridor as maglev carts and trucks whiz past. He hugs the wall, looking for a hallway or small corridor. He spots a small narrow hallway, but it's on the other side of the four-lane corridor with vehicles speeding past. He needs to time his run, or he'll be New Arcadian roadkill. Rick stands poised to dash across the busy road, waiting for a large truck to pass.

Now! He runs across one lane, pauses—standing erect, on his toes in-between lanes—as a maglev cart cruises past in the second lane. He dashes across the second lane and into the third lane behind a brown shirt on a Maggie. Rick startles the brown shirt, and the Maggie almost hits a cart.

One more lane to cross. A cart is approaching fast. Rick darts across the lane ahead of the cart as it whizzes past. The right front bumper of the cart hits his hip. The impact sends him spinning through the air. He lands on the cold hard tiles, rolling to a stop at the base of a steel bollard—a yellow-painted steel pole used for collision protection, installed at corners of corridors. His right leg hurts. He sits on the cold floor, examining his injury. He tore his slacks and scraped his leg, but there wasn't much blood. No broken bones, but he'll have a nice bruise.

He pushes himself to his feet and moves into the dark maintenance hallway. The floor is cement, no cold orange tiles. He checks the doors of locked rooms as he limps down the hallway. Rick is sore and exhausted. His existence since he left home is a confused blur. Has he been in the city for a few hours, or has it been days?

Sliding to the floor, he attempts to gather his thoughts. He needs to get his bearings, so he can find the Surface Integration room and the Rail Station. His thoughts wander to home. The kids. Courtney. His grant. An asteroid storm is coming. Rick drifts to sleep.

"Hey, jerk wad." Karl kicks Rick's foot. "Wake up, dickhead," Karl says as he leans down, slapping Rick upside the head. Rick wakes from a deep sleep. He looks around, unsure of where he is. "Rick, wake up."

Rick looks up to see the face of his friend. It occurs to him this might be the first time Karl has addressed him with his real name. Rick looks up at Karl with a dopey smile. Rick has never seen Karl concerned about anyone but himself. Karl is a self-assured, well-educated, self-affirmed, know-it-all, who is undeterred by whatever mission or purpose he aims. Taking an interest in another person's plight is not a trait people would associate with Karl.

Rick surveys the face of his friend with glassy eyes of half awareness. Karl looks older than his years. He has creases around his eyes. His face looks drawn, haggard. He still has the same Karl unkempt hair and scraggly three-day beard, now with a touch of gray, and he wears the ever-present suit jacket.

Karl can see Rick is slow to wake. "Are you OK?"

Rick scoots up to sit taller against the wall. "Yeah. Thanks."

"What the hell are you doing in here, ass wipe?" Karl asks in the friendliest way.

Rick isn't sure he can trust Karl. They were friends in college, but Karl works with these people. Rick is considering whether to tell Karl his plan to get to the Rail Station when Karl speaks.

"If you want to get home, you're going the wrong way, buddy." Karl's statement stuns Rick. He has never heard a simple, considerate sounding sentence from his friend.

"Yeah, I got lost in these hallways. How did you find me?" Rick asks cautiously to see if Karl is sincere.

Karl pulls a tiny dot from under the collar of Rick's tunic. "I put a tracker on you, dimwit. How else could I find you? Can't let you wander around the city like a drunken puppy. The Black Guard will catch you and you'll never get out of here. You need to get your ass to the Rail Station and hop the speed rail to L.A., I mean Edendale, before anyone knows you're gone. Fucking moron. How hard is that?"

Rick beams. He holds his arm out. "They took my band." Rick taps his naked forearm. "City map won't load. I can't call, stream, or project a page." Rick chuckles, poking at his bare arm.

"Hey, you silly bitch. You know you're on city atmosphere, right? Don't you feel it? The Delirium?"

"Delirium. What's Delirium?"

"Sodium Psychochloroldexahydrite or something. I don't remember the exact name. They call it the atmosphere. I call it Delirium. We put in the air to help with circadian rhythm problems. Since you can't tell day from the night in this place, it messes up your biological clock. Some people can't sleep, while others are fine until one day, they can't take it and crack up. Next thing, you see them curled up in the fetal position crying or worse, they go completely mad. Atmosphere was supposed to be the cure. We pumped the gas into the city, but it didn't work. We didn't know what to do. The entire project would fail if team members were at risk of going crazy. But it all changed one day when a much higher dose got pumped into the city by accident. In minutes, the city changed. The air felt clean and clear. Everyone was happy. No more problems. No more depression or craziness. People under the effects of Delirium are peaceful and happy. It dampens other emotions, but helps people focus on work. A little extra gas and ta-da, it's fucking peace and quiet in New Arcadia. That's the way the colonel likes it. Delirium makes people content and compliant. Utopia!" Karl explains. Rick nods slow acknowledgment.

Karl reaches into his jacket pocket and pulls out a small metal tube. "No worries, I've got the cure!" His eyes twinkle as he lifts the tube to his mouth, sucking lightly.

Rick reacts. "You have a pipe! Smoking is illegal."

Karl hands the pipe to Rick. "It's been illegal for a decade. So, what? Do you want to wander around the city all gooney eyed, or do you want to get home, fart-face?"

Rick takes the pipe from Karl, takes a long deep draw, and coughs.

"Careful there, hophead. That's almost pure nicotine. It can be harsh. Luckily, something as simple as nicotine counteracts Delirium. The Black Guard use D-Nox rings for the same reason.

Nose rings aren't my style." Rick hands the pipe to his friend, but Karl pushes it away. "You keep it. You'll need it until you get topside."

Once again, it's as if a sheer fabric that was fogging his view lifts from his head. He takes a short draw on the pipe, then puts it in his pocket and nods to Karl. "Thanks." Karl nods back.

Karl leans against the wall and slides down next to Rick, then removes his band and hands it to Rick. "Here, asshole. You stole my band." Rick laughs, taking the band.

"It won't react to your voice, but it will get you access to the Rail Station."

"Great! I can use the city map and walk." Rick uses the band to display the city map.

"Why use the map when a Maggie can take you?" Rick gives Karl a strange look. Karl yells, "Maggot!" Nothing happens. Rick is impatient and starts to skootch up the wall to stand. "I can use the map and walk to the Rail Station." Karl lifts his hand to stop Rick. "Patience." After a few moments, Karl points to the end of the tunnel. "Look, it's here."

A Maggie, painted white with a red racing stripe, appears, floating in the corridor at the end of the hallway. Karl helps Rick stand, and they walk to the Maggie. Karl points at a small control panel at the front of the Maggie, between the footholds.

"It's unregistered. Touch this button to code your voice and you'll have control of this Maggot to go anywhere in the city," Karl instructs without touching the button.

Rick presses the button, and the machine control responds, "Maglev... logging. Training voice for control. Speak after the tone."

Rick speaks. "Maglev, Maggie, this is the voice for control. Slow, Left, Right, Fast, Map, Stop." Rick speaks the words he expects to use. The Maggie makes a ready tone. Rick steps up on the Maggie, placing his feet in the footholds. The Maggie rocks for a moment before stabilizing.

Karl grabs Rick's arm, looking at him with a brooding face. "The Colonel sent me to bring you back. Too bad you fought back, stole my band, and got away."

"Thanks, Karl. You're a true friend."

Karl takes a step back and wipes an eye. "Well, what are you waiting for, idiot? You have a family to save. Don't make me remind you I saw Courtney first. Get moving, numb-nuts."

"Don't you want to come with me? You can get out of this place and away from the colonel. I have a safe place back home. You don't have to stay."

"Nah, I made my choices. I'll pay my price. You followed the rules and your heart. You deserve everything, the beautiful wife, kids, and the house with the picket fence. If I can do one good thing, it's helping you get back to your life. Now, get away from me, jerk-wad. Vamoose!"

Rick stands steady and erect on the Maggie, then barks a command. "Maggie, go to Surface Integration Storage." Rick waves at Karl as he speeds down the busy corridor.

Karl is in shock. No one has ever called him a true friend. He stands at the end of the hallway, at the edge of the busy four-lane corridor. Carts and levitating trucks speed past.

"Well, I'd better make this look good," Karl says, as he steps calmly into the main corridor. "Oops," he utters just before a speeding truck smashes into him.

Chapter 24: Railroaded

Wednesday Evening–New Arcadia

Rick gets the hang of riding the Maggie by himself. The maglev is a transport nom, intelligent enough to self-navigate to a location, but also uses anti-collision sensors and inter-vehicular communication protocols to control speed, spacing and lane changes to arrive at the destination. The result is a speedy, yet fluid ride through the corridors of the underground city.

A speeding utility truck hit Karl and dragged him twenty yards. The self-driving trucks have anti-collision systems, but they're designed to avoid collisions with other vehicles, not to avoid humans stepping into traffic. Karl's body lays twisted on blood-splattered orange tiles. Traffic stops. Alarms sound.

The Maggie cruises the main corridor and down a small tunnel before stopping in front of the Surface Integration Storage room. Rick hops off the Maggie and hears an alarm. Guards will search for him; he needs to move fast. He opens the door. The room is dark, but lights come on as he enters. He moves cautiously until he is sure no one is in the large room. He walks through a demonstration room designed to train people how to live on the surface after the disaster.

Rick walks past the demo room and into a large warehouse with rows of tall metal racks stocked with supplies and equipment for over 100,000 survivors.

The City Guard, in their sky-blue tunics, are the first to arrive at the scene of the accident. One look at the broken body lying on the cold tiles and it's obvious the person is dead. The eyes of a City

Guard glow as he views his VUE contact lens. He touches the air to contact the morgue requesting a body wagon.

Another guard kneels over the body. He takes photos of the dead person, then straightens the fingers of one hand to get a scan of the palm and fingerprints. A photo of Dr. Karl Wetzel appears in his VUE. The doctor is a silver tunic. The City Guard alerts the Black Guard.

Rick runs down a row of the warehouse racks, reading the descriptions on the boxes looking for gear he might need. He grabs a backpack, a KA-Bar knife, and a medical kit. He spots a box of machetes. Rick doesn't expect to be whacking large vines in a jungle but grabs the large blade and slides it in the backpack.

Rick's pants are ripped. The colonel and the Black Guard will look for a silver tunic; he needs a change of clothes. He spots a box marked KEVLAR X9GRS SKIN SUIT. Pulling one out of the box, he finds that the material is thick and composed of several layers, yet feels like lycra.

The description on the box reads *Kevlar/Graphene woven mesh ballistic resistive skin suit*. Rick strips off his clothes and pulls on the bulletproof suit. In nearby boxes, he finds black slacks and a black tunic to wear over the skin suit. He stuffs his silver tunic and torn slacks deep in the box of black tunics. He then grabs a pair of boots and pushes his deck shoes into another box.

Black Guard Control receives information on the death of Dr. Karl Wetzel, a silver tunic. Images of the accident and the report appear in Kobalt's VUE. The colonel sent Dr. Wetzel to look for Dr. Munday. Now, Wetzel is dead. Kobalt does not hesitate. He taps the air. "Black Guard. APB on Dr. Richard Munday, a silver tunic. Capture and relax on sight."

As Rick runs through the warehouse overhead lights above each row come to life as he stuffs items in the backpack. He finds a flashlight and a blanket. Jogging down another row, he grabs MREs (Meals Ready to Eat) and energy bars.

Rick talks to himself as he rummages through the warehouse. *"I might be over thinking this, but I don't know how long it will take to get home. If all goes well, I hop on the Electro-Rail and I'm home in a few hours. But since I left home, nothing has gone as expected. Better to be a good scout and be prepared."*

Running through the final rows of the warehouse, he picks up a bundle of military-grade 550 Para-cord, a fancy name for a strong rope, a fire-starting kit, and a canteen for water.

Platoons of Black Guard stream from their hidden quarters, riding beefed up maglevs. These shiny black Maggies are sturdier and faster than normal maglevs. Thirty-Two Black Guard split into groups of eight, each group heading in a different direction; all in search of Dr. Richard Munday.

The alarm stops. Rick runs through the demo room and glimpses himself in a mirror. He stops to view his image. He wonders if he can get to the Rail Station unnoticed. Rick jumps on the Maggie and speeds through the underground complex to the Rail Station.

A Black Guard investigator arrives at the scene of Dr. Wetzel's death. He examines the body and goes through Karl's pockets. In one pocket, he finds a vial of a viscous fluid. The investigator bags the vial and dictates a note into his band. The victim wore glasses, now broken. They are refractive, used to improve vision, not VUE lens. He adds the glasses to the evidence bag. The victim wore a wristwatch. It's a Patek Philippe, an expensive old watch that only keeps time. The investigator removes the watch and slides it into the pocket of his slacks. He pulls up Karl's file. Karl used a Smart-Band. The investigator makes a note; the victim's band is missing.

The Maggie speeds Rick to the Electro-Rail station. Rick hops from the Maggie to the tiled floor, adjusts his backpack to hang from one shoulder, and walks casually hoping he won't be noticed.

Karl's band is on his forearm. Entrance to the expansive station requires walking through a gantry. Rick strolls around watching people enter and exit. There is no turnstile or gate. You don't need money or a ticket. The system must wirelessly connect to people's band or VUE. Green LED lights flash overhead as each person passes through.

Rick assumes that if an unauthorized person walks through, red lights flash, alarms sound and bad things happen to the violator. He rubs Karl's band. Karl said he would need the band to enter the station. Rick prays it works as he walks through the gantry. No alarms or red lights. No Black Guard. Relieved, he walks into the massive station, trying not to look lost.

People he walks past look down and move away. He wonders why everyone is so shy. He also avoids eye contact and walks to the mezzanine over-looking the Electro-Rail vacuum tubes and platforms. The Rail Station is busy with passenger and cargo cars arriving and departing. Rick wanders along the mezzanine, which traverses the width of the Rail Station. Signs along the mezzanine mark stairways leading down to passenger platforms.

Rick becomes transfixed watching the activity in the Rail Station. He catches his mind drifting. He needs to focus, so he reaches for Karl's pipe and takes two quick drags. In a few moments, his mind is clear.

A group of people gather at a monitor. Rick stands behind them, trying to read the tube schedule. When the people notice him, they disperse. Rick thinks it's strange, but he doesn't want to talk to anyone, anyway. He wants to get home.

Rick scans the schedule, looking for a passenger car heading to Edendale. The destinations have names like New Elysian, Ambrosia, Nod, Edendale, and New Dakota. New Dakota is the only name that sounds like a real place. Rick recalls the map he saw during the orientation video with routes leading to Las Vegas, Denver, Seattle, Atlanta, and Los Angeles.

As Rick tries to decipher the destinations and schedules, a man stands next to him. "Where are you heading?"

Rick answers without looking at the man. "To New Los Angeles."

"New Los Angeles? You mean Edendale?"

"Oh yeah, Edendale. I'll never get used to the new city names." Rick tries to make lite of his mistake. The screen flashes with schedule updates. A rail car destined for Edendale will depart in forty minutes.

"Yeah, we all do that sometimes. Did you get leave, or did they transfer you?" the man asks.

Rick looks at the man. He is Black Guard. Rick almost panics but realizes the black tunic and black slacks he wears makes him look like Black Guard.

"Oh, I got leave. My mother is dying. Three-day pass." Rick lies. He hopes Black Guards get three day passes when their mothers are dying.

The guard slaps Rick on the back. "Lucky for you. Oh… sorry about your mom, though. I'm stuck here. You know we're code red, right? Nuclear War alert. They say it's not a drill, but I'll believe that when I see the mushroom cloud, right?"

Rick shrugs. "Yeah, code red, doesn't get more serious than that. Guess I lucked out, except for my mom, of course." Rick tries to look sad. He doesn't want to linger, so he turns away.

"Hey," the guard calls out.

Rick stops.

The guard gives Rick a look over and taps his nose. "Where's your D-Nox?"

Rick must think quick on his feet. He's glad he cleared his mind with the puffs off Karl's pipe. "Oh, I took it out. The ring freaks out Mom. I think she has some bad memories or something. I don't want to scare her."

"Oh man. That must have hurt!" the guard says, cringing.

"Stung like the devil, man. You wouldn't believe it." Rick says, holding his nose.

"You better watch the atmosphere, even in the rail cars."

Rick taps his arm. "I'll be all right. Got the patch."

"There's a patch? Wow. These guys think of everything. Hey, you know when you get there, you can't get topside to visit your mom. Movement to the surface is locked down, at least until they cancel the alert."

"Oh? Right. My mom, ah, she lives in the new city. She operates food actualizers in the cafeteria. No need to get topside. That's how I got leave."

The Black Guard nods approval but is distracted by his VUE. His gaze is focused above Rick's head. Rick prepares to run.

The Black Guard is entertained by what he's seeing in his VUE. He looks like a smiling blind man. "Oh man, it's a bad day for Silvers. One got mowed down in the west corridor and there's another one on the run."

Rick wants to flee, but if he makes a scene, he's dead for sure.

The guard moves his fingers in front of his face to answer a call. "No, sir. I checked the map. There are no silvers in the station. OK, sir. Right away, sir. I'm on it," he says.

The guard adjusts his head to focus on his surroundings as if he's suddenly recovered his vision. "I gotta run, have to guard the entrance. No one gets into the station. Hope your mom is better. You're a lucky bastard." The guard runs to the entrance.

Captain Kobalt sent out an entire Black Guard company in search of one man, and they have come up empty. Workers wearing VUE lens or bands are easy to track. Kobalt checks Munday's file. It confirms he doesn't have a VUE, and his band was confiscated upon arrival.

The atmosphere in the city makes people more compliant. Incidents are rare. Black Guard has not needed to track down an individual until now. Kobalt messages his lieutenants. "*Start door-to-door checks of residential and office areas.*"

They are code red. The asteroid storm is about to arrive. Kobalt knows this is not a drill. It aggravates him that his guard can't find and relax one man. What will happen if all hell breaks loose? He must maintain control. He doesn't want to suffer the wrath of Cruikshank's fury.

Kobalt reviews the investigator's report of Dr. Wetzel's death in his VUE. Dr. Wetzel's band is missing. Could Munday have stolen the band? Kobalt runs a locate on Wetzel's band.

Kobalt calls his Black Guard. "He's in the Rail Station. All units to the railway station. Now!"

Rick watches the friendly Black Guard run off. He is sure this is the most excitement the guard has seen since his arrival in New Arcadia. Rick needs to find a place to hide until the passenger car for Edendale departs.

He walks down the stairs to a passenger platform scouting for a hiding place. At the rear of the platform, a walkway runs the length of the Rail Station connecting the platforms to a large storage area. Rick moves down the walkway to the far end of the station. The area is dark and quiet, stacked with empty freight cars. He ducks between a row of rail cars just as his band displays a recorded video of Karl.

"Hey, dumb shit. Someone just ran a locate on this band. They know where you are. Ditch the band." Karl must have hacked the system to notify him if anyone tracked the Band. Rick removes the band.

"Thanks, Karl, for saving me. Again."

Rick runs to the back row of rail cars and tosses the band in an empty freight car. He runs through the storage area toward the stairs he walked down, watching for Black Guard.

Black Guard platoons' stream through the Rail Station entrance. As each guard passes through the gantry, red lights flash and alarms sound. The Black Guard carry weapons that look like paintball guns. Passengers and workers scramble to avoid the swarm of guards. Rick moves to the front of the storage area where he can see most of the station. He crawls under an empty freight car, inching forward, so he can see what's happening, yet careful to remain out of view.

Guards move through the station and onto the passenger platforms. A group of guards split off and run to the far end of the Rail Station. Rick resists the temptation to move, waiting for the right moment to act.

He hears a commotion at the far end of the storage area. "We've got you. Come out now."

The guards have located Karl's band. A few moments later he hears. "He's not here. It's just the band."

The big, bald man Rick saw knock out the distraught blue-tunic strides through the gantry. The Black Guard leader sizes up the situation. He sees the melee of people trying to avoid the guards. His guards are not taking charge of the situation.

"All teams. Relax everyone. Relax everyone in the station. Now!" Kobalt shouts the order.

Guards fire their weapons into groups of people. The guns make a high-pitched swoosh sound when fired, propelling venom filled darts with airbursts. Passengers and workers fall silently to the floor all over the station.

Kobalt scans the large station for Dr. Munday as Black Guard squads move, relaxing people.

"Team One and Two, sweep the cargo and freight car storage areas. Teams Three and Four, move to the far platform, fan out, and move forward. If he's hiding out there, you will drive him to me!"

Rick scoots out of sight, under the rail car, as teams of Black Guard run past his position to the far platforms. Rick notices a passenger car moving to platform number five. Three people stand at the end of the platform, anxiously hoping the car will whisk them away before the Black Guard reaches them. Rick hopes they succeed because, in that instant, he decides to join them.

Most of the Black Guard are in the depths of the storage areas or searching the dark, unused platforms, but it wouldn't be long before they reach him.

Kobalt receives a call from the colonel. "Have you captured Dr. Munday? If you cannot contain this situation, I will transfer you and your Black Guard to the surface."

Kobalt paces in frustration. "We have him trapped in the Rail Station. He will be relaxed and, in our custody momentarily, sir."

Rick sees the tough bald guy turn away. He's talking to someone on his VUE. This is his chance. Keeping low, Rick sprints to the track. He catches up to the moving passenger car. He runs, crouching along the far side of the car, out of Kobalt's view, then scurries to the front of the car ducking under the aerodynamic nose as the car slows. The car comes to a stop along the platform and the door slides open. Two men and a woman hurry into the car. Rick lifts himself from the track onto the raised cement platform, stands and walks to the door.

When Rick enters the car, the woman passenger sitting at the rear of the car screams. The man next to her tries to quiet the woman.

The other male passenger stands holding up his hands. "We did nothing. Please don't relax us."

The man holding the woman calls out, "My wife and I just want to get home. Please let us go."

Rick raises his hands to show he isn't carrying a weapon. "I'm not Black Guard. I won't hurt you. Stay calm. I'm going wherever you're going." Rick sits down in the front row, placing his backpack on the floor.

Kobalt ends his call with the colonel, then scans the Rail Station. Turning his view, he realizes there are no people on platform five. There are no bodies relaxed on the cement, and a rail car is now at the platform. He's about to call his guards when one of his men climbs from the track to the platform and enters the car. He hears a scream. Kobalt smiles.

The guard doesn't exit the car. Kobalt senses something strange about the guard who entered the car. He runs across the mezzanine toward the platform. While running, he alerts his guards. "He's in the rail car. Everyone to platform five." The door of the passenger car begins to close. As Kobalt runs down the stairs, he reaches into a pouch on his belt, pulls out three metal balls, and throws them high in the air. Buzz-Bee's.

Once the metal balls are in the air, they automatically engage and fly with a high-pitched whirring sound. Openings on the top and bottom are intake and exhaust of miniature turbofans that power the flying spheres. The ports around the diameter support camera, sensors, and weapons. Kobalt uses his VUE to control the Buzz-Bees and see what they see. Kobalt points to the closing door of the passenger car and the Buzz-Bees fly to the car. The door is almost closed. Kobalt flicks his hand signaling the Buzz-Bees to fly faster. Two of the Buzz-Bees make it through just as the door closes, the third smashes into the door. The crashed Buzz-Bee whines as it zips across the cement platform, falling onto the adjacent track where it buzzes and ricochets off the platform walls.

The passengers are frightened of Rick's presence. He tries to set them at ease. "I want to get home, just like you. I'm heading home to my wife and kids. Where is this car going?"

The frantic woman is crying and cannot answer. Her husband holds her. The other man answers. "This car is going to New Zion. Then I transfer to Nod. I'm not sure where they're going," he says, tipping his head toward the couple.

The husband is about to respond when there is a loud smack and the whining of Buzz-Bees. The passengers look to the front of the car as two Buzz-Bees fly in just as the door slides shut. The Buzz-Bees hover, making their whining, whirring sound and the woman screams again. This time no one outside the rail car can hear her, except Kobalt, who sees and hears everything in his VUE.

The passenger car advances into the airlock. Turbines rumble. The environment surrounding the rail car becomes void, a vacuum. Black Guard swarm to the platform. The turbines spin down as Kobalt screams into his VUE. "Stop this thing. Stop it now!"

A reply comes from rail control. "Air lock launch door is opening. We can't stop it." The car launches. In a flash, the car shoots down the tube, disappearing into the rock wall.

Kobalt stands on the platform surrounded by his Black Guard as the rail car disappears, but he isn't watching the car; his eyes are locked on the images in his VUE. Munday sits at the front of the car, with three passengers locked to their seats by the sudden g-force of the rocketing car, stunned by the sight of the Buzz-Bees.

Kobalt smiles. "Sitting ducks." Kobalt flies one of the Buzz-Bees to the rear of the car while the second Buzz-Bee hovers near the front. The woman screams once more. The Buzz-Bee fires hitting the woman in the face, just below her eye. She cries, clawing at her face trying to remove the venom pumping dart, then falls silent. The

Buzz-Bee fires darts at the two men, hitting them both in the chest and they slump in their seats in paralyzed sleep. Thin screens at the front of the car play a video with cheerful music welcoming passengers and providing mundane information about the trip.

Rick watches the Buzz-Bee fly over the passengers. When it shoots the woman, Rick reaches into his pack and grips the handle of the machete. As it shoots the men, Rick pulls the machete from his pack, stands up holding the large blade like a baseball bat and swings at the Buzz-Bee hovering near him. Kobalt is so focused on the passengers he doesn't notice Rick stand behind the second Buzz-Bee. The machete blade hits the flying metal ball with a *ping*, sending it smashing into the railcar's wall. The damaged Buzz-Bee's turbine whirs with a grating sound.

As the wounded Buzz-Bee flies out of control, Kobalt fires six darts, all of which fly wildly bouncing off the wall or sticking into empty seat cushions.

Kobalt curses and directs the remaining Buzz-Bee toward Munday, who is standing in the aisle holding a machete. Kobalt advances the hovering Buzz-Bee forward slowly, careful to stay out of machete range. He fires a dart hitting Rick in the chest. Munday falls between the seats. Kobalt laughs victoriously.

"Rest peacefully, Dr. Munday."

Rick feels the dart hit him in the chest. He dives between the row of seats to escape the attack. He looks at his chest. There's no dart; the skin suit saved him. He reaches for his backpack to use it as a shield.

If he cowers in wait, he'll be an easy target, so he does the unexpected and jumps to his feet with his machete in one hand, backpack shield in the other. The Buzz-Bee advances toward him. Rick swings at the whirring ball and misses. The Buzz-Bee shoots a dart. Rick covers with his shield and the dart sticks in the backpack. Rick steps into the aisle, swinging his machete like a madman, his shield covering his face. The Buzz-Bee zips left and right, zigzagging through the air as it evades the swinging blade, then moves back to hover at the rear of the car.

"Why isn't he relaxed? It doesn't matter; there's no place for you to go Munday. When the rail car arrives in New Zion, I'll have a regiment of Black Guard waiting. But I'm not done with you yet. I will not lose to some skinny scientist," Kobalt says to himself, then moves the Buzz-Bee in for a final attack.

Rick stands in the aisle, watching the flying orb hover at the rear of the car. The machete hangs at his side, but he keeps the backpack shield ready to guard against dart attacks.

The Buzz-Bee races through the air toward him at waist level. In less than three seconds, the whirring orb hovers two feet in front of him. Rick instinctively moves the pack to cover his groin area. The Buzz-Bee hangs in the air for a second, then instantly rises to eye level. Rick swings the machete in a forceful upward motion. The flat side of the blade hits the Buzz-Bee just as the Buzz-Bee—*ping*—fires, sending a dart skimming past Rick's cheek as the orb smacks into the metal ceiling of the rail car like a bug hitting a windshield. The Buzz-Bee falls to the floor. It's disabled, but not out of commission.

The dart hits the wall and falls to the floor. "That would not have been pretty," Rick says as he squashes the venom pumping dart under his boot.

Kobalt screams. His move was perfect. Munday was going down. "Damn you, Munday."

Kobalt motions for the Buzz-Bee to fly. The injured bee lifts off the floor in a wobbly hover. The Buzz-Bee rises again to eye level, then speeds in jerky motions toward Rick. Kobalt fires. A mechanical *plink, plink, plink* sound comes from the whirring ball. Munday stands his ground, wiping his brow as the Buzz-Bee hovers a foot from his face.

"Arrgh!" Kobalt is shooting blanks. He motions his hand forward fiercely. The Buzz-Bee zips forward at top speed, hitting Rick in the forehead.

"Ouch!" Rick howls, rubbing his forehead. "No blood, but I bet that'll leave a mark."

The Buzz-Bee hovers, unsteadily, a few feet away. Rick drops his backpack, grips the machete, and swings. "Second inning. Batter up!"

Smack! The Buzz-Bee flies the length of the railcar, smashing hard against the back wall before falling to the floor and going silent. Rick jumps up and down with his hands in the air, cheering for himself as if he'd knocked one out of the park.

The display in Kobalt's VUE goes black. The Black Guard standing around Kobalt groan.

"You are safe now, Munday, but that car has only one stop, and I guarantee you will not leave that rail car alive."

Rick looks around the car. The three passengers are asleep. The video screens are now streaming a popular show. A readout across the top of the screen shows the rail car's speed at 720 miles per hour and arrival in New Zion in two hours, twenty-five minutes. Rick recalls the map he saw of the new cities. He believes New Zion is near Denver, Colorado. He hopes he's right. New Zion is not Los Angeles, but at least he's headed in the right direction.

Colonel Cruikshank watched the confrontation between Dr. Munday and Kobalt on his office screen, connected to Kobalt via the captain's VUE. "Kobalt! How could you let him get away? You are captain of the Black Guard. You can't capture one scrawny scientist!" The colonel scowls.

"There is nowhere for him to go. Black Guard will capture and relax the doctor when he arrives at New Zion, sir."

Cruikshank pounds his cane on the floor. "No! You and your elite guard will take the Scramjets to New Zion. You will take Dr. Munday into custody. I don't trust Lieutenant Astatine. He borders on incompetence. No mistakes. Munday must be controlled. There will be no chaos or disorder in the new cities. I will not stand for it!"

Kobalt touches the air in front of his face. "Elite Guard. Report to Scramjets. We launch immediately."

Rick stands in the aisle with the machete at his side waiting to be sure the battle is won. His heartbeat slows as the adrenaline subsides. He drops into the front seat, slides the machete into his backpack, and lays the pack in the seat next to him.

He is safe for now and moving toward home, but he doesn't like his chances once he arrives at New Zion. Black Guard will be there waiting for him. Even if he can evade the guards, the city is on lockdown. He lies across the seat, using his backpack as a pillow and takes a nap.

The elite guard glide in formation on maglevs to the hypersonic Scramjet launch facility. The cavernous launch center is high and wide with rocky unfinished walls, unlike the domed rooms of the city. Three streamlined jets are lined up wing tip to wing tip, each one on a separate magnetic launch track, ready to fly. Besides the pilot and copilot, each jet has space for six passengers.

The jets are hypersonic hybrid Scramjets capable of reaching Mach 6. Their speed enables them to traverse the US continent in forty minutes, or circumnavigate Earth in six hours, making the jets the perfect rapid response vehicle.

Kobalt stands in the center jet's doorway. "To New Zion!" He shouts thrusting his arm into the air, then ducks through the low doorway disappearing into the jet. The elite guard file into the jets.

Reinforced cement doors slide open at the top of a mountain. An Electro-magnetic launcher thrusts the hypersonic Scramjets on tracks bursting out of the mountaintop access at six hundred miles per hour. Once airborne, the turbine engines engage propelling the jets to an elevation of sixty thousand feet. The distance to Denver is too short to reach maximum speed, so the jets travel at Mach 3 without firing the Scramjets. The elite Black Guard will land in Denver less than thirty minutes later.

Chapter 25: Broadcast

Denver, CO–Wednesday Evening

Jin leaves his workstation at 5:15 p.m. and exits the secure office. He typically works much later, but he has Becky on his mind. He puts his normal glasses in his locker, slips on his band, then his VUE lens and notices two calls and a voice message from Curtis. Once Jin is out of the building, he touches Becky's image.

Becky touches in. "Hey, you're off work early."

"We have plans tonight, right? I got off work as early as I could."

"No. I promised my mom I would help her with shopping for Saturday night. We're having dinner at my parents' Saturday, remember?"

"Sorry. Work's been crazy. Dinner, Saturday night, your parents' house. Got it. Can't wait."

"It's nice to know you were thinking of me, though."

"I'm always thinking of you. I love spending time with you. When we're apart, I can't wait until we're together again. But, if you're busy tonight, I guess I'll catch up with Curtis. He's called me three times. It must be something urgent."

"You are such a sweetheart Jin Goldberg. I'm a lucky girl to have you. But next time we're together you must promise me one thing."

"Sure, what?"

"Tell me why you had the nickname, Box as a kid."

"Oh God. Anything but that. I never want to hear that name again. Wait. I think Curtis is calling. I have to end the call now," Jin laughs.

"You promised!"

"Geeze, Beck. If you insist on knowing all the horrible things about my childhood, I'll have to see you before Saturday. How about later tonight?"

"I want to know everything about your childhood. Are you up for a late dinner at my place? You see what Curtis is up to and I'll do some extra shopping for us."

"That sounds great. Let me know when you get home. Curtis will be fine. He probably discovered a new asteroid and is excited to share the news. Maybe he discovered he's wrong about all those asteroids, a hundred thousand miles out. Anyway, can't wait to see you."

"I'm curious to hear what Curtis is up to," Becky says before touching out.

Curtis checks news feeds and forum chatter. There is nothing about the destruction of Perth. There are no news reports, no rumors or scuttlebutt. Everything is quiet. Can he be the only one who knows the truth outside of Australia?

Curtis trusts Marcus. They've never met in person, but Marcus has been active on the forum for years. They have hunted for asteroids together. What reason would Marcus have to lie about something like this? The photos he sent look real, and someone cut his transmission. It really spooked Curtis when they asked for his call sign.

Where is Jin? Curtis hopes he isn't on a date with Becky. He might never call.

With time on his hands, Curtis works to confirm Marcus's information. Curtis googles restaurants in Perth; places that will be open at this hour. Busy signals answer each call. He checks the phone directory in Perth, chooses a few names at random, and calls the numbers. Busy signals again. He wants to call Marcus but doesn't dare.

Something is going on. Phone lines are down or blocked. The news is being censored. People in Perth need help. The world needs to know what's happening.

Jin's image appears on screen. "Finally," Curtis says as he touches in.

"Hey, Curt-man. What's up?" asks Jin.

Curtis can think of many responses, but this is not the time to be petty. He needs Jin's help to get the news out, so they can help the people of Perth. After what happened during the ham radio transmission, Curtis didn't dare take the chance that their voice communication could be monitored for keywords and phrases. Jin has told him that the NSA monitors conversations in over one hundred languages, but he doesn't think Klingon is one.

Curtis speaks the words in Klingon that mean "I am honored to see you again." This isn't exactly what he means to say, but it's the closest translation he can come up with.

Jin laughs. It's been years since they spoke Klingon.

"First, you leave a voice message in Klingon, now you're doing it in person. Curtis, what's going on?"

Curtis speaks forcefully in the harsh language, telling his friend to "Speak Klingon or die."

Jin isn't sure if Curtis is playing or serious. "Come on, man. This is what you called about? It's been a while since—"

Curtis interrupts him. "Silence! News for you only. Speak Klingon or die."

Jin pauses, then bends at the waist toward his thin screen. "I bow before you," Jin says in Klingon, a response of submission. He then adds, "Begin again."

Curtis is glad he has Jin's attention. He takes a sip from his Giant Gulp Cup and speaks in the gruff jargon. "A city down under destroyed. Meteor. Received SOS by QSO. Marcus sent. News lied. Government cover-up"

Jin replies in the TV series language, "Marcus? Meteor. What City?"

Curtis continues speaking Klingon. "City of Perth destroyed. Not fireball. Meteor explosion. I have photos. No news. Perth needs help."

Jin lets his brain translate for a moment, then "Oh shit," in English. "Oops, send photos and call back on the IP tunnel."

Curtis has a direct IP tunnel into Jin's home network. He copies the image files to Jin's system and uses encrypted video over IP for a video call with Jin.

Jin checks the photos. "You're sure this is downtown Perth?"

"Yes. I checked maps and images of the city. It's definitely Perth, or what's left."

"It looks like an explosion destroyed the buildings, and it's obvious people are dead. That doesn't mean it was a meteor. How did you get these?"

"Marcus. He sent an SOS using Morse code. He said voice frequencies were being monitored, and the net was down. Then his

QSO went dead, and somebody asked for my call sign. I freaked and called you. I figured if anyone knows what's going on, it's you NSA pukes. You guys monitor everything," Curtis explains.

"And you thought it was safe to speak Klingon over the phone?"

"Don't tell me you guys listen for Klingon."

"How do you think I got the job?"

"Oh man. Don't psych me. I'm already freaking." Curtis nervously sucks on his Gulp straw.

"Relax. Klingon is safe. But you're right. If there was a disaster of this magnitude, I, and the other NSA pukes, would know about it."

"I knew something was going on. I'm not a conspiracy nut. I told you!" Curtis says.

"If you are right, and the government is blocking this news, it's being done at a very high level, and there aren't many levels above my team."

"Marcus said it was a low altitude meteor explosion. The asteroid activity is high. You saw it yourself during the sky storm. I'm sure more asteroids are incoming. Why would the government spooks want to cover this up?"

"I don't know. Let me dig into this. Sit tight."

"I'm not going anywhere." Curtis stuffs a handful of Doritos in his mouth.

Jin pounds away on his keyboard. "I'm running a scan through a data center housing high-level government servers. There is no mention of any destruction or death in Perth."

"No surprise there."

"I know you trust Marcus, but I'm running the photos through a program that checks pixel by pixel to see if software like Photoshop altered the images." Jin has the results a few seconds later.

"The photos are clean. These are real. Now you've got my attention."

"I told you, man. Marcus is the real deal."

"Let's go to Australia, virtually. I'm using a software tool to gain sleuth-like access to Australian government servers. If there's a disaster in Perth, I'll find evidence in their Emergency Management system. Bingo! The Australian Government has dispatched all police and fire personnel to Perth's city center. Oh, and they've called up military troops to provide support for rescue operations."

"Ok, you've got proof. Now what? What can we do to help?" Curtis asks. Jin rocks back and forth, his fingers moving across the keyboard as gracefully as a piano aficionado. "Whoa! Jin's in the zone. That's the computer genius I know."

Jin replies without looking up from the monitor. "Ah, sneaky. I see what's going on. Somebody installed an advanced spoofing bot that blocks all the outbound ports! Everything looks normal to local operators, but in effect, the bot ropes their systems off from the rest of the world. They've blocked the entire country with a giant firewall."

"That's why there's no news from Perth?"

"Exactly. News and requests for help look like they've transmitted, but in fact, never get past the firewall. Nothing gets out."

"The Australian authorities must wonder why nobody has offered to provide aid."

'I'm sure they'll figure it out, but they're in the depths of the crisis. All hands-on deck. This must have been done by a faction inside the US government or another rogue government, but why? Who would want to keep the disaster secret?"

"The world needs to know. If there are more asteroids coming, there's more destruction on the way. We're the only ones who know what's really happening. We need to tell people," exclaims Curtis.

"Agreed. Can you write a document describing the Perth incident and warn people of more asteroids?"

"I'm on it. What do we do after that?"

"You post the news and images on low key sites, like small city news pages and blogs. Avoid large news sites. We don't want your posts to get censored or kicked. Tag the articles with keywords for search metadata. I'll send a message to everyone," Jin states, as he rocks and speed types.

"See. I wasn't exaggerating. Now, it's team Curtis and Jin working together, just like the good ol' days."

Jin doesn't respond.

"All right." Curtis takes a quick sip from his Gulp Cup. "I'm working up a list of news sites. You're sending a message to everyone? Wait, what do you mean by everyone?" Curtis asks.

Jin replies, "Everyone. Call you back in a few. I need to work on this."

Forty-five minutes later, Jin and Curtis are on a video call using their encrypted IP tunnel. Curtis gives his update: "I'm ready to distribute the news story and images. I'm using an app called Tunnel GuruVPN, which will mask my location while I post the photos and the news article on the news sites. I also hacked into the server of a company that feeds small town news sites. That should help."

"Great Curtman. I've translated your news article into several languages and encrypted the photos and the news article in a worm. I will install the worm on telecommunication servers around the world. Once installed, the worm will proliferate and spread on its own. It's the best way I know to broadcast news about the destruction of Perth to people around the world."

"Wait, whoa. You can do that? You've got scary skills, man."

"I was well trained. Here we go." Jin's fingers move at a blur across the keyboard. "This will get a bit convoluted, but I think it's best we hide our tracks, don't you?"

"Ah, yeah, sure. Who knows that happened to Marcus after his transmission got cut off?"

"I don't have time to fully ghost the trace, but nobody will have time to dig too deep. I've logged into a server in a data center in Guatemala City. I'll use this server to jump to a server farm in Germany. After that, we're on our way to a server in Croatia, then we tunnel our way into a telecommunications server in the United Kingdom. I want the message to originate in a legitimate country without being traced back to us."

"That is some crazy shit, man. How does this get the message to everyone?"

"All right. I'm in the British server. Now I'm installing the worm. The worm uses hooks in a common communication virus. Common to employees of NSA, at least. The virus lives in all mobile devices undetected by users. Every text message sent or received moves through a telecommunication server. I've programmed the worm to install on any device that sends a text message on any of the common message platforms in use."

175

"But how does it get to everyone?"

"That's the fun part. When a user sends a message, that user receives the photos and news article. The virus, already on their phone, will then forward the photos and news to every contact in the person's Smart-Band or VUE lens. When those contacts receive the photos and message, their device forwards the packet to everyone in that person's contact list. You see. It spreads exponentially."

"There are hundreds of millions of text messages sent every day. This will spread like wildfire," says Curtis.

"More like billions of messages sent a day. This will proliferate rapidly. OK, I'm moving from the UK to France. Dropping the French version on France Telecom. Moving on, I've dropped the German version. Now, let's share the Arabic version in Dubai and Riyadh." Jin rocks gently as he types furiously. "Let's give the Chinese a taste. I'm dropping the worm in Beijing, Shanghai, and Shenzhen. Next up, the Spanish version goes to Mexico City, Madrid, Barcelona and Buenos Aires, and finally, we drop our little friend in the US on Verizon, AT&T and T-Mobile, and I'm backing out."

"That was fast. How do you know it will work? Have you done this before?" Curtis asks.

"Yeah, something similar. It's kinda my job. It will work. Patience, it's 7:10 p.m., Denver time. That means it's 2:10 a.m. in the U.K., and it's 9 a.m. in China." Jin stops rocking and leans back in his chair to observe his efforts.

A few minutes after loading the worm into the UK, hundreds of users receive the broadcast. There are tens of billions of text and photo messages sent around the world each day. As the worm loads on phone after phone, it spreads from one person to hundreds of people, then thousands, then hundreds of thousands, and so on.

"Now what?" asks Curtis.

"Now, nothing. Our work is done. I'm heading over to Becky's. She's fixing dinner. Don't worry. By morning, most everyone will have received the message at least once. Unless it's someone like you who has no friends."

"I have friends. Wait. Becky can cook. I bet I get the message before you!"

Devices around the world ping, vibrate, and beep as they receive text messages and the worm. An Egyptian man walking down a street in Cairo reads the news in his VUE lens. While he reads, his phone sends the message to his five hundred contacts. A young woman walking on the Bund, in Shanghai with her boyfriend receives the broadcast five times in less than a minute. A young boy riding an electric scooter in Mexico City crashes, blinded by messages flooding his VUE. In a few hours, phones have broadcast the message millions of times. With each ping of a text, the message is broadcast to hundreds more people, sharing news of Perth, and warning of more asteroids falling to Earth.

Mike McCoy

Chapter 26: Fly the Rocky Skies

Wednesday Night

Kobalt and his elite Black Guard use the Scramjets as fast transport, allowing them to be anywhere on the planet in a few hours. Kobalt has used the Scramjets, flying to any location requiring control. Meteor events increased in recent months. Whenever a meteor event involved humans, Kobalt and his team flew in to control the scene and keep the event out of the news, as they had in the wetlands of Myrtle Beach, South Carolina, early that week. The Scramjet is not a warcraft. The advanced jets were designed for speed. Scramjets are stealthy at high altitude, flying higher and faster than conventional aircraft traversing the globe unnoticed.

The trio of Scramjets soar in formation through the sky at sixty thousand feet, well above commercial aircraft. Kobalt sits behind the pilot in the open cockpit, looking out the forward window, still upset that Munday got away. This trip would be unnecessary if his guard had relaxed the slippery scientist before Munday entered the rail car. The skies ahead are clear.

High above the Scramjet formation, a rocky meteor enters the Earth's atmosphere. As an asteroid in space, the rocky mass had followed a stable orbit for billions of years until something unseen disrupted its rotation, causing the rock, and millions like it, to fall through the solar system. Now the rock, pulled into the grasp of our planet, enters Earth's atmosphere, and becomes super-heated. The space rock's fragile composition cannot withstand intense heat and pressure. It bursts into a thousand fragments glowing against the evening sunset.

That rocky orb is not alone. Hundreds of space rocks follow, all with different shapes, sizes, and compositions. Some asteroids are rocky rubble piles, loosely congealed pieces of dust and rock, spinning together through space, while other asteroids are solid metal, composed primarily of iron and nickel.

A group of meteors enter the atmosphere above the jet formation. They come in fast. The aircraft systems pick them up. Alarms sound.

"Jack, we have multiple incoming. Who's firing at us?" asks the pilot.

Alarms continue to sound as the copilot checks radar, sensor readings, system monitors, and exterior cameras. "I'm tracking several objects, but they're coming in too high, and way too fast to be any conventional threat. We're not in danger. Look up there." The copilot points out the front window.

Kobalt pushes himself between the pilots to look out the cockpit window. A tight grouping of fireballs moves across the sky above them.

"Look, they're spreading out," says the pilot.

"Wow, what a sight. There must be twenty separate asteroids," reports the copilot.

"Meteors," corrects Kobalt.

"Based on their speed and rate of decent, looks like the West Coast will have a meteoric sunset," says the copilot.

"The forecast tonight is partly rocky with scattered atmospheric explosions," the pilot jokes.

"Get us to New Zion." Kobalt growls.

"We're almost there. Slowing airspeed, decreasing altitude. We have a turn in thirty seconds. We'll be on the ground in five minutes," the pilot states.

As the jets turn, three fireballs streak across the sky from the east. One fireball explodes in a brilliant flash. A second fireball disintegrates much less dramatically, burning up and disappearing in a silent puff. A third fireball stays together. The pilots and Black Guard watch the meteor crash into empty farmland. The impact sends a plume of dirt and smoke high into the sky.

Chapter 27: Bluster or Muster

Wednesday Evening–Washington, DC–9:30 p.m.

Vice President's Office

Ex-vice president Cliff Baker pours himself an ample shot from a half empty bottle of Makers Mark bourbon whiskey, then fills Mitch Campbell and Jerome Hargrove's glasses. "This ARC crap cannot stand. Where's Charles? He's the tactician. The master strategist. He'll dream up some legislation to fix this."

Mitch lifts the glass of whisky to his lips. "Charles is busy with the Japanese. The Minister of Disaster Management is in the city for meetings. We can't create new legislation. The House and Senate no longer exist. Any new legislation will require support from the Arcadian council. They won't give up the power they've just gained."

Cliff swirls the brown liquid in his crystal glass and then drinks it bottoms-up. "Screw the Arcadians. I'll form a new government without them. We still control the military. We have the power."

Mitch leans back in his chair and takes another sip, then points to Cliff. "Do we control the military? Do we hold power or do the Arcadians? We don't know who Cruikshank has his hooks into. He has a lot of influence."

"I'll schedule a meeting with the leaders of the House and Senate first thing in the morning and get this moving before the Arcadians can make any moves. I'll make sure we have the military with us. We will reinstate the Constitution before anyone hears about the damned ARC Amendment being signed. What will the Arcadians do, start a war?" Cliff Baker asks.

Jerome Hargrove follows up on Cliff's idea. "Since we have the opportunity, we can make a few changes to the Constitution. Why have all those amendments, anyway? I mean, bring it up to date. You must admit, some ideas the Arcadians have are intriguing. The Constitution is what, three hundred years old? Wait… three hundred years old? That doesn't sound right." Without waiting for anyone to respond, Jerome uses his VUE to check the age of the document. His fingers flick at the air in front of his face as he types on a screen only he can see.

Mitch acts like he's about to throw his whiskey glass at Jerome, but drinks it instead. He leans toward Cliff and says in a half whisper, "I'd hate to waste good whiskey on the idiot. How did he ever get to be a cabinet member?"

"The party owed his uncle a huge favor. I've taken him under my wing. This way, I can always depend on his support. That's more than I can say for most," Cliff replies. His band vibrates and dings, receiving multiple messages as he leans forward to reach for the whiskey bottle. Seconds later, Mitch receives multiple messages.

Jerome's calculations are interrupted by incoming messages. He mutters, "Sweet Jesus, Mary, Mother of God. What on Earth happened?" He moves his finger, flipping through images of Perth in his VUE. "They're dead. Thousands are dead. Oh, my." He gulps and sobs.

Cliff and Mitch view the images and read the text. They look up from their bands at the same time. Mitch wears a steely face of arrogance. Cliff's face exhibits shock and disbelief.

"This says there is an active effort by the US Government to cover up a meteor explosion that destroyed Perth. We are the government. We aren't covering up anything. I didn't even know…" Cliff was beside himself. "How did things get so out of control?" He swirls the bourbon in his glass and again drinks it all, bottoms-up.

Mitch scowls at Cliff. "That's right, Cliff, have another shot of whiskey. That's your answer. Dull your senses to the issues and delay acting, while others take control and manipulate the system to their own ends. You're all bluster and no muster. Look how that's turned out. We are no longer the government. You are no longer the vice president. The Arcadians have taken over and you let them do it right under your nose."

Cliff sinks into his executive chair, clenching the armrests as he realizes Cruikshank has played him the fool. "It's that evil bastard Cruikshank. He's always slinking in the shadows, whispering conceit in unsuspecting ears, playing people and the system. Advising the president. My god, the man's been in senior positions during the past three administrations."

"Yes. Cruikshank has been a tireless, patient man. Now, he wields the power. Power you allowed to slip through your fingers. You knew the president wasn't well. I told you to act. So, what will you do about Cruikshank? Bluster? Cry and complain? Or will you muster your allies and act? You've lost your chance at the presidency. You've lost the country. What will you do about it, Mr. Vice President?"

Cliff stands to show he accepts Mitch's challenge.

Cliff touches his band and calls the Secret Service command post. "Locate Colonel Cruikshank, Russell Thompson, and any other known Arcadians, and arrest them. Search the White House and their personal residences. Put out an APB with DC Police."

Jerome stops swiping his fingers in the air for a moment. "The president will be with Cruikshank and Thompson."

Cliff continues. "And if the president is with them, arrest him, too." There is a pause. "Arrest him for treason and the attempted coup of the United States of America. Find them and arrest them all. Call me when it's done."

Jerome removes his VUE and stares at Cliff Baker. "How can you arrest the president for a coup of his own government?"

"By signing that damned ARC amendment. It's treasonous by its very definition," Cliff yells, fueled by whiskey and adrenaline.

The effects of the toxic mix cause Cliff to stumble, but he steadies himself, putting both hands on the surface of his desk. He glares at Mitch and touches his band to call Tug Grimes, Secretary of Defense.

There's a long pause as he waits for Tug to answer the call.

Jin knocks on Becky's door. Becky pulls the door open and steps to the threshold. "Wha… You're wearing a dress and you did something with your hair," Jin says, as he gives Becky a slow head-to-toe examination. "I smell perfume. You're wearing make-up on your–"

"Is it too much? I never do this. This is so not me," Becky says nervously as Jin stares at her lovingly.

Becky's lower lip trembles. "I, I just thought tonight could be special. I know it's stupid. If you don't like it–"

"Becky, you're amazing. I am the luckiest guy on Earth." Jin says, as he wraps his arms around his girl.

Becky embraces Jin. "I know I'm being silly."

"Shut up and kiss me." They kiss passionately, with wanton lust.

Becky can't find the words to describe how she feels. She lingers in the warm, soothing contentment of being held in the strong arms of her man, kissing him deeply.

Jin looks into Becky's eyes. "I never thought this could happen to me. I'm really good at math, but that never got me the girls. Seeing you in the doorway, so beautiful, wanting me, it's incredible. For the first time in my life, I am truly in love." He pauses and gently kisses Becky's plump lips, then says, "I'm in love with you." They kiss deeply.

Becky leads Jin by the hand through her townhouse. They pause at the dining table. "This looks wonderful. Candles and everything. It smells great, Beck."

Becky tugs on Jin's hand, pulling past the dining room. "No need to rush dinner. I'm taking the day off tomorrow."

"Oh?" is all Jin can think to say.

As Becky leads him to her bedroom, he says, "I'll call in sick."

Dinner is cold, and the candles burned to the wick when they eat, but it's the best meal they've ever had. They finish a bottle of wine and go back to bed.

Chapter 28: High Alert

Washington, DC–9:50 p.m.

Tug Grimes is dining with his wife at one of Washington DC's finest restaurants. It's a rare evening. The Secretary of Defenses' busy schedule rarely allows for a quiet evening out. Tug's wife, Joan, planned the special date night; Tug had promised not to miss it.

The restaurant is bustling with the Capitol Hill elite. It's a favorite location for legislators and lobbyists. Joan looks around the large dining room and spots Secretary of State, Joyce Pritchett. Tug recognizes several members of Congress and a few other cabinet members scattered around the restaurant. Charles Adams and a group of Japanese men occupy a large table near the front.

"You could have chosen a quieter spot for our night out. I thought you wanted something intimate," Tug inquires.

"It's close to the White House. I knew if I chose this restaurant, I'd have better odds of you keeping our date," Joan answered with a sly smile. "Besides, it doesn't hurt for all the power brokers to see you out with your wife. It humanizes you."

"Humanizes me?" Tug's band vibrates. He reaches to touch in, but Joan puts her hand on his arm. Tug looks at the display, then looks to Joan. "It's the vice president. He never calls this late. It must be something urgent." Tug hesitates.

"My loyal, disciplined, military man. Your dedication is why I love you. I just hope Cliff Baker leaves some of the evening for me… us."

Tug touches to accept the call. Cliff is talking as soon as Tug touches in. "Tug, I need you and General Mahon in my office in an hour. It's urgent. You know I wouldn't be calling you if it weren't—"

"Mr. Vice President, it's late. I'll give Jack a call and I'll be there as soon as he can join us." Tug wants to finish dinner and spend time with his wife. He promised tonight to her and intends to keep his promise. "Sir, if it's about the Perth messages, we can get to the bottom of that—"

Cliff interrupts Tug mid-sentence. "It's about the damned ARC. I need to know if you stand with me and the United States of America. Do you honor the oath you took to protect it, or are you with those Arcadian bastards?" Cliff stops talking, letting silence hang in the air.

The question catches Tug off guard. No one has ever questioned his honor or loyalty. "Sir, I am the Secretary of Defense of the United States of America. My duty is to serve the president and our fine nation. I do not recognize any government called Arcadia, and never will." Tug sits straight, almost at attention.

"OK. I thought so. But, glad to hear it, just the same. Get yourself and Jack here ASAP. We need to fight this."

"Yes, sir, as soon as we can, Mr. Vice President."

Tug stops the call and winks at his wife. "Sorry, dear. One quick call." Tug places a call to General Jack Mahon. The call is not answered. Tug tries again with the same result. He squeezes Joan's arm affectionately. "Jack isn't answering. He's probably having dinner with his wife and kids. Let's order dessert."

"Don't you have to call Cliff back?"

"After dessert, dear. If I call too soon, he'll think I didn't try hard enough," Tug says with a wink.

A sudden jolt and violent shaking overtakes the building, sending plates in the kitchen smashing to the floor. Windows shatter. Women scream. The ceiling buckles, sending slabs of plaster to the floor. Heavy chandeliers in the dining room swing wildly and crash to tables below. When the shaking starts, Tug grabs his wife, pulling her with him under the table.

A rolling wave passing through the ground follows the strong jolt of the quake. Tug thinks for a moment that he's on a ship at sea. The rolling and shaking last a few violent seconds. All is quiet for a moment before the fire and security alarms in every building across the city go off. Seconds later, police and fire sirens blare. A massive earthquake has struck Washington, D.C.

Tug lifts his wife from beneath the table. The dining room looks like it was bombed. People rush for the exit. Some people limp from wounds. The air is full of dust. Chandeliers that haven't fallen hang by thin wires. Large pieces of the ceiling are missing, exposing the rafters above. Tug holds Joan close. He leads the way carefully, allowing others to pass them to the crowded front doors.

They walk past a couple sitting motionless in their booth along the restaurant wall. A heavy wooden beam fell onto their table. The table gave way, severing the legs of the couple, as it crashed to the floor. Tug can tell by their skin color that the two are dead. Joan gasps at the sight. They look like nicely dressed ceramic dolls, sitting still and lifeless. Tug pulls his wife forward.

Tug Grimes is not one to panic. He is patient. People have jammed the doors of the restaurant. Tug hangs back. One beam has fallen, but the building is not collapsing. Tug hears a distant rumbling sound. The sound becomes a deafening roar. Joan looks at Tug with fear and horror in her eyes, as the front of the building explodes under the force of a tremendous gust of blazing hot wind, sending their bodies flying across the shattered restaurant.

The wind strips the roof off the one-story brick building, flying away into the darkness. Bodies of people at the front of the restaurant explode with the glass and bricks. Tug loses his grip on Joan's hand as the blast hurtles them through the air. Tug's body hits the back wall of the restaurant as it collapses, cushioning his fall. Tables and chairs pile over him in a heap of debris. It's over in seconds, but it takes the old military man a few minutes to push the pile of rubble off his body.

"Goddamn. That was a big one!" Tug says as he pushes a table off him. He tries to stand. His side hurts. "Ouch, damn it! Feels like I broke a few ribs." He coughs, clutching his side.

The air is thick with dust.

"Joannie, where are you, girl?" he cries out. He hears a weak cry from under a jumble of tables, chairs, and accumulating dirt. Gritty dirt is everywhere, piling up deeper by the second. "Hold on. I'll get you out of there," Tug says, as he pulls furniture and bricks from the area where he hears his wife crying.

He pulls a chair from the pile and sees the dirty face of his wife. She's in pain. When she spots her man, the grimace on her face becomes a shaky smile. "I think my arm is broken, but I guess I'm OK."

Tug digs through the debris to get his Joannie free. She extends her good arm. He lifts her, putting an arm around her waist to steady her, as he tries not to show how much pain he is in. Blood drips down Joan's dirty face from a cut on her forehead.

"My girl sure is a sturdy broad," he says. Joan's arm was in an unnatural position, looking ghastly. A grisly bloody bone is sticking out. "You look all right, except that arm. We'd better get that fixed up. Can you walk?" Tug asks, helping his wife move through the debris. Tug coughs again, trying to ignore his pain.

Joan limps forward, held by her husband. "I don't think I'll recommend this restaurant to my friends."

Tug smiles. That's his girl. "What? It's the perfect spot for an adventurous date."

"I'll admit, the service was explosive, but you never got your dessert."

Tug holds his wife tighter. "I'm just glad we were together when whatever the hell this was happened."

Tug stands under the dusty sky in the middle of what was one of the finest restaurants in Washington, DC. He looks around surveying the destruction and yells out to no one in particular, "What in the hell just happened?"

As if in answer, Tug's government-issued black SUV rolls up, stopping in front of the blown-out building. His driver steps over what remains of the brick wall that was the front of the restaurant, trudges through the debris, and makes his way to the Secretary of Defense and his wife.

"Are you all right, sir?" The driver asks as he rushes to help Tug with Mrs. Grimes.

"We're alive, Dennis." Tug notices his driver has made it through the explosive episode without a blemish. "My, don't you look spiffy. How'd you get through this without a scratch?" "I parked in the structure down the street. The reinforced cement wall protected the SUV. Let me help you. We need to move; fallout is accumulating fast."

They hobble out the front of the building and into the SUV. Tug and Dennis make sure Joan is comfortable on the rear passenger seat. Tug gets in next to her. Dennis puts the SUV into four-wheel drive and gets the vehicle moving through the accumulating dirt.

Tug taps Dennis on the shoulder. "Get to the White House, pronto!"

The city is wrecked. The rock and brick facades of buildings have fallen, leaving heaps of debris scattered across sidewalks and into the streets. Gas mains are broken. Fires flare in hundreds of buildings. Police cruisers and fire trucks across the city get stuck in the gritty fallout, now a foot deep.

Tug surveys the damage. He hopes in the light of day it won't be as bad as it looks now, but he knows he's being optimistic. The city is in ruins. What was not blown over, now burned. The quake lasted only seconds. The city could have survived that. It was the super-heated blast of air, traveling five hundred miles per hour, that blew this major world capital over like a stack of Jenga blocks.

Joan gazes at Tug's rugged face. A face that remains calm and confident in the face of death and destruction. "Should you call Cliff, now?"

"I need information before I call. He'll expect me to know what the hell happened." Tug touches his band. NO SERVICE flashes. Tug leans forward to his driver. "Dennis, do you have the sat phone?"

Dennis pulls the sat phone from its charging cradle and hands it back. "Here you go, Mr. Secretary."

Tug calls his office at the Pentagon. No one answers. Next, he calls the Deputy Secretary of Defense, Clive Armstrong. He doesn't answer. He calls Jack Mahon again. No answer. Tug is getting pissed off. "Where the hell is everyone?" He calls *The Watch*, part of the State Department's Operation Center and someone answers.

"Hello. This is Tug Grimes, Secretary of Defense. Do you folks know what the hell happened?"

"Mr. Secretary. We have reports of a massive explosion of undetermined origin, southwest of Baltimore BWI airport. I-95 North and the 495 Capital Beltway are closed or jammed. We have no additional information, sir."

"That was one hell of an explosion. There was a major earthquake, followed by a high-speed air blast that ripped DC apart. There's more than a foot of fallout covering everything. It will be tough for emergency vehicles to get around town. I saw burned bodies in the rubble. Check for radiation. Are we under attack? Who the hell would nuke us?"

"DC ripped apart, sir?"

"Buildings are down. Fires everywhere. The death toll will be huge. I've seen ordinance. Hell, I've had it fall all around me, but nothing like this. The city is ruined."

"Sir, per our emergency protocol, I have sent an alert to all branches of the military, all security forces, Homeland Security, and FEMA, but I'm only getting a response from local authorities. I've checked, and our networks are intact. Cellular circuits are down, but satellite and fiber are up. No one is responding. It's strange, sir."

"Very strange. You and your team keep calling. I want you, or the officer in charge, to call me as soon as you have confirmation on what the hell caused the explosion. We are on high alert. Understood?"

Tug calls Cliff Baker's office. The call takes longer to connect than normal, but Cliff answers. "Tug. What the hell was that?"

"I'm trying to get a handle on it, Mr. Vice President." Tug updates the vice president on the information he has learned.

"What kind of explosion? It must have been huge. The White House shook like a baby rattle. Secret Service swooped in and moved us to PEOC. Come to the EBR when you arrive." Cliff pauses for a moment and asks. "Were we attacked?"

"If I didn't know better, I'd say it was nuclear. My gut tells me it isn't, but for the life of me I don't know of any bomb, other than a nuke, that can cause the damage I'm seeing here. We'll be there in twenty minutes. Can you have a medical team meet us? Joan is injured. There are other strange things going on. I think it's best to discuss in private."

Chapter 29: Seeds of Humanity

The six Arcadian cities are on red alert and buzzing with activity. Citizens, according to their tunic color, move to emergency stations and prepare for an imminent nuclear attack. They have built the cities and prepared for the possibility of attack. They practice the red alert drill monthly. The drill has become routine.

Citizens are excited to run through the drill; Now that Operation Hard Shelter is operational, the experiment will last two years, after which everyone will return home to their families. The work is rewarding, and the pay is generous. Living in the underground city is free, so most people plan to emerge topside with ample savings. This drill is different, though. The experiment is underway. People are excited, yet hopeful. It's just a drill.

Colonel Cruikshank sits at his desk in his elegant, neo-modern quarters. He views a call with General Mahon as he massages his aching leg. The few muscles in his thigh that remain are hard and knotted. His agony is intense, but the colonel will not show his pain. Pain is an old friend. Unwelcome and uninvited, but a frequent visitor.

"Jack. Now that Arcadia is the legitimate government of the land, I would like to extend an invitation for you to be a founding member of the council, alongside Jon Anderson and myself."

"It will be my honor and a privilege to serve on the council. I am here at New Arcadia in the bunker on level three with my men. I'll move down to the city once the storms begin. Everything is going according to plan. FEMA is prepared to provide support to the topside population."

The colonel winces in response to a torturous muscle cramp. "It pains me, but there will be no help for the topsiders. No matter what you have prepared, it will never be enough to sustain the population. Let them loot, fight, fuck, and kill one another as they starve off. Humans will destroy whatever the asteroids don't. We will offer no aid. Your men must protect the city perimeters against any survivors who may happen upon us. I will not have topsiders mixing with the few and fortunate. Secure the city perimeters. That is your mission."

"That's different from what we've said in presidential briefings. I want to confirm we're on the same page. We've made plans."

The colonel chuckles. "Politics and poppycock, Jack. We had to tell them what they wanted to hear. Politicians wouldn't have known what to do if we had told them the truth."

"Of course. OK. We will proffer no aid. No one knows about the cities. The locations are secret. It won't be difficult to defend the cities."

"I knew you were the right man to sit on the council, Jack," Cruikshank laughs wickedly.

General Mahon hesitates before joining the colonel in a conspiratorial laugh.

The colonel senses a vibration and freezes. His eyes widen, and ears perk as his smile fades. He hears a deep rumbling sound rushing toward him just before it hits. *WHACK!* The tremendous sound of a collision hits the underground city. Books fly off shelves. A statue of a samurai, dressed in combat armor, falls to the floor. General Mahon is still laughing when he is knocked off his feet by the tremendous jolt. The city's main dome vibrates like a bell. The quake passes through the floor of the underground city like a rolling wave, knocking people off their feet.

Cruikshank touches a thin screen. "Sky Command, report. Were we hit?" Before the commander can respond, the colonel opens another call. "City control, damage report." He touches the screen again, opening a third communication link. "Kobalt, double the City Guard, and I want Black Guard patrolling the cities. Put down any discontents, but keep it quiet."

Reports flow in. "Sky Commander here, sir. We tracked an impact in Maryland. It was quite large. Washington, D.C., and surrounding areas are affected. We received a significant seismic jolt from the impact. We will monitor and update you with more information as we have it."

"I'm dispatching Black Guard platoons in all the cities, but I will have them remain in the background. The City Guard and Medical Service teams will keep order. Black Guard will monitor and react if needed, ensuring everyone remains calm. We're about to land at New Zion. I'll report once we arrive," Kobalt advises.

"City Control here, sir. We have some scattered minor damage, but nothing significant to report. The building management system set off alarms. We're shook up, that's all. We're resetting sensors and sending out repair crews."

The tremendous jolt agitated the citizens of New Arcadia. Fear and anxiety grip the city. Many people fear there has been a nuclear impact. Is this why the experiment became operational? Workers huddle in groups at their assigned posts.

The projected billboards scattered throughout the city continue to display motivational messages on the city walls. City music plays cool jazz. The music plays louder than usual. A voice comes over speakers. "Remain at your stations. We experienced a seismic event. Minor damage has been reported. If you need assistance, call The City Guard or Medical Services."

Zsoldos enters the colonel's office. "That was a big one. I'm getting constant updates. Looks like the party is over for Baltimore. Washington D. C. will survive, but it's severely damaged," he reports.

The colonel sits quietly at his desk. He feels redeemed. His planning and efforts are paying off. "The first test of many. We face challenges ahead."

"Sir, I think it's time for your announcement."

"I agree. Make the preparations. Increase levels of city atmosphere for all cities to keep everyone at ease. I'll be ready in ten minutes."

"I'll meet you in the press room."

Medical Services teams patch up the cuts and scrapes. The City Guard answers questions and calms the masses. Black Guard discreetly relax a few miscreants, quietly removing the offenders.

Evening in New Arcadia becomes daylight. City music plays an upbeat military march. Projected billboards in the six cities display the image of the colonel, flanked by Arcadian CEO Jon Anderson. It looks as if the colonel and president are standing on the balcony of a palace. Cruikshank wears a white military uniform, his chest full of gleaming medals, his shoulder boards crowned with gold braid. He wears a white peaked military cap to cover his thinning hair.

The colonel stands with arms extended in gracious inclusion.

"Fellow citizens. Many of you have worked diligently for years building the new cities, preparing to withstand the greatest test humankind could ever face. Worldwide nuclear destruction. Mankind causing the extinction of man. We have prepared well. Congratulations to you all."

Cheers erupt.

The colonel quiets the masses.

"I have seen war. I have tasted death. I've inhaled the futility of destruction, twisted metal, burnt flesh. My boots have waded through streams of flowing blood and stepped over young bodies trampled in mud. The commanders of the Four Wars fight endless battles to win empty victories at any cost. We choose to passively defend. We will save life. We implemented a strategy to save humanity and we will emerge victorious."

The citizens gaze at the billboards with rapt attention.

"Today our grand experiment officially began in haste. Not because of the Four Wars. No, not the wars. Nuclear destruction is not our fate. There is a new enemy. An enemy God commands. We felt the power of this new enemy tonight from a seismic quake experienced by all in New Arcadia. Do not despair. We are well prepared, and we shall succeed. Because we planned, we will live."

The colonel pauses. Citizens in the cities speak in hushed tones asking who is this new enemy? What does the colonel mean?

"All of you, everyone in the six cities, we are Arcadians. Together, we have created a harmonious environment for personal growth and enrichment. You are a new society. We brought nature with us; it surrounds us. We live in these hard shells with abundant plant and animal life. In time, we will emerge from our underground pods to repopulate Earth. It is the goal of Arcadia to create a better life for all. We will become a more humane humanity, living harmoniously together with nature, reaching mankind's full potential. That is the promise I make to you. You are Arcadians."

The colonel leans against the marble banister. In reality, it is a wooden pole, but with some video magic to the citizens of Arcadia, it is an elegant marble balustrade on a palace balcony.

"My good citizens, an asteroid impacting Earth's surface caused the earthquake in New Arcadia. We prepared for nuclear destruction, but the true enemy we face is a storm of asteroids plunging toward Earth, pushed by the hand of God himself.

Instead of nuclear winter, Earth faces destruction by thousands of asteroids bombarding the planet. The outcome is the same. The end of mankind. We built the Arcadian cities to ensure that you, the best representatives of the human species, will survive. You are the few and the fortunate. You are the seeds of humanity."

Cruikshank hears a gasp of fear echo through the cities. Even though the city atmosphere dulls emotions, the news stuns the city occupants. A few panicked screams echo through city tunnels, but most people don't react. City Command increases the level of atmosphere in the cities.

The City Guard receive instructions in their VUE lens to chant, "We are the few and the fortunate." The Guard chant, repeating the familiar phrase. "We are the few and the fortunate." Victorious music plays.

City Guard are dispersed among the population in all the cities. "We are the few and the fortunate," they chant.

Tensions dissipate. Medical Service teams join in on the chant. "We are the few and the fortunate." The Black Guard withdraws to the shadows. The chant catches on. Citizens join the City Guard, stomping one boot on the floor, then shouting, "We are the few and the fortunate." Stomp.

The enthusiasm gains momentum as more citizens join the chant and stomp. "We are the few and the fortunate!" The cities vibrate with the sound of seven hundred thousand boots pounding the orange-tiled floor, followed by the echoing chant. "We are the few and the fortunate!" Stomp. "We are the few and the fortunate!" Stomp.

Chapter 30: Dark Cluster

The Los Angeles 210 Freeway–7:15 p.m.

Rob is driving back from Primal Pastures, in Murrieta. Wire cages filled with baby chicks, pigs, and lambs are loaded in the back of his old Chevy Suburban. Rob bought Ethan his eggs and bacon, just as he had promised.

The baby chicks and pigs will grow quickly. The hideaway will soon have eggs every morning, and in a few months, the pigs will become bacon. Rob worked with the staff at the farm to buy boy and girl piglets and lambs to produce for more piglets and lambs. He also bought baby hens and rooster chicks, so they will have chickens to produce eggs and raise others for meat. Lambs were an afterthought. First, they're cute. Second, if Courtney and the kids are to build a new life after the storms, sheep have been an integral part of domestic life for millennia. The sheep will be valuable for their future.

Uncle Rob's phone beeps and vibrates. He never went in for one of those arm band phones, the kind Rick and Courtney like, or those glasses, the executives and bankers made popular. Rob still carries a big smartphone. It's old, but it works.

He looks at the screen. Seven messages! More messages than he receives in a week. Rob reads the messages. They're all the same. Photos of Perth. News of a government cover-up and a warning of more asteroid events. Rob checks a news website. The report of a meteor destroying the city center of Perth is the top story.

Rob turns on the radio. The story of the Perth meteor is being reported non-stop. The news agencies are having difficulty locating experts to provide information on asteroids and cannot reach officials in Perth for comment. Without additional information, the reporters state the news is unconfirmed and comment on the unusual manner the news of Perth went viral.

Rob stays in touch with some astronomy groups and occasionally visits the forums. Rob calls an old astronomy buddy Ted Strickland. If anyone knows what is happening, it will be Ted.

"Hey, Ted. It's Rob Munday. I suppose you've seen the news. What do you think?"

"Ol' Rob Munday. The old codger who used to be my friend. I can't believe it. Good to hear from you. It's been too long. What got you to crawl out from under your rock?"

It's true, Rob hasn't talked with Ted for a few years. He's glad they're still on speaking terms. "Crawl out from under a rock?" He chuckles. "Well, I guess you could say that. Sorry for being out of touch. Have you heard this Perth news?"

"Have I heard the Perth news? How could I miss it? The only problem is they keep showing the same damn pictures. There's no new information and no news coming from Perth. It's strange if you ask me, Rob. The whole thing smells like a hoax."

"I'm most curious about the warning of more asteroid events. Do you think it's possible?"

"The messages. Everyone got those, and I mean everyone. Some people received them hundreds of times. The news says the volume of messages brought down some VUE nets."

Rob is talking on the phone while concentrating on driving through heavy traffic. He tries not to change lanes quickly or brake too hard, lest he have pigs and chickens tumbling around inside his old truck. "But Ted, what do you think about the prediction of more asteroid events? Have you seen any evidence on the forums? What are you guys seeing out there?"

"You know, we've been shut out of all the government and university telescopes, so we've resorted to using our own scopes. Some forum members are reporting strange goings-on. Some of it I don't believe."

"What strange goings-on?"

"Well, one guy says there are objects in the asteroid belt out of their normal orbits. Another fella reported a dark cloud, out past Mars. There's a group who says they confirmed that dark cloud a few days ago but described it more like a dark cluster. They say it's wide and is now closer than Mars. See what I mean? Strange reports. Now we have this Perth message which, if real, the government tried to cover up. Why do you suppose they'd want to cover up such a catastrophe?"

Rob thinks for a moment. *Objects in the asteroid belt out of their normal orbits. Dark Cluster. New meteor showers. "Turbulence."* Rob kicks himself for not making his own observations, but he's been obsessed with preparations for the hideaway. Now, people are observing a dark cluster heading toward Earth. This does not sound good.

"Why would the government hide the fact that an asteroid destroyed a major metropolitan area? One reason I can think of is, they know more asteroids are heading our way, and they don't want worldwide panic. That's why, Ted."

Ted gasps. "Oh, my!"

Rob hears something on the radio that catches his attention. "Hold on, Ted. I think there's a news update." Rob turns up the volume on the radio so Ted can hear.

"I repeat. We have reports of a massive explosion near Baltimore, Maryland. People felt the shock wave as far south as Richmond, Virginia. We have reports of major damage in the nation's capital, with many buildings damaged and fires throughout the city. We have no updates on the number of injuries. We are receiving reports of fireballs and impacts in other parts of the country. We are working to confirm those reports. We will interrupt regular programming when we have more details. Repeating our top story: a major explosion has rocked East Coast cities north of Washington, D.C. We are working to get a statement from a White House spokesman, but our inquiries have gone unanswered. Get all your news here as it happens on KFI AM 640."

Rob lowers the volume. "Ted, I think your dark cluster got closer. I suggest you and your family locate an old bomb shelter or the basement of a building and move in. Gather enough supplies to settle in for a while. If this cloud or cluster is heading our way, find suitable cover or kiss your ass goodbye. I predict the weather in the coming days will be very rocky."

Ted's voice becomes low and sullen. "My wife passed, thank God. I wouldn't want to put her through something like this. I must call my son and his wife. Take care, old friend. Thanks for calling."

"Thanks for the information, Ted. I've got to get my family to a safe place. You be sure and do the same," Rob says before realizing Ted dropped the call before he said goodbye. Rob focuses on traffic as he presses the accelerator. He's convinced time is of the essence. He must get his family to the hideaway as quickly as possible.

Rob calls the Martinez brothers. When Rodrigo answers, all Rob says is, "Rodrigo. It's time to rock-and-roll." Rodrigo isn't exactly sure what Rob means, but he's received hundreds of messages on his band, so he has an idea of what Rob is referring to.

"Now is the time? Is it really happening like you always said?" Rodrigo asks, then curses under his breath.

Rodrigo and his brother, Eddie, have worked with Rob for the past three years building the hideaway. Rob told them stories about his fear of a future disaster. Rob knew the Martinez boys never believed a disaster would require such an extravagant enclosure. No matter what they believed, they worked hard and without complaint. Rob promised that if a disaster ever occurred, the Martinez brothers and their immediate families would have a safe place to stay.

"Rodrigo, I think the event in Perth was the start. It might be a few hours or a couple of days, but I'm convinced more asteroids are coming. The news just reported a huge explosion near Washington, D.C. We need to get moving. Gather any materials needed for last-minute touch-ups. Grab your wife and kids and get to the hideaway. Call Eddie and tell him the same. Remember, immediate family only. I've got a truck full of pigs and chickens. I will unload, then pick up Courtney and the kids."

Rodrigo curses again as a million thoughts race through his mind. Rob told them to be ready to move to the hideaway at a moment's notice. Neither Rodrigo nor Eddie believed they would ever move into that place. He has not packed. He's sure Eddie hasn't packed either.

The brothers told their wives about the hideaway. They always tell their wives about the jobs they work on, but never told them they might move in one day. How is he going to explain this to Isabel? How can he get her to believe what he's about to tell her? They need to pack up, leave their home, and move into an old converted mine! Rodrigo curses again. He touches his band to call his brother.

Chapter 31: War Paint

Pasadena–7:30 P.M.

Rob drives as fast as traffic and the old SUV loaded with chickens, piglets, and lambs allows. He calls Rick's band, but it goes to voice mail. "Hey, Ricky boy. I hope your presentation went well. After you've finished showing off to all those science types, call us. We miss ya, boy."

Rob needs to call Courtney to tell her he's taking her and the kids to the hideaway. He doesn't want to upset her. He doesn't want to fight. Danger is eminent. He hopes Courtney will understand and cooperate. It will be a tough call. He sets his phone on the passenger seat. He tells himself he'll call in a few minutes.

The radio continues to play in the background.

The epicenter of the explosion is southwest of Baltimore, outside the city center. Power is out in Baltimore, Washington, D.C., and surrounding cities. Hundreds of fires have erupted. We have reports of many injuries, but we have no death toll. Ash or dirt is accumulating and is nearly two feet deep, making travel impossible on the streets of Washington, D.C. News crews cannot reach the site of the explosion. Fallout has jammed the roads, burying cars and trucks in the accumulating dirt. We advise everyone to stay in their homes.

Rob rehearses in his mind what he will say to Courtney. He hopes the call will go as well as it does in his head. Waiting longer won't help. He resolves to make the call. He reaches for the big smartphone as rings.

Courtney is calling. Rob answers. "Sweetie. Did you hear from Rick?"

Courtney inhales, about to speak, but pauses. The air is tense. Rob can sense she's upset. "Did you get those messages on your phone?" Courtney asks almost in a whisper.

Rob nearly steers off the road. The swerving truck makes the piglets squeal. "I got the message several times. What happened in Perth is terrible."

"The news says there was a huge explosion near Washington D.C. Rick is there." Courtney cries.

"Courtney, dear, don't worry. Our Ricky boy knows how to keep his head down. He'll be fine. Just you wait. We'll hear from him soon. Hey, I picked up a load of, ah. I was going to unload, but I'll stop by if that's all right," Rob says, trying to think of a way to tell Courtney about the hideaway.

"OK," is all Courtney can say. Her tears become convulsions of uncontrollable sobs. She braces herself on the kitchen counter to keep from collapsing to the floor.

Alyssa hears her mother crying and rushes to the kitchen. "Mommy, Mommy. What's wrong?" Alyssa holds her mother. "Is it Daddy? Is Daddy, OK?"

Courtney wipes her tears and manages a quivering smile. "Daddy's OK, baby." Courtney pushes herself up. "Uncle Rob is coming over."

"That's right, dear. I'll be there as quick as I can," Rob confirms.

Alyssa is excited. "I saw the messages on my VUE. Is the shit hitting the fan, like Uncle Rob said? Are we going to stay in Uncle Rob's cave?"

Courtney's ears perk when Alyssa mentions the cave. Courtney bites her lip. "Uncle Rob, did you fix up that old cave? Is it safe?"

"Courtney dear, yes. It's fully prepared and safe. You'll see. I want to take you and the kids there; at least for tonight, until we know what's what."

Courtney exhales. "I'm scared, Rob. I'm ready to have some help, even if it means spending the night in a cave. Okay, the kids and I will get ready." She ends the call.

Courtney looks at Alyssa, who is still clutching her. "Pack your things, honey, enough for a few days. We're going to sleep in a cave!" Courtney exclaims in a defeated tone.

"Does that mean we can miss school?" asks Alyssa.

"Yes, I guess you can miss school. Get packed, and tell Ethan to pack a suitcase, too."

Alyssa runs to her room, excited about missing school and the adventure of sleeping in the cave. Alyssa answers from down the hall. "Ethan went to Chris and Allie's house." Courtney hears Alyssa, but her answer doesn't register.

Courtney tries to pull herself together. She needs to pack and prepare; Rob will arrive soon. She looks around the room, thinking about what to pack. She is drawn to family photos on the living room wall. She stands in front of her large wedding picture, lifts it off the wall, and clutches the framed photo to her bosom. She forces herself not to cry, but can't control the tears streaming down her face. She pulls photo after photo from the wall, stacking them on a living room chair.

Instead of exiting the highway and heading up to the hideaway, Rob stays on the 210 freeway. The livestock will have to make room for Courtney and the kids. They'll go to the hideaway together. Rob is afraid there isn't much time. If meteors are falling on the East Coast, it won't be long before Los Angeles is at risk. He speeds past the exit that takes him to Courtney and the kids. He needs to make one quick stop before picking up the family.

He races up Loma Alta Drive and turns onto the dirt road leading to his house. The truck fishtails around the corner, eliciting clucks, bleats, and squeals from the livestock. He guns the gas up the steep driveway, speeding past the house, driving to the back of a large metal garage next to the house.

Rob jumps out of his old Chevy Suburban and runs to a large sliding door. He pushes the door open, then runs through the garage, pushing open the large door at the front. He drives the Suburban into the tall metal building, stopping directly beneath a large object hanging from the high beams of the garage. A large gray tarpaulin covers the object. Rob pulls on a corner of the tarp. Once he gets it moving, it's easy to pull the cover off the object hanging above his truck. Rob gathers up the falling tarp and pushes the bundle of fabric to the side.

He walks to a steel upright rising to the ceiling of the garage. Mounted on the upright is a control box leading to a winch mounted high above. Rob pulls the power switch and then punches the down button. The winch whines and chains clink as they move over gears. Slowly, the object lowers onto the Suburban. When it's low enough, Rob grabs an edge of the object, moving it to align properly. The object locks onto mounts Rob had welded on the Suburban's roof. Rob checks the mounts and connects a cable harness for electronics. "She might not be pretty, but she'll do the trick." He ducks under the edge of the object covering his truck. His door won't open all the way, but he shimmies into the driver's seat.

He drives out of the garage with the shell of an X-37B shuttle completely covering the old Suburban. The X-37B was an unmanned miniature version of NASA's space shuttle that made many secret, long-term orbital flights until they cancelled the program and replaced it with the larger X-37C. Rob bought a gutted-out test version and removed the wings, leaving just the shell of the spacecraft which fit snuggly over the Suburban, leaving only the tires visible beneath the space crafts' shell.

An X-37B has no windows, so Rob outfitted the exterior with Ultra HD wide-angle cameras, and mounted 8K screens on the interior of the spacecraft to mimic the truck's windshield and side windows. With the orbiter locked in position, the screens are in the perfect location for driving. Rob drives carefully down his steep driveway and out to the main road, getting used to handling the truck with the extra weight. Soon he is comfortable and confident, driving his customized rig.

When he gets on the freeway, his odd-looking vehicle gets strange looks, curious stares, and honking horns. Rob is on a mission. He doesn't have time for gawkers and complainers. "Out of the way. No photos. This is top-secret government property," Rob says with a laugh.

Rob is having the drive of his life. It doesn't occur to him that his vehicle is nearly two lanes wide. Even though he removed the wings, the wing mounts jut out, adding almost a foot on either side. He swerves through traffic, laughing at the cursing jeers and vulgar sign language of other drivers.

He planned for this moment, but was never sure the time would come when he would use this contraption. He's excited, he's scared, but feels vindicated. All his work and preparation may pay off.

The space shuttle covered Suburban is almost at the exit to Rick's house when the sky brightens with a blinding white light. For a moment, everything looks like a photo negative. Rob thinks the screens have burned out. Blinded drivers hit their brakes. Through the shell of the X-37, Rob hears screeching tires, honking horns, and crunching metal on metal sounds as cars smash into one another.

The cameras adjust and the screens inside the Suburban display the scene outside. A small European car has stopped in front of him. Rob hits the brakes, but the nose of the X-37 protruding in front of the truck makes it hard for Rob to judge distance. The X-37 rams the tiny car, pushing it into the car ahead of it, causing a three-car pileup. The condition of the squashed car surprises Rob.

"Now that's what I call a sub-compact. Sorry, Mr. Fiat."

Car horns stop honking when meteorites and spherules of hot molten rock traveling at forty thousand miles per hour slam through cars and trucks on the freeway. Car windows shatter. Rocks and pieces of hot iron pierce cars and unlucky drivers.

Molten spherules hit the top and side of Rob's truck, but the X-37 shell shields him and his livestock. Rob listens and waits as the spherules hit, but nothing pierces the protective covering over his truck.

"Hot damn! Now, that's American engineering at its finest."

Rob puts the Suburban into reverse, freeing the X-37's nose from the rear of the crumpled Fiat just as a fierce wind burst through the cars. The blast of wind sends the small European car over the edge of the highway, tumbling to the street below. The ferocious wind tosses semi-trailer trucks like toys.

Rob looks ahead. Vehicles jam the four-lane highway for as far as he can see. Wrecked cars and trucks are all around him. Some cars are steaming; others are on fire. Dead cars surround the few functioning cars, making it impossible for them to move. One car moves back and forth, ramming the cars surrounding it, trying to find a way out of the maze of wrecks.

Rob is in the exit lane, with two hundred yards to the off ramp. He moves the truck forward, driving on the shoulder to get around the wrecked cars. Rob punches the gas to get as much speed and momentum as possible. As he drives forward, the wing mount on the driver's side slices and gouges the sides of the stalled cars. "Oops. Just a little body damage, easy to repair. Pardon me. I've got passengers to pick up." He guns the gas again, sideswiping, gouging, and shoving cars out of his way, until he reaches the off ramp.

Once he's free of the highway, he finds the roads are strewn with idle cars and dazed people standing in the street. Some people try to help the injured. Rob wishes he could assist, but he's got to get to Courtney and the kids.

A few miles more, and Rob will arrive at Rick and Courtney's house.

Ethan isn't home to hear that they will sleep in the cave, or he would have been the first one packing a suitcase. Ethan is at Vanessa's house, three blocks over. Vanessa was the babysitter, or as his dad explained it, the night he left for Washington, D.C., their security guard.

Vanessa's younger siblings, Christopher, and Allie are friends of Ethan and Alyssa's. They know each other from school but had not known Vanessa was their older sister. Ethan has never been to Chris' before, but spent the afternoon at his house to play games after school. Ethan came home for dinner and then made excuses to go back to Vanessa's... He meant Chris' house. He said he wanted to play with the kids again, but secretly he wanted to be around Vanessa.

The other reason Ethan wants to visit is because Vanessa's family has a Glide-pad. Glide-pads allow users to walk, run, jump, or slide in any direction, mimicking realistic, real time in-game movements sync'd with VUE game environments and objects.

The kids are playing Dodge It. Ethan is on the Glide-pad. He must dodge objects thrown at him by the other kids sitting across the room on the couch. The players can conjure all kinds of objects to throw at him. He ducks, jumps, lunges, and rolls to avoid whatever is coming at him. He's trying to set a record. If he can beat Chris's score, he'll replace him on the couch next to Vanessa.

The game is getting more difficult. Chris throws fireballs at Ethan's feet while Vanessa tosses bowling pins at his head. If he jumps too high, he'll miss the fireballs, but get bonked in the head by a bowling pin. Allie is throwing rotten tomatoes, but her aim sucks.

Chris changes tactics. He throws spears waist high in fast succession. Ethan slides on the Glide-pad under the spears, escaping certain skewering, then rolls over to face his attackers, laughing and praising his accomplishment. "He glides and slides to win!"

His score is about to eclipse Chris's high score. Ethan is confident he will be the new champion as the final seconds tick down. Then, the image of a rotten tomato smashes into his face, covering the VUE lens. "Allie! You killed me!"

There's a loud crash from above. Seconds later, a blast shakes the house. The windows blow in from the blast, sending shattered glass flying across the room. Ethan feels the shock and the hot wind. He pulls off the VUE and looks up toward the loud crash. He spots four golf ball–sized holes in the ceiling. Speckles of dust dance in the light falling from the holes. He lays still on the Glide-pad across the room from the couch. His eyes follow the dancing dust down to see Vanessa, Chris, and Allie motionless and silent, dead on the couch.

Ethan slides to the edge of the Glide-pad. He stands and stares at the faces of his friends. Vanessa sits silently on the couch, still beautiful. A red spot on her chest blossoms wider. A deep pain grips Ethan in his gut. A pain he's never felt. A pain that draws tears. He wasn't hit by the meteorites, but was cut to his core. He wipes away a heavy tear running down his smooth cheek and runs out of the house.

Ethan heads home in the orange glow of dusk, running as fast as he can. The neighborhood is a mess. Windows of cars and houses are smashed. Trees are blown over. He jumps over a fallen palm frond as he runs. There are holes in the street and holes through cars. People come out of their houses to see what has happened. Some limp about, bloodied with injuries from meteorites or broken glass.

Tears stream from Ethan's eyes as he races home. The pang of loss is not lessened by the horror of destruction he witnesses. A house is missing its roof, another has so many holes in the walls, it looks like there was a police shootout. It is eerily quiet.

Ethan runs around the corner. He panics. *Mom, Alyssa, are you hurt?* The damage on his street is markedly less, but he's filled with guilt and fear. He left home. He wasn't there when the meteor struck. He wasn't there for them. He prays they aren't dead.

Courtney should pack. Rob will arrive any minute, but she can't stop herself from looking through family photos. The life she dreamed of and worked so hard for is over. Rick is missing, asteroids are falling; her way of life is being destroyed.

She is flipping through a book of baby pictures when the meteor blast hits. A bright flash of light comes through the front window. Dusk turns to the brightest of days. Then comes the blast, a huge explosion. Seconds later, the house is rocked by a fierce hot wind. Windows in the kids' bedrooms shatter. Alyssa screams. "Mommy! Mommy!"

Courtney is shocked into action and rushes to Alyssa's room. Alyssa cries, trying to shake glass out of her hair. "Get it out. Get it out." Courtney holds her daughter's head in her hands. Alyssa has several shards of glass in her face.

"Hold still darling." Courtney calms her daughter as she plucks the glass from the girl's pearl-white skin. Blood wells up, replacing the glass.

"That's the last one. You'll be all right." Courtney soothes Alyssa as she picks glass from Alyssa's long blonde hair. The glass piercing her face didn't hurt until her mother plucked the pieces out. Alyssa sobs.

"Did you pack everything you need?" Courtney asked softly. Alyssa nods. Courtney checks the bag and puts a few more things in Alyssa's suitcase.

"Where's Ethan?"

"I told you. He went to Chris and Allie's house," Alyssa answers through her tears.

Courtney slumps and sits on the floor in a daze. Her husband is missing, and now her son is absent. Courtney is running on fear and adrenaline. If she stops to think about Ethan being missing, it will paralyze her and there is no time for that. "Go to his room and pack his duffle bag. Hurry, Uncle Rob will be here soon. We need to leave," orders Courtney.

"We can't leave without Ethan," Alyssa cries.

"We'll go by Chris and Allie's with Uncle Rob. We won't leave him behind. But I need you to pack his bag."

Alyssa wipes her face. Blood mixes with tears streaking her cheeks. "OK, but I'm not packing his underwear."

"Alyssa, pack everything he will need for at least a week, including his underwear. We don't have time for this, baby. Hurry, I'm packing for Daddy, too," she says, zipping Alyssa's suitcase closed.

Courtney puts Alyssa's bag in the living room, then goes to the master bedroom to pack for herself and Rick.

Alyssa grudgingly goes to her brother's room to pack his things. When she finds his undershorts, she picks up each pair daintily with two fingers, careful to only touch the elastic band. She finishes packing, zips his duffle, and carries it to the living room.

Alyssa sets the packed suitcases by the front door while Courtney stacks family photos in a cardboard box when she hears a loud metal on metal scraping sound.

Alyssa rushes to the front window. "Mom. You better come see this. A spaceship just landed in front of our house!"

Courtney opens the front door and steps to the porch with Alyssa standing beside her. Courtney watches the strange sight of a spacecraft coming to a stop in front of their house. In her heart, she hopes it's her husband, Rick, finding his way home to her and to his family, but her imagination is getting the best of her.

"Honey, stand behind me."

Courtney cannot believe what she's seeing. Are space shuttles still flying? Should she be afraid? All she knows is that caution is appropriate. She's still questioning herself when Alyssa runs from behind her toward the strange spacecraft.

"Uncle Rob, Uncle Rob," Alyssa cries, running to the strange vehicle. Courtney panics for a moment before the image of Rob walking around the rear of the craft registers in her brain. He bends down with open arms to greet Alyssa. He snatches her and lifts her, giving her a big squeeze and a kiss on her bloodied cheek.

Courtney stands with her hands on her hips, looking like a determined woman. She looks down from the porch at a smiling Uncle Rob. "Really? You show up to save us in the Space Shuttle?"

"You're darn right. That baby saved my life on the way here, and she'll protect us on the way to the hideaway. I got her cheap… at what you might call a government spacecraft rummage sale. She might look silly, but if there's another blast, you'll be happy we have her. Let's load up and get out of here."

Courtney doesn't argue or hesitate. She ducks inside the house, returning with a suitcase in each hand. Alyssa grabs her suitcase and Ethan's duffle. Uncle Rob reaches to take a suitcase from Courtney. She hands him both. "I have to get my photos," she says, running back to the house.

Rob and Alyssa go to the rear of the space vehicle to load the suitcases into the old Suburban hidden beneath the X-37 shell.

As Ethan runs down the street, he encounters a strange sight. A spaceship is parked in front of his house! It looks like the ancient space shuttle. Ethan recognizes it because he has a model hanging from the ceiling in his room.

As Ethan gets closer, he sees Alyssa and Uncle Rob loading suitcases into the ship. Alyssa spots Ethan running and jumps up and down screaming, pointing at Ethan. "There he is! There's Ethan! Hurry, Ethan!"

As Courtney walks out of the house carrying the box of family photos, she was so relieved to see her son she almost drops the box. The sight of Ethan stops her in her tracks. New tears freshen the moisture on her face.

Rob yells out. "Glad to see you, boy. Help your mother and let's go!"

Ethan rushes to the porch steps, taking the box of photos from his mother. As they walk to the spaceship, Ethan faces his mother. "I'm sorry, Mom." New tears gush. "I should have been here when—when it happened." Courtney hugs her son. He's shaking and crying. She hugs him tighter as he tries to talk through his convulsing tears. "I was so afraid it hurt you and Alyssa."

"We're fine, baby. Uncle Rob is here for us. We're going to his cave. We'll be safe there." Courtney speaks in a whispered, loving tone to her son.

Ethan cries as they walk to Alyssa. He looks through his tears at his twin sister. He observes her wounds and the streaks of dried blood on her cheeks. He smiles between his sobs and asks, "Is that your war paint?"

Alyssa can't see her face. She doesn't realize blood is smeared across her cheeks, but she feels the stinging pain and will not let the comment go without response. "Yes! I am fighting the war and helping Mom while you're out playing with your girlfriend, Vanessa," putting an emphasis on the word *girlfriend*.

Ordinarily, Ethan would not let such an offense go unanswered. He'd retaliate in good sibling rivalry fashion, but this time he walks to Uncle Rob, handing over the box of photos, allowing Alyssa's assault to go without physical or verbal response.

Rob takes the box, shuffling the suitcases and animal cages to make room as Ethan stands stiff and silent. Rob finds a spot for the box and secures the rear doors. "OK. Duck under the shell and squeeze into the truck. Let's get moving," orders Rob. He observes Ethan's quiet demeanor. "Ethan, you're riding shotgun. Men in the front. Women in the passenger row."

Courtney and Alyssa have no qualms about the seating arrangement and scurry to their places. Rob starts the truck and hits the gas, catapulting the spacecraft down the street. Rob chuckles as he pushes the gas harder, grinding and screeching past cars and trucks lining the road. At the end of the street, he turns on to a wider street, zigzagging past abandoned cars.

"The freeway is a mess. We'll take the side streets till we get to Azusa Avenue. No worries though. We'll be at the hideaway soon."

Uncle Rob navigates the X-37 covered Suburban past wrecked, crashed, burned-out cars and buildings along the streets of Pasadena. They drive through death, seeking safety in a hideaway dug deep inside a mountain. A place he gambled on, forsook his reputation for, and risked sanity to prepare for his family. He drives, thankful they have a safe place to go.

Ethan sits quiet and still in the front seat of the Suburban. His tears have dried, but he wears guilt like a plaid shirt. Courtney and Alyssa sit close together in the passenger seat. Courtney stares at the destruction on the video screens. Alyssa turns around to look at the piglets, lambs, and chickens.

Rob observes Ethan. He is quiet, staring ahead, caught up in his thoughts. He looks suddenly grown up. He doesn't look like a silly little boy anymore. "You OK, boy?" Rob asks. Ethan doesn't answer. Rob swerves to miss a big truck burning in the middle of the road. He looks at the stoic boy. "Had a rough day? We all did. You'll be all right. We'll get to the mine, and we'll all be all right. It's my promise, boy." Ethan turns his dirty face streaked with dried tears to his uncle and gives a small nod. Rob nods back.

A bright streak in the distant eastern sky cuts through growing darkness. The streak lingers as it races across the sky, appearing in the front, then the side video screens. It seems to move in slow motion, then explodes in a bright white flash, turning screens pure white before fading to black.

Rob turns the strange space vehicle on to Foothill Boulevard as another streak crosses the sky and explodes in a blinding flash. This one is faster, closer, and louder. Moments later, the sound of hundreds of rocks pelting the top and sides of the X-37 reverberates within the safe cocoon.

Rob thumps the dashboard with his hand. "They said I was crazy. Today, crazy is good. Hang on kids, we'll be there in no time." Rob guns the engine. The X-37 covered Suburban chugs up the road with black smoke pouring out of the exhaust.

Chapter 32: Allies and Foes

Washington, DC–12:10 A.M. Thursday Morning

The drive to the White House is slow. Wrecked and burning cars block the roads. Debris from toppled buildings spills into the streets. Fire trucks, ambulances, and police cruisers struggle to move around the city in the deep, gritty fallout.

People bewildered by the strange events crowd the sidewalks, stepping clumsily through the thick dirt. They don't understand what has happened. The air is hot. Dust rains down. This is not a peaceful and tranquil storm. Rocks and fragments up to five feet in diameter fall randomly from the sky, slamming into cars, buildings, and people.

The twenty-minute drive to the White House stretches past sixty minutes. The dirt is now nearly two feet deep. The black four-wheel drive Suburban advances slowly in soft deep grit. Dennis drives judiciously, careful not to get stuck behind wrecked cars. Tug is anxious. They aren't far from the White House, but they're moving too slowly. Tug looks at his wife. She gazes out the window with a blank stare.

Tug has not let a minute go to waste. He's been on the sat phone the entire time. After several calls, he has a grip on the big picture. "Dennis, quit pussyfooting. Get us to the White House, posthaste, or I'll toss you out and drive this rig myself."

Dennis does not require additional motivation. He drives on the sidewalk to the end of the street, then turns right on to Seventieth Street NW. They are now just blocks from the northwest gate.

The large Suburban drives around the barricades at Seventieth and Pennsylvania Ave NW. The wind knocked over the guard shack, but Marines stand post. One of the Marines waves the vehicle through and minutes later, it comes to a stop outside the West Wing, where a medical team waits to greet the Secretary of Defense and his wife.

211

Tug helps the medical team get Joan onto a gurney. "These fellas will take care of you. I need to see Cliff. I'll check on you soon." Tug leans down and gives his wife a soft peck on her dusty, blood-streaked cheek. Tears well up in reaction to her husband's unusual public show of affection.

U.S. Secret Service personnel led Tug to the Deep Underground Command Center. Video screens cover the walls displaying news streams. Tug looks across a large conference table and observes Cliff Baker, Mitch Campbell, and Jerome Hargrove, all looking exhausted. Tug assumes they have been working tirelessly to assess the cause of the explosion, gather damage reports, and direct recovery efforts. He doesn't know they are battling the effects of a whiskey drunk that's wearing off.

Cliff Baker drowsily looks across the conference table. "Tug! You made it. Tell us what you know. Where is General Mahon?"

Tug stands rigidly at the end of the long conference table. "The city is in ruins. What didn't topple over is burning. Two feet of gritty fallout blankets the city. Most vehicles can't get through the stuff."

Jerome wakes when he hears the word fallout. He pulls off his VUE in panic. "We've seen the dirt piling up on the news reports. It's fallout? You mean it was nuclear?"

Cliff jumps in. "You said it wasn't nuclear. You're saying it was an attack?"

Tug is too tired for overreacting politicians. "Gentlemen, I am using the term fallout to describe debris that results from an explosion. It could be from a big bomb or a volcano. I believe we can rule out the volcano, so the fallout accumulating across the city is from one hell of a huge bomb, or something else. As I said before, I don't believe it's nuclear—just my gut feeling. It's too early for radiation burns to appear. If we're dead three days from now from radiation sickness, you'll know I was wrong."

Jerome hurriedly checks his VUE and types in the air, apparently searching for the effects of nuclear radiation. A few moments later he mumbles, "Oh, my. Oh, dear."

Mitch ignores Jerome's hysterics. "So, if it's not nuclear, what caused so much damage? Certainly, no conventional weapon I've ever been briefed on."

Tug voices the thoughts nagging him since the explosion. "Remember what the president was rambling about. The sky is falling. A storm is coming. Must get underground. He also mentioned Perth and the earthquake in Chile."

Cliff chugs black coffee, hoping to shake off his hangover. "Those were the ravings of a demented man. He's sick. He didn't know what he was saying."

"I beg your pardon, sir. There is no other reasonable explanation. We now know an asteroid destroyed Perth. The message we received warned of more impacts. Tonight, Washington is in ruins. What other conclusion seems likely?"

Mitch reacts as if a light switch flipped on. "An asteroid hit us. He said a storm is coming. Could he mean an asteroid storm? Are more coming? Is it possible?"

Cliff is startled into awareness. He feels like he's been drenched with a bucket of cold water. The effects of whiskey are replaced with anger. "What else did that fool say? Get underground. Get to the new cities. The new cities. It's Cruikshank. He knew. That's what he wasn't telling us. That bastard knew this was coming and didn't warn anyone."

Jerome looks to the vice president. "In his defense, Cruikshank told you to find a deep hole and stay there."

"So, if an asteroid storm is coming, we must assume Perth and D.C. are not the last of it. It seems Cruikshank and his cronies planned for this. Where did he go? They built city's underground. Is that where he took the president?" asks Mitch.

Cliff slams his fist on the table. "The Arcadians. The few and the fortunate. He is saving them in underground cities, leaving the rest of us sitting ducks in an asteroid storm. I told you he's an evil bastard."

Tug remains standing at the end of the conference table. "We need to learn more about what's happening. I've been making calls. Gentlemen, we have other problems. I could not reach General Mahon, but I have spoken with the Secretaries of the Army, Navy, Air Force, and Commandant of the Marine Corps. The Army and Navy are with the Arcadians. The Air Force and Marines are with us."

Cliff struggles to remain composed. "Cruikshank worked to overthrow the government. Now he controls half the military. I admit it, the old bastard has out maneuvered me at every turn. I'm running ten steps behind that rusty old colonel. But this is the United States of America, dammit, not Arcadia, and I mean to keep it that way. We can still turn this around. We need to up our game. Get a full cabinet meeting here at once or as many that are alive and ready to fight with us. Call JPL and NASA. We need control of telescopes and satellites so we can see what's headed for Earth. Get Homeland to secure food and oil reserves. Locate underground bunkers for our personnel. Where is Charles? We need his input—"

Tug interrupts Cliff. "Charles didn't make it. Charles and Joyce Pritchett were at the same restaurant as Joan and me. Both are dead. Several others are dead or severely wounded. Sorry, Cliff. I know he was a good friend."

Cliff Baker sinks in his chair, letting his chin fall to his chest.

"I'm sorry to report most of Homeland isn't with us. I don't think Charles knew. Many of the departments under Homeland are with the Arcadians. It's like he had the whole thing pulled out from under him."

Cliff lifts his head. "Well, I know what that feels like. Charles Adams was an honorable man and a great asset to America. We will sorely miss him." Cliff pauses a moment before continuing. "All right. It's time we get ahead of the situation. We need to gather information and formulate plans. We need to protect and save as many resources and lives as we can."

Jerome pipes in. "This meteor storm is actually good cover for the ARC problem. All the news outlets will report the disaster. News of ARC won't see the light of day."

Mitch gives Jerome kudos. "Smartest thing you've said all night."

"I agree with your line of thought, Mr. Vice President. I've been working to get in touch with JPL." Tug Grimes touches his band. "Gentlemen, I have Dr. Donald Simmons online. He was, until recently, the acting director of JPL. As you know, JPL is closed because of budget cuts. Let's see what he can tell us."

Tug swipes his hand, and the image of Dr. Simmons appears on a large, thin screen. "Dr. Simmons, I apologize for the late call. If you've seen the news, you know we have a major disaster here in Washington. We need your input. We believe an asteroid caused the disaster. If it was an asteroid, are more coming? Please give us your opinion."

Dr. Simmons looks to be crouching behind his desk in a dark room. Long black uncombed hair and large dark eyes make him look paranoid. When he notices the vice president, he looks more frightened. "How did you find me? My band has blocking codes. You shouldn't be able to reach me. I'm not traveling to any of your seminars, if that's what you have in mind."

"Dr. Simmons. We aren't calling about a seminar. There's been a terrible disaster. We need your help."

"Too many of my best engineers and scientists went missing attending your conferences. Lured away, never to return. What am I supposed to think when Washington calls?"

"Dr. Simmons. I can assure you that the US government did not authorize those actions. We need your help and expertise. What do you know about these asteroids?" Cliff Baker implores.

Dr. Simmons' look of paranoia changes to a look of, I told you so. "A disaster in Washington? That's what it takes to get someone in power to listen? We've been reporting the potential danger of an asteroid bombardment for months to Homeland Security to FEMA to the National Security Advisor. But our reports fell on deaf ears. Then our director and the last of our project managers went to seminars. Most haven't returned. Our resources were systematically reduced over the past five years. Funding cuts forced us to lay-off staff. We closed monitoring stations and shut down missions. You cut our programs and budgets, then cut them again until we had to close the facility. It's as if someone didn't want us to warn people."

Mitch jumps in. "Dr. Simmons, we understand your anger and frustration. There are people who have worked to undermine the government. We've got to move past that and focus on solutions. You said asteroid bombardment. So, you've answered our question. More asteroids are coming. How many? How long will this last? We've got to know what we're up against to create an action plan to save as many people and resources as we can."

"I need to get space-based and terrestrial systems up immediately. We need people and resources. We need fresh data on the number of asteroids and comets moving our way."

Cliff replies excitedly. "Dr. Simmons, you've got it. You'll have our full support. How long is this going to last? How bad is the situation?"

215

"Mr. Vice President, I will send our last report. It's almost four months old, but we warned of a potentially catastrophic asteroid bombardment lasting from several weeks to three months. Homeland told us measures were being taken to protect the public, but they never told us what measures they were taking. They ordered us to not release the information to news outlets, then gutted our staff and shut down our facilities. They said they would make announcements at the appropriate time. I'd say, it's time." Dr. Simmons lets out a deep sigh.

Tug leans in to show a sense of support for the troubled doctor. "Dr. Simmons, thank you for your candor and honesty. Representatives of the Air Force will contact you and provide you with the personnel and support you need. I authorize you to call up all JPL personnel. Get them back to work ASAP. Contact me directly with news and updates on the asteroid weather report."

"We'll kick start NASA. We'll have a Marine detachment posted at JPL headquarters to make sure you have no trouble. You have a direct line to me any time you need it," Cliff offers.

"Thank you, Mr. Vice President and ah… sir, sirs. Thanks to all of you. I'll pull a team together and get an update ASAP."

Cliff Baker stands, the whiskey consumed earlier, now converted to adrenaline. "Gentlemen, we have a long night ahead. Tomorrow will be a longer day. Get everyone here now! I don't care if they walk through knee-deep sludge. I want everyone here. We need to get on top of the damage reports. Schedule a press conference warning people of the asteroid storm. We need experts advising people how to protect themselves. We need to secure food, water, and fuel. We've got to find out where these Arcadians have us outmaneuvered and get in the game."

Cliff pauses for a moment to look around the room. He hoped more people would have been there to see him acting presidential. "Where is my assistant? Let's get on this!"

Chapter 33: Munday's Hideaway

Uncle Rob drives up the curvy San Gabriel Canyon Road, past the San Gabriel Reservoir, then turns onto East Fork Road, which follows the San Gabriel River into Shoemaker Canyon.

The road narrows, and the pavement becomes gravel. As they drive deeper into the canyon, the road degrades to a dirt track through the wilderness.

The extra weight of the X-37 strains the old truck. After five miles of driving through huge potholes and traversing the shallow river three times, the dirt trail takes a sharp right turn. The truck drives up a long steady rise before the road widens and levels out.

As they crest the hill, the screens inside the old truck display the image of an arched bridge spanning a canyon. There is a large flat gravel area in front of the bridge and an old, rusted shipping container on the left. Rob brings the Suburban to a stop. The white cement bridge glows in the bright beams of the aircraft lights mounted on the X-37.

"Wow, that's cool," says Alyssa.

"Did somebody misplace a bridge?" asks Courtney.

Rob is tickled by their reaction. "It's the Bridge to Nowhere."

Ethan's mood has not changed, but he can't hold back his interest in the strange bridge. "Because it's in the middle of nowhere?"

"Because it leads nowhere. See, it's a dead end," Alyssa says, pointing.

"You're both right. A long time ago, a road was being built between the San Gabriel Valley and the small town of Wrightwood on the north side of the mountains. During the winter of 1938, there was a flood that wiped out the road. The bridge construction was already complete. After the flood, they gave up building the road, so here sits a bridge in the middle of the canyon, leading to nowhere. I present the Bridge to Nowhere."

The kids and Courtney laugh and Rob laughs with them.

"For many years, the road was no more than a narrow hiking trail. Weekend hikers and bungee jumpers were the only people to visit this lonesome bridge. That old shipping container stored bungee jumping equipment."

"Bungee jumping. I wish we could try that," says Alyssa.

"Before there was a bridge to nowhere, do you know what the San Gabriel River was known for?"

"Fishing?" Ethan offers.

"Nope. Gold mining."

"Gold mining. Here? I thought they did all the gold mining in Northern California," says Courtney.

"People have mined the San Gabriel River, off and on, for over one hundred and fifty years. In the early 1930s, there was a small village with huts and shops for miners. There was a large mining excavation in the riverbed a mile downstream from the bridge. Mines were dug into the mountainsides. The gold rush didn't last, neither did the village. The flood of 1938 wiped out everything, including the road. Then in 2023 some guy discovered a large gold deposit, and gold fever was back! The road we just traveled was re-built."

"I wouldn't call that much of a road," Courtney declares.

"Well, like most gold strikes, it soon went bust, and they stopped maintaining the road. Now, we drive over the bridge and we're home."

"Is the bridge safe?" Courtney asks in a concerned tone.

"Rock solid. They built this bridge to last. It's in great shape. I drive across almost every day," Rob says, as he slowly drives onto the bridge.

"On the far side of the bridge, we take a quick right turn, or we'll drive directly into the side of the mountain." Rob maneuvers the sharp turn, drives sixty feet to the end of the dirt road, and stops. He leaves the aircraft lights on, pointing up the canyon.

Everyone piles out of the old space shuttle and looks around. "Here we are. Great spot, isn't it?" says Rob.

"I thought we're going to a cave. I don't see any caves around here," says Ethan.

"Well, it's called a hideaway. It's supposed to be a secret, so I made it hard to spot. It's tough to see during the day, so if you don't know where to look, the entrance is nearly impossible to see in the dark. I don't want strangers showing up without an invitation. Follow me." Rob grabs a flashlight and leads the group along the trail lit by the aircraft lights. The rocky trail hugs a steep hillside that drops nearly straight down, one hundred feet to the river below.

Courtney stays next to the space shuttle. "That looks dangerous."

"It's perfectly safe, dear," Rob says.

Rob walks along the trail until he disappears beyond a rocky outcropping. Thirty yards past the outcropping, there was a narrow recess in the mountainside populated with large bushes and small trees. The trail continues past this point. A hiker would walk past the recess and continue walking up the canyon.

Rob stops at the bushy recess and calls out. "Come on! It's just in here."

Alyssa runs back to her mom.

"Hurry, Mom," Ethan calls to encourage his mother.

Alyssa holds Courtney's hand, pulling her mother along the trail. As Courtney walks, she notices the trail is wider and less scary than it looked. Alyssa and Courtney make it around the rocky outcropping and find Rob and Ethan waiting for them.

Instead of continuing down the trail, Rob walks into the bushes growing in the recessed area along the mountainside. He reaches into a bush, inserts a key into a lock, and pulls open a cyclone fence gate with plants growing on it. The gate and steel fence posts are painted to match the color of the dirt and rocks, camouflaging them. The cyclone gate is built into the mountainside, covering the entrance. Rob pulls the gate open wider to reveal the entrance of the mine.

"This is so cool." Ethan jumps with excitement. "Can we go inside?"

"That's the idea. You can prop the gate open with that stick behind you. Let's go!" Uncle Rob leads the way.

The entrance is dark and the rock roughhewn. Rob beams a flashlight into the mine. Five feet inside the cave is a wooden door painted gray, secured with a heavy chain, a big lock and warning signs. One sign reads DANGER DO NOT ENTER. Another sign has skull and crossbones, with a chemical insignia underneath the words: DANGEROUS GASES - SUDDEN DEATH WILL OCCUR. A third sign looks official, posted by the County: UNSTABLE - CAVE-

IN–DO NOT ENTER. Pasted on the door is an old, yellowed newspaper clipping with a photo of a young man, and an article describing how he died in an old mine, presumably this one.

"We are not going inside there. Rob, this is quite enough. Kids, we're going back," Courtney says in a panicked tone.

"Relax. sweetheart. I designed this to scare people away."

Courtney shudders, feeling goosebumps on her arms. "Well, it's working."

"See the little altar." Rob moves the beam of his flashlight to an altar mounted in a small niche carved out of the rock wall. "Nice touch, don't you think?" The flashlight illuminates burned candles, a statue of Mother Mary, and dried flowers placed in the small niche. Rob laughs as he unlocks the chain.

"Just one more door till you see the living quarters."

Alyssa and Ethan are pushing to move forward. "Kids backup, don't crowd your uncle," says their mother.

Courtney stands rigid with her arms crossed talking to herself. "Is he crazy? This is all crazy. We're in a damp, dark, abandoned mine that might collapse on us any second and he's taking my children inside."

The kids follow on the heels of Uncle Rob as he moves through the rough-cut tunnel. Courtney moves only because she doesn't want to be alone in the dark.

"They dug this mine into a mountain of solid granite. I assure you, it won't cave in. It was dug in the early 1900s to mine gold. They found veins of quartz and gold running through the granite. They dug deeper and deeper, following the veins, mining out the gold ore. They must have done well. The mine has two levels and goes nine hundred feet into the mountain. They abandoned the mine in the 1930s before the bridge was constructed," Rob explains as they walk deeper into the mine. "I bought the mine four years ago and have been working on this little project ever since."

Rob comes to a steel door welded to iron braces embedded in the cave walls. The door looks like one you would see in a submarine with a metal wheel that turns to unlock the door. A lock and chain secure the wheel.

Rob removes the chain, turns the wheel, and pulls the heavy door open. "I call this the blast door. It's three inches of solid steel built into the cave wall. I got it secondhand from a scrap yard. It used to be on a navy ship. Nothing is getting through this door. Hopefully, no one uninvited will ever venture this far." He looks at Courtney, who seems in shock. "Hopefully, the threat of death by cave-ins and toxic gas will keep most people out." Rob laughs.

Courtney nods agreement.

"Come Inside, let me show you our humble mountain retreat." Rob steps across the threshold of the blast door and flips the lights on.

A rocky tunnel comes into view. Overhead LED lights hang every ten feet, illuminating the mine shaft. The tunnel is tall and wide. The floor is solid granite; roughhewn but flat. The air is cool. The walls are damp. A small gutter cut into the sides of the floor drains away the dripping water. Ten feet down the tunnel is an opening the size of a large bedroom cut into the left side of the mine. The room is brightly lit. A large wooden worktable sits in the center of the room. Gun lockers line the walls of the room.

"This room is the armory. If we ever need to defend ourselves, I've got guns, ammo, and a few surprises. Hopefully, we never need it, but you never know what will happen when people are desperate. You'll notice more rooms like this one along the mine shaft. Come along. The room on the right is for general storage, clothing, blankets, and sundries," Rob explains as they walk through the tunnel, passing a carpentry workshop with a worktable, wheelbarrows, ladders, saws, and other tools.

The mine shaft curves sharply to the left before they enter a large room with a high ceiling. The room is a long, wide, rocky gallery. The ceiling is twenty-five-feet high, giving the space a dramatic ambiance. The granite ceiling and walls glisten in the bright lights. Thin veins of white quartz run the length of the room along the ceilings and walls.

"This is the main gallery. It's a natural structure inside the mountain. Have a look around. I'm not the best at decorating, so I copied pictures of a model home."

Courtney spins slowly around, looking at the amazing room that features an expansive wood floor with large area rugs surrounded by groupings of modern couches and chairs. Ethan and Alyssa explore the room.

221

"Hey. There's an entire wall covered with thin-screen," shouts Ethan.

"We have a thousand movies and TV shows stored, ready for viewing," added Rob.

"Mom, look! There's a library filled with hundreds of books— actual books," Alyssa cries.

"I love the dark wood shelves and the wooden ladder, too," says Courtney.

Beyond the living room are two long dining tables with benches; each table large enough to seat a dozen or more people. Decorative chandeliers hang over the dining tables. Ethan stands in front of two large windows cut into the rock wall, parallel with the dining tables. "Whoa. We have windows. I thought we're in a mine. I can see the bridge outside, and there's the river. Hey? Isn't it nighttime?"

"I designed these windows to make the place seem larger and to bring the outside in. Each window is a whopping thirteen feet wide by eight feet high. They aren't real windows, but they look realistic, don't they? Rest assured; we are in the mine. I have cameras mounted several places outside, and I have many stored live motion landscapes. The windows will help us feel like we're someplace other than inside a mountain. If you don't like the view of the canyon, we can change it. Watch this," he explains.

The windows instantly display a live scene of the Oregon coast, with waves crashing on a rocky shoreline. "There you go. You now live at the beach. The perspective gives you the perception of looking out the front window of a beach house." Rob turns with his arms stretched wide. "This is the main gallery. What do you think? Do you like it?"

"Rob, this is amazing. It looks like a hotel suite. I admit it's not what I expected to find inside a cave," Courtney says, as she strolls through the gallery. "How did you ever get the money to—"

"Courtney, sweetie, if I'd told you and Rick what I was doing up here, you'd think I was crazy. So, I kept the project under wraps. You would have tried to stop me."

"We certainly would have stopped you. You built a house in a cave just in case a disaster struck? This is too much. How much did this cost?" asks Courtney.

"But it came in handy tonight, didn't it, Uncle Rob?" Ethan states, as he moves around the room, testing the furniture.

"Yes, siree, mister. I built this place because I believed Earth at some point would suffer a major catastrophe. I didn't know if it would happen in my lifetime or the children's. I felt I needed to prepare a refuge. The asteroid impacts are horrible. At least we're safe, and we will survive this," Rob explains.

"I can totally live in here," Alyssa says as she runs to a couch and plops down on the cushion.

"Well, you haven't seen it all. Gather round my desk." Rob directs them to the far end of the room where he has a control center with a large monitor mounted on the wall over a large desk. "From here we can check the status of various systems throughout the mine complex, such as power generation, water filtration, irrigation, air conditioning, lighting, interior and exterior cameras."

"Cool," says Ethan.

"I'll give you a quick overview of the hideaway layout. You'll have plenty of time to explore things on your own. The hideaway is a fully self-contained, self-sustaining environment. That means it will take care of us as long as we take care of it. Watch the screen as I describe the features of our hideaway. Just past the main room is the galley. There is a fully furnished restaurant style kitchen with a pantry, food prep area, and a walk-in refrigerator. I got all this cheap at a restaurant supply bankruptcy sale," Rob says cheerfully. "After the galley are the living quarters with nicely furnished rooms." The thin screen displays an image of a bedroom.

"That looks cozy," says Alyssa.

"There are several rooms like this along the main shaft. The goal was to develop an environment that allows up to fifteen people to live comfortably for several years."

"Years! Did you say years?" Courtney asks.

"Prepare for the worst. Just in case, dear," Rob says, in a consoling tone. "The living quarters include personal hygiene areas with toilets, showers, sinks, and what not. We've got his and hers, but it's somewhat communal. The showers and toilet stalls are private."

"Well, if we have to stay here a while, at least we'll be clean," says Ethan.

"That will be an improvement for you," Alyssa teases.

"Hey." says Ethan.

"We equipped the hideaway with ample water storage, water filtration, recycling, and composting systems. Solid waste makes great fertilizer. Just wait and see."

"Who is we, Rob? You and who else?" asks Courtney.

"What? We, oh..." Rob stammers.

"You couldn't have done all this work by yourself. Who helped you build all this?"

"Oh, Martinez Construction. Very nice young men. Eddie and Rodrigo. They're smart engineers and very handy. Couldn't have done it without them. You'll be meeting them soon. The deal was, if we ever need to use the hideaway, the Martinez brothers and their families will join us. I got a big discount on the work. Part of my negotiation. They are sworn to secrecy about the location and the capabilities we've developed here," Rob explains.

"We have to share our cave house with people we don't know?" Alyssa asks.

"Yes, dearie. Don't worry. They're very nice people. Rodrigo has a boy about your age. I think Eddie also has kids, so you'll have playmates while we live here," Rob says with a wink. "Look here on the map. There are stairs to the lower level, where the more interesting parts of our environment are located—."

"Oh yeah. I saw it on the blueprints. We have a garden and a farm," cries Ethan.

"That's right, son. The garden and farm make use of other galleries, like the main gallery. These are natural spaces in the mountain. Kind of like giant bubbles in the granite. Luckily, we didn't have to excavate much to create the spaces. We installed special grow lights down there so we can grow all sorts of fruit and veggies. We've got orange, apple, and lemon trees, and your typical garden veggies. We've got to work together, but we can grow enough food here to keep everyone well fed and nourished," Rob instructs.

"Especially if we're vegetarians," says Alyssa.

"I am very impressed, Rob. It seems you've thought of everything," Courtney says.

"Well, we aren't finished. There are a few more things to tell you about before we unpack the truck and get moved in. The farm contains livestock pens and a chicken coop." The screen displays an image of the farm in a rocky gallery with a low ceiling.

"A farm with a red barn and everything. Wow, Uncle Rob, this is cool," says Ethan.

"Well, the barn is cheeky, but no harm, no foul. You'll be unloading the chickens, pigs, and lambs and putting them in their pens, young man. You said you wanted bacon and eggs."

"So, we won't be vegetarians?" asks Alyssa.

"You can if you want. I'll eat eggs and bacon," Ethan says, pushing his sister aside to get a better look at the farm.

"One last treat to show you. I call it the Atrium." The thin screen displays images of a circular room with a low, narrow entry. The roof of the gallery is like a cathedral rising to a peaked ceiling at least sixty feet high. Lights around the perimeter of the floor point up to the ceiling, illuminating the room in a rainbow of colors. Embedded in the walls are wide ribbons of white quartz and veins of gold sparkling in the light. Soft, peaceful music plays in the background. A bench sits at the center of the gallery.

"We stumbled on this gallery when we enlarged the opening to the farm. Good thing the miners never found this room. They would have mined the gold, destroying this masterpiece." Courtney and the kids stand silently in awe of the room.

"It's beautiful," says Courtney.

"I love it," says Alyssa.

"If we're cooped up in this cave, this will be a nice spot to spend some private time. It's beautiful, Rob," says Courtney.

Ethan doesn't grasp the concept of peace, solitude, or quiet time, so he tugs on Uncle Rob's hand to get his attention. "The map shows a door at the end of the mine shaft. What's that?"

"It's a back door!" exclaims Alyssa.

"No, I bet it's an escape hatch," counters Ethan.

Rob stands, shaking his head.

Courtney puts a hand on Ethan's shoulder and squeezes. "There is no back door or escape hatch. Is there, Rob? What is it?" Courtney asks cautiously.

Ethan, using his finger, traces the map of the hideaway, silently mouthing the words of the environmental systems, then pauses, turns his head and squints.

"Is this what it looks like when he's thinking?" Rob asks.

"I'm not sure. We've never seen him think before," replies Alyssa.

"It's the power station," the boy says enthusiastically.

"Right you are," says Rob, surprised by Ethan's guess.

Ethan looks like he's thinking again. "But what type of fuel? We can't store enough gas or diesel, besides the exhaust would kill us. We're in a mine, solar is out. You said we can live here for years. So, what's the power source?" Ethan asks.

"Quite a quandary. It was one of the biggest problems to solve. But, thanks to government budget cuts, I got my hands on this beauty."

The screen displays a small room with a cylinder that is shorter and fatter than a typical water heater found in American homes. Attached to the cylinder is a large metal box. A shaft runs between the metal box and a generator. The generator has a thick cable running to a power inverter and junction box.

Everyone looks at the water heater contraption with confusion.

"What is it?" asks Alyssa.

"It looks like a big battery," says Ethan.

"Well, it is like a battery of sorts. It generates heat, which moves fluid in that metal box. The moving fluid turns the generator and voila! Let there be light," Rob explains.

Ethan examines the sophisticated yet simple contraption. "Ah. Is this what I think it is?" Ethan asks, with a puzzled look at Uncle Rob.

"It's a simple process. A chemical reaction that creates heat, discovered over one hundred years ago, involving very hot salts. There are no moving parts in the module. It can generate more power than we will ever need for up to twenty years, based on our expected consumption levels."

"What kind of salt exactly?" asks Ethan.

"Well, um, it's a natural reaction," Rob says, as he moves to whisper in Ethan's ear. "It's Uranium Hydride at a 10 percent level." Rob pauses. "It's self-contained, self-monitoring, factory-sealed, fully shielded, incredibly stable and safe."

"Uranium," Ethan says loudly.

"Uranium! Robert! You're exposing my children to radiation!" Courtney screams, freaking out. Courtney grabs Alyssa and Ethan by the hand and moves rapidly through the main gallery toward the blast door.

Rob chases after them. "Sweetie, it's incredibly safe. Maybe I shouldn't have mentioned the uranium part." Rob catches up with Courtney and the kids and stops them. "Courtney, relax. I've studied every reactor type."

"It's a nuclear reactor?" shouts Courtney, as she marches through the blast door, pulling the kids behind her.

"Honey, slow down. Let me explain. It's not the kind of reactor used in old power plants. Universities have used this type of reactor for research and NASA has used them in spacecraft for decades, with no accidents."

"I was beginning to relax. But, underground farms and nuclear reactors, preparing all this to live underground for who knows how long. I can't! I won't live like this!" Courtney sobs.

Alyssa comforts her mother. Courtney trembles. Rob stands in front of the girls with his hands on his hips.

"I know. It's a lot to absorb. I think you are scaring the kids more than my nuclear reactor did."

Courtney looks down at Alyssa. Alyssa looks up with wide eyes as she tightens her arms around her mother's waist. Alyssa asks, "Are you gonna be OK, Mom?"

Ethan tries to soothe his mother's fears. "Don't worry, Mom. It's like we're in a nuclear submarine cruising under the seas. Nuclear submarines don't blow up or meltdown or whatever, do they, Uncle Rob?"

"No. Not that I know of."

"See, it's the same, except we're cruising under a mountain in a mine shaft instead of underwater in a submarine. At least we can breathe and go outside if we need to," Ethan rationalizes to help calm his mother.

"Courtney, I didn't mean to shock you or the kids. The technology is stable. It cannot go supercritical or meltdown. It's not possible. It's a fully sealed, self-contained system and does not emit radiation. It's safe to stand next to the device. If it wasn't safe, do you think they would have built it for the Explorer Three manned space mission?"

"You mean Explorer two? I've never heard of Explorer Three," says Courtney.

"Work on Explorer Three was almost complete when they canned the project. After Northrup canceled the project, they had spare parts lying around. I borrowed the power system."

"Borrowed?" questions Ethan.

"Well, I checked it out for research. They weren't going to use it, and it solved our power problem," Rob explains.

"I don't think you can check out nuclear power systems like library books, Robert," says Courtney.

"Well, I did, and they haven't come asking for it, so finders keepers!"

"See Mom. It's just like living in a submarine," Ethan says.

"With much better furniture and bigger beds!" exclaims Alyssa.

"But we need a periscope," Ethan says.

"I'll show you that later," Uncle Rob says with a wink. "Let's get moved in."

Chapter 34: De-Railed

After Rick's battle against Captain Kobalt and the Buzz-Bees, he settles into a comfortable seat at the front of the railcar to take a nap. He has a couple of hours to relax before arriving in New Zion. He takes a few drags on Karl's pipe to clear his mind.

The Black Guard will wait for the car at New Zion station. The odds are low that he will make it out of the rail car before being relaxed. He will be captured and confined. Rick knows all this. He also knows he will never stop. He will never give up. Somehow, he will get home to Courtney, his children, and Uncle Rob.

The rail car speeds along, moving nearly as fast as a bullet through the smooth underground tunnel to New Zion. The vibration of the rail car traveling at 720 miles per hour is like a soft massage. He falls into a deep slumber and dreams of battling the Black Guard.

The railcar is speeding through the smooth dark tunnel in a near vacuum at seven hundred twenty miles per hour when the car suddenly slams into one side of the tunnel, bounces off and slams into the other side of the tunnel, making horrendous metal screeching sounds. The rail car goes from 720 miles per hour to a grinding halt in seconds.

Rick flies three feet, smashing into the metal wall at the front of the car. The bodies of the passengers at the rear of the car cartwheel over rows of seats, breaking bones and slamming into the front wall of the railcar.

Rick lies on the floor. One of the male passengers' smacks headfirst into the wall. The limp body falls on Rick. He pushes the dead weight off him. The power has failed. It is dark and silent. He reaches around in the dark to find the flashlight in his backpack.

Rick checks the wrecked car using his flashlight to locate the other passengers. He spots the husband and wife. Their bodies are twisted, and limbs contorted, most assuredly dead.

Kobalt and his Elite Guard arrive in the underground city of New Zion. Maintenance personnel scramble to the jets, moving them to large elevator platforms that lower the Scramjets to an underground hangar and maglev launch facility below Front Range Airport.

Lieutenant Astatine is present to greet Captain Kobalt. Astatine is a tall, slender man with dark hair and a thin, manicured mustache. He is the leader of the New Zion Black Guard. "Welcome Captain. We will go directly to the Rail Station in my maglev car."

Kobalt and Astatine enter the car. The Elite Guard follows in a levitating troop carrier. The vehicles move briskly through the New Zion corridors, passing large caverns filled with cattle and other animals. Kobalt views the cows in large corrals. "Now I know the source of the smell I detected when I arrived. I hope all of New Zion doesn't suffer from this stench."

"Don't worry about the smell. The livestock pens are far from the main city. But be sure to thank us the next time you enjoy a real beef steak in New Arcadia," Astatine replies.

After several minutes, the maglev car and troop carrier arrive at the Rail Station. Captain Kobalt and Lieutenant Astatine walk smartly through the station as the guard march in formation behind them.

Astatine receives a call on his VUE from City Command. "Lieutenant, we have an alert on the New Arcadia tube."

Lieutenant Astatine relays the news to Kobalt. "There's a problem with the rail tube. I'm touching you in with City Command."

Kobalt reacts. "Commander, what's the problem? Where is Dr. Munday?"

"We're investigating," the commander replies. "We received an alert of sudden pressure loss and power failure in the tube. All traffic has stopped on this line. The railcar Dr. Munday's is on has stopped somewhere between the cities. We've launched inspection drones down the tube from both cities to investigate the mishap. I'm expecting an update at any moment."

Kobalt touches the air, opening a connection to Colonel Cruikshank. "Colonel, we have arrived in New Zion. Dr. Munday's rail car was to arrive in twenty minutes."

The colonel smiles and claps gleefully. "Good, Kobalt. He's all yours now. Don't let him slip past you this time."

Kobalt stands on the platform of the New Arcadia line. He studies the dark tube. "I said, was to arrive. City Command has advised us of a tube failure."

"I'm receiving the update now," reports the City Commander. "The drone sent from New Zion is reporting a cave-in somewhere under Nebraska. A cave-in would explain the vacuum loss and power failure."

"Cave-in? Could the rail line have been hit by a meteor?" Kobalt speaks his thought out loud.

"That would do it," says the commander.

"Don't assume an asteroid has done your job, Kobalt. I want a full report and body count," Cruikshank demands.

"We watched meteors impact somewhere in the mid-west while we flew here." Kobalt pauses in thought. "Derailed by a meteor? Where are you, Dr. Munday?"

"Dead, I hope, sir," Lieutenant Astatine says.

"If he's not, we'll make sure he wishes he was." Kobalt raises his fist as he moves past his men.

The Elite Guards respond with a "Hoo-ah!" and form up behind the captain as he exits the Rail Station.

Chapter 35: Moving In

Rob and the kids unload the Suburban, putting the cages of chickens, piglets, and lambs onto wheeled dollies, so they can push the cages along the mine floor to the main gallery. Once the animals, suitcases, and boxes are inside, Rob moves the X-37 covered Suburban to the gravel area on the other side of the bridge. If it's safe tomorrow, he'll move it farther down the road. The location of the hideaway is a secret. A space shuttle parked at the bridge is likely to draw more attention than Rob wants.

Rob carefully conceals the mine entrance, closing and locking the camouflaged chain-link gate, locking the wooden door with the warning signs, and then secures the heavy blast door. It's a cumbersome process, but necessary for their protection.

As he walks into the main gallery, he sees the kids playing with the animals. Alyssa is poking her hand through the cage, trying to pet the lambs. Ethan is chasing the piglets from one side of the cage to the other, making them squeal and Ethan laugh. Courtney isn't in the room.

"Where's your mom?" Rob asks the kids. Ethan motions with his head toward the kitchen. Rob walks quietly to the galley and watches Courtney rummaging through the cabinets, frantically moving, and rearranging the plates, cups, and bowls. Rob stands silently, but Courtney must sense his presence because she turns to face him. Long strands of hair fall in her face. She slowly pulls them back, smoothing her hair. Her face is flushed, and her eyes are red.

"I didn't know how you'd want the cupboards organized. We just tossed stuff in there. This place could use a woman's touch."

Courtney drops to a chair at the kitchen table. "How long will we be in this place? I want the life we had. I want Rick. Where is Rick?" She pauses and gulps in air, ready to cry. Slowly she asks, "Do you think he's dead?"

"Our Ricky boy, he's a smart one. He'll survive. I know he will."

"I can feel him. If he were dead, somehow, I would know, but I'm scared. I'm so scared."

"The important thing is we're alive. We have food and shelter, and we have each other. We'll make the best of things and create good lives for the children. We need to be strong for them." Rob looks Courtney in the face and then wipes a tear from her cheek. Courtney attempts a smile.

"It's best we stay busy. Me and the boys, we did the best we could. Reorganize to your heart's content. And our boy, Rick… well, I'll bet he'll be coming back to us as soon as he can." Rob gives Courtney a hug. "Just as fast as he can. You'll see."

Courtney nods. "I'll be fine. If he tries to call, can he reach us?"

Rob is about to answer when he's interrupted by a loud crash, followed by screaming kids in the main gallery. Rob runs into the main shaft. He's cut off by Ethan chasing piglets, followed by Alyssa chasing the lambs down the shaft, past the living quarters.

Alyssa cries out excitedly as she runs toward the lower level of the mine. "Don't worry. We'll catch them."

"Chase them into the farm. You can run them right into their pens." Instructs Rob. He turns to Courtney. "Well, that's one way to move the livestock into the mine."

He pauses. "See? They'll find their fun here. They'll be OK." Courtney forces a smile as she dries her eyes with a tissue.

Ethan and Alyssa chase the piglets and lambs to the farm, working to herd them into pens. The lambs are easy. Alyssa gets most of them into the pen. Ethan snatches one as it scurries away, then hands the fluffy little lamb to Alyssa.

The piglets are more of a challenge. Ethan chases them around the farmyard, grabbing them one by one. He chases each one to a corner of the farmyard to trap them, then grabs the plump little pig. The last piggy runs to hide behind a stack of pallets. Ethan gets on his knees and tries to coax the little pig out of its hiding place. He holds his hand out, rubbing his fingers together as if he's holding a treat for the piglet while calling for it. "Here, piggy, piggy. I've got something nice for you. Here, piggy, piggy."

The piglet edges out of the hole, hesitating for a moment to see what the treat might be. The piglet charges, biting the treat. But it's not a treat. It's Ethan's finger! Ethan lets out a loud, howling scream. The piglet runs. Ethan lunges, trying to grab the pig, but it slips out of his hands and runs across the farmyard.

Ethan shrieks, lying on the ground, crying. Alyssa runs to his side. "What's the matter? Did it bite you?" Ethan screams between sobs, gulping air as a river of tears stream down his cheeks. Alyssa kneels on the ground, hugging Ethan, rocking him. "Did it hurt you? Where does it hurt?" Alyssa pulls at his hands to examine his fingers. There is no blood. "What happened, Ethan? It's just a stupid little pig." Ethan's body shakes. He can't stop sobbing.

Alyssa holds him, smoothing his hair. Ethan slowly calms and between sobs, he speaks breathlessly. "They're dead. All dead. I should be dead!"

"Who's dead, Ethan?"

Ethan shudders as he sputters out the names. "Van-Vanessa. Chris and Allie."

Alyssa gasps. "What? You were at their house. They're dead?"

Ethan's eyes focus on the darkness of the mine. He sits still, looking at nothing. "We were playing Dodge It. I was on the Glide-pad. There was a loud, crashing noise. I saw little holes in the roof. I watched the dust sparkle and dance in the beams of sunlight. It was kinda beautiful, you know? I followed the sparkling dust to the couch where they were sitting." Ethan pauses, gulping the cool air of the mine. A heavy tear rolls down his cheek. "They were dead. All of them on the couch. I would have helped them, but there was nothing to do. It was over in a second. I just stood there looking at her." Ethan pauses. "I thought of Mom and you, and I ran." Ethan shakes and sobs again.

Alyssa hugs him. "It's not your fault. There was nothing you could do. We're safe. That's what matters."

Ethan sits silently, staring into the darkness being held by his sister.

"I know you have a crush on Vanessa."

"I do not!"

"I'm not teasing. It's sweet. You felt love for her. She died. Now, you're crying for her. It's romantic. I wonder if anyone would cry for me?"

Ethan slowly wipes the tears from his eyes and looks at the sweet, smooth face of his twin sister. "I'd cry for you."

"Not you! You have to cry for me. I'm your sister. I mean, you know… I wonder if anyone would cry for me, the way you cried for Vanessa," Alyssa ponders.

Ethan stands. "I think George Richards likes you." Ethan smiles, anticipating his sister's reaction.

"Ew yuck! Not Plump George. Anyone but him," Alyssa cries out.

The siblings walk together to the upper level.

"Don't tell Mom or Uncle Rob that I freaked out. Mom is scared enough," Ethan says, wiping his face, hoping to hide the evidence of his sorrow.

Alyssa nods agreement. "We are all scared. She's worried about Dad. I am, too. I hope he comes back soon."

"Dad won't forget us. He'll be back. I know it," Ethan says, trying to sound confident.

Chapter 36: A New Dawn

Rick moves to the railcar door. He finds an emergency panel; removing clear plastic housing, he pulls the emergency release. The door seal pops open, creating a small gap between the door frame and the sliding door, but the door does not open.

Rick lodges his machete in the gap, using it as a lever while pulling the handle. The door slides open. He flashes his light through the opening, but all he can see is tunnel wall. The space between the railcar and tunnel wall is too narrow to squeeze through.

Rick uses the flashlight to examine the carpeted panels along the front of the passenger cabin. A lower panel is removable. He drags the dead man's body down the aisle, so he can access the panel, then uses his Ka-Bar knife to pop the panel from the wall of the railcar, hoping to find a way out. Behind the panel is a small hatch marked TECHNICIANS ONLY.

Rick figures in this case he's qualified. He turns a handle and pulls the hatch open, revealing a crawl space. He scrambles in, holding the flashlight in front, dragging his pack behind him. Electronic panels line crawl space walls. A few feet ahead, there's another panel marked EXIT SHAFT.

The hatch has two handles. He sets the flashlight down, grabs both handles and turns. Nothing. He pulls both handles; the door doesn't budge. He gathers his strength and pushes. The seal breaks and the hatch door swings down with a whoosh, sending Rick sliding headfirst onto the track below, followed by his flashlight and backpack.

Rick crawls from under the nose of the railcar and stands on the tracks, using the flashlight to survey the situation. The wrecked train blocks the tunnel, so he leaves the rail car behind and walks along the dark tunnel, scanning with the flashlight, looking for what caused the train to stop so suddenly. The tunnel looks normal, except for a crashed railcar and the power failure. Everything looks as he imagines it should. The tunnel is a smooth cement tube with rail tracks mounted on metal risers embedded in the cement. Everything is spotless.

Rick talks out loud to himself. "Well, good news is I don't have to deal with Black Guard while I'm trapped in a tunnel in the middle of God-knows-where-America. But what am I going to do? Walk all the way to New Zion?"

As he moves down the tunnel, he sees dirt scattered between the tracks. "Dirt? Did someone make a mess in the colonel's tunnel?" As Rick moves down the tunnel, he sees more dirt and rocks strewn across the tunnel floor. The debris grows thicker. Rick walks faster, aiming his flashlight down the tunnel until he comes to a wall of dirt, rocks, and broken cement. "A cave-in. Well, that explains things."

Rick crawls up the dirt, pulling chunks of cement out of the way, trying to reach the top of the broken tube. He loosens a rock, which causes more dirt and rocks to fall into the tunnel. He rides a small avalanche of debris down to the tracks. "Guess I'm not digging my way out. Something powerful must have caused this."

Rick scans around with his light. To his left, half-buried in dirt and rocks, is a door marked TUNNEL MAINTENANCE. Rick stands dumbfounded. "Huh. The colonel and that fat white guy sure are smart. If there ever was a tunnel that requires maintenance, X marks the spot," Rick laughs at his stroke of luck, rushes to the door and digs with his hands, pushing dirt and rocks away. He uses his machete as a shovel to dig out the door.

Once the dirt is cleared away, Rick uses his light to study the door, finding it doesn't have a lock and there is no handle, just a small round hole. He wonders if the hole is for a large key. He pushes a finger into the slot, cautiously feeling around inside. He squeezes his hand through the slot and finds a button. He pushes the button. Nothing. He pushes the button and the door at the same time. It doesn't budge. Rick pushes the button and uses his other hand to pull on the door. It moves slightly. He pulls harder and the heavy door creaks open.

The open door reveals a small round chamber with a metal ladder. "No dirt. That's a good sign." Rick steps to the ladder, pointing the light up illuminating metal rungs embedded in the cement wall of the round chamber. The rungs continue up beyond the beam of the flashlight. "Up is good." He secures the machete and flashlight in the backpack and slings the pack over his shoulders, tightening the straps.

He climbs hand over hand up the cold, damp steel ladder in pure darkness, through spider webs sticking to his face and hair. After a couple minutes of climbing, he rests. Wiping his face of the spidery threads, he then pulls the flashlight out the backpack and points the beam upward, seeing only endless rungs. He stows the light and climbs steadily, resisting the urge to wipe his face or to warm his hands. He pulls his body up, hand over hand, rung by rung. The cold iron rungs suck the warmth from his hands. He loses feeling in his fingers but reaches into the blackness for the next rung above him. His hand finds the rung, but his fingers will not grip, slipping from the rung. His weight shifts, causing his foot to slide off a rung, and his body dangles held by a single hand. He wills himself to grip harder while his feet frantically search for a foothold, knowing if he loses his grip, he will fall to his death. His foot finds a rung, and he pushes himself up.

His hands ache with pain. He stops to rest, putting his right hand under his left armpit to warm it while gripping the rung with his left hand. Once his right hand is warm, he uses the same method to warm his left hand. Upward he climbs. The tunnel is cold, but he drips sweat. The backpack grows heavy. He adjusts the pack, then climbs.

"Whoever designed this maintenance shaft is a complete idiot," Rick grumbles.

After seventy more steel rungs, Rick pulls himself onto a cement platform next to the ladder. He lies on his back, staring at the blackness. He does not need the flashlight. The blackness feels close. The ladder continues.

After a short rest, Rick stands, gripping the ladder. He looks up. "I just hope the maintenance man left the door open up there." He clambers up fifty more cold steel rungs and finds a larger platform. Climbing out of the shaft and stepping away from the ladder, he switches on his flashlight to see he is standing in a ten-by-ten-foot room with a cement floor and corrugated steel walls. The ladder he climbed comes out of a hole in the middle of the floor. Other than the maintenance shaft, the room is empty. One wall is an industrial metal roll-up door. Rick tries to lift the roll-up door, but it's locked from the outside.

The air is warm, but there is a breeze. Rick points his light toward the breeze. One of the corrugated metal walls is bent, creating a narrow opening. Rick moves to the tear in the steel wall and flashes his light through the opening. The hole leads to another room. Boxes and clothes are strewn about. The room is lit by predawn light and is open to the outside.

He points his light away from the opening to provide enough light to see the bent metal wall, but hopefully not bright enough to give away his position. He grabs the corner of the bent metal and pulls. A few hard tugs and he makes the hole wide enough to squeeze through. He lies on his back and uses his legs to push away boxes on the other side of the wall. Rick listens. Silence. He tosses his backpack and flashlight ahead of him, then crawls through the hole. The roof and one wall of the next room are missing. Clothing, papers, and boxes litter the room.

Rick gets to his feet and steps into the early light. He's outside. He's free. He takes a deep breath, dust in the air makes him cough. Surveying the area, he walks along a wide dirt path between buildings. On his left and right are rows of industrial metal doors. He walks along the row of damaged storage units. An incredible force has bent the corrugated steel walls. Something has torn the roofs off several of the units and spread debris across the ground. He walks on old clothes, paper, and old photographs. He passes a naked antique doll, its ceramic head cracked.

He walks transfixed, drawn to a grouping of headlights and silhouettes of people on a rise ahead. He walks toward the new dawn light.

Chapter 37: Sworn In

Thursday–Early Morning

White House DUCC (Deep Underground Command Center)

Vice President Cliff Baker and his small team worked through the night. Cabinet members and staff members of the press, a few senators and congressmen straggled in, one by one during the night, making their way through the chaos of the city. It's early morning and people crowd the Command Center. These people know it is their duty to get to the White House during a crisis. Others arrive, believing they can help. Some have come knowing that the underground complex offers protection and refuge.

News reports and damage assessments stream in from a variety of sources through the night. By early morning news helicopters are flying over the enormous crater in south-western Maryland, surveying the damage from Baltimore to Washington, D.C., and beyond.

Cliff Baker's Chief of Staff assistant and his aides are missing or have not arrived. His press secretary, a young brunette woman, presents the vice president with a stack of papers. "Mr. President, here's your speech with the latest revisions. We need to move to the press room. You'll be on in a few minutes."

"Thank you, Sheryl. A little hasty referring to me as Mr. President." The soon-to-be President Baker moves with the young woman. She walks ahead, guiding him to the press room. Cliff breathes deeply. "I'll give the speech a quick review before we start. Has Judge Sanders arrived?"

"Chief Justice Sanders is waiting for us. I don't think I'm being hasty. President Baker sounds nice. It will be official in a few minutes," the young woman says.

The press room is abuzz with activity. The TV crew and reporters make last-minute preparations to cover the news conference. Senator Mitch Campbell, Tug Grimes, and Jerome Hargrove have cleaned up and are all handshakes and smiles.

Cliff Baker greets everyone and takes his position behind a podium with the presidential seal. The podium stands before a blue background, flanked by American flags. He scans the text of his speech, then nods to the press coordinator. She speaks into a wireless ear-mounted microphone. Seconds later, the director signals his crew. One of the crew stands between the camera and the podium holding up his hand with five fingers open then speaks: "We are live in five, four…" He silently finishes the countdown with hand signals until he has a closed fist, then ducks out of the way pointing to Cliff Baker, the next President of the United States.

"Fellow Citizens, the areas of Maryland, northern Virginia, and Washington, D.C., are suffering from the destructive effects of a devastating meteor impact. The damage will surely be in the billions of dollars and deaths in the hundreds of thousands. It is with sincere grief and sadness I must report President Anderson is missing and presumed dead. President Anderson was among many of our nation's leaders and representatives lost in last night's devastation. To maintain the continuity of government of our great nation, the law mandates I be sworn in as acting President of the United States. Chief Justice Sanders will conduct the oath of office."

Cliff Baker steps out from behind the podium. Justice Sanders stands next to Vice President Baker. It's a tradition that the oath of office is taken while placing one's hand on the Bible. In a strange twist, Senator Campbell and Secretary Hargrove stand in front of Justice Sanders, holding the US Constitution between them. Cliff Baker puts his hand on the Constitution while reciting the oath.

Cliff Baker repeats after Justice Sanders. "I do solemnly swear that I will faithfully execute the office of President of the United States, and will, to the best of my ability, preserve, protect, and defend the Constitution of the United States, so help me God." The room erupts in applause.

Mike McCoy

"Dear citizens, I swore the oath to you, the citizens of the United States, holding my hand on the Constitution instead of the Bible. The Constitution is the defining document that enabled the greatest country mankind has ever known to grow and flourish with freedom for all. I swear to preserve and protect a constitution under siege. A Constitution some would toss away with idle promises of something better. America is not perfect, but for nearly two hundred seventy years, it has been the best country the world has ever seen. Together, using this platform that has worked so well, we will work together to make it better. Not by tossing it away, but by building upon the foundation of the Constitution and the great blessings bestowed upon us by our founders. Preserve, protect, and defend. I swear that to you, on my life." The room explodes again in loud applause and cheers.

Mitch Campbell smiles in admiration. He kicked Cliff in the ass, challenging him. Cliff accepted the challenge and now stands before the nation as its leader. Mitch steps over to Cliff and shakes his hand. "Congratulations, Mr. President." Several others shake the president's hand before President Baker quiets the room to speak again.

"America is under attack, but not from a foreign government. The universe is sending asteroids and meteors crashing down on us. The greater Washington area is suffering from a large meteor impact. We have reports of impacts in Los Angeles and other parts of the country. I can confirm the impact in Perth reported yesterday. Scientists from NASA and JPL have advised us that this is the beginning of an asteroid storm. We are working with these experts to assess the severity and duration of this unusual event. We cannot predict the timing, frequency, or location of incoming asteroids. However, we are working to gain more information as quickly as possible. I am told that many of these space rocks will burn up or explode high in the atmosphere and never hit Earth. Watch and listen to local news streams for updates and instructions from your local government officials. We will advise citizens of locations providing resources and protection. We face a new and unusual challenge, but working together, man to man, woman to woman, we will survive the asteroid storm and become a stronger people and a stronger nation. Stay tuned to news reports. Good day and God bless." President Baker bows slightly with genuine humility, then waves as he walks from the podium. He does not take questions from reporters in the room. The news streams switch to reporters who will analyze and parse every word said.

President Baker and key staff are hurriedly ushered back to the underground command center, shaking many hands, and slapping backs in praise along the way. The mood is upbeat and celebratory. A new president has been sworn in. People enjoy the bright moment amidst death and destruction. Structure and order are restored. People dare to hope. A mid-level staffer works his way through the people and approaches the president. President Cliff Baker accepts the staffer's hand. "Mr. President, your acceptance speech. You killed it, sir. It's one for the history books."

"Thank you, son," says Cliff Baker. Son of a small-town auto mechanic, now President of the United States of America. Cliff basks in this moment of supreme victory and accomplishment. He looks at Mitch and gives a confident nod.

All the computer screens and wall-sized thin-screens in the command center switch from news reports to the image of Colonel Cruikshank. The haggard face of a white-haired old man fills the screens. He looks older and more wrinkled than the day before in the cabinet room. His sharp blue eyes are now gray, but still fierce and keenly focused. He moves his gaze slowly, as if he's examining everyone in the room.

"Congratulations, President Baker. However, your claim on the highest office is misguided. Your president, the CEO of Arcadia, is alive and well. He is here with me."

The camera pans to the right, showing Anderson in the flesh. Anderson looks forward with a blank expression. His eyes dark and dull. The excitement in the Command Center instantly deflates. "I have President Anderson with me for his protection. After last night's event, I believe being under my care is well-advised."

Cliff is instantly red hot. "You and Anderson are traitors. He wouldn't have left the White House unless he was under your

243

influence. You convinced him to throw away the Constitution and kidnapped him. Where are you?"

"We are safe, thank you. You and your people are not. I am pleased that you survived last night's impact. As you have seen firsthand, there is a storm coming and its effects will be catastrophic. After the asteroid storms, a new world will rise from the destruction. The goal of Arcadia is to create that new world, saving humanity and preserving the accumulated knowledge of mankind. Because of our efforts, humankind will thrive once the storm recedes," the colonel states coolly.

Cliff shakes his hand at the screen. "You bastard! You knew. You plotted and prepared for years without sharing your information. You're causing the deaths of millions of people. You're saving yourselves while you could have saved millions."

Cruikshank sighs. He shakes his head, his tight lips curl into a smile. "Billions. Well, certainly hundreds of millions will die. If not directly from meteor impacts, you will die of starvation and disease. The new world will not sustain a population of billions. Alas, we can save only the few selected to live in our new cities."

People in the command center rally around President Baker. A woman cries out, "You can save more people. You could have saved us all. If someone had warned us; given time to prepare. People deserve a chance to live."

The colonel looks sullen. "Human nature as it is would not have allowed it. If we warned the world, everyone would have suffered chaos and murderous destruction at the hands of our fellow beings. Watch your news. You'll see, it's already happening. As always, man is at the mercy of his fellow man."

Cruikshank then pauses, as if in thought. "I warn you this. Find deep holes—caves, caverns, sewers—and pray if you are of a mind to do so. The storm will last months. Nothing will be spared. We know you have attempted to access telescopes and satellites. Looking skyward will not help you now. However, we will not impede your efforts, no matter how futile." The colonel raises his right arm, bent at the elbow, his fist at his chest in salute. "Praise

Arcadia." The screens and monitors in the Command Center switch back to news streams.

Looting and mayhem ensued minutes after the president's announcement of the asteroid storm. People in cities large and small swarm into grocery stores to stock up on food and supplies. Knowing death is about to rain down from heaven, people don't wait in line to pay for goods, they take what they need. Chaos spreads across the country, as mothers and fathers frantically gather food, water, and supplies for their families before someone else steals it.

Chapter 38: Hitchhiker

Thursday–Early Morning

Rick is drawn to the activity in the distance. Lights from police and fire vehicles flash dimly, dulled by a dusty fog. Inches of dirt cover the ground. He can make out a narrow road; raised above the rest of the landscape. He walks to the flashing lights. The sun is rising with a burnt orange hue.

Rick approaches carefully. He doesn't expect to see Black Guard here, but doesn't know where here is, so caution is in order. The last thing he needs is to get captured and taken to New Zion, or worse, back to New Arcadia. As he walks to the lights, more cars and trucks zip past, heading to the site. People exit their cars and rush to see what has happened. Rick stands among people marveling at a crater in the ground. At fourteen hundred feet in diameter, it looks enormous. The impact is fresh. Wisps of steam rise from the dirt.

As the morning sun rises, it dissolves the deep shadows in the hole, revealing a two hundred fifty-foot-deep crater. There is no fiery molten rock at the bottom, just smoldering dirt. Rick observes the police and emergency personnel. They're standing around talking. No one is injured. There is no damage, except for a giant hole in the middle of a field. The officials and city folk are looking at the crater and talking amongst themselves.

Rick stands at the crater's edge and understands what happened to the railcar. A meteor impacted Earth directly over the path of the high-speed rail, smashing the tube, cutting power, and sending a burst of air down the tunnel, causing the railcar to derail.

More people arrive to ogle the crater. It's something most people would never expect to see in their lifetime. The local people view the crater as a curiosity. Rick sees it as a warning.

A group of young men, in their twenties, arrive in pickup trucks and run to the edge of the crater, gathering near Rick. "Oh shit! Look at that crater. I told you it was an asteroid," says one of the young men.

"Whoa, that 'oid musta been huge!" says another.

"I heard asteroids have gold and diamonds in em. I bet there's a huge meteor buried down there!" a third young man exclaims.

"Remember when my family went to the Diamond Crater in Arkansas. That crater has tons of diamonds. My brother found a bunch," says a fourth man.

Two of the young men run to their pickup, returning to the crater's edge with shovels. "I'm digging me some diamonds," says one of the young men holding his shovel.

"Not if I get there first, sucker. Finders keepers. Whoo-hoo!" says the shovel-wielding man, as he goes over the edge and runs down the steep slope into the crater. His competitor follows, jumping off the raised rim of the crater, landing on both feet in the soft dirt, stumbling and almost falling forward as he runs down the slope, shovel in hand, yelling after his friend.

"Those diamonds are mine, Wyatt. Gold and diamonds, here I come! We're gonna be rich!"

The police chief watches the two men run into the crater and yells after them. "Wyatt and Benjamin; you two be careful. This here is Wagner's land. If you find anything, you need to take it up with Mr. Wagner, ya hear!"

The other two young men stand next to Rick. He can tell they are anxiously considering whether to join their friends. He knows he shouldn't say anything, but he can't help himself. He turns to the young man who told the others about Diamond Carter. "You know, the Crater of Diamonds, in Arkansas, isn't a meteor crater. It's volcanic."

The young man looks at Rick, surprised to see someone he doesn't recognize; someone not from town. "Huh?" He frowns at Rick for attempting to spoil his fun. He runs into the crater, yelling, "It's volcanic!"

Rick calls out to the young man running down the crater's slope. "I don't mean this crater is volcanic. This is clearly a meteor impact, and I suspect you'll be seeing more craters like this soon." Rick looks to the last young man who is contemplating his run into the crater.

The young man pauses. "More craters? What do you mean?" he asks with a frightened expression.

Rick is afraid of sounding like a crazy lunatic, so he chooses his words carefully. "This is the beginning of a massive asteroid bombardment. You need to find protection from the asteroid storm; someplace that will shelter you from the impacts."

The young man looks at Rick as if he's speaking Chinese. "You're fucking crazy, man. You one of those doomsday fanatics? Bomb shelters and shit? Where you from? You ain't from round here, I know that." The young man stares at Rick for a moment. His questions don't require a response. Rick can tell the guy is trying to sort things in his brain. Then he runs over the edge of the crater and down the slope, calling after his friends. "Leave some a them diamonds for me, assholes!"

Rick realizes that the crater is entertainment for these people. They have no concept of the coming danger. How could they? They will misunderstand anything he says. What he believes is about to happen is beyond most people's comprehension. Maybe Colonel Cruikshank was right; you can't warn people. Rick turns away from the crater's edge and walks to the highway.

Rick walks along the two-lane highway. Inches of dirt cover everything. He can just make out the asphalt ribbon. He surveys the flat, dry landscape surrounding him. The air blast from the meteor's impact has laid the trees flat. Power poles lie like fallen dominoes. Everything, once green, is now brown. It feels good to walk. The air is clearing. It's a sunny morning. He has renewed confidence and hope. Even if he walks home, he will get there.

Cars whip up clouds of dirt as they pass. The novelty of the crater is waning. They've seen what there is to see. It's a hole in the ground. People go on with their day. A white sedan passes slowly, then stops fifty yards ahead. The driver leans over to the passenger side and pushes the door open.

Rick runs to the open door and looks in to see a thin-faced man with long gray hair. "Need a ride, brother?"

"Sure. Thanks," Rick says, as he sits in the passenger seat.

The driver sticks out his hand. "I'm Keith. Where you headed?" he says, as the car moves down the highway.

Rick is instantly comfortable. There's something about the man's calm presence that sets him at ease. Rick takes the driver's hand in his own. The grip is strong and warm. "I'm Rick. Thanks for the ride. I'm heading to Los Angeles. Back home to my family," Rick says.

"Los Angeles? Well, I'm afraid I can't get you that far. I'm driving to town. I can drop you at the Greyhound AutoBus station. Not sure when the next bus comes through, but you can ask them."

Rick considers taking a bus to Los Angeles, but without his band to pay for a ticket, no paper money, and no ID, the bus is not an option. "I'll just keep hitching rides. Probably faster than waiting for the bus. Thanks, though."

The driver stares at the narrow highway, observing the morning light. "Beautiful morning, isn't it? Dusty, but beautiful. Did you like the new addition to the local landscape? I guess God figures we need a conversation piece. Gives the townspeople something to gab about."

Rick fidgets in his seat. The last person he told of the coming disaster ran into a crater. Rick must try again. If he can save lives, it's his duty to do so. Wasn't that his argument with the colonel?

"Keith, I don't want to frighten you or appear like a weirdo, but please listen to what I am about to tell you."

Keith wrings his hands on the steering wheel. "Isn't that how weirdos always start their stories?" Keith laughs. He looks at Rick, who is not laughing. "Sorry, but you stepped into that one. Go ahead. Shoot."

Rick turns in his seat to face Keith. "I'm an astrophysicist. I work in a lab at Cal Tech. That crater, your new landscape feature, was caused by a meteor falling to Earth from space. The short story is, there will be a lot more meteors. The Earth is entering a period of heavy asteroid bombardment. There will be hundreds, maybe thousands more impacts like that. The entire human race is at risk. We are all in grave danger." Rick pauses, waiting for Keith's reaction.

Keith doesn't say a word; instead, he reaches in his pocket, pulls out an old smartphone and hands it to Rick.

"I know. I got the message, just like everyone else. In fact, I received the same message one hundred times or more. Annoying, if you ask me."

Rick flips through the photos and reads the message. "Thank God. Somebody got the news out about Perth. You say everyone got this message?" He hopes Courtney and Uncle Rob received the message.

"Yes, everyone. Most likely dozens of times. I thought it might be a hoax until we got our very own crater. The TV news is constantly talking about Perth, but I don't watch. The wife watches," Keith explains.

Rick realizes he has a smartphone in his hand. He can call Courtney! He cradles the phone as a prized object. "Do you mind if I use your phone? I need to call my wife. I've been out of touch for a few days."

"Sure. Go right ahead. She must be worried sick."

Rick pokes at the screen. When he sees digits, he realizes he doesn't know her number. He usually asks his band or touches his wife's image to call. Rick speaks a voice command requesting information, but the call does not connect. He tries again. Nothing. He notices a message on the screen: NO SERVICE.

Rick hands the phone back. "No luck?" Keith asks.

"No Service. The blast must have knocked out cell towers. I should have known it wouldn't work."

"Power's out in town as well."

Keith doesn't seem upset by the news of an asteroid storm which puzzles Rick. Meteors are falling from the sky. There is no power or phone service, yet the man driving the car appears calm.

"Meteors destroyed Perth. You have an impact crater near your town. I have warned you there will be more impacts. Aren't you afraid?"

Keith smiles peacefully. "Why be afraid? I have faith in God. His will be done. We're not in control. His landscaping project proves that, don't you think?"

Rick studies the man, who speaks with a tranquil smile and bright blue eyes before replying. "I agree we are not in control, but you can gather supplies, find protection. You can prepare to survive what's coming. The people at the crater acted like it was an amusement. Come see the big hole. Yep, that's a big hole, now get home. If everyone got the message about Perth, don't they understand more destruction is coming?"

"You are certain more meteors will hit?" Keith asks seriously.

"I'm very certain. It would take too much time to explain, but I have it on high authority. Earth and every living creature will suffer over the next several weeks," Rick states emphatically.

Keith nods. "High authority, eh? I didn't tell you. I'm the pastor of a church in town. I know a thing or two about high authorities. But you're right. If there are more coming, I need to help protect church members and townspeople. How do we hide from asteroids?"

"I know a place that should be safe." Rick looks around at the stark countryside. A town comes into view. There is less dust. The trees are green, houses and buildings are not far off. "What's the name of your town?"

Keith answers proudly. "Burwell, Nebraska. Population: twelve hundred and forty. Your escape to the great outdoors, Calamus Lake, and home of Nebraska's Big Rodeo."

"Nebraska?"

"I realize Nebraska isn't the glamour spot of the country. Most people pass us by. We kinda like that. Let's us live in peace."

The car pulls off the highway onto a road, then down a dirt driveway, coming to a stop in front of a one-story brick house. "You say you know a safe place for our people?"

"Back at the storage facility. There's a unit with a ladder. You can get hundreds of people down—"

"Tell you what. Come on in the house. You'll meet my wife, Haylee. Have some breakfast and tell us all about where we need to get to. Then we'll let you go on your way to your family."

Rick follows Keith into the small house. Haylee works over a gas stove. The two men sit at the kitchen table. She pours coffee and serves up a hearty country breakfast. Rick tells Keith and his wife about the ladder in the storage facility and the rail tunnel below. "The tunnel isn't wide, but there should be plenty of room."

"Getting people together will be difficult with the power out and phones down. We'll need supplies and provisions. How long you expect we need to stay in the tunnel?"

"This landscaping, as you call it, is just beginning. I don't believe the main event has started. The bombardment might last a few weeks or a few months. I honestly don't know. But I am certain the frequency and intensity will grow stronger before it subsides." Rick

251

stops talking when he notices Keith's blank stare, which he takes to mean "Just answer the damn question."

"Plan for a month," Rick answers succinctly. Keith nods, showing appreciation for the simple answer.

Haylee sets a small plate of food for herself on the table and joins the men. Keith sums up the plan for her. "Honey, all we have to do is convince the townsfolk that rocks will fall from the heavens. They should all climb down a hole and live in a tunnel for the next month."

"Sounds simple enough, dear."

"You know, I feel the lord has put it on my heart to preach a sermon this Sunday on natural disasters. It reminds me of Isaiah 45:7: I form light and create darkness, I make well-being and create calamity, I am the Lord, who does all these things. More coffee for you, Rick?"

Rick covers his cup with his hand to signal no more coffee. "The sermon sounds wonderful, as long as you promise you'll be giving it from inside the tunnel."

"Sunday is just a few days away. We need time to prepare, and with the phones down, it's the best way to gather the congregation to give them the message."

"Keith, you can't wait. More impacts could come without warning. You must find safety. If not for yourself, think of Haylee and your church family," Rick pleads.

Haylee stands, taking the plates from the table. "Concerning that day and hour no one knows, not even the angels of heaven, nor the Son, but the Father only. It will take you longer to get home than to get the entire town of Burwell down that hole," says the pastor's wife.

Keith winks at his wife. "That's right. Come on. Let's get you on your way to saving your own family. May he give you the desire of your heart and make all your plans succeed." Keith leads Rick to an old blue pickup parked under a carport. "Take my truck. She's old, but she'll get ya there. The tank's full. Should get you to Denver before you need to refuel."

Haylee tucks a wad of one-hundred-dollar bills into Rick's hand. "This should buy you enough fuel to make it home."

Rick is grateful. "It's too much. Are you sure?"

"We're sure. We'll be sitting in a hole for the next month, while this old truck is getting blasted to smithereens by space rocks. Better to let you get some use out of it."

Rick opens the door and climbs into the truck. He puts both hands on the steering wheel and his foot on the brake. The normal process to initialize an older AutoCar. Nothing happens. Rick shakes the steering wheel and gives a voice command. "Start." Nothing. "Drive to Denver, Colorado." Again, nothing happens.

He looks around the ancient truck interior. Rick gives Keith a troubled look. Keith reaches into the truck and turns the ignition key. The gas engine starts up and roars with power. "Like I said. She's old. You still remember how to drive yourself?"

"Oh, sure. I just. Yes. I can drive myself. It'll be fun. Like old times."

Keith uses the hand crank to roll down the window, then closes the truck door. "Just head back out to the 91 East, then south on Highway 183, and follow the signs to Denver. You should be there in about six hours. It's a ten-hour drive from Denver to Las Vegas, then you're nearly home. By this time tomorrow, you'll be holding your wife and kids in your arms."

"Keith, Haylee your saints. How can I ever thank you?"

"You just saved the whole town. It's the least we can do to thank you. Drive safe."

"Now, be sure to give your kids a hug from old Keith and Haylee," says Haylee.

Rick thanks them again, then drives the old blue pickup out of the carport and down the dirt driveway. Keith and Haylee watched Rick drive down the dusty road until the truck was out of view.

"It's a great joy to help another human being. He seemed kind of pushy though about this asteroid situation. It must be that big city stress."

"He seemed sincere. I'm glad we could help him get home," Haylee says.

"I'm not so sure about rounding up the townspeople and herding them into a tunnel. Meteors falling from the sky are frightful, but moving everyone underground for a month seems like an overreaction."

"Take it up with the mayor and the police chief. They'll know what's best for the town," Haylee says as she walks back into the house.

Keith looks to the pale blue sky. It's a beautiful morning. Birds fly from tree to tree. Small butterflies flutter in the soft breeze. Keith is known to take long pauses and gaze in wonder at the beauty of God's creation. Haylee's screams from inside the house startle him from his reverie.

"Keith. Keith, oh God. Come see! Oh, dear lord," Haylee cries.

Keith rushes into the house. "The power's back on," mumbles Haylee, as she stands in front of the TV, holding her hands over her face.

Keith freezes as he watches the news report. *"An area northeast of Washington, D.C., was struck by a large meteor."* Video streams from a helicopter news crew flying over a huge crater. The immense area of destruction caused by the impact is hard to comprehend.

"The crater is over three miles in diameter, but the damage extends many miles beyond the crater. The epicenter was the town of Laurel, Maryland, approximately fifteen miles from Washington, D.C. Everything for miles beyond the crater is buried. The only objects we can identify are buildings tall enough to rise above the deep fallout and whatever lies above the dirt is burning."

The helicopter flies away from the crater to Washington, D.C. The cameraman pans over the landscape. Dirt covers everything. The landscape, for miles past the crater, looks like a midwestern town wiped out by a tornado. Pieces of human existence—houses, cars, clothing, and home appliances—are strewn around like trash.

The news switches to another reporter standing in front of a broken Washington Monument. *"The base of this time-honored monument stands, but the top third of the tower has toppled to the ground. Everywhere around me buildings are burning, and two feet of dirt covers the city. The death toll may surpass two hundred thousand."*

Keith holds Haylee tight and kisses her cheek. Keith speaks softly, staring at the news report. "Rick is right. We need to get the town into that tunnel. I'll drive to the police station and talk with Chief Harper."

Haylee stands silently, staring at the TV, nods in agreement.

Chapter 39: Harpoon

Thursday–Washington, DC

President Baker sits at a desk on a studio set built to look like the Oval Office while on a video call with the governors of every state.

"Governors, thank you for attending this briefing. You must all urgently act to prepare for the asteroid storm. I am instructing each of you to use every resource available in your states to save as many people as possible. Find protection underground: old air-raid shelters, basements, parking structures, or sewers if they're the only choice. Initiate martial law. Call up military reserves, police, and fire departments to help move people and supplies to any available shelter."

Governor Scott Hayes of Georgia speaks. "Mr. President, I've placed calls to the base commander at Fort Benning, but I'm not getting any response."

The president's face displays frustration, but his voice remains confident and commanding. "We've had communication issues with some branches of the military. I will resolve this. You have little time to get sheltered. We expect the bombardment to intensify in the next twenty-four hours. Make use of church volunteers, Boy Scouts, Girl Scouts, the damned Moose Lodge if you must, but get moving. We need to save as many people as possible."

Governor Dora Crawford of California calls out. "Twenty-four hours' notice before the destruction of our society? Is that the best our government can offer? We've already had impacts and deaths. Didn't NASA or JPL know about this? Will you support funds for disaster relief?" she asks.

"I don't want to denigrate President Anderson, but there are indications he and some of his cabinet knew this was coming; however, they chose not to share that knowledge." Grumbling and hisses come from the governors. President Baker shakes his head and waves his hand to show he will not engage in debate. "You have my promise, good news, or bad. I will share it with you. Focus on getting people to safety. Get instructions to your citizens over streaming services. Use any alternative methods you have, even broadcast TV if you still have broadcast stations in your area. There is no time for discussion or special requests. You all must act. Encourage a calm, swift movement of your citizens. We don't want more panic and looting."

The governors erupt with a series of questions. With fifty governors and their staff talking all at once, the president hears only noise. "Quiet down. Quiet now!" the president shouts to get everyone's attention. "It is likely we will lose communications as the storm intensifies. Some areas will lose power. No matter what happens, or how bad it gets, you are the governors of your states. You have a responsibility to lead your people. We are the United States of America. Nothing, not even an asteroid storm, will put us asunder. Be strong. Use every local resource and asset to get your people to safety. That is all."

The governor of Wyoming shouts over the clamoring voices. "Every state and man for his-self!" His image drops from the screen. One by one, video screens turn black as the governors touch out of the call.

President Baker steps away from the set and his press secretary escorts him to the Command Center. "That was great, sir—short and to the point."

President Baker hurries into the Command Center. "What do we have next?"

"We have an update from Dr. Simmons at JPL. They have several ground and space-based telescopes working now," Sheryl reports, reading from a screen projected from her band.

"I pray we have some good news for a change."

Cabinet members and military leaders crowd the room. Staff members move to make way for the president, allowing him to sit at the large conference table. Cliff nods to Tug Grimes, Mitch Campbell, and others around the table. Air Force Major Anthony Cortez stands at the front of the room. A huge video screen covers the wall behind him. Once the president sits, Tug signals the Major to begin.

"All right, let's get started. JPL, the National Reconnaissance Office, and NASA have worked frantically to get their systems online to provide a realistic idea of what we are in for, and sorry if

I'm jumping ahead, but it doesn't look pretty." The major shuffles nervously, aware that he might have broken protocol.

President Baker waves him on. "That's all right, Tony. This is not the time for political double-speak. Let's cut it to the bone. We need to know what's coming at us."

Major Cortez gives a stoic nod. "I'll let Dr. Simmons explain."

The image of Dr. Simmons appears on the screen. The president doesn't hesitate. "Dr. Simmons let us have it, full bore. No, sugarcoating. What are we up against?"

"It's worse than our simulations predicted. We've only had a short time with our systems up, but we've spotted dozens of new comets and large clusters of asteroids moving through the inner solar system, heading toward Earth. There are thousands of objects, ranging from ten meters, which will burn up in the atmosphere, to objects one hundred meters and larger, which will impact and cause damage like we've seen in the DC area. Bombardments will occur daily, coming from the east, traveling westward, in a wide swath covering North America to south of the Equator. Events will occur from late afternoon until early morning with varying intensity. The same is happening around the world. We are tracking several impacts across Asia, the Middle East, and Europe. The intensity will increase over the coming days. While the number of objects is greater than predicted, this is the event we expected and reported earlier. However," Dr. Simmons pauses longer than expected. The room doesn't breathe in anticipation of the doctor's next words.

"However, what, Simmons?"

Dr. Simmons bites his lower lip before speaking. "We have identified an asteroid. Well, we've identified thousands of new asteroids and comets, but one designated as 2039 JZ966 is particularly alarming. Our calculations show the asteroid will cross Earth's orbit in three days."

President Baker looks to Major Cortez, then to Tug. Both faces are blank. "That seems to be a common occurrence these days. What's special about this one? Dammit! I said cut it to the bone, Doctor." The president looks at Simmons with an angry scowl. Dr. Simmons sinks into his chair.

Tug jumps in. "Mr. The president, asteroid JZ966, is a potential Earth-killer. It's over one kilometer in diameter. That's ten football fields wide. If it makes a direct impact anywhere on Earth, it will kill millions and blast enough debris into the atmosphere to cause an impact winter lasting several years, causing death and starvation around the world."

Everyone in the room gasps. A young aide runs to exit the Command Center. President Baker stands and points at the door. "Nobody leaves. That news does not leave this room. Nobody moves until we have a solution."

"President Baker is right. We have the brightest minds in this room. We need a solution to save as many lives as possible," adds Mitch.

Jerome pokes his fingers in the air, manipulating searches on his VUE, making whimpering sounds as he reads. "Dear Lord, three days. Three days to die. Oh, my."

Cliff loosens his tie. He could use a shot of that Maker's Mark whiskey but knows such an act wouldn't look very presidential. "Tug, you and the major obviously have had this news for some time. What options have you come up with?"

"Sir, Major Cortez briefed us on this just minutes ago, during your video conference with the governors."

"Well, let's come up with options now. Can't we launch a rocket and push it out of the way before it gets here?"

Mitch helps finish the president's thought. "He's right. I remember a decade ago. We funded a NASA project to deflect asteroids. It used laser beams or something. Can't we use that system?"

"Potentially. With several years of warning, we can deflect an asteroid by changing its trajectory. We have developed and tested several technologies for planetary defense. But any technology to accomplish this takes years. We have days," Dr. Simmons explains.

Jerome's hands dance through the air in front of his face. He makes a final poke and two slow finger strokes, as if scrolling through text. "Ah, ooh. Maybe it will work," he says under his breath, yet loud enough for everyone to hear.

"What is it, Jerome? Can you please stop twiddling your fingers for a moment?" Mitch asks.

Jerome removes his VUE lens. Ignoring Senator Campbell, he looks at Tug and says a single word, "Harpoon," then returns the VUE to his face and resumes flicking his fingers in the air.

Tug looks at Major Cortez quizzically. The major shuffles uncomfortably. "I've never heard of Harpoon. Secretary Hargrove, send me what you have on it."

Jerome flips his wrist, and the Harpoon file appears on the major's band. He scans the document for a few moments. "All right, Harpoon, which is a classified mission, by the way," the major says, firing a sharp glare at Jerome. "Is an asteroid intercept spacecraft, an experimental mission, funded by the office of National Planning, under the National Preparedness Assessment Division of FEMA, which is part of Homeland."

"The project sounds sufficiently buried under layers of government agencies. No wonder nobody's heard of it," says Mitch.

"There have been no budget appropriations for a space mission. Budget cuts shut down NASA and JPL. Yet, some obscure agency under Homeland can manage a clandestine space program. This smells like something that bastard Cruikshank would cook up," remarks President Baker.

Mitch realizes he interrupted the major. "Sorry. Please continue," he says, signaling the major to proceed.

Cortez reads the document projected from his band. "The concept is to launch a spacecraft called a Hypervelocity Asteroid Intercept Vehicle at a target asteroid. The space vehicle has two parts, separated by a long boom, or as they named it, Harpoon. The leading portion is a kinetic impactor that creates a crater in the asteroid. The second part of the spacecraft contains a nuclear explosive device."

Jerome flicks his fingers in the air, moving his head around like a blind man. "And?"

The major looks at Jerome. "And what?"

Jerome swivels his chair to face the major. "And Harpoon is scheduled for a test launch in ten days. Can't we move the launch up by, say, seven days?"

Major Cortez looks stumped. "I have no idea. It seems I'm at a disadvantage here."

"Let's be clear about the potential of this harpoon device. If I understand correctly, the explosion will push the asteroid away from Earth. Is that correct, Dr. Simmons?" asks President Baker.

Dr. Simmons' face twists with concern. "I'm not sure you understand Harpoon's mission. The aim of an HAIV, such as Harpoon, is to destroy the asteroid, not deflect it."

"You mean Harpoon will blow up the asteroid? Why didn't you say that?" shouts the president.

"It wasn't my suggestion. It was his!" Dr. Simmons says, pointing at Jerome. "No one asked for my opinion until now."

"I damned well am asking you now! Is this harpoon thing a good idea?"

Dr. Simmons has a stern look on his face. "As I stated earlier, deflection missions take years, if not decades. This will require some study, but if Harpoon is ready to launch, it is likely our best chance for a planetary defense mission. However, based on the size of JZ966, it could take several harpoon devices to disrupt the asteroid."

"Several Harpoon devices? You said Harpoon would blow up the asteroid with a nuclear bomb! A nuclear bomb against an asteroid. How many could it take?"

"I said nothing about Harpoons capabilities. Obviously, I don't know yet. I've just learned of this device. Depending upon the launch vehicle, the characteristics of the nuclear device, the size, shape, and density of the target object, it could require forty simultaneous HAIV impacts to destroy an asteroid the size of JZ966."

"Forty asteroid smashers. That's crazy. How can we ever hope to save the world from this beast?" asks the stunned president.

"We have to try," a woman's voice calls out from across the Command Center.

"Yes, we must try. We have to try," other voices in the room echo.

"Of course we will try. Dr. Simmons, what will it take?" asks President Baker.

"I need to study the mission plan to ensure we can re-target Harpoon for JZ966. We need to run orbital dispersion simulations and modeling. Obviously, there are many unknowns. Our objective will be to destroy the asteroid or break it into smaller fragments."

The room is silent as people in the Command Center contemplate launching a nuclear weapon in space to destroy an asteroid. Cliff Baker breaks the silence. "Jerome, do some digging. Find out where the Harpoon tests are taking place."

"What else do you need, Doctor?" asks Mitch.

"More time. You people are expecting the impossible. We must acquire scans from space telescopes to determine JZ966's density and composition in advance of the launch. We need data to determine the number of impactors required and select optimal target locations for the nuclear explosives to have the highest degree of success. This assumes that there is more than a single Harpoon device. If there's only a single system, any mission to destroy JZ966 is doomed to fail. We have years of work to complete in two days. You people shut down JPL, now you expect miracles."

Tug works to change the direction of the discussion. "Dr. Simmons, we're all faced with impossible tasks today. We'll learn more about Harpoon and help determine if we have a mission or not."

President Baker puts down his notes and rises from his chair. "Dr. Simmons, we need to know that asteroid backassward. We must destroy this beast. Ladies and gentlemen, the universe has issued Earth a death warrant. It may be in our power to see that warrant is not served. We have a short window to save our country... dammit, to save the world. There is no time to waste."

The room buzzes with activity as people move quickly into small work groups. Mitch is pleased. He walks to President Baker. "Good job, Cliff... ah, sorry, Mr. President. I guess you work best on whiskey hangovers and no sleep."

Cliff chuckles. "It's amazing how a crisis helps you focus."

Tug Grimes rolls up a small thin-screen and stuffs into his satchel. The president calls him over. Cliff speaks in a low tone so only Tug can hear. "Tug, we need to save as many American lives as possible. That means getting people underground." Tug nods in agreement.

The president continues. "Who controls the largest underground sites scattered across the continent?"

Tug returns with a devilish grin. "I would have to say the Arcadians."

"I suggest we plan for the Marines to overtake, and occupy, the Arcadian sites. Swarm those underground locations and get people underground. The few and the fortunate be damned."

"You don't have to ask twice. That old colonel always rubbed me the wrong way." Tug signals the Commandant of the Marine Corps to follow him as he moves to the door. "We'll have an action plan tout suite, Mr. President," Tug says, as he leaves the room.

Cliff is confident the gears of the US government machine, at least the components not absconded by Colonel Cruikshank, are working. He is proud of his first hours as president of the United States. He's barely slept. He should be exhausted but is full of energy. The day is just beginning. He spots his secretary at the far end of the room and calls out, "Sheryl, what's next?"

Chapter 40: Cave Mates

Thursday Morning

Rob sits at his control center, checking systems and reading news reports. Ethan plays a game called Hopscotch, Bomb Watch on his VUE. He hops around the main gallery, avoiding exploding blocks on the floor. Occasionally he steps on a bomb and launches his body onto a couch. Alyssa reads a book from the library. It feels strange to hold the paperback book in her hands and turn the aged, yellow pages.

Courtney works in the kitchen where she has discovered a well-stocked refrigerator and prepares breakfast. They eat at one of the long dining tables, huddled together at one end.

Rob can see Courtney is still having a tough time adapting to the new environment. "Excellent breakfast, dear. We've all had a big shock. At least we're landing on our feet. We'll get back out in the world when it's safe."

A tear runs down Courtney's cheek.

Rob frowns. "I didn't mean to upset you, dearie."

"It's just, all the things that our society taught us are important, everything we strived for: money, career, fashion, social status, all those worldly things we love so much. It will all vanish. It was all meaningless. I know it's silly, but I can't help but mourn the life we're leaving behind." Courtney wipes her tears away. "I'll be fine. I just need time."

She reaches out to hold the hands of her children. "At least we're together. Thank you, Rob. I don't know what we would have done without you."

"And the hideaway," adds Ethan.

"This is a chance to learn what is truly important. Family. Family is what matters. Family is never meaningless," Rob says, in a sober tone.

A loud alarm sounds. Courtney nearly jumps out of her skin, letting out a frightful squeak.

Rob runs to his desk, checks the security monitors and calls out, "Everything's fine. That's the front door alarm. It's Rodrigo, one of the Martinez boys. Remember, I told you about them." Rob silences the alarm.

Courtney steps to Robs desk and looks at the video screen on the wall. Several people are walking through the mine shaft toward the blast door. "Let's greet our new cave mates with a nice welcome." Rob says, taking Courtney's hand. Rob pulls Courtney to the heavy door. Ethan and Alyssa follow closely behind.

Courtney seems unsure of what's happening. "Our what?"

Rodrigo greets Rob as he steps through the blast door. Rob hugs Rodrigo. "Welcome, Rodrigo, welcome. I'm glad you made it. I expected you last night. Did you have much trouble?"

Rodrigo wears a sour face. "When I got home last night, I told Isabel we need to move the family to a hidden place inside the mountain. For our protection, I told her. But she doesn't want to leave the house. She knows about the meteors in Pasadena, but Long Beach is far from Pasadena. Nothing happened in Long Beach. Everything's OK. When we got those Perth messages. We thought it was a joke. When she saw the news about Washington, D.C., she asked me to bring everyone here! Stubborn woman."

Rob looks behind Rodrigo to see several family members. Rodrigo moves aside, allowing his wife to step through the door and into the main shaft. Her eyes dart around questioningly, trying to size up the strange place her husband has told her about.

Rob can see that Isabel is nervous. "Is this your wife, Rodrigo?"

"Yes. My wife, Isabella," Rodrigo offers. Isabella stands next to her husband, allowing the others to move through the blast door. A series of people carrying heavy bags and boxes of food stream through the door and file into the main shaft. Rodrigo introduces each one as they step through the steel door. "This is Inez, my wife's sister, and her husband, Edgar." Edgar nods politely as he steps past. "And this is my wife's mother, Maria, our daughter Mary, our son Carlos, and Inez and Edgar's daughter, Clara." Everyone smiles politely as Rodrigo introduces them.

Courtney is taken aback by the number of people, but she smiles and attempts to be courteous, greeting them all. "Such a lovely, large family. I'm sure there's room for everyone. We were just saying that family matters the most," she says, haltingly.

"Let's get your gear inside, then I'd like everyone to gather in the main gallery. We'll get the living quarters assigned. I'm sure everyone will be comfortable." Rob works to herd the group down the mine shaft to the main gallery.

Rodrigo and his family drop their bags in the large room, then leave to get another load from the truck. Edgar grabs a cart in the supply room to load with gear. Rob catches Rodrigo by the arm and pulls him aside. "Where's Eddie? Have you heard from him?"

"I called him. He knows we are here. He said he will join us, but his wife can be difficult. Even more stubborn than my Isabel."

"People don't believe they're in danger until it hits them on the head. I suppose if people never saw rain, it would be hard to sell umbrellas. I hope Eddie can convince his wife. I have a feeling yesterday's asteroid events are just the beginning. The next several days could get much worse," says Rob.

Rodrigo nods agreement, then walks to the entrance of the mine to bring in more supplies. "Oh, how many people would Eddie consider immediate family? I guess I should have asked before. It's just that we have somewhat limited space and resources, and well…"

Rodrigo pauses for a moment before answering. "I don't know. Maybe ten or twelve," he says, adding people in his head.

"Oh, my!"

As the Martinez family returns to the main gallery, the Munday kids sit at the far end of the long dining table, shy of the strangers filling the main gallery. Alyssa scoots closer to Ethan and whispers to her brother, "I was hoping it was Dad."

Ethan quietly agrees. "Me, too. Now the mine is full of people we don't know."

The children's apprehensiveness creates tension in the room.

Rob plays host. "Ah, here we are. Everyone, this is Ethan and Alyssa. Courtney and Rick's offspring. You've met Courtney. Rick should be along soon. Ethan and Alyssa, this is the Martinez family. At least part of the family. Remember, I told you Rodrigo and his brother Eddie built the hideaway with me."

Ethan mentally counts the new arrivals. "Part of the family? There's more?"

Rodrigo smiles and is about to speak when Rob interrupts him. "Rodrigo's brother, Eddie, and his family will join us. They should arrive any time now." Rob says moving his glance from Rodrigo to the kids, to Courtney, and back to Rodrigo.

Alyssa moves to stand with her mother as she sizes up the Martinez family. "I think we're gonna need a bigger cave."

Ethan walks across the room and stands in front of Carlos. Carlos is a year older and three inches taller than Ethan. Ethan holds out his hand. "I'm Ethan. What's your name?"

Carlos shakes hands with Ethan. "Carlos," he says, flatly.

There's a pang in Ethan's heart, but he forces a smile. "I'm glad you made it here safely. Welcome to Munday's Hideaway." Ethan's gesture breaks the tension. Everyone feels welcome and starts the work of settling in.

Chapter 41: Denver

Thursday Morning–Denver, Colorado

Jin and Becky slept until late morning, lazing in bed, chatting, and cuddling. Becky is in the shower while Jin checks the news on his band. The news of a meteor strike near Washington, D.C., shocks him.

Becky walks out of the bathroom, wrapped in a towel. Jin is sitting on the bed with his back to her. "Jin, honey, what's the matter?"

Jin turns to her with a panicked expression. "We need to pack and find cover as quickly as possible."

"What happened? Is it about the Perth photos?"

Jin stands unconsciously naked and moves to the bathroom. "Worse. A meteor hit Washington. The President announced that Earth is in an asteroid storm. We need to find a safe place. I'll take a quick shower. Get dressed and pack as quick as you can."

Becky doesn't know where they will go, but she's done a lot of camping in the Colorado Mountains. She runs around the house, grabbing gear and dumping it on the living room floor: sleeping bags, a tent, rope, cooking gear, knives, and boots. By the time Jin is out of the shower and dressed, she's adding food and water to the pile.

Jin walks into the living room and sees the pile of gear. "Wow, woman, you move fast!"

Becky smiles, pushes a strand of hair from her eyes, and keeps moving. "I figure we'll pack everything in your truck—it has more room than my car. I guess we'll be camping out somewhere so…" Becky motions to the pile.

Jin hugs Becky tightly. Her heart beats rapidly. She struggles, trying to move, but Jin holds her until she calms. He whispers in her ear. "You're so wonderful. I want to ravage you right here on top of the camping gear."

Becky huffs. "Rolling around on boots and cooking gear in the middle of an asteroid storm might get us killed."

"I don't care. I've loved. I've been loved. Dying in your arms would be death of a life fulfilled."

Becky pushes him away. "You'll die alone, sucker. I'll be long gone. I don't plan to die at the mercy of some random rock falling from the sky. I'd rather live in a cave and be the last living human couple on Earth. Then make love like rabbits; working to repopulate the planet with our babies." Becky grabs a backpack off the floor, goes to her room, and stuffs it with clothing.

Jin stands in the living room, proud of the woman he loves, until he's prompted by a voice from the bedroom. "Get moving. You need to find me my cave." Jin grabs the sleeping bags and tent to load in the truck.

Jin and Becky finish loading the gear. Jin touches home and his truck drives via the fastest route.

"We'll drop by my house to grab my clothes and gear. While we're driving, let's run some searches for caves and air-raid shelters. We need to find a safe place, but one with food and water nearby."

Jin's truck pulls into the assigned parking spot at his townhouse. "I'll just be a minute," Jin says, exiting the truck and running, two steps at a time, up the stairs to his townhouse. While waiting in the truck, Becky locates listings for storm shelters in the Denver area, checking each shelter to see which ones provide the best protection and resources for an extended stay.

Jin quickly returns to the truck wearing a heavy backpack and both hands carrying duffle bags. He loads the bags into the back of the truck and jumps in.

"Well, you pack fast. Another plus in your favor. I might decide to keep you," Becky says.

"I have an emergency, go bag packed in case of a storm or natural disaster. I hadn't planned on an asteroid storm, but same idea. Do you have a spot picked out?"

Becky is about to answer when Curtis's image appears on Jin's band. Jin touches in. Curtis is very excited and animated. "Did you see what happened in Baltimore? The devastation is incredible. The death toll could be a million. At least we got our message out. I hope we warned some people in time. Our message went massively viral worldwide! Now all the news is about DC, but we did our best. We were right, asteroids are impacting all over the place. If we weren't anonymous, we'd be frickin' famous. Oh hey, Becky."

Becky leans toward the band before Jin has the chance to respond. "Yeah. It's so cool to have asteroids smashing into Earth killing people. Its great people had like five seconds' warning."

Jin looks cross-eyed at Becky and tries to calm the discussion. "We did the best we could with the information we had. The bad news is that impacts are increasing around the world. We're searching for a location to ride out the storm. Curtis, you'd better find some deep cover for yourself. Becky has a list of potential locations. We're sorting through them now."

Curtis replies. "Becky, you're right. If we knew sooner, we could have saved more lives. There was a news blackout. Without us, there wouldn't have been any warning at all. I just hope we helped save some people."

"I know you did your best, Curtis. Sorry for being snappy. If the world knew, they would surely thank you guys."

Curtis accepts Becky's apology with a tilt of his head, then his eyes go wide, and he types rapidly.

"Hey. I know a place. Get to the Denver airport. There are underground fortified shelters under the terminals and outlying buildings."

Becky quickly reviews her list. "I have the airport on my list, but it's farther than other locations, and may not be best for food and water."

"I've spent way too many hours researching the fabled underground structures of the Denver airport. There's a lot of mystery surrounding that place, but I can tell you with confidence, there is an underground, reinforced structure under the United lost baggage warehouse, on Undergrove Street. The LSG Sky Chefs building is across the parking lot. LSG Sky Chefs prepare meals for a thousand flights per day. The building is a hundred thousand square feet of food and water storage. These facilities are not at the main terminal, so off the radar for most people. You'll have food and shelter without competition from others."

Becky looks up from her list and gives Jin a quick nod of agreement.

"Sounds good, Curtis. I guess we'll be staying at the airport until further notice. How about you? You'd better get to a safe place. Henderson, Nevada won't be spared from the asteroid storm."

Curtis sucks the straw of his Gulp cup, but it's empty. The straw gurgles with air bubbles. "Don't worry about me. My old man was an end-of-the-world prepper. He built a steel-reinforced cement bunker twenty feet underground next to the garage. It's stocked with food and water, designed to support a family of four. I'm good."

"Stay safe, buddy. So, the structure you're talking about is under the United building, but food is in the Sky Chef building? That means we have to leave the shelter and move to another building to get food?"

"Yes, it's two different buildings, but they're just across a parking lot from each other. The asteroid storms are arriving in the afternoon and continue through the night. There will be plenty of time to get out and explore during the day."

Curtis pauses for a moment then adds, "You could stock up there, then head to my house, I mean, when the impacts die down. You can move during the day. I have plenty of room and supplies for us." Curtis peers into the camera looking like a sad hairy puppy dog longing for company.

Jin hesitates. He is most concerned about protecting Becky. Becky looks at the image of Curtis. "Sounds great, Curtis. We'll stock up on supplies at the airport then head your way. I can't wait to meet you in person." Jin doesn't argue with her plan.

Jin's truck steers onto the highway. "Curtman, we'll get to you as soon as we can. We might have to dodge a few meteors on the way, but we'll get there."

Rick has been driving for hours. Traffic is light, but the journey is taking longer than expected. The truck doesn't go very fast, and Rick doesn't want to push the old pickup too hard. He listens to the radio. Every channel carries non-stop news of the disaster in Washington, D.C. There are reports of multiple impacts in the Los Angeles area and impacts in Europe and Asia. Rick wants to hear more about Los Angeles, but the reporting is a regurgitation of every detail about Washington.

The news reported that the Los Angeles impacts occurred in the foothills of the San Gabriel Mountains. That's Pasadena! Rick worries about his family. His gut tells him they are OK, but his gut can't stop his mind from worrying.

People ride in AutoCars going about their daily business. Rick wonders why they aren't frightened? Why aren't they preparing for the storm? Maybe Washington, D.C. is too far away. Maybe they don't think it affects them. Rick is sure that people don't understand the amount of destruction a heavy asteroid bombardment will inflict on Earth.

It's late in the afternoon when he approaches the Denver Metro area. Reaching Denver is a great accomplishment. He is closer to home. Closer to Rob, the kids, and Courtney.

Rick stares out the window at the Rocky Mountains. They are a stark contrast to the flat grasslands he has driven through all day. Once he gets to Denver and fills the truck's gas tank, he'll drive through the Rockies on the way to Los Angeles.

A flash of an immensely bright light blinds Rick. He steers straight ahead and presses the brakes to slow. He hears cars crashing.

As he regains his vision, a delivery van swerves and overturns directly in the path of his pickup. Rick presses the brakes harder but can't avoid smashing into the chassis of the overturned truck. The impact smashes his head against the steering wheel. Another car crashes into the rear of his truck, whip lashing his head into the rear window. After coming to a stop, Rick sits in the wrecked truck, bracing for another impact. Blood streams into his right eye from a cut on his forehead. He wipes the blood away. His head and body are hurting, but nothing is broken. He looks out the driver's side window and sees three yellow lights streaking through the sky, followed by puffy white trails headed in his direction.

Rick tries to open the truck door, but it's blocked. He scoots across the bench seat, leans back, and kicks the passenger door with both legs. The door swings open with a metal creaking sound. He grabs his backpack and jumps out of the truck. The highway is blocked by wrecked cars and trucks. Dazed people wander around the crashed cars. A man limps from his burning car while trying to make a call on his band. Another man stands outside his car yelling; apparently, he'll be late for an important meeting.

Fireballs are coming. There is no time to waste. Rick spots an overpass one hundred yards ahead. If he can just get under the base of the overpass, it will provide some protection from the fast-approaching meteors. Rick runs as fast as he can, zigzagging and dodging wrecked cars. He passes a man and a woman standing by their wrecked car.

"Run! Follow me to the overpass," he calls out as he runs.

He sees a woman sitting in her car, crying loudly. "Get out of your car. More asteroids are coming… run to the overpass," he says as he pulls her door open, encouraging her to follow him. She doesn't move. Rick can't stop to explain. After hesitating, he runs. Rick is twenty yards from the overpass, running as quickly as his legs allow, weaving around cars and jumping over debris littering the highway.

Fifteen feet from the overpass, a burst of heat and light fills surrounds him. Rick shields his eyes for the second time in two minutes. His skin is on fire from the heat of the exploding meteor. Blinded, he trips, falling to the pavement. He braces the fall with his hands, feeling his skin being scraped off his palms by the rough roadway. His knees take the rest of the impact as he skids on the pavement. He is in pain. He doesn't move. Blood drips down his face from his head wound. His body is sore, but his brain is still working.

"One meteor down, aerial explosion, two to go," he thinks as he lies on the roadway waiting for explosions and death to arrive. Rick's face rests on the pavement. One moment, he feels the texture of rough cement against his cheek and the smell of road oils; the next he is being dragged under the overpass.

The face of a young Asian man leans down. "Can you move? We need to get up the abutment underneath the overpass as high as we can. Ready?"

Rick tries to stand as the young man lifts him. Rick summons the strength to move as he and the young man scramble up the cement ramp to the abutment. Their bodies spill into a narrow crawl space where the ramp of the abutment meets the supporting base of the overpass.

The sky erupts as the second meteor explodes just a few thousand feet above the surface, disintegrating into a million pieces. The blast sends rocks ranging from a few feet in size down to spherules no larger than a pebble traveling at twenty-eight thousand miles per hour, slicing through cars, trucks, and human flesh. The pieces of exploded meteor keep moving until something can stop them, which is usually several feet of earth.

Rick and the others who made it under the overpass hear metal being crushed and pierced. A meteorite crashes through the overpass, leaving a gaping hole in the center of the bridge. The people hiding in the abutment wedge themselves deeper into their protective space as rocks and dirt blast through the underpass.

The third meteor does not explode in the atmosphere. The fiery rock crashes into a grassy field three miles away. There is a mighty sound and the ground shakes. The impact sends a plume of dirt high into the air. A hot blast of wind follows the explosion.

Rick rests his back on the cement foundation of the overpass, sitting with his knees scrunched under his chin. A line of people are crowded in the cramped space. He wipes the sticky, slowing stream of blood from his eye and looks at his scraped hands in the gray light, picking sand and pebbles out of his wounds.

The pastor's old truck is wrecked. Rick allows himself a moment of despair, wondering how he will make it home. Denver is a long way from Pasadena.

Rick feels a hand on his shoulder. "Wow. I guess we made it just in time. Too close if you ask me." The man notices Rick staring at his hands. "Are you OK? Looks like you have a nasty cut on your forehead. That will leave a scar."

Rick raises his gaze slowly to the face of the young man who pulled him to safety, answering slowly. "Yeah, scraped my hands and knees. Thanks for your help."

Rick leans forward to look out beyond the overpass. "I'd be mincemeat if I'd stayed out there." Rick spots a car bumper riddled with small holes, lying in the road just beyond the overpass. "That must be what I tripped over. You saved my life. That was very brave."

"We tried to save people—to warn everybody—they must have received the message a hundred times. I don't know why people aren't taking the warning seriously. We told them more were coming after Perth. With DC, it's obvious. People need to find protection or they're all going to die," the young man says.

Rick is astonished. "You tried to warn everyone? What do you mean?"

The young man sits taller, pulling a young woman sitting next to him closer. "My friend Curtis got a message and photos from our friend in Perth, over ham radio. There was no news of the destruction. I know it sounds crazy, but I believe the government was covering it up. We had to get the message out to warn everyone. My name's Jin. This is my girlfriend, Becky." Jin extends his hand. Rick looks at his bloodied hands. Jin pulls his hand back.

"You sent the message about Perth?"

"Jin and Curtis tried to warn everyone. There just wasn't enough time," says the young woman.

"I'm Rick Munday. Nice to meet you. I'm glad someone got a warning out. I hope my family received it in time. You're not crazy. The government blocked the news about Perth. They covered up more than that. They've known asteroids were coming for a long time; at least part of the government knew and did nothing to warn people."

Becky is curious about the man Jin saved. "How do you know this? Who are you?"

"I'm an astrophysicist from Cal Tech. I did a preliminary study as part of a grant proposal. My findings showed that Earth might go through a period of heavy asteroid bombardment. I didn't know it would actually happen. It was just a hypothesis. I was in Washington for a seminar. I learned that a faction of the government was covering up the news of Perth. This group knew the asteroid storm was coming and worked to save only themselves."

Rick pauses for a moment, reviewing the events in New Arcadia. He decides it's too much to share with people he has just met. Rick tries to stand, but the ceiling is low, so he hunches over. "Thanks for your help. I need to keep moving. I need to get to my family in Los Angeles." Rick starts down the ramp to the highway.

Some people who found protection under the overpass walk down to the highway, while others are too frightened to move. The only people alive are those who found shelter under the overpass.

Rick pauses halfway down the ramp and calls out. "This is just the beginning of a major asteroid storm. It could last weeks or months. Gather your loved ones and find shelter. Get hunkered down before everyone goes into panic mode. There's no telling what people will do when they realize what's happening and get hungry."

Jin watches Rick limp down the ramp. Becky jabs him in the ribs.

"Go after him," she urges. "He's injured. If he's on his own, he might not make it through the night." Becky pulls Jin closer. "Ask him to join us at the airport to rest before he moves on. He knows all about this. I bet there's more we can learn from him."

Jin nods to Becky. "OK, I'll ask him to join us."

Jin and Becky grab their backpacks and scurry down the ramp. Rick walks on the highway, weaving through wrecked cars, trucks, and bodies toward Denver.

"Mr.... ah, Munday. Wait." Jin runs to catch up with Rick. "Becky and I know a place near the airport with food and protection from the storm. Would you join us for the night?"

Rick stops walking. He wants to keep moving, but he's tired and sore. "It is getting late, and I need a safe place for the night. Your offer sounds nice, thanks."

The sound of cars and trucks snaking through the wreckage disrupts the silence on the highway of death. A semi-truck leads a caravan of vehicles through the impact zone. The semi pushes damaged vehicles from the roadway, making a narrow path for others to follow. Slowly, the large semi clears a lane lined with wrecked cars and trucks through the destruction.

A steady line of vehicles pass them heading toward the airport. Becky steps out in front of a large truck and waves her arms. The truck has no choice but to stop. Becky speaks to the driver. After a minute, Becky motions for Jin and Rick to get in the truck. Moments later, the three of them are moving toward the airport. Traffic beyond the impact area speeds up, driving as if nothing had happened.

The truck driver is a heavyset guy who looks as if he hasn't shaved for a week. He wears a khaki hunting vest with more pockets than anyone would ever need, an old baseball cap, and sunglasses. The truck has a strange, indescribable smell. While not well-kept, he seems to be a good-natured fellow.

"Nasty weather we're having today, ain't it?" Without waiting for anyone to respond, he continues. "Thank God, I stopped to piss back thar at the Love's Travel Stop. I just missed getting plastered with those space bb's. I'm not in need of any ventilation. Thank you very much!" Rick thinks some ventilation might be just what the truck needs, still trying to decipher the source of smell in the truck. He's about to respond, but the trucker continues his monologue.

"Lots of cars heading the other way, leaving the airport. I bet the airport just closed. Somehow, I'm guessing, exploding space rocks and aero planes don't mix. Who-ha!" The trucker laughs and chortles gleefully.

"I'd expect every airport in the country will close, based on the number of meteors in the past twenty-four hours. Maybe the FAA finally got around to issuing a warning," Jin says.

The trucker drives anxiously, scanning the road, watching for oncoming cars crossing lanes. "I'm dropping my load at the Lufthansa Cargo building, then heading as far from here as possible. If you want to get to the passenger terminal, you'll have to catch another ride."

Jin reviews the map in his VUE lens and spots the Lufthansa building just down the street from the United warehouse. He swipes his hand to display the map on his band and nudges Becky, pointing to the map.

Becky speaks to the driver. "Oh, we're heading to the United baggage warehouse to meet my brother. He works there. That's on the way, isn't it?"

The truck driver looks at Becky. His eyes squint as he examines her with suspicion. "I think your brother might not be telling the truth. I don't think you'll have much luck finding him unless he's a lost bag." The truck swerves to avoid an oncoming car. "I don't know what you kids are up to. I don't much care, anyhow. I don't need a fancy story. I'm gonna unload my shipment and get the hell outta dodge."

The truck stops at the corner of Undergrove Street, in front of a building marked United Baggage Storage. There are several cars in the parking lot and a group of people being led to the front door, guided by men in black uniforms.

"Now that is strange. I have drops here once or twice a week and the only car ever parked here is Terresa's. She's the only employee, and she ain't your brother!"

Rick recognizes the uniforms. Black Guard. "You're right. Something strange is going on. Can you drop us at the next building?" Rick asks.

The truck driver stops in front of the LSG Air Chefs' building as another car pulls into the United building's parking lot. The trio jumps out of the truck and walks to the LSG building.

"The parking lot is empty," Rick observes.

"Maybe they went home early," Becky says.

"Let's check the front door," says Jin.

Rick pulls on the door, but it's locked. Jin spots a security pad. Using his VUE, he moves his hands in front of his face.

Rick is curious. "Can you get us in?"

"If it has a network connection, I can get us in."

Becky gives a proud, confirming nod.

Twenty seconds later, a green LED flashes on the pad and the door buzzes. Rick pulls the door open with a look of astonishment.

"How did you do that?" he asks as they walk into the building.

Jin doesn't answer; He is in awe of the huge brightly lit building filled with equipment that robotically prepares meals for thousands of airline passengers each day. The group walks down a line of food preparation equipment.

"I work for the NSA. I can hack my way into almost anything," Jin finally answers.

Rick gives Jin a surprised look. "Nice work."

"It doesn't look like anyone's here, but some machines are still running," Becky comments, looking around cautiously.

"The system looks highly automated. They probably don't have a large staff," Jin notes.

Several mechanized, automated production lines that prepare airline meals fill the large building. The equipment processes individual meal components, then places bowls and plates filled with food onto trays. A mechanism inserts the filled trays into the familiar food trolleys pushed by stewards up and down the aisles of aircraft. Two of the lines are still operating. With no workers to manage the trollies, trays full of food exit the machine crashing to the floor, one after the other.

"Looks like they left in a hurry," notes Rick.

"Exploding meteors make people scatter fast," says Jin.

Becky points to the pile of food on the floor. "It looks like Chicken Cordon bleu."

"Wow, this must be the business class line. It smells good," says Rick.

Jin opens the door of a nearby trolley and pulls out food trays, handing one to Rick. "Dinner is served."

"There's the employee break area. We can eat there," says Becky, taking a tray from Jin.

Rick digs into the airline food as he observes Jin and Becky. They seem like a nice young couple, but Jin's admission that he works for the NSA concerns Rick. The NSA is a division of Homeland Security. Is he part of the conspiracy?

Rick looks Jin in the eye and asks, "You work for Homeland Security, but you and your friend sent the message about Perth. Somehow, that doesn't add up because it was people at Homeland who blocked news of the asteroid storm."

Jin swallows hard. "The NSA has technically been a division of Homeland for the past decade, but we're very autonomous. I monitor communications traffic. We use algorithms to watch for trends. I had no idea the government was blocking news until Curtis contacted me about Perth."

Becky interrupts. "They search for asteroids as a hobby." Jin nods. She then adds, "It's how we met."

"Hmm, actual star-crossed lovers. Could be a first," Rick says.

Jin straightens. "Hey, I confess, we're nerds. That's it. No conspiracy here."

Jin pauses for a moment, waiting for Rick's approval. Rick doesn't give it. He stares at Jin and Becky, hoping his gut feeling is right about the couple.

Jin continues. "There must be a team inside Homeland working with a spooky high level of security to block their activity from my group. When Curtis told me about Perth, I hacked into Australian servers and discovered how communications from Australia were being blocked. I realized someone very high up was controlling the news. I knew we had to get the information out to the world."

"Spooky is right. They call themselves Arcadians. They knew the asteroid storm was coming and hid the information, even from our government, to protect themselves. Unfortunately, I have experienced firsthand what these guys are capable of. There's nothing you or I can do about them now. The shit storm is here. I don't care about the politics—I just want to get home to my wife and kids."

"Government be damned. Nothing matters more than saving the ones you love." Jin puts his arm around Becky. "We're heading to Las Vegas to meet up with Curtis. Other than Becky, he's the only family I have, and he has nobody but us."

Rick pushes his food tray aside. He tells Becky and Jin the story of his experience in New Arcadia. He tells them about Colonel Cruikshank, the underground cities, and his escape from New Arcadia on a high-speed rail headed to an underground city named New Zion. He tells them about the meteor impact that interrupted his journey, the nice preacher, and his drive to Denver.

Then, in a guarded tone, he tells Jin and Becky, "Those men escorting people into the baggage storage building were Black Guard, just like in New Arcadia. I think the Denver airport might be New Zion." He points his finger down, indicating that the city could be below them.

Becky perks up. "The United building… Curtis told us it has an underground structure."

"If the rumors about the Denver airport are true, Curtis will be very excited to learn his conspiracy theories weren't fantasy, after all," Jin says.

"I can't wait to meet your Curtman." Becky nudges Jin.

"Incredible. The amount of money and planning this must have taken. Colonel Cruikshank masterminded the entire thing and kept it a secret all these years. It's amazing," says Rick.

A distant sound rumbles through the cavernous building. Becky raises her head to listen. "Is that thunder?"

The thunderous sound grows louder, closer, and more frequent.

Rick's ears perk as he studies the sounds. "I don't think that's thunder!"

The sound of a huge explosion rocks the building. The cement floor heaves and the building rattles. The ceiling lights sway.

Rick reaches for his pack. "Kids, we'd better find cover. The sky is falling."

Becky and Jin grab their gear and run for the door. Becky touches the side of her glasses, switching to VUE mode as she runs.

"I'm pulling up the plans for the building next door. There's an elevator and stairwell in a maintenance room."

"Seems odd for a one-story building, doesn't it?" says Jin, as he reaches for Becky's hand while running. After a moment, he adds, "Hey, how did you get those plans?"

"You're not the only one with hacker skills. Oh, and Curtis helped me."

The trio pushes through the door into the night. The sky is lit up with glowing meteors and shooting stars. Several meteors explode in the lower atmosphere, sending shock waves through the air.

As they run across the parking lot to the next building, Becky grips Jin's hand tighter. "Wow, the sky really is falling," she says in a terrified tone.

Chapter 42: Tribulation

Thursday–Burwell, Nebraska - Late Afternoon

Pastor Keith talked with the police chief. The crater outside of town and the news from Washington, D.C., had raised concern, but people in this part of Nebraska can be stubborn. It was not until the vice president appeared on TV, declaring himself president, and announcing a nationwide state of alert that the chief went into action.

The chief dispatched patrol cars using bullhorns to instruct the residents of Burwell to meet at Riverside Park. The chief went to the grocery stores in town and commandeered truckloads of food and water. The chief enlisted the help of the Boy Scout troop and store workers to load the trucks.

It was late in the afternoon when the town of twelve hundred souls gathered in the parking lot of Riverside Park. School buses fill the parking lot, ready for the trek to the rail tunnel.

People gather in groups. The Methodist church huddles together. Members of the Church of Living Waters gather in another part of the parking lot, across from the Catholics. People who work together at the feedlots, the grocery stores, and other local businesses who aren't churchgoers cling together in their own small groups. The police chief stands on the back of a flatbed truck.

"People of Burwell, thank you for your orderly assembly. We are a solid community. We need to stay that way. This is a scary time. I don't know what's ahead of us with these asteroids, but the best course of action is for all of us to get underground for protection. Remain calm and we'll get through this. I'm sure you've all heard about this tunnel. Now, we've been out there to check it out. I guess you also heard about the ladder. Good news is the boys found an elevator. Bad news is that dirt buried the tunnel door. We have a crew down there digging it out and we have a diesel generator on site. The elevator will be ready soon, so we can all get down there faster and with more comfort."

There's a sigh of relief from the crowd. Everyone had heard about the long ladder. Most dreaded the climb. The chief waits for the commotion to die down, then speaks again.

"You can bring one suitcase, per person, and a sleeping bag. That's all. We have food and water donated from Dukeman's and Affiliated Foods. We thank them for their support. Whatever else you brought, leave it here. Won't do you no good. It's a narrow tunnel and there isn't room for lots of crap." A man in the crowd waves his hand vigorously to get the chief's attention. The chief points at the man. "Chris White."

"Chief, I got a folding chair. Is that all right?"

"If I say yes, then everyone will go off scrambling for folding chairs. Y'all listen up. One suitcase and a sleeping bag. That's it, for now. Don't panic about comfort items. We'll have time to grab more of what we need as time goes on. We want everyone safe and secure ASAP. So, hold your questions."

The chief looks out at the crowd. Most of these people he grew up with and has spent his life with. They can rebuild the town. He won't let some asteroid from space kill his people.

"To keep things orderly, we are loading into six buses. Drop whatever you don't need and line up. Buses will rotate every twenty minutes, which should allow most of the first load to get down the elevator before the next group arrives. We'll have everyone out there in less than two hours. If you leave and drive out there, you'll be the last in the tunnel, so be neighborly and patient." The first busloads of people clamber onto the buses.

Haylee and Keith huddle with their congregation. Everyone is nervous about what's happening. They pray. Haylee takes a head count. It's been hours since the police cars went around town, but Frank and Debbie Brown are still not at the park.

Haylee pulls Keith aside. "Frank and Debbie aren't here. What should we do?"

Keith feels responsible for his congregates. "Some people are stubborn; others are plain stupid. Frank might well be in the stupid category. Nevertheless, my duty is to shepherd all the lambs of our flock."

"Maybe they just need assurance that they're loved and accepted. We can't leave without them."

"It'll take some time for these buses to get everyone out to the tunnel and back. I'll drive to Frank's place to get him and Debbie. I'll be back with them before the last bus leaves," Keith says.

Haylee looks at her husband adoringly. "You are my Rock."

Keith pulls his wife to him, giving her a tight hug and a deep kiss. He looks deeply into her eyes.

"You're a strong, smart woman." Keith lingers for a moment, inhaling the smell of her hair. "If I'm your rock, you are my Mother Earth."

The path to the car is littered with items not allowed in the tunnel. Keith notices a copy of the book Straight Up: 10 Ways for Christians to Prepare for the Rapture, laying in the dirt, its pages fluttering in the wind.

Keith drives to the Browns' house. It's just a few minutes out of town, on the way to the reservoir, off Dam Road. The Calmus River runs along the north side of town. Keith gazes at the lazy river most of the way to the Browns' house.

Keith pulls up to the house. The place looks quiet. Frank's submarine, resting on wood mounts, has a more finished appearance than before. He walks to the front door and hears voices arguing inside.

"I'm not going down into some tunnel. God spoke to me. Woman, why don't you believe me? I built it for you. To save you!"

"Frank Brown, you're a goddamned fool. I've known it since we were young. If it wasn't for Thomas, I would have left you long ago. It's been one crazy scheme after another your whole life. I stayed for Thomas. You know that. I've barely hung on since he's gone. I will not get into that tin can you made." Her voice trails off.

"Thomas has been dead for five years. You haven't left me. If you stayed for him, why are you still here? I loved him too. He was my son. You're not the only one who loved him. I am a fool, I know it. But this fool loves you, woman. I want to protect you. God told me how and I built it. I built it for you. For us. It's time. It's nearly time. I know it."

Keith feels like an awkward eavesdropper. He's about to knock on the door when Frank bursts out of the house, almost bulldozing Keith.

"Keith. What are you doing out here? I thought everyone headed to your tunnel."

Keith staggers backward, hoping not to fall. After a few steps, he steadies his stance. "The whole town is in the park. They're taking busloads of people out to the tunnel now. They found an elevator, so getting down will be easier."

Frank stares at Keith indignantly. "And you came out here to fetch me and Debbie, I suppose?"

Keith smiles his country pastor smile, sincere and folksy. "Well, sure Frank. We want everyone to be safe. We wouldn't go down there without you all."

Frank stands firm. Debbie walks onto the porch. "Well, we ain't going, are we, Debbie doll?" Debbie stands without reply. Frank points at Keith. "God has mysteries. You said that, Keith."

He turns and marches to his submarine as he speaks loudly. "He put it on my heart and in my brain to build this thing. So, I built it. I didn't ask why. He compelled me. There must be a reason. So, thanks, but we can't go to your tunnel, Keith."

Frank climbs up the wood mounts, opens the hatch, and squirms inside. He flips switches and turns knobs. A humming electronic sound emanates from the strange craft. His head bobs into view. Frank looks to Debbie, then cocks his head as if listening to something unheard.

"There isn't much time. Debbie doll, get in here with me. There's plenty of room, you'll see. I made it comfortable for you."

A bright spot appears in the clear eastern sky. The light in the sky grows larger as it moves closer. Frank is the first to see it and points.

"Debbie, it's coming. It's time. Get in here, baby. You'll be safe. You'll see."

Debbie and Keith look where Frank is pointing. The glowing orb grows larger and brighter. The fireball flies at a low angle toward Burwell; the light burning brighter as it grows closer. Keith tries to follow the meteor's crash to Earth, but he's blinded by the intense light. There is a thunderous sound as the meteor smashes into the base of the Virginia Smith Dam, which holds back the Calmus Reservoir.

A violent jolt in the ground knocks Keith and Debbie off their feet. The submarine rocks on its mounts but does not fall. Keith and Debbie attempt to stand as the ground cracks and splits in violent convulsions.

Keith regains his vision. As he looks around staggering in a daze, a hot blast of air, moving six hundred miles per hour, sends him flying. Keith hits the roof of the neighbor's overturned car, over seventy feet from where he stood. He rolls to the ground, afraid to stand, and surveys the destroyed landscape. The blast blew Frank's house away. Foundations, pipes, and water heaters are all that remain of neighboring houses. The wind tossed cars like toys and knocked the sub off its mounts. The sub lays in the grass on its side. Keith can't see Debbie anywhere.

The top hatch of the sub is dug into the dirt. No matter how hard he pushes, Frank cannot force the hatch open. He calls out to Debbie. He saw her fly into the air. He moves frantically inside his sub, looking out the windows, trying to locate his wife or the pastor. All he can see is destruction. He yells and pounds on the sub, but no one can hear him.

Covered in dust, Keith struggles to stand. The wind was so intensely hot it blistered his face and arms. Blood drips from his ears. He slowly inspects the destroyed landscape. He looks to the sky with awe and wonder. Far in the eastern sky, four more bright spots appear. Raising his hands toward heaven, he calls out. "And the stars of heaven fell unto Earth, even as a fig tree casteth her untimely figs, when she is shaken by a mighty wind." The four bright spots blaze in the sky. Two of them explode overhead, bursting into millions of bits.

Keith staggers through the debris, yelling, "And the kings of the Earth and great men, and the rich men, and the chief captains, and the mighty men, and every bondman, and every free man, hid themselves in the dens and in the rocks of the mountains, and said to the mountain and rocks, fall on us and hide us from the face of him that sitteth on the throne, and from the wrath of the lamb."

As Keith cries out, tiny bits of exploded meteor moving at twenty-eight thousand miles per second zip through his body. Small spots of blood slowly appear on his shirt, face, and arms. The small spherules pass through the pastor's body and keep moving, his nervous system not registering the pain.

Keith drops to one knee and haltingly recites. "And lo, a great multitude, which no man could number, hmm, stood before the lamb, clothed in white robes. And, and whence they came? These, these are they which came out of the great tribulation and washed their robes, made white in the blood of the lamb."

The force of the meteor that hit the base of the earthen dam pushed a tsunami-like wave of water up to the reservoir. When the wave of water lost its upstream momentum, the water in the reservoir traveled downstream with great speed. The rushing wave of water burst past the broken dam. Eighty million gallons of the Calmus Reservoir swept over the fish hatchery at the base of the dam and barreled down the river unabated toward the town of Burwell.

Keith hears roaring thunder in the distance but pays it no mind. He continues his recitation, mixing scriptures. "For there will be a great tribulation. No flesh will be saved. The sun shall be darkened. The moon shall not give her light. Concerning that day and hour, no one knows!" Keith stands, limping, blood oozing from tiny holes all over his body. He shouts incoherently. "Not even the angels of heaven, nor the Son, but I know. I know. You want a sign? You want signs? I don't need no rapture book. Tribulation is now!"

Debris covers Debbie, but slowly pushes her way out. She is two hundred feet from where she once stood. In the distance, she spots Keith staggering with arms outstretched. His face turned to the heavens, shouting. She limps toward Frank and his submarine.

She hears the thunderous roar. She watches a tremendous wave of water sweep over Keith. The torrent carries him away with ruined cars and broken houses. The deluge hits the submarine an instant before taking Debbie away with the flood waters. Her body turns and twists, submerged in the frothy, dirty surge traveling at great speed with incredible force.

Frank can't see the wall of water coming, but when it hits, the water lifts the sub, and it moves with the current. Turning over in the fast-moving water, the craft rights itself. Frank tumbles inside his boat. Water gushes through the unsecured hatch until he pulls it down and turns the wheel to seal it. He scrambles to the captain's seat, hoping to steer the craft, but the torrent of water carries the sub bobbing uncontrollably through the rapids heading toward town.

Frank sees cars, wood, and debris floating in the murky flood waters. The Calmus River makes a big bend just north of town. The sub moves with the force of the raging water as it sweeps over the riverbanks and sweeps across the town of Burwell.

Frank's sub bobs and bounces in the turbulent water as it sweeps across the town until the sub smashes into the wall of a building becoming lodged with other refuse accumulating as flood waters push and swirl around the blockage. Frank's sub is stuck, surrounded by debris, while the main force of the flood continues to savage the small town.

When the townspeople saw the first meteor approaching, many fled the park running in panic.

As the other meteors hit, people ran to their trucks and speed away. But Haylee keeps her flock together. The buses return, and a driver signals frantically for her group to get on his bus. Haylee pushes her people on board as the flood waters sweep around the bus. Some try foolishly to outrun the flood, only to be consumed by the muddy surge.

The flood waters seek to rejoin the river at the edge of the park.

The flood churns against the bus, moving it with the flood. The bus floats awkwardly on its side, pushed by the turbulent water, moving it across the park until it smashes against a large cottonwood tree. Water rushes around the bus, holding it against the massive timber. Haylee shudders as she watches bodies float past.

Soon, the flood waters calm and recede as they spread across the park, rejoining the lower Calmus. Haylee climbs out of the broken

Mike McCoy

bus, stepping to the soggy grass, followed by her congregation. Haylee surveys the desolated park, then looks to the heavens clutching her bosom. "My dear Keith."

Frank opens the hatch and crawls out of his sub. Trash, ruins of the town, and the stark white flesh of drowned bodies are piled around him. Frank cannot see another living soul. He sits on his wrecked submarine and cries.

Part Three–New Zion

Chapter 43: Hunkered Down

Thursday - Evening

Fires from heaven rain down on mankind, turning the moon bloodred. The sky reverberates with explosions and the ground groans from thumping impacts. Fires scorch and mountains tumble as the hail of heavenly rocks spreads across all the land, leaving desolation in the storm's wake.

Rick, Becky, and Jin crouch in front of the double glass doors at the entrance to the United building as Jin works on the access panel. Becky stares awestruck, witnessing the thunderous ruination of all that mankind has built. Rick is anxious as Jin works, his fingers turning and poking rapidly in midair, hacking his way past building security.

"What's taking so long?" Rick asks.

Jin looks up momentarily. "Access to this building is tougher than the one across the street. Some custom encryption, but I'm getting close."

Rick puts his hands to the tinted glass doors as if he is holding field glasses and presses his face to his hands to look inside. The lobby is dark and empty. No Black Guard.

A tremendous explosion rips through the night. Rick turns to face the direction of the blast. A scorching hot air burst, smashes their bodies against the building. Rick's back crushes against the glass door, cracking the glass. He covers his face to shield against flying dirt and small chunks of cement.

Becky's shoulder slams into the cement wall of the building. She whimpers in pain, then cries out frantically, as she watches the LSG building blow apart.

"Jin, hurry. We were just in there. If we hadn't gotten out... Oh, God."

The force of the blast rips a handicapped parking sign out of the ground, sending it flying. Rick, unable to move, watches the sign fly toward him. He braces in anticipation of being wiped out by the flying sign and metal pole. The sign pole flies in an arch like a spear and sticks in the grass three feet from him. The sign end penetrates the grass with the pole and the cone-shaped cement base suspended in the air.

Rick runs to the sign, hefts the heavy metal pole and yanks the sign out of the ground. He grips the pole like a lance and charges to the double glass doors. The end of the pole covered in its cone of cement acts as a battering ram. Rick aims for the right side of the double doors, hitting it dead center just above the metal push bar. The glass door shatters, sending shards of glass across the lobby floor. The sign pole hangs awkwardly through the metal frame of the door. As the glass door shatters, the access panel beeps, green lights blink, and the door unlocks.

Jin shouts, "Got it!" Raising his arms as if he scored a touchdown.

Rick sneers at Jin.

Jin, proud of himself, smiles and shrugs his shoulders.

Becky pushes past them and enters through the unlocked left door. "Great teamwork, boys. Let's find the stairwell before we get plastered by a meteor."

The door from the lobby to the main building is open. Behind the door is a vast warehouse with rows and rows of multi-level racks filled with suitcases of every shape and color. The team uses flashlights and Becky's building layout to find the maintenance room. A sign: No Admittance–Maintenance Personnel Only, is on the door. The door has an access panel like the one at the entrance. It takes Jin only seconds to hack entry into the maintenance room door.

"Not much of a maintenance room. It's just an elevator and a stairwell," says Jin.

"But it's our stairwell," says Becky.

"Good job, Becky," says Rick.

Halfway down the first flight of steps, Jin stops to dig in his backpack. He pulls out a small black box and switches it on. A red LED flashes. Seconds later, the LED changes to solid green and he sets the box on a step. "OK, all set," he says. Becky moves down the steps. Rick and Jin follow.

"What was that?" Rick asks.

"It's a satellite relay link. Terrestrial data is out. No data, no news, no communications. The transceiver will give us access to satellite data in the stairwell."

They run down the stairs in search of safety from the raging storm above.

"Let's not go down too low. I want to make sure we have a strong signal while we work," says Jin.

The team settles in at the fourth level down, sitting on the steps in the dark stairwell. The sounds of the sky storm now a gentle rumble. Jin and Becky go to work on their VUE. Becky checks the news streams while Jin accesses Homeland Security systems. He scans for updates on FEMA emergency response, military orders, troop movements, and inter-agency transmissions, hoping to learn anything that will help them plan their move to Las Vegas.

Rick feels like a third wheel. He doesn't have a VUE or a band. He is tired and bruised, but he won't let physical pain keep him from reaching his family. He shines his flashlight down the stairwell. The stairs go down into blackness; a blackness that swallows the beam of his flashlight. A tinge of fear runs up his back as he stares into that darkness. Just hours ago, he escaped the underground city of New Arcadia. Now he stares at blackness that may lead to New Zion.

Rick turns away from the dark to see Becky and Jin sitting shoulder to shoulder, light escaping the edges of their VUE, illuminating their faces as they sweep their fingers over invisible screens.

"You whiz kids come up with anything?"

Becky looks at Rick through her lens with the VUE glow lighting her smiling face. Jin keeps working. "I've been reading news streams," she says. "The asteroid storm is moving east to west in a wide path covering the northern hemisphere. Some places are getting hit hard while other towns are untouched. There are reports of destruction across Europe and Asia. No news on how far south the storm goes, but since Perth got hit, I guess it's the entire planet."

Jin jumps in. "Great update, Beck. Here's what I have. President Baker held a video conference with all fifty state governors this morning, telling them it's every man for himself. The states are pretty much on their own."

"So basically, he told the governors, 'Sorry about no warning and by the way we have no plan, so bend over and kiss your asses goodbye,'" Rick says, facetiously.

"I bet the president and his staff are well-protected. Just think of all the people who are dying because of our incompetent government," says Becky.

"It seems the new president knows about your Arcadian friends and doesn't like them much. I'm picking up chatter from military sources... hold on a sec," Jin says.

Jin types and swipes the air while Becky and Rick wait. Jin talks to himself, or maybe it's a conversation with his Lens. "Oh, really? This is good. Is there more detail? That helps. Brilliant."

Rick doesn't like being left out of the conversation. "What is it? What's so brilliant?"

Becky adds, "Share, share."

Jin smiles. "I like this new president. You told us the Arcadians have several underground cities. Apparently, admittance to the Arcadian party is strictly by special invitation. President Baker wants to crash the party. He intends to swarm the underground cities with as many people as he can."

"That would save thousands of lives," Becky says.

Rick considers the idea. "Uninvited guests will mess up the colonel's plans. His few and fortunate be damned."

"See, it's brilliant. Screw with the Arcadians and save people at the same time," says Jin.

Rick's mind is scheming. "Maybe we can help the new president with his plan. Have they located all the cities? I saw some maps. I might help fill in the blanks."

Jin checks his VUE. "They have two underground cities located. They've been trying to locate the Arcadian servers to learn more, but no luck. They're planning to attack the cities with the US Marines, but it will take several days for them to deploy."

"That'll be too late. People are dying. This needs to happen now!" Becky pleads.

"Becky's right. Another night of impacts and all communication systems will be down. There'll be no way to get a message to people. It might be too late, already."

Jin swipes his finger through the air, then presses an invisible button. "OK, desperate times call for desperate measures. We got a message out, once, maybe we can do it again."

"I just hope people react this time," says Becky.

Curtis answers Jin's call. "Hey, Jin. Where are you guys? I hope you're safe. I think the asteroid I discovered just landed in my backyard."

"We're hunkered down in a stairwell below the building you recommended. Thanks for that tip, man. It saved us. Are you safe?"

"Yeah, I'm in my old man's bug-out shelter. I hope this is over soon. I'm not sure my soda supply will last." Curtis raises his Gulp cup, shaking it to show it's empty.

He tries to scoot along the floor of the shelter like he does in his house, but the chair doesn't roll. "Damn, oof." Curtis hefts himself out of his chair, walks to a shelf stocked with Coca-Cola, grabs a big bottle, and strolls back to his desk.

"Curtis, we need your help. We need to get another message out."

"OK, sure. What do you need me to do? Oops, I mean, chay' jIQaHlaH," Curtis asks how he can help in Klingon.

"No need for that, Curtman. I installed an extra layer of encryption to our VPN. Nobody will listen in on our calls."

"Thank god. Speaking Klingon is rough on the old larynx," Curtis says, then hacks a cough.

Jin swipes to display the call on the projected display of his band, so Rick can see and interact.

"Curtman, we believe the rumors of the Denver airport having an underground base are true."

Curtis is smug. "I knew it. I've been giving you the evidence for years."

"But not a base. A city. This is our new friend, Rick Munday. He escaped from a city named New Arcadia. We think this stairwell leads to a city complex, deep below the Denver airport."

Curtis sucks on the straw of his Gulp cup, as if it's a pacifier, then exclaims, "Are you shitting me? I told you! Didn't I tell you? You thought it was all a bunch of conspiracy theories. Oh, my oh,

God. I need pizza. The conspiracy nuts had it right all along. Bazinga!"

"Curtis, these cities are new. A secret part of the government built them. They call themselves Arcadians," Rick explains.

"Oh wow. Arcadia… that's a Greek reference to a civilization living in harmony with nature, a utopian ideal. Arcadians. That's so sick!"

"The guy in charge is sick, if you ask me. He, and his followers, knew the storm was coming and built the cities to survive," says Rick.

"A secret sect of the government working to protect a selected few. Who would believe this could actually happen? It does sound like one of your conspiracy theories," adds Jin.

"The best conspiracy theory I ever heard." Curtis hums the melody of the X-Files theme song.

"Curtman, I'm sending you code keys for access to secure Homeland servers. We need to locate all the access points in every underground city. We'll hack the security at every location so people can enter. Then we broadcast a message advising people to move underground for protection from the storm."

Becky jumps in. "We need to work fast, so we can save as many lives as possible."

"Hey, you know me. I'm always up for a challenge, but that's a huge ask. I know you have super-high-level access. Won't these Arcadians have servers, separate from the servers where you have spook-level access? How do we find them, let alone hack them? We don't even know their locations. It could take weeks," Curtis says. His hand trembles as he refills his Gulp cup.

"We've got to try," Becky pleads.

Jin types in the air. "Curtis, I've sent you the key codes. You have a faster, more stable connection than I do. Gain access and link me to the government systems, and we'll work together. Rick will work with Becky to build a list of cities. We'll confirm the locations and points of entry. Let's get busy!"

"I've scoured every server, in every data center I can think of, but I can't find anything that leads us to the Arcadian servers. We're stuck," Jin says in frustration.

"I can remember four of the cities and one they said was under construction, but I know there were more," says Rick.

"Even if we knew all the city locations and accessed their systems, we've got to be careful how we do this. If we hack their security before people are at the doors, they'll have time to change the codes and lock us out indefinitely. This will never work, guys. We need help and I need brain food," says Curtis. He pushes himself out of his chair and goes in search of snacks.

"We've got to do something. I'm sure there's a clue. We just need to think. We know some city names. We know the general locations. Do a search. Maybe there are data centers near the city locations? Search for major construction projects over the past five years? Come on boys, think! There must be a way to find the Arcadian systems," Becky says.

"I'm checking for data centers. Good idea, Beck," says Jin.

"I'll run a search for construction projects," Curtis reports.

"What else? What else? Rick, is there anything more you can remember about the cities?" asks Becky.

Rick stares at Becky until she becomes uneasy. "What is it? You're starting to creep me out."

Rick slowly verbalizes his thoughts. "A friend helped me get time on a restricted system to conduct research for my grant. He gave me an access code. I didn't know it then, but he was working with the Arcadians. In fact, he lived in New Arcadia. Maybe..."

"How did you communicate with him?" Asks Becky.

"By e-mail, we—"

Jin interrupts Rick. "Did you save the e-mail?"

"Do you remember the code?" asks Curtis.

"I save all my e-mails. The code should be there."

"OK, give me your cloud credentials," says Jin.

"You got it... let's see you get spooky," Rick says.

Jin types in the air so fast, his fingers blur in the dim light. After minutes of fierce finger blur, Jin slows his typing. "Curtman, do you see this? We're in the Arcadian network."

Curtis crunches on a stack of crackers, crumbs falling on his desk. "That wasn't just an access code. That was the golden key to a big-ass backdoor," Curtis says, with dry cracker mouth. He grabs his Gulp cup to wash down the dry, crumbly mess.

Rick thinks of his friend. "Thanks, Karl. You saved the day again."

Jin and Curtis work incredibly fast. It's as if they anticipate each other's thoughts.

"I have the city list," says Jin, displaying the list on his band.

Functioning Occupied Cities
New Arcadia–near Washington, DC
New Zion–below Denver airport
Edendale–Los Angeles
Halcyon–Las Vegas
Ambrosia–Sacramento
Nod–Seattle

Cities Under Construction–semi-operational
New Dakota–near Sheridan, Wyoming
New Elysian–White Mountain National Forest, Maine
Empyrean–Atlanta
New Atlantis–near Mobile, Alabama

"Confirming geo-locations, building a quick database," mumbles Curtis.

"Sending blueprints."

"Scanning blueprint entry points."

"Entering entry points into your database," says Jin.

"Wow, these guys have a lot of dirt on government officials. There are hundreds of folders here," exclaims Curtis.

"Check security system," directs Jin.

"Right. On it. But look at this collection of photos and documents. They could black-mail almost every politician with this stuff," says an amazed Curtis.

"Won't matter who screwed what, if they're all dead."

"Right. Oh man, each facility has its own unique encryption key for city security. This will be tough to pull off," Curtis observes.

The Curtis and Jin continue to work at a rapid pace. Rick and Becky watch.

"Are they always like this?" Rick asks.

"They're practically brothers, but I've never seen them mind meld before."

"I think we'd better let them work. I'll explore the stairwell. I need to feel useful," Rick says as he stands.

"Wait," Becky calls out.

Rick pauses. Becky digs through her bag and pulls out a small plastic box. She opens the lid, exposing an Ear Dot. She hands it to Rick. "Ear Dot remote. Sorry, I don't have an extra VUE for you, but at least we can communicate. I'll link the audio to my lens while you explore."

Rick puts the small device in his ear. "Thanks," he says before disappearing down the dark stairwell.

Jins moves index finger; a long slow press. "OK, here's a summary. We have—"

"Wait, let me patch in Rick," says Becky.

"Huh? Where did he go?" Jin asks, looking up from his VUE.

"He went to explore. He's linked to our comms," Becky explains.

"Hey, glad this thing works. I'm down twenty-five floors. I think I'm getting close to the bottom," says Rick.

"We have good data on ten facilities. Six are fully functioning and habitable. The other four are under construction but can protect people. We have the entry locations, maps, and system schematics for all the cities," states Jin.

"And we have confirmed locations of other government underground facilities at Cheyenne Mountain, Weather Mountain, Dulce Base, and other military bases. All the usual suspects," says Curtis.

Rick hustles down the stairs, working up a sweat in the stagnant air of the stairwell. "Great job, guys. Let's focus on the six functioning cities. We need to overwhelm the Arcadians with thousands of people."

"Why are you so keen on overwhelming the Arcadians?" Curtis asks.

"Cruikshank is a control freak. Those few and fortunate, the people in the new cities. The colonel lied to them and drugged them into submission. If we swarm the cities, it will mess up his plan to control the future of humanity."

"Besides, the six cities are closest to large population areas and our best hope to save the greatest number of people," Becky adds.

"OK, but we still have a huge problem. There's no way we can control all the entry points, secured doors, and elevators at six facilities simultaneously. Once we mess with their systems, they will change the encryption codes and according to the schematics, they can drop blast doors all over the place to secure themselves, keeping intruders out, meaning us," Curtis explains.

"Is there a way you can hack the doors without them noticing?" asks Rick.

"One or two doors might not get noticed. Multiply that by hundreds when you count all the elevators, stairwell doors, and blast doors. We'll set off a bunch of alerts. Curtis is right. This is a huge task. We need a lot more people than Curtis and me to pull this off," Jin explains.

Becky elbows Jin. "Oh, and Becky! Sorry, babe. Even with Becky, we can't manage it. We need a team of people for each city, especially once they know we're inside. We need to monitor their system changes when they try to lock us out so we can trace our way back in. Not to mention, it will take hours to get thousands of people into the cities. It will be tough, no impossible, to keep control for that long." Jin takes a breath. "It would take a full-fledged hack-a-thon to get people inside," Jin finishes.

"Hack-a-thon? Hmm," Curtis muses.

Becky leans against the stairwell wall. "We need a gang of people solving puzzles, opening doors, fighting off an enemy who is defending their fort. It sounds like a multi-player role-playing game."

"Unfortunately, this isn't a game. We're talking about life and death for hundreds of thousands of people," says Rick.

"Wait a minute. What are you thinking, Beck?" asks Jin.

"If there were hundreds of people playing a game, opening doors to underground cities, saving the world or rescuing a princess, they could give us access to the cities without knowing what they were doing."

"Forget saving the world. I would do it for a fifty-million-dollar prize," says Curtis, swirling a half-filled Gulp cup.

"You'd do it for a few liters of soda," Jin laughs.

"Hey, that hurts. If this storm goes on for too long, I might run out of soda. That would truly be a sad day. But maybe Becky is right. If I had more time, I could write a game using the maps we downloaded. If enough people played, it might work. But it would take me a month to get a game demo running."

"I can get the prize money," Jin offers.

"You can get fifty million dollars?" Curtis asks.

"I can grab funds from a government asset forfeiture account. You know, funds seized from drug smugglers, illegal arms traders, and money launderers. I don't think the government will miss it," Jin says.

"You can do that? Why didn't you tell me this five years ago?" Curtis asks.

"Money will have no meaning by the end of the week. That video game is a great idea, but we're in the middle of an asteroid storm. Do you think people will play a game with the sky dropping on them?" asks Rick.

"They will. The gamers I know, as long as their net doesn't go down, will watch streams and play games while their house is collapsing around them," says Curtis.

"He's right, Rick. Gamers live for this stuff. Don't worry, they'll play," adds Jin.

"Fellas, I'm at the bottom of the stairwell. Thirty-five floors down. The door here looks more like a bank vault than an entry door. The panel says Amradyne 176G. Better program the hack for this door into your game."

"I can pull up schematics on that door. Hold on," says Jin.

Jin shares the schematics with Curtis. "Oh, geeez. We're gonna need a few thousand players if all the doors are like this."

"Get on it, boys," Rick says, examining the door with his flashlight.

"Curtis, what are you thinking? How do we handle this?" asks Jin.

"Maybe instead of writing a new game, we modify an old game. You remember my friend Aman. His brother Raj and I were friends when you were away at college."

"The guy that died when he fell into Grand Canyon?"

"That's horrible," says Becky.

"Yeah. It was sad. But since then, his older brother, Aman and I have become great friends. We've been messing with an old indie game called Colony Revolution. I don't think it ever got launched. I doubt anyone has ever heard of it, but I like it."

"Can we use that game to control the cities?" asks Jin.

"I think it will work. I'll ask Aman to help. He's an ace programmer, and he manages a company with hundreds of software engineers," says Curtis.

"Hey! Maybe he can get his programmers to help," says Jin excitedly.

"Do it!" exclaims Becky. The rumble from above grows louder, causing the stairwell to vibrate.

"It's getting nasty outside. I'm not sure people will make it through another night of this," says Jin. He looks up the stairwell as dust fills the air. Becky reaches for him, and they hold each other tightly.

Darkness surrounds him, his thoughts wrestling. Instead of hitchhiking across the country or stealing a car to drive home, he stands at the entrance of New Zion, staring numbly at the door. It beckons him, daring him to enter.

He wills himself to turn away and launches himself up the stairwell. He touches the Ear Dot. "Becky?" he whispers.

"Rick, are you OK? Are you coming back up?"

"Yeah, I'm on my way. Hey, can I make a call with this thing?"

"I can make a call and patch the audio through."

"Please search Courtney Munday."

"Of course, on it. I talked to my mom and dad. They're safe. They'll try to get to New Zion in the morning."

"I'm sure they'll be fine, Becky."

"Checking for the number. Connecting."

"You've reached Courtney Monday. Did I miss your call? I am so sorry—."

"The line dropped. I'll try again."

Becky tries again. Rick hears silence followed by a series of beeps, then a recorded voice saying, "All circuits are busy. Please try again."

"Can you try Robert Munday?" Once again, he hears an all-circuits' busy message.

"I'm sorry, Rick. If they're like you, I'm sure they've found someplace safe."

"Becky?" Rick asks solemnly as he walks up the blackness of the stairwell.

"Yes."

"I know you want to save everyone. I'll help if I can, but come daylight, I need to be moving towards home."

"I understand. I'm sure your family misses you terribly."

It's almost 9:00 p.m. in Henderson, Nevada when Curtis calls Aman.

"Curt-tis, buddy. How's it happening, bro?"

"Sorry if it's too early, but I need your help."

"Hey, no problem. Any seven days, twenty-four-seven you are family. For anyone else, I would say I haven't had my cha and marmalade. But for Curt-tis, you were a brother to Raj. You are family to me any seven days. What's up?"

Curtis takes a deep breath. "OK, one hundred percent of everything I'm gonna tell you is real."

Chapter 44: The Game

Friday Morning

A video-stream of the Governor of the State of California, Dora Crawford, appears on every connected device in the state. People watch her on electronic billboards, digital signage, TV screens, Smart-Band, and VUE.

"Citizens of California, we have planned for your protection from the asteroid storm. We have built underground facilities in Los Angeles and Sacramento. You are now receiving detailed directions to these locations via Smart-Band and VUE lens. You are to make your way, with great haste, to the underground facilities. We have food, shelter, water, and amenities for your comfort. Pack lightly. We have everything prepared for you. Be patient, remain calm and courteous to your fellow citizens. We have room enough for everyone." The video ends with the governor's welcoming smile. The message repeats five minutes later.

The governors of every state near an Arcadian city broadcast similar messages. A video stream of the governor of Colorado plays on every communication device in Colorado. The message instructs people to move to the entrances of an underground city, named New Zion, located under the Denver airport.

The governors of Virginia, Delaware, Pennsylvania, and New Jersey direct their citizens to the once-secret entrances of New Arcadia. People move. Millions upon millions of people gather what they can carry and move to underground cities across the country.

President Baker is being briefed on the status of the planned US Marine attacks on the underground cities. "Sir, we have now confirmed the locations of three underground cities, including New Arcadia, Cruikshank's location," explains a Marine commander.

"When will you attack?" asks the president.

"We'll be ready in three days, sir. We are allocating men, equipment, and planning logistics. We have teams assessing the locations to prepare our plan of attack. All preparations are ongoing."

Sheryl interrupts the briefing. "Sir. Excuse me. You've got to see this." She motions her hand over her band, flicking a finger toward a wall-sized screen. The messages from the governor of Colorado and a dozen more governors fill the screen. Everyone in the Command Center stops working to watch the streams. Even Jerome Hargrove pauses, his finger poking to watch.

The governor of Delaware, a rather fat man, whose jowls shake as he speaks, is the first to call the president to complain. "That is not me. I broadcast no such message."

"That's obvious. You're much thinner in the message, Daryl," Jerome says in jest.

"That is uncalled for. We have a catastrophe of worldwide proportions, and one of you is trying to be funny." The governor scowls. Jerome sinks into his chair. Cliff Baker shakes a scolding finger at Jerome.

More governors call to complain. Each governor's image appears as they call in. The governors erupt in anger, talking over themselves.

"Who could have done this?" "Our images were hijacked." "I never authorized this message." "Where are they telling people to go?" "This will cause more havoc." "Who's running this country?"

President Baker stands and yells, "Silence!" The room quiets. "Commander, I think you'd better move up your plans. I want Marines at those sites now! Governors calm down. We will sort this out..."

Mitch watches the streams and counts. He turns to the Marine commander, who was briefing the president. "Commander, have your teams watch the videos carefully and monitor the Smart-Band messages of each state. It seems whoever created these messages has identified more locations than the three in your briefing."

Cliff Baker leans over to Tug Grimes. "Tug, your people need to get a handle on this. Find out who's broadcasting these messages. First it was the Perth news, now this. Are they trying to help us, or do they have their own agenda?"

Tug nods then signals the Commandant of the Marine Corps and the Secretary of the Air Force to follow as he moves out of the room, presumably to find a quieter place to chew out his command staff.

Curtis spins around in his chair, pumping his Gulp cup into the air as he cheers. "It's working! They bought it. People are moving to the underground cities."

"Your government at work!" exclaims Jin.

"We couldn't have done it without Aman and his company's software engineers hacking and programming at breakneck speed," says Becky.

"Oh geeze, my development teams are happy to work on a fun project for a change. Oh my, I tell you they're really loving this," says Aman, cheerily.

"Good job, everyone but we're just getting started. What's next, Aman?" asks Rick.

"We've tapped into security cameras all over the airport. People are gathering at the entrances in the airport terminals. I can see at least three hundred people in the building and parking lot above you and more are coming. I'll send a message to their bands, directing them to the stairwell once you are out of there."

"Guys. I'm still not sure this will work," says Curtis.

"Why not? What's the problem?" asks Rick.

"If we open the floodgates, the city security system will go nuts and they'll shut us down before we get started."

"But we planned for that. The game will crack the new encryption codes," says Becky.

"Which will take time," says Jin.

"We need a head start. A way to get people in the city before the Arcadians know what's going on," says Curtis.

"You're just bringing this up, now?" asks Rick.

"Hey, it's been a long night. I can't think of everything," cries Curtis.

"Cool it, guys. We're so close. There must be a way," says Becky.

"Hang on. I'm pretty sure I can open the door at the bottom of the stairwell without setting off any alerts, but I need to do it from the door," says Jin.

"Pretty sure?" asks Rick.

"No way. You'll get stuck down there. You'll never get back up here with a horde of people moving down the stairwell." says Becky.

"I'm sure. I can do it. Sorry, Beck. I've got to be at the door. There's no other way. I can open the door and get hundreds of people in the city before the Arcadians know we have invaded them."

"Nice to know you, kid. Once you get that door open, I'll be on my way home," says Rick.

"If you're going down there, I'm going with you," says Becky.

"No, Becky. It's dangerous. I've got to do this alone," Jin insists.

"You kids are cute. Damn it. I'm gonna hate myself. I've got an idea how to get a bunch of people into New Zion," says Rick.

"Why will you hate yourself?" asks Becky.

"Because it means I'll be delaying my trip to Los Angeles. Curtis and Aman, I need you to make some changes to that game."

Rick, Becky, and Jin hustle down the stairwell toward the entrance of New Zion. "I swore I'd never enter an Arcadian city again. At least I'm doing it on my own terms, this time. I hope this plan works," says Rick.

"Don't your plans usually work?" asks Jin, huffing down the stairs.

"In theory, yes. It's the unexpected things that mess plans up."

"Great. I'm sure nothing unexpected will happen this time, right?"

"We're ready to go. Let us know when you get to the bottom of the stairwell," says Curtis.

"We count over seven hundred people in the building and parking lot above you. The governor's message worked really super well," says Aman.

"How about the large equipment elevators on the other side of the airport? Are they ready?" asks Becky.

"Heavy One and Two are loaded. Five hundred people in each. Ready and waiting," Aman confirms.

"Let the game begin," says Jin.

"We're halfway down the stairwell. Send down Heavy One and Two. The Black Guard will respond to the breach, sending troops to the far side of the city. Once we're at the bottom unlock the maintenance room door so the stairwell fills with people," Rick says, reconfirming the opening gambit.

"Thanks, everyone. You're saving thousands of lives today," says Becky.

Tug Grimes huddles in a conference room down the hall from the Command Center with the Marine Commandant and the Secretary of the Air Force.

Tug looks sternly at the men. "Forget your planning and assessments. Get your troops and assets moving. Plan and adapt as you go. We don't have days. The president wants people in those cities posthaste. Colonel Cruikshank has the Army under his control. They've had time to prepare. Expect heavy opposition. Our objective is to overwhelm and overrun their positions, assist civilian access to the cities, and protect them once they're in."

General Mark Davidson, Commandant of the Marine Corps, points to a map. "OK, Los Angeles or whatever the hell they call it is the easiest. We're moving men and equipment from Camp Pendleton. We have reconnaissance drones overhead now. Our forces will arrive within four hours. We'll also send troops to Sacramento, but it will take more time to convoy up Interstate 5. We also have troops and equipment moving to New Arcadia as we speak. They're coming in from Camp Lejeune."

"Good. Get it done," says Tug, watching a map of the Arcadian cities update with new locations. "What about the other cities?"

General Casey, Secretary of the Air Force, jumps in. "We have men and equipment moving from Buckley Air Force Base to the Denver airport. It's just twenty miles up the road. Buckley is home to all branches of the military. We have rounded up and detained all Army and Navy personnel stationed at Buckley as a security precaution, and we have set up a statewide no fly-zone. The Army at New Zion has a small fleet of aircraft and several air defense emplacements. We've been monitoring their activity and have allowed the Army to believe they control the airspace over the Denver airport. We can easily take out the Army's aircraft and air support. We will control the airspace over the airport within the hour. We're pulling cadets and staff from the Air Force Academy to help control the public in the airport terminals. We've got New Zion covered."

Tug wants to instill action. "Use every resource available to get the job done. Commandeer equipment and invoke martial law, conscript men if you need them. Do whatever it takes. We don't know what you will be up against, but I can guarantee Cruikshank will put up a fight to keep his New Arcadia."

"Get ready for the hottest action in Crypto-eSports. We are minutes away from the launch and first ever tournament of Colony-Revolution Coup. News of this game burst on the scene just hours ago, but the fifty-million-dollar purse has attracted the biggest names in the Crypto action scene. I'm Ceylon Junglefoul, your lively host, for what is sure to be an adrenaline-filled epic day of gameplay."

The caster announcing the game is a tall, thin, Sri Lankan man with a thin face and a sharp nose. He wears an outlandish bright blue suit with broad orange lapels. His blue-and-yellow hair looks like a nest of bird feathers. Ceylon Junglefoul's gaming broadcasts and tournaments garner millions of followers worldwide.

Gamers who play and watch game streams are extremely dedicated. Even the threat of an asteroid storm doesn't deter the fervent gaming audience. News of the game surfaced early that morning on Tweaknet, the most popular gaming network. They scheduled the first tournament before anyone has even played the game, creating a heightened frenzy among the players.

"Mr. Meteor, one of the game developers, is on stream with us to explain the game. Mr. Meteor, tell us, why are you launching Colony so suddenly? We haven't seen a beta, a press release, or any news of this game until this morning."

Mr. Meteor sits in a dark room, only his silhouette visible. His voice is garbled to mask his identity. "We want Colony to receive the attention it deserves. Launching the game with a tournament and generous prize money will bring awareness to its unique and exciting game play," he explains.

"Your unique launch method is generating lots of attention. We have hundreds of players ready and three million people viewing the stream. But why all the mystery Mr. Meteor? Do you have something to hide, or is your secret identity part of a publicity stunt?"

"This is not a stunt. The tournament is very serious. You've received the fifty million, correct?"

"Yes. We have the prize money. Well, tell us more about the game."

"Colony Revolution-Coup has maps and puzzles of large underground ant colonies. A rogue force has overtaken your ant colony. You must regain entry and get your entire ant population into the colonies. Teams of six will work to decrypt system codes, fight to open doors, hold open blast doors, and control elevators enabling access to the colony. You must maintain access until your entire population inhabits the colony. The teams will work against a very advanced humanlike artificial intelligence or AI that will do everything in its power to keep you from your goal."

"There are hundreds of teams. There aren't enough colonies for everyone to play. Will they be competing against one another?"

"Yes, and no. The game starts with one team per colony selected by lottery. Each team will work to secure their colony. Teams will fight against the AI. If the AI blocks a team's progress, for example, by changing the security system encryption codes, the game is open to all teams. Every team works to crack the new encryption. The team that cracks the code replaces the previous team. Equal opportunity for every team to play. Colony populations will vary in size, but the team that secures the highest percentage of their population, minus fatalities, will be the winner. Expect the unexpected. You will be challenged. May the best team win!"

"Thank you, Mr. Meteor. Let's turn to the main stage where we see six teams, selected by lottery, to be the first players in the tournament. The teams look ready. Let's see who wins!"

The game stream is computer-generated and designed so the teams appear seated on the stage of a huge stadium filled with screaming fans. In reality, teams could be anywhere around the globe. Individual team members are likely sitting at home alone in their bedrooms. Home viewers can watch the stadium view, click through the various colony maps to watch the team of their choice, or follow the casters who comment on game play.

"Joining me today is TORPEDO! We'll be calling the game bringing you the best Colony-Revolution Coup action!" exclaims Ceylon Junglefoul.

Computer generated cheers follow the news that Torpedo is casting the game. Torpedo is a fan favorite. Instantly, three hundred thousand fans send their approval with thumbs-up emojis. The ratings for this show are already through the roof. Anticipation for an exciting game is mounting.

"TA-DA. I'm TORPEDO! I'm stealthy. I'm sneaky. You won't see me till you meet me. KA-BOOM! Hi, hiya, hey. WE GOTTA GAME! Hey. HEY!"

The action starts fast. Junglefoul gets the casting rolling. "Team Liquid Metal from New Delhi, India, is off to a fast start. A large ant force has accumulated at several entrances of the colony map named New Zion. It looks like their first move is to gain control of two huge elevators."

Players view movement of ants on the colony maps. If they hope to control blast doors and elevators, they must gain access to the cities' control systems. Teams need to hack and decrypt security codes to unlock doors and passages to get the ant population moving.

"Get going boyos. You gotta crack the system's control code to make those up and downs get moving. Your ants are waiting. Team Liquid Metal get cracklin'," calls Torpedo.

Two massive elevators, each filled with hundreds of ants, move downward. Liquid Metal members look surprised.

"That's a great move by Liquid Metal. They will get hundreds into their colony with this move. What a huge advantage so early in the game," says Ceylon.

"Early days, but cheeky. That seemed too easy."

"All the initial action is happening at New Zion. Look! I can see hundreds of ants moving down a stairwell," Ceylon comments.

"Let's flip the dipper. We have ants piling up on another map. Massive piles of them buggers are pushing in on the grounds surrounding New Arcadia. South Korean Team Twin Dragons are working their cracklin' magic. They be a knock, knockin' on the door, but the no entry sign was flashing. Unlike New Zion, it's gonna take some time for the Twin Dragons to get their ants moving."

"Heavy One and Two are moving. Thirty seconds until their doors open on New Zion," Aman says, updating the status for Rick and his team.

"The game is on. We've got the best Crypto-gamers online working to crack the Arcadian codes," says Curtis.

"Good job, Mr. Meteor. My man Curt-tis, you did really super great! You explained the game but kept the mystery and intrigue alive. Just what we need to attract the best players to the game," says Aman.

"That was fun. I'm like the undercover whistle blower of the Colony-Revolution Coup!"

"You have real star power, Curt-tis. After this is over, you can be an actor. No fooling. I wouldn't lie to you, Curt-tis—your family," says Aman.

A blue tunic in New Zion City Command works at his control console. Since the city went on lockdown, it's been quiet. City Command has become a boring place. There was a report of a broken door at one of the topside entrances the previous evening, but the Black Guard chose not to investigate. The asteroid storm was active around the Denver airport. They assume the broken door is storm damage.

A sensor flashes showing Heavy One and Heavy Two large equipment elevators are moving down to the city. The blue tunic runs a system check. All systems show they are on lockdown mode, but sensors indicate movement. He checks the cameras in the large elevators. The cameras are out. Everything has been quiet. City systems are running well. The blue tunic hesitates before asking for help. He tries to get the attention of his supervisor, who is casually roaming the room chatting with the staff. "Supervisor! Miss, please look at this," the blue tunic requests, raising his hand to get attention.

The supervisor seems bothered by the request. "What is it?" She saunters to the blue tunic.

"Not sure, miss. It could be a system error.
Sensors show movement of Heavy One and Two, but all other
systems show them stationary," he says, pointing at his monitor.

The supervisor nudges the blue tunic to the side so she can poke
at the monitor. Indicators show the elevators moving, now almost
to city level. She pokes away but cannot gain control of the elevator
movement.

The elevator is dark and cramped, but they can tell the elevator is
moving downward. There is pushing and jockeying for position.
People flooded into the large elevators seeking protection from the
storm. More people pressed in as the elevator doors began closing.
Bodies press so tightly together that breath is scarce. Humanity,
compressed in a metal box, descends to the unknown. You can
smell sweat and fear. You can sense the anxiety in the black unseen
eyes of the face pressed next to yours.

The mechanical sound of the platform lowering stops with a
bang and a thud. Movement halts, leaving only silence. Silence
followed by the ache of anticipation. Angst followed by panic.
People scream and cry as hundreds press against the unopened
doors. A metal clanking sound. Silence.

Gunge. gunge, gunge, gunge, gunge. The huge metal doors slide
open. The press of bodies spits the first ones out. They fall to the
floor, then get trampled by the hundreds streaming after. People run
out of the large elevator into a huge corridor.

Several bodies, mostly small children, are on the floor of the
elevator, crushed or suffocated during the descent. Two bodies
along the back wall died standing. The limp bodies now freed slump
heavily to the metal floor.

The second elevator is about to open.

The blue tunic watches his supervisor rapidly poke controls on
the screen with no response. The elevators arrive at city level. More
blue tunics gather to watch. The supervisor gains control of a
camera in the corridor, monitoring the elevator doors.

Slowly, the doors open. They see hands pressing through the
opening. The doors have opened ten inches when the first person

pops out. It looks like the elevator ejected the body by some force. More people are expelled as the doors open, pressed by a great mass. A woman leans down to pick up her child. The mother and child disappear under a wave of people. Others trip on the bumpy surface of the city's tile floor. The stream of humanity escaping the metal box sweeps over them.

The blue tunic gasps at the terrible sight. The supervisor touches an alarm and then pokes the air to make a call.

"Black Guard, alert. We have intruders at Heavy One and Two," the supervisor announces.

A Black Guard responds. "What type of intruder? We are locked down."

The supervisor sits frozen, watching hundreds of people trample over fellow humans. Women, children, and old people lay lifeless on the tile floor and inside the huge elevator.

The blue tunic responds to the Black Guard. "Hundreds of people in Corridor 40 exiting Heavy One and Two."

The Black Guard triggers an all respond alert. Black Guard platoons stream out of their stations across the city riding military style Maggies, all moving to converge on Corridor 40.

The elevator doors close, and the huge platforms move toward the surface.

"We're at the bottom of the stairwell. Jin's working on the door," Becky reports.

"Black Guard are moving to Heavy One and Two. I've unlocked the maintenance room door. People are moving into the stairwell. Now, it is up to Jin to get that door open without setting off an alert," Aman advises.

Jin works carefully to unlock the security door without attracting a welcoming party of Black Guard. "I've just about got it, guys."

Seconds later, an LED on the Armadyne 176G security door turns from red to green, followed by the sound of metal bolts retracting. "Rick, help me pull the door open. I had to disable the motor to avoid detection."

Rick and Jin pull the heavy door open while Becky restrains the growing mass of people in the stairwell.

"Move left once you're through the door. Hug the wall so you don't get swept away with the crowd," Rick instructs, as they pull on the heavy door.

Becky faces people on the stairs holding her arms wide. "Stop! Stop. Wait until we have the door fully open. Everyone will enter the city safely."

The people on the bottom flight hold back a stairwell full of desperate people pressing to get down the stairs. "Stop! Wait. You're already safe," Becky tells them again. Calls for patience echo up the stairwell from people at the bottom.

When the heavy door is fully open. Rick calls to Becky. "I'll hold them back. You and Jin go first."

Rick replaces Becky, holding back the undulating mass of people packed in the stairwell. Becky darts through the door, followed by Jin. They move left with their backs to the wall, sidestepping to move away from the door.

Rick sees them move. He holds his arms out wide and steps back, back, back through the doorway. He locks eyes with the people standing on the bottom flight of stairs. "OK, now!" Rick scurries to the left, joining Jin and Becky ten feet from the door.

People push, shove, and press their way into the city. A steady stream of people rush down stairwell invading New Zion.

Four platoons of Black Guard riding maglevs converge at the elevators in Corridor 40. Captain Kobalt and Lieutenant Astatine direct the Black Guard troops.

"Relax all invaders. I don't want anyone to wander around the city. You will contain this situation," orders Kobalt.

Kobalt's elite guard, which accompanied him from New Arcadia, hover patiently awaiting his orders.

Black Guard Platoons One and Two surround groups of elevator people moving in the corridor. Black Guard shoots and relaxes everyone in range of the advancing platoons. People freeze when they see others dropping to the ground. Two Black Guard fire large-barreled weapons that look like grenade launchers. The shots go high into the air before the canisters burst above the crowd, releasing clouds of gas. Two hundred people collapse to the floor. The Black Guard platoons dismount their Maggies and advance down the corridor, stepping over unconscious bodies, firing continuously, dropping bodies to the cold tile floor.

At the other end of the corridor, Black Guard Platoons Three and Four launch gas canisters, hundreds more drop to the floor. The Black Guard platoons advance through the corridor, moving toward Platoon One and Two, trapping and relaxing everyone caught between the Black Guard forces.

"The Black Guard has their hands full on the other side of the city." Curtis says excitedly.

"Heavy One and Two have arrived topside. Another load will arrive in at city level in two minutes," states Aman.

"Good. I hope that will keep the Black Guard occupied for a while," says Rick.

"Team Liquid Metal is getting the hang of things. They just opened doors at two stairwells and elevators. Go team! People will enter the city from several locations," announces Curtis.

Captain Kobalt stands in front of the closed doors of Heavy One, surveying the bodies lying on the tiled floor. No one weeps for the dead. They look like crumpled rag dolls tossed aside by a toddler tired of playing with them. Kobalt walks to the trampled woman who died while trying to pick up her daughter. A few feet away lies the body of her child. The tyke still reaching out for her baby doll. Kobalt stands over the child.

His face tightens. "Two minutes. People can't take care of each other for two minutes. Selfish, thoughtless, humans," he says to himself.

Suddenly self-conscious, he notices Lieutenant Astatine watching him. Kobalt lifts his heavy boot and crushes the head of the baby doll.

"Captain, the elevators will arrive again soon," says Lieutenant Astatine.

"Surround them and hit them with gas cannons. Round up any runners. Give them rehabilitation, fifty-year doses." Kobalt walks from the elevators as Black Guard troops arrange the heavy gas cannons.

Lieutenant Astatine quick steps to walk alongside Kobalt. "I have City Command." The video call appears in Kobalt's VUE.

"What the hell is happening? I thought the city was on lockdown," screams Kobalt.

"We are, or we were then Heavy One and Two started moving. We can't control them. We now have alarms at several entry points. Elevators are moving and stairwell doors have unlocked. People are entering the city from everywhere. I believe we have been hacked, sir," reports the City Command officer.

"Hacked? Then hack them back! Reset security systems and set new encryption codes. Follow your breach protocol. Why do I have to tell you this?" shouts Kobalt.

"Yes, sir. I never thought we would need——." The officer stops herself, then continues. "It will be done, Captain." Kobalt hears the City Command officer calling out orders to her staff before she stops the call.

Kobalt glares angrily at Lieutenant Astatine. The young lieutenant cowers. Kobalt touches the air to call Colonel Cruikshank.

"Colonel. New Zion has been breached. We have topsiders entering the city. It appears someone has hacked the city systems."

"Hacked? How could Astatine and his City Command let this happen? We have security protocols for this," Colonel Cruikshank shouts.

A call from General Mahon interrupts the colonel's call with Kobalt. Mahon's image appears in Kobalt's VUE and on the colonel's office screen. "Intruders have cut the New Arcadia perimeter fences in several places. Thousands of people are crossing the campus parklands. They're headed for city entry points. Did you send out invitations?"

"Invitations? I did not send out any damned invitations. What are you talking about? Your forces must protect our cities!" Cruikshank screams.

"We've intercepted messages from state governors instructing citizens to move to the cities. The existence of the cities is a tightly held secret, yet our locations are now being broadcast to citizens across the country. Either you changed plans without informing me, or someone has exposed us."

"Impossible! Even if someone has discovered our locations, your mission does not change. General, you are to secure the perimeter of New Arcadia. Your troops must protect and defend the cities. That is your mission. Stop all approaches. New Zion has been breached. Why aren't your men protecting New Zion?" screams the colonel.

Mahon stumbles over his words. "We prepared to defend secret cities. Fighting off a flood of people was not the plan." The general pauses. Seeing he will gain no sympathy from Cruikshank, he changes tack. "Our troops are holding strong at Edendale in a standoff against the Marines. There have been no intrusions into Edendale. At New Zion. We have troops in the airport terminals, and we control the airspace."

"General, someone has hacked New Zion systems allowing topsiders to enter the city. It appears there is a coordinated effort to disrupt our systems and invade our cities," Kobalt says, succinctly.

"How can that be? No one knows the cities exist. How could they find us? New Arcadian computer systems are closed off from other networks. How could anyone hack us?" asks the general.

Cruikshank is fuming and thinking out loud. "Yes, who could have hacked New Zions's systems? Cliff Baker couldn't have gotten his people organized this fast. The man can barely manage his calendar. It can't be Dr. Munday... Munday is dead."

Chapter 45: Freaky Dink

Rick, Jin, and Becky move swiftly, yet cautiously. Using the city map and guided by Curtis, who is monitoring city cameras, the trio makes their way through the corridors of New Zion. Rick leads them to the end of a narrow passageway that opens onto a main corridor.

"OK, we take a quick left, then the Black Guard armory is just ahead."

Rick edges around the corner, then jumps back as a large contingent of Black Guard artillery glides out of the armory. Rick, Jin, and Becky watch as the artillery mounted on autonomous vehicles moves down the main corridor.

"I'm glad we didn't walk into the middle of that," says Rick.

"We led people into the city to save lives. Instead, all the people from the elevators are dead because of us." Becky grieves.

Rick tries to calm Becky. "They're not dead. They will sleep for a few hours. The Arcadians call it being relaxed. They'll be fine. The colonel doesn't use bullets or explosives. I guess he doesn't want to ruin his cities."

"Curtis, are we good to go? Can you see if anyone is in the armory?" asks Jin.

"You're good. The armory is clear. Black Guard is moving all their equipment to the other side of the city. Get moving," says Curtis from his bunker.

Rick runs down the wide corridor and into the armory, followed closely by Jin and Becky. They enter a large, empty room.

"Everything's gone," says Becky.

"Don't worry. I'll find what we need." Rick scrounges through boxes on storage shelves. "We need to change clothes. Put on these are skin suits. They'll protect you from relaxation darts." Rick tosses the skin suits to Becky and Jin.

They change clothes, pulling on Black Guard slacks, tunics, and black boots over the skin suits. They give each other a once over. Becky does in a pirouette to show off her new attire to Jin. They both giggle like silly kids. Rick hands Jin and Becky black kepi hats to complete the Black Guard attire.

"The skin suits aren't very comfortable. They're thicker than I imagined," says Becky, adjusting her tunic.

"Just a few details to complete the package," Rick says as he rummages through inventory on the shelves.

Rick moves from shelf to shelf until he finds what he's looking for. He removes three metal rings from a temperature-controlled enclosure marked D-Nox. He holds two rings in one palm and holds the third in his other hand. "Hey you two. Come over here. I've got something you need."

Jin and Becky watch as Rick holds a chromium U-shaped ring in front of his face. Flesh-colored appendages wiggle from the ends like they're trying to climb out of the metal ring.

"Is that alive?" Becky asks squeamishly.

"Not sure what they are," Rick says as he inserts the squiggly ends into his nostrils. Rick shivers slightly as the fleshy arms wiggle up his nose. "Tickles though."

"Aww no. I am not sticking one of those in my nose," Becky says.

"You both must feel light-headed. You were just giggling. It's the city air. It's mixed with a gas to make people compliant. The nose ring emits a chemical antidote. Not to mention, it completes the look of a Black Guard. It's easy. Jin, show Becky," Rick says, offering the nose rings to Jin.

Jin picks one up. The small worm-like arms wiggle. Jin laughs anxiously as he slowly puts the ring to his nose. "I don't think I will like this." He inches the ring closer to his nose with anxious anticipation. The wiggling arms stretch up and wriggle into his nostrils. Jin shakes his head and rubs his nose. "I think I'm gonna sneeze."

"You next, Becky. It's not as bad as it looks. Come on," Rick says encouragingly.

Becky picks up the ring, shuddering at the thought of sticking worms up her nose. She closes her eyes with a grimace. She puts the ring to her nose, letting out a soft squeal as the small fleshy fingers find their home.

Jin smiles at Becky. "It looks good on you, Beck."

Becky smiles and curtsies, then stops herself. "What did I just do? This is not like me at all."

"Like I said, it's the city atmosphere. You'll be all right. Give the D-Nox a few minutes to kick in," says Rick.

A few feet away, a charging rack holds several sets of Black Guard military style VUE, which feature a large wraparound lens.

"Jin, can you switch VUE control cards for yourself and Becky to these and get one set up for me? I'll work on getting weapons."

Jin goes to work on the VUE lenses while Rick moves to another part of the armory.

"Freaky dink. Team Liquid Metal put your right hand in and shake it all about. Do the hokey pokey and turn yourself about! They landed the two big elevators again only to have the entire load wiped out by the opposing force. Not looking so easy for team Metal," says Torpedo, excitedly.

"That's right. Team Liquid Metal got crushed at the big elevators, but they are making great progress with small elevators and stairwells. Hundreds of ants are streaming in through those less obvious entrances. Great tactic," adds Ceylon.

"Over at New Arcadia, the Twin Dragons be learning from team Liquid Metal. They've cracked control of small elevators at several points in buildings above the city," Torpedo reports.

"It's about time. They have tens of thousands of ants piling up at the entry points and ants have spread across the huge campus, waiting to flood in and win their colony back. I see movement! Maybe they can catch up to team Liquid Metal."

"You speak too fast, Bird Man. Set your eyes on this," says Torpedo, pointing to the New Arcadian map.

"My God. Enemy forces are coming out of hidden bunkers at ground level, pushing the ants back from the entrances. They're blocking ant movement. What's that? They are installing a barrier around the buildings. Oh my," gasps Ceylon.

"Tricky dicky. Mr. Meteor said there would be challenges. This game is overheating. The teams need to work their moves and grooves. This one's a toughie."

Colonel Cruikshank sits in a cushioned chair in his private spa. President Jon Anderson sits next to the colonel with a dull, flat expression, looking forward at nothing. It doesn't appear the president knows where he is or what's happening around him. Russell Thompson fusses over the president, making sure he is comfortable.

Colonel Cruikshank looks frail. His skin is gray and wrinkled. His hair is thin and lifeless. His eyes are gray, sunken into his skull. He waits in his chair, rubbing the tight, thin thigh muscle of his bad leg.

"I prayed for peace, yet they force a battle upon us. We must be strong and at the ready. Nothing like a good spa to invigorate the body and clear one's mind. Right, Jon?" the colonel says to the once-vibrant politician. The president doesn't answer.

A spa attendant connects tubes to the president's scalp plugs while another prepares fluids that will pump and pulse through the man's brain.

"We have prepared a special protein-scrubbing enzymatic mixture for this session, Mr. President. It should be more effective than your last treatment." The president doesn't appear to comprehend the attendant's statement.

"A new treatment. That's sure to bring you around, Jon. I hope they don't bring me a skinny one again. I need to feel the surge of youth in my veins to prepare for battle."

A door opens with a commotion on the opposite side of the spa. An attendant holds the arm of a youth struggling in the doorway. Another attendant attempts to keep hold of the youth's other arm. The boy fights to free himself, shouting, "Let me go! Get off me!" The attendants forcibly drag the boy across the room to the waiting chair while the boy thrashes to get free.

The colonel watches with excitement. "It's about time you brought me one with some fight in him. Look at the boy. A fine specimen." The colonel spies the boy's fit body. "Ah yes, this one looks ripe and ready. Relax, boy. Join us for the spa. Ha—ha-ha!" The colonel practically licks his lips.

The attendants struggle to get the boys' flailing arms and legs strapped in the spa chair. The boy's fierce black eyes meet the colonels. Their vision locks. The boy sees weak, wanting dry old flesh. The colonel grins, expecting to see fear. Instead, he sees deep strength and contempt.

The colonel breaks the stare. "Let's see how you hold up, boy. Attendant, get this started. I've got barbarians at the gate."

The attendant slides a long thick needle up the vein of the boy's muscled arm. His angry expression transforms to violation. Blood flows.

Hot, angry blood surges into the colonel. His body jerks. The colonel closes his eyes and groans, allowing the steamy youthful elixir to fill his veins.

The attendant pushes a relaxing lozenge between the boy's lips. The boy spits it across the room and struggles to get loose of the straps. Then the boy recognizes the president sitting next to the colonel. Being in the same room with the president stuns him. Blood streams out of his body. He feels sluggish. He resigns himself to observe the spa treatments in silent horror.

"You've got spunk, boy. General Mahon could use some of that. Topsiders broke through the perimeter fence attempting to enter my city and he does nothing to stop them. I must monitor the man constantly. He has no initiative. Rumor has it the Marines will be here soon. I'll need my strength, or rather your strength, ha-ha, to help the general fight them off. I will allow no one to invade New Arcadia."

Colored fluids gurgle through tubes attached to the president's skull. The president is dull but looks peaceful as the procedure progresses. Suddenly, his eyes shoot wide open, and his head shakes violently. His mouth opens, allowing inaudible gasping sounds to escape. His head shakes harder and his body spasms tearing the tubes out of his head. Loose tubes of colored fluid squirt wildly in the air, splashing the colonel. Blood splats across the boy's face. He squirms in disgust, unable to wipe his face as the thick goo dribbles slowly down his cheek. Blood and colored fluids stream out of the president's scalp plugs, drizzling down his face.

Attendants rush to shut off the machine and stop the squirting fluids as a massive amount of red goo gushes from every hole in the president's head. His wide eyes droop shut, and the body relaxes. The president is dead. Russell rushes to the president's side, but there is nothing he can do but hold the dead man and grieve.

The colonel watches the scene of the president's death without reaction. Watching death overtake a friend is something he has seen many times. He says in a quiet tone, "Goodbye Jon, my dear old friend." He then yells at the attendants. "Wipe this mess off me!"

The colonel cannot focus on death. He is reveling in his own transformation. His skin has tightened and glows with the tone of youth. His eyesight has sharpened; his irises once again are piercing blue. His muscles have absorbed the youthful plasma, becoming taut and strong. His hair has thickened and returned to its youthful brown hue.

The parabiosis process is complete. The colonel views the boy. He is gray and gaunt. His black eyes look too large for his thin face. His hair is dry and thin. The boy turns his head weakly. The colonel sees a tormented face confronting him with hatred and scorn.

Attendants unstrap the boy and help him stand. The boy shakes them off, standing awkwardly by himself. Slowly and unsteadily, he shuffles to the door. An attendant holds the door open for him. The boy holds the door frame to right himself, then turns to the colonel.

"You are the lowest kind of thief. Stealing youth is your curse, not your cure."

The attendants pull the boy from the doorway.

The colonel bounds out of the soft chair, feeling strong and sturdy.

"We shall see, won't we, boy? I have more important concerns than worrying about unruly youth. I've got uninvited guests to deal with." The colonel presses past the attendants and exits the spa.

Rick trots back to Jin and Becky loaded down with weapons and arranges them on a nearby table. Jin hands Becky a Black Guard VUE lens, then hands a lens to Rick.

"Try these. The Black Guard sets were lock coded for city-only access. Curtis helped me unlock and activate them for universal access."

Rick pokes his finger in the air, then swipes and pokes again. "Control for voice. Code for motion control." Rick makes standard VUE lens hand motions to calibrate the unit. "This is great. I feel human again."

Rick hands Becky and Jin utility belts. "Put these on. You've got a handgun, extra magazines of relaxant darts, and a few other toys in there." They each touch a button on their belts to sync the belt with their lenses enabling visual, motion, and audible control of the belts.

Rick calls out. "Mags. Over here."

Three military style maglevs zip to them from the back of the armory, stopping directly in front of the Black Guard disguised trio. Jin and Becky stare at the hovering platforms. Rick steps on one maglev, putting his feet into the footholds floating in front of the young couple.

"They're easy to ride. You rode skateboards when you were kids, right?"

"Sure," says Becky.

"I never skateboarded. I was more of an indoor boy," says Jin, grabbing Rick's arm to lift himself onto his Maggie.

Jin gets both feet in the footholds but is bent over, clinging to Rick. The Maggie sways from the uneven weight. Jin straightens, and the maglev stabilizes.

Rick gives Jin a soft push to move the Maggie forward. Jin leans left, and the Maggie turns left, moving in a wide circle around the room. "Hey. Look at me!" The Maggie speeds up and Jin screams. "Oh, no! Ahhh." His arms flap as he flies around the room, trying to maintain his balance.

Rick laughs. "See, you're getting the hang of it. Don't try to balance. The Maggie will do that for you. Just relax and lean." Jin continues his awkward ride in wide circles.

"Now Becky, you try it," says Rick.

Becky steps onto a Maggie. Rick holds her hands as she gets into the footholds. Becky wobbles until she's balanced, then slowly sways right, left, back and forth, testing her weight. She leans forward and rides quickly to the far end of the room, turns slowly and rides swiftly back. "Not bad once you get the hang of it."

Rick applauds. "You're both doing great. Jin sling this over your shoulder and you'll be a real Black guard." Rick hands Jin a rapid-fire machine gun and an extra magazine. "Now we ride through the main city to the Electro-Rail Station and hope there's a rail car heading west soon."

Jin brings up the city map in his VUE. "If we pass for Black Guard, I think we can make it."

"Let's head out," says Rick, leading the way on his Maggie to the main corridor. Jin and Becky look awkward for a few moments, but quickly get the hang of cruising on the maglevs and catch up to Rick. Soon, the trio is gliding smoothly along the corridor to the city center.

Becky checks the Rail Station status. "Guys, we have a problem. All rail activity has stopped."

"Curtis, can you and Aman get control of the Rail Station?" Jin asks.

Curtis appears in all three VUE's. "Wow. You all look tough. Checking the rail system. Oh no, no, no. This is bad. They're resetting the security systems."

Aman joins in. "They are on to us. They know they've been compromised. No worries. We expected this. We will regain system control. That's why we have the teams playing. It shouldn't take long."

"We'll keep moving to the Rail Station. Hopefully, a team will hack the system by the time we get there," Rick says as he glides into the large domed city center.

All movement in the game stops. Elevators halt and blast doors drop, closing off corridors. Stairwell doors swing shut and lock. Ants get trapped in stairwells and elevators. Ants that made it into the city are being taken off the game maps.

Players are dismayed. Some pound their keyboards while others raise their hands in confusion. One player pounds his head with both his fists in frustration.

"Blimey. Did the game servers take a tumble? The maps all locked up. What happened?" asks a stunned Torpedo.

"This is it! The moment hundreds of teams have waited for. The game AI reacted to the colony intrusions and reset its security. It's open season! Every team gets a crack at hacking colony security. Teams who gain control of a colony replace the teams that got locked out," explains an excited Ceylon Junglefoul.

"Crikey! This game is living up to the hype. Something new at every turn. Look at all the team's cracklin' now. Which mates will be next to play Colony-Revolution Coup?"

Mike McCoy

Chapter 46: Extra Company

Los Angeles Wednesday-Friday

Friday Morning

The west coast of North America, from Juneau, Alaska to Santiago, Chile, suffered through a devastating night of fire from the sky. Streams of red, yellow, and green smoldered in the sky as asteroids ravaged the city of Los Angeles throughout the night.

Many meteors flew far out over the Pacific Ocean. Others exploded brilliantly in the sky, followed by air bursts and rocky debris destroying houses, buildings, cars, and roads. Large space rocks crashed through the atmosphere, slamming into Earth, wreaking havoc on the cherished objects and things built by man. The meteor blasts devastated the neatly arranged homes and streets of modern suburbia scattered across the continent. Homes, buildings, shops, and malls burnt to the ground, leaving only ash and bone. Burned-out washer/dryer units and water heaters are the skeletons of a once vibrant society. Untold thousands died that fiery night.

Everything is not destroyed. Everything is not dead. The storm may have destroyed a building or house may while the next building stands untouched. Entire areas remain miraculously the same as the day before, but it isn't the same.

Sirens howl. Smoke from a thousand fires fills the air. Power and data networks are out in many areas, rendering bands and VUE lens useless. AutoCars, noms, and actualizers sit idle, unable to receive instruction. Survivors emerge at dawn. Some take advantage of the chaos to loot stores. Some wander aimlessly while others sit alone in their homes crying.

For most people, the reality of their world is entirely digital. Life is a stream of data enabling social connections, work, meal preparation, transport, and entertainment. Life as they know it is out of service, destroyed by fiery rocks crashing from the sky. Life has ended before death arrives.

The one form of communication still working this morning when others have failed is AM radio. The government requires Smart-Band and VUE lens designs to include AM radio for emergency messaging. Most people don't know their device has a radio, but this morning, for many, the single shining ray of hope comes from a tinny voice transmitted over an amplitude-modulated radio wave.

The governor's voice announces that people can find shelter in an underground city called Edendale, built beneath the tall skyscrapers in downtown Los Angeles. She tells people there is food, shelter, and room for all. Everyone from Los Angeles and Orange counties are instructed to make their way to this new city prepared for them. The message provides directions to several entrances of the underground city. The governor directs people in Northern California to another city, named Ambrosia located under Sacramento.

Everyone receives the message, and it's rebroadcast every five minutes. Roads jam quickly. Vehicles of every type converge from all directions in downtown Los Angeles.

As people arrive downtown, they leave their autos and move to the underground city entrances. The line of empty cars and trucks becomes so long that all movement on the freeways stops. Freeways become clogged for miles and miles with abandoned vehicles. There is no choice but to abandon transport and walk. A parade of people of every type, color, shape, and size slowly wander their way toward the hope of shelter and safety.

Wednesday Night–Los Angeles

When Eddie Martinez arrives at his house, the night of the Pasadena meteor event and announced to his wife Selena that they will leave their perfectly good undamaged home to go live in an old mine. A weird project she didn't fully comprehend, funded by some old lunatic. She flatly refused.

"Rodrigo is heading up there with Isabella, Inez, Edgar, and the kids. We need to go. It's happening just like old Rob said," Eddie pleads.

Selina looks down at her newly manicured nails turning her hand this way and that, studying the deep red hue applied by the manicure nom. She slowly looks at Eddie with a flick of her head that tosses her hair over a shoulder. "We're meeting Gloria and Louis for dinner and drinks. We haven't seen them in ages. Louis booked a table at Le Domaine. I've been dying to go there. God knows you won't take me, so we're going. Get cleaned up and dressed."

"Baby, did you see the news? Look what's happening in Baltimore. It could happen here! An asteroid blew up in Pasadena, killing people, wrecking cars, and buildings. You act like nothing happened. All you think about is trying to keep up with Gloria, to see who can outdo the other. I'm trying to keep us alive, not see who has the prettiest dress and the best hair. God damn!"

"The news said those asteroid things happen once in ten million years, or something. It's like Baltimore hit the lottery, and Pasadena got five numbers out of six. Once in a bazillion million, odds it will ever happen again. Old Rob's crazy. You said it yourself. I can't believe Rodrigo fell for all his mumbo jumbo. Come on, honey. It's just one dinner. If you want to show me that cave, we can drive up Saturday." Selina ends with a seductive twist of her wide hips.

Eddie and Selina went to dinner with the Robles. No asteroids exploded or crashed into the restaurant. Everyone survived the evening.

The only person injured was Eddie, who suffered taunts and jibes as Selina told Louis and Gloria all about the project to convert an old mine into a doomsday hideaway. She told them its location in the mountains, how Eddie and Rodrigo work with a crazy old man to make an end-of-the-world shelter, and how Eddie came running home insisting they move into the cave. Eddie reminded Selina the project was a secret, and she shouldn't tell anyone about it. His statement only caused more laughter and ridicule.

Thursday morning, the sun rose brightly. It was a beautiful day. Eddie worked alone on a home remodel project. The work went slower without Rodrigo. Eddie didn't mind working late. He was in no rush to get home. He still suffered from the burn of humiliation from the previous night.

When Eddie arrived home, it surprised him to see several autos parked in front of his house. As he walked through the front door, he dodged nieces and nephews running around the living room playing VUE games. When he entered the kitchen, he found his wife and her sister having a loud, excited conversation on a video call. A puck on the kitchen counter projects the images of several women.

Selina excitedly repeats her description of the hideaway. "Oh, my God! I swear it's a real cave house carved into the side of a mountain. Eddie said its huge. It's not that far away, just north of Arcadia. It has a farm inside with real crops like lettuce and corn." The group of women on the call soak up the gossip like wet sponges.

"It's next to that bridge to nowhere. Just ask your lens. You'll see. It's across the bridge, right Selina?" adds Margot, Selina's sister, who is apparently familiar with the story.

"Great, first you make me look crazy in front of Gloria and Louis at dinner. Now you're telling all your friends. OK, yes. I built a secret cave house. Your husband works for a crazy old man. How do you think we paid for this kitchen?" Eddie says angrily. He motions over the puck; the projected screen evaporates, ending the call.

"Eddie! Those were my friends," cries Selina.

"You love making me look stupid, don't you?"

Margot raises a finger and tilts her head. "No, she was making Rodrigo look stupid. He's the one who dragged his family up there."

Eddie never cared for Margot. He refers to her as Selina's stupid sister. He reserves little patience for her, but if he picks a fight with Margot, he will suffer a thousand cutting words from his wife later that night. He doesn't want to ruin his evening, so he bites his tongue.

Eddie looks at his wife. "Why is she… why is everybody here? What's going on?" Eddie asks.

"Honey, I told you. It's Junior's birthday. I would never try to make you look silly, baby. George and Hector are in the back. Join them. Hector brought real steaks. Have a beer. Relax, babe."

"I don't like you telling your friends about the mine. Rodrigo is taking care of his family," Eddie says before leaving the room.

Margot waits until Eddie is out the door. "The secret mine," she says in a spooky tone. Selina and Margot break out in laughter.

Hector and George stand at the barbecue holding beers. Hector wears a white apron and a chef's hat. He holds tongs in one hand, waiting for the right moment to flip his steaks.

"I'm grillin' these babies with tender loving care, Georgie. One hundred percent Grade-A, USDA Prime beef steaks. The real thing not from a food actualizer. Tonight, we feast!" Hector and George high-five each other. Eddie grabs a beer and joins them.

Hector holds his beer in salute. "Eddie! I got to give it to you, man. You kept that place secret all this time. You never told us one thing about it."

"And you got Selina to keep your secret, at least until now. That's incredible," adds George.

"Anyone who can get my sister to keep a secret for three years, man. That's an accomplishment," says Hector before guzzling down half a bottle of beer.

"Respect," says George as he downs an entire bottle.

Eddie tips his bottle back, taking a long slow drink, and then looks up to the sky. "I know crazy Rob is crazy, but he's such a nice guy. So genuine and down to Earth. He has a passion, you know. You get sucked into it." Eddie pauses.

"And I heard he pays really good," says Hector, chuckling and motioning with his tongs.

"It's a fun project. The place is cool. The old man thought of everything. You could live in there for years," Eddie says, looking at the darkening sky.

Eddie spots an object in the sky. It looks like an aircraft flying faster than normal. Lights flash like aircraft lights. One light becomes three, then six, now twenty, then whatever it was silently breaks into hundreds of long streams of light. George sees it and nudges Hector to look up. Hector, busy with his perfectly timed steak-flipping, ignores the nudge. Eddie isn't sure what he's seeing. Did a plane blow up in the sky? The pieces aren't crashing; they continue to move across the sky.

George points to the sky. "There's another one… Oh, and another. What the hell? Hector, look!"

Hector flips the last steak and looks at George, who's pointing at the sky. Hector looks up to see the sky burning with a dozen fiery rocks.

"Oh shit! Crazy Rob was right. Selina!" Eddie yells for his wife as he runs into the house.

A meteor explodes over Long Beach, making a tremendous sound like nothing they've ever heard. Seconds later, a burst of burning wind sweeps through the backyard, blowing the chef's hat off Hector's head, singeing his hair and eyebrows as his apron flutters in the hot wind. More meteors explode in the sky, crashing into distant houses and neighborhoods. Hector leans over the barbecue, protecting his steaks.

"Hector, we've got to get out of here. Come on, man," George shouts.

Hector stalls until George grabs him, pulling him into the house as more asteroids fill the sky. Hector whimpers as he leaves his steaks on the grill.

The rest of the night is a frantic blur. Eddie insists everyone drives to the mine. Hector leaves his children, Hector Junior, and Claudia, with Eddie and Selina while he drives to pick up his wife at the hospital where she works as a nurse. They agree to meet at the mine.

Eddie, Selina, Margot, George, their two kids, Angel and Princess, and Hector's kids, Junior and Claudia and Grandma, all pile into Eddie's large truck. Eddie drives the city streets, assuming the freeways will jam as the asteroid storm continues.

The firestorm intensifies. The sky looks like a puffy gray cloud blanket embroidered with red and yellow streaks. Eddie is now driving through downtown Los Angeles. He takes Second Street and continues East under the 110 Freeway. Fireballs crash into the tall skyscrapers, concert halls, and county buildings that loom over the roadway. The sight of the buildings disappears as the truck enters the Second Street tunnel under Bunker Hill. The white tile walls of the tunnel gleam with the reflection of the trucks' headlights. Eddie pulls over and stops two hundred feet from the end of the tunnel, intending to take a short pause from the destruction.

A fast-moving car honks and swerves around Eddie's truck. As it speeds out of the tunnel, the car gets pelted with molten spherules.

The car, riddled with holes, crashes into a cement wall. The driver never exits the car.

Eddie and family spend the night in the tunnel. Several other cars also find refuge in the iconic Los Angeles tunnel. The firestorm recedes before dawn. Eddie wakes with first light and pulls out of the tunnel. Broken glass, metal, and chunks of cement litter the city streets. The tall buildings stripped of their glass exteriors look like iron skeletons.

Eddie navigates the city streets, avoiding the freeways. Progress is slow as they make their way through East Los Angeles. As he turns onto Huntington Drive, everyone in the truck receives a message from the governor telling them to find shelter in Edendale below downtown Los Angeles. Selina begs Eddie to turn around and follow the governor's instructions, but Eddie does not turn around. He's finally picking up speed. He isn't going back.

Forty minutes later, they are driving up East Fork Road. When the truck finally approaches the Bridge to Nowhere, they see what looks like a space shuttle parked on the side of a wide gravel-covered area. The boys, Angel and Hector Junior, are excited, hoping to explore the spacecraft that surely crash-landed in the mountains. Eddie notices the wheels below the craft and smiles to himself. Crazy old Rob made it to the hideaway.

Eddie eases his truck onto the cement bridge, drives across and parks on the dirt patch that is the end of the road. He leads his wayward band along the narrow trail as quickly as they will go.

Selina and Margot help their mother and the boys heft suitcases. Princess carries her dolls and Claudia carries a box. Eddie moves to the hidden entrance, unlocking the cyclone fence gate and opening the wooden door. As he moves deeper into the mine, the steel blast door opens. Rodrigo stands in the door with open arms to welcome his brother.

Eddie hugs his brother. Rodrigo speaks softly in his younger brother's ear. "I'm so happy you all made it. How is it out there?"

As Eddie releases the hug, his smile fades. "The city is destroyed. Thousands are dead. People don't understand what's happening. Edendale is the only hope for most, but I don't believe it can take everyone."

Rob stands behind Rodrigo and counts the number of people in the narrow tunnel. "We've been watching it on the streams. They say more than a million people are trying to crowd into the mysterious underground city. Who would have thought to build an underground city as protection from an asteroid storm? And you called me Crazy Rob! Ha-ha!"

Eddie and Rodrigo laugh nervously.

The line of people standing in the mine shaft looks shell-shocked and hungry.

"Eddie, let's get your family inside. They look exhausted. Please come in. Welcome. Welcome, everyone." Rob greets each one as he gestures for them to walk past him down the mine shaft and into the main gallery.

"Eddie, you have such a large family," Rob says as he counts nine people, including Eddie.

"This is Junior and Claudia. They're the children of my wife's brother, Hector, and his wife, Jean. Hector and Jean should arrive soon," Eddie says, patting the children's heads as they walk past him.

Rob counts on his fingers. "That will make eleven, plus the twelve we already have. Oh, my. I think we need to modify the sleeping arrangements."

The new arrivals straggle into the large main room, dazed and out of sorts. Isabella and Inez rush over to hug Selina, Margot, George, and the kids. Courtney and Maria carry food to the large dining tables. The kids—Alyssa, Ethan, Mary, Carlos, and Clara, who are already friends—walk together to greet the new kids, welcoming them to their new home in Munday's Hideaway.

Mike McCoy

Chapter 47: Gymnasium

Friday–New Arcadia

A dozen boys aged nine to thirteen live in Gymnasium. They exercise, fight, play, eat, and sleep in Gymnasium. The only time any of them leaves is for the spa. The selected boy leaves Gymnasium full of youthful energy and returns drained, nearly dead.

The gym attendant carries an anemic boy to a bed and starts the rejuvenation process. He administers intravenous fluids of a mysterious concoction enabling the boy to recover his strength and vitality.

Zekiel has observed the other boys' condition when they return from spa. They never speak of what happens. Maybe they're ashamed or refuse to remember the process that robs them of their youth. Zekiel believed they were drugged.

Other boys, when selected, walk passively and go silently to face their fate. When the attendant chose Zekiel, he did not go quietly. He fought the gym and spa attendants. He refused the lozenge stuck between his lips. It took the shock of seeing the president's head explode and brain goo splashing his face before Zekiel submitted.

When the process was complete, he was near death. Old, tired blood slogged through his veins, robbing him of strength. He felt hollow. He nearly fell trying to stand, yet refused help. He steadied himself and shuffled to the spa door. Only when he was in the hallway and the door closed behind him did he allow the attendants to help him return to Gymnasium.

Zekiel lies in his bed. A needle once again pierces his vein. This needle delivers fluids to nourish his wasted body. There is no easing the torment of his soul. He remembers every horrifying, disgusting moment. He is not ashamed. It hardens him.

When Gordon, the gym attendant, moves away from Zekiel's bedside, the boys rush to check on him. Boys who have not been to spa push close, wanting to know everything. Boys who have been through the process stand back warily, waiting to hear what he will say.

James and Davey are the first at Zekiel's bedside. At nine years old, they are the youngest boys. They've never been to the spa. "Are you OK, Zekiel?" asks James.

"You look sick," says Davey.

"Did it hurt?" asks James.

Nolan pushes to the front of the group and speaks eagerly. "Gordon says you'll be on your feet in no time. Gordon said he's never seen a stronger boy. Gordon said—"

"Gordon, Gordon," Aiden sings the name, interrupting Nolan. "I bet Gordon's real proud. Zekiel made it back alive. Success! Now fix him up and use him again. Gordon should have you spa next."

Nolan steps back sheepishly. He is tall and older than many other boys. At twelve years old it's odd he's never been to spa. Some boys say he's Gordon's favorite, others whisper other reasons Nolan is never chosen. No one really knows why he's passed over for spa.

Zekiel is thirteen, making him one of the older boys in Gymnasium. He, James, and Davey were the newest students. The colonel arranged for the Gymnasium to be at full occupancy before the storms began.

Boys destined for Gymnasium were sourced through the State of Virginia's Department of Social Services foster care program. They carefully study potential specimens through a rigorous series of tests and physical examinations. The genetic makeup of the boys must closely match the colonels. Blood types must match and lab tests for viruses, liver function, anti-aging hormones, and genetically screens for over 300 diseases. Students selected for Gymnasium are exceptional examples of the human species.

Aiden crouches at Zekiel's bedside. "You'll feel better in a few hours, but it takes a week to recover. Look at Will. He did spa a few days ago. He's better already." Aiden nods at Will, a thin, eleven-year-old who stands at the end of the bed. Will scrunches his face at Aiden.

Aiden continues. "Or you can drag it out longer, fake it. If you look weak and tired, Gordon won't pick you. Ask Owen. He's been faking for weeks." Aiden points to a shy, quiet boy who stands away from the group. Zekiel laughs weakly but stops laughing once he notices Owen isn't amused. Owen steps back but stays close enough to hear Zekiel's report if he gives one.

Owen is ten. When he arrived at Gymnasium, he was a happy, lively boy full of energy, joking and playing with the others. Gymnasium was better than any of his foster homes. When he returned from spa, he spent a full week in bed. The next boy selected for spa, a boy Owen knew from foster care, never returned to Gymnasium. Owen didn't speak for two weeks. Gordon thought Owen was faking and selected him for spa ahead of others.

When Gordon carried Owen back to Gymnasium, his limbs hung limp, near death. He languished in bed for weeks. When he recovered, he kept to himself. He rarely speaks and usually sits alone in a corner of the room, hands in his lap as he rocks silently.

"See, you'll be better soon. Aiden knows," James says encouragingly.

"What happened? Why did they make you sick?" asks Davey.

Zekiel doesn't want to answer. He doesn't want to think about spa. Now he understands why the others don't talk about it.

Zekiel pulls Aiden closer. "I'm never going to spa again. We gotta get out of here."

Aiden moves close, lowering his voice. "Are you crazy? You can't say stuff like that. Not to mention it's impossible. The gym is locked tight. Gordon's the only one who can open doors."

"I'll get out. I'll die before I spa again."

"There's no place to go, anyway. Did you forget? Underground city, thirty floors down, asteroid storms outside. Besides, it's our duty to aid the colonel in the service of New Arcadia."

"Screw New Arcadia. I won't help that youth-stealing bastard ever again," vows Zekiel.

Thin Will spoke in his tweeny voice. "He looks old and mean, but he's not so bad. He needs us."

"I know how you feel, Zekiel. I felt the same way. This was your first spa; you'll snap right back. It's not so bad. You get used to it. Just go with it," Aiden says, trying to comfort Zekiel and not scare the younger boys.

"It's awful. You don't know what it was like," Zekiel says, grabbing Aidan's arm.

Aidan laughs. "I've been to spa five times. I know exactly what it's like. You've been once and you're ready to run."

"No. The colonel did spa with President Anderson. They put tubes in the president's head. Then he started jerking. They liquefied his brain, and it squirted out all over the room." Zekiel instinctively wipes his face where the bloody brain goo splashed. Zekiel looks at Aiden and the boys. They're staring at him, waiting for him to continue.

"President Anderson is dead. He died in spa. The colonel sat there smiling. He barely said goodbye, like a dead president is nothing."

"Oh shit," says Aidan.

"Shit," the boys echo.

"People are trying to invade New Arcadia. The colonel said barbarians are at the gate."

"What's that mean?" asks James.

"I'm not sure, but he said the Marines are coming! They want to invade the city. The colonel will fight them!" Zekiel exclaims.

"OK, that's different from my spas. I usually suck on the lozenge and zone out, waiting for it to be over, knowing I'll feel like shit for a week."

"If people can get in, maybe we can get out," Zekiel says.

Nolan shakes and coos. "Ooh. Ooh. No. No, Gordon will be mad. You're bad boys."

Aidan stands quickly, grabbing Nolan by the shoulders and shakes him. "Not a word. Not a whisper, understand. Gordon won't be mad if he never knows. If Gordon finds out, I'll make him send you to spa. Who knows, you might not come back."

Nolan shakes with fear. He nods understanding and shrinks away.

Owen leaves the group, sits in his corner, clasps his hands in his lap, and starts rocking.

Mike McCoy

Chapter 48: Crypto Wars

Friday-Frederick Maryland

The messages broadcast by the governors directed hundreds of thousands of people to New Arcadia. VUE maps show the underground city near Fort Detrick in Fredrick, Maryland. A large business complex of eight four-story buildings at the center of a large parkland campus sits on what was once one hundred seventy-five acres of farmland. The city of New Arcadia is far below the business complex. The property runs along Yellow Springs Road and Christopher's Crossing, with residential subdivisions on three sides.

A grassy berm protects the perimeter. The height of the berm hides the existence of a ten-foot-high cyclone fence ringed with concertina wire. Behind the fence is a deep, grassy moat that circles the entire property. Behind the moat are a second fence and a perimeter road.

Entry to the complex is a two-lane road straddled by sentry buildings and vehicle barriers to control access. The entry road crosses the perimeter road and continues across the parklands until it descends below the east building to what looks like an underground parking structure.

When cars began arriving by the hundreds, the vehicle barriers and sentry buildings staffed with army soldiers stopped the cars from entering the main gate. As the line of cars and trucks grew on Yellow Springs Road, people got out of their vehicles and began exploring the perimeter, discovering the ten-foot-high fence.

A man used his side cutters to snip through the fencing. Once he and his family were through both fences, he gave the side cutters to a pair of eager teenagers who ran along the fence, cutting openings for other people.

Hundreds of people ran across the perimeter road and into the parklands of the building complex. They found the doors of the buildings locked. The glass doors were smashed, and people ran through the halls of deserted buildings. Their VUE lenses led them directly to elevators and stairwells that would take them far below the surface to safety in the underground city.

They struggled to open the secured stairwell doors and operate elevators, pressing buttons, and praying for entry. People continued to stream into the buildings, filling the halls as they pushed for position. Long lines of humans stretched out from the buildings winding across the parklands.

Crowds gathered at the tall metal roll-up doors at the base of the two-lane ramp leading to the underground parking structure. They banged on the doors, begging for entry.

Disappointment and anger swept through the crowd. The governor had instructed them to come for their safety and protection. They gave up everything, bringing their families to seek sanctuary from the terrifying asteroid storms to find the city locked. Hope is fragile.

People sat in the hallways, in their makeshift lines, hoping someone would let them enter. Elevators ding as their doors slide open and stairwell doors unlock with a click. People frantically push their way into the lifts and down the stairwells. There was a mad human stampede to enter the city.

Then everything stopped. Nobody knows how many people entered the city before the elevators stopped and Army troops began pushing people out of the buildings. Soldiers cleared people out of the halls and stairwells of the building and now stand guard blocking entrance.

Colonel Cruikshank swaggers into City Command, swinging his cane in a cheerful mood accompanied by Zsoldos. "I trust you have regained control of the city systems, Commander. We can't have New Arcadia overrun by topsiders the way they invaded New Zion."

"No, sir. Only a few people gained access. They were relaxed and moved to quarantine. We immediately followed protocol and reset the system security with new encryption codes. We are again on full lockdown."

The colonel shows approval as he scans the room. Cruikshank nods to Zsoldos. The portly man moves to a thin screen. "Look here, our systems are being flooded by network intruders pinging and prodding the servers. They are working to hack our encryption or find a back door to gain access. You must continually reset encryption codes. You must work smart and fast to stay ahead of them. From the looks of it, this is not the work of one or two nerds in their mothers' basements. We're getting hit by hundreds of crypto-hackers." Zsoldos pauses as he pokes the screen several times. "And they are good." Zsoldos points to several blue tunics. "You, you, and you two over there. This is a crypto war. You must keep our system secure. Use every tactic, spoof our IP addresses, reset our DNS servers, plug every hole in our system or they will gain access. Work fast and keep on your toes."

A blue tunic sitting nearby monitoring exterior camera systems voluntarily gives a report in a frantic tone. "Tens of thousands of people have surrounded the buildings and assembled in the Parklands. Thousands more are making their way here. Sir, if they breach the entrances again, they will flood the city in minutes. Even the Black Guard won't be able to put them all down."

Colonel Cruikshank smacks the metal tip of his cane on the cement floor. "Where is our General Mahon?" the colonel shouts. The image of Mahon appears on a wall-mounted screen. The general appears stressed and frustrated.

"Where is my perimeter? If you would have defended our perimeter and repelled the invaders from the start, we would not have topsiders filling the Parklands," shouts Colonel Cruikshank.

The general has a sour look on his face. "Apparently, your design of the New Arcadia perimeter did not contemplate one hundred thousand people walking onto the campus Parklands. You assured me the cities were secret. What would you have me do, fire on civilians?"

"I expect you and your men to do what is necessary to protect New Arcadia. Shoot them, bulldoze them, if that's what it takes. They're dead regardless. What does it matter lead, meteors, or starvation? The result is the same. It's just a matter of timing."

The general winces. He looks ready to fire a heated reply but seals his lips, pausing to for search for new words. "My troops have moved people out of the buildings and stairwells. We are constructing a new perimeter fence to keep people away from the buildings."

Air Force Academy–Colorado Springs, CO

A group of twenty cadets stand in the Quadrangle, more familiarly called the Quad: a large grassy field at the center of buildings in the cadet area of the US Air Force Academy. The iconic cadet chapel sits on the eastern edge of the Quad.

The cadets stand next to a TX-200 advanced Air Force trainer and listen to an instructor. "This fine aircraft is the latest supersonic trainer. For those of you who wish to become Air Force pilot candidates, your training may lead you to JSUPT, or Joint Specialized Undergraduate Pilot Training, where you will have the chance to strap on this baby." The instructor affectionately pats the side of the aircraft as he speaks.

A loud alarm sounds followed by an announcement over a loudspeaker. "All cadets and staff. Assemble at Stillman Field immediately. All cadets and staff are ordered to assemble at Stillman Field. You will receive further instructions at assembly."

Five minutes later, twelve hundred cadets and five hundred staff members stand in formation on Stillman Field. Fifty buses are parked behind the bleachers.

An officer stands at the center of the tall bleachers. "We have been ordered to aid civilians at the Denver Airport. You will all load into buses. It is a one-hour drive. You will receive assignments during the ride. This is a humanitarian effort to help protect as many civilians as possible from the asteroid storms."

The cadets and staff line up to fill the buses in an efficient and orderly manner.

Black Guard reinforcements arrive at Heavy One and Heavy Two. City Command followed the security protocol and reset the system encryption codes, blocking entry to New Zion. Teams of Black Guard move up the stairwells to collect stragglers. The last load of elevators is arriving.

As the elevator doors open, the mass of people see they're surrounded by heavily armed Black Guard. Guards escort the people to waiting levitating buses parked in a ring in front of Heavy One and Two. It's easier to move people awake than handling relaxed bodies. The bodies of those trampled to death lay where they fell for all to witness. Anyone who makes a sudden move or does not comply is relaxed.

Kobalt turns to Lieutenant Astatine. "Now your city is under control, Lieutenant. I expect you to keep it that way."

City Command appears on their VUE lenses. "In the confusion, people entered the city from several locations. There are hundreds of people in Corridors four and fifteen."

Astatine responds, trying to regain control of his command. "Send two platoons there immediately. Heavy One and Two are clean-up operations now."

"Sir, there is a strange situation near Elevator seven, and the supporting stairwell, on the south side of the city," reports City Command.

"What situation?" asks Kobalt.

"There was no sign of elevator movement or breach of the stairwell door, but hundreds of people are in Corridor ten. They must have entered through the stairwell."

"That's on the opposite side of the city. How many got in?" asks Kobalt, gruffly.

"At least six hundred before we caught the problem. We could not secure the stairwell door, so we dropped blast doors at both ends of the corridor. We've trapped most of the topsiders between the blast doors. They should be easy to sweep up."

Kobalt looks at Astatine with renewed disgust.

"There's something else strange, Captain," says the City Commander.

"There are many strange things happening in New Zion today. What else?" Kobalt asks angrily.

"Were any Black Guard ordered to the Rail Station?"

Lieutenant Astatine looks aghast, unable to answer. "There was no such order given," replies an irritated Kobalt.

"I have three Black Guard on maglevs moving swiftly to the Rail Station, sir."

"Black Guard deserters?" asks Kobalt.

"All Black Guard are accounted for, sir."

"Maglev's running for the Rail Station while we're distracted on the other side of the city. It can't be. They said he was dead. His rail car crashed. It's not possible. How could he have reached New Zion?"

Astatine looks confused, unable to follow Kobalt's meaning.

A rare event occurs. A smile slowly forms on Kobalt's face. "It's got to be Munday. He's the one behind this. It's time for this to end, Dr. Munday."

Kobalt calls to his elite troops. "Teams Four and Six, make sure we have all topsiders secured. Team One and Three, with me to the Rail Station! Lieutenant join me. This should be fun."

Lieutenant Astatine spins his maglev around, moving quickly to catch up with Kobalt.

Rick, Jin, and Becky glide to the Rail Station. Jin and Becky, now comfortable on the Maggies lean into the curves as they speed through a large domed room then enter the corridor leading to the Rail Station.

"Curtis, we need an update. Can you get us in a rail car heading your way?" Rick asks.

Curtis pokes at screens checking city status. He sends a private message to Aman.

"Aman, I've got nothing. We've lost control of doors and elevators. City Command is actively fighting us. There's nothing I can do. We've got to help Rick. It won't be long before they discover us in their system," Curtis says frantically.

"It's all cool, bro. City Command has the control for now. Let them fight the hackers. The hackers are on the outside trying to get in. City Command is not fighting us. We are effectively on the inside of their network. We have root access and we've masked our secure tunnel super-well. We're cool if we stay under the radar. If we take control of the Rail Station, they'll be on to us and lock us out. Then our gang would get trapped for sure," Aman explains.

"We can't leave them hanging. We've got to do something," says Curtis desperately.

Someone pokes Aman in the ribs. He turns to see the smiling face of his cousin. "Hey, cuz. What's happening, bro?" Aman asks in his sing-songy voice. His cousin leans in and whispers in his ear.

Curtis hears Aman saying, "Oh? Ah, really, now! Oh my. You don't say. But can you make it work?"

"What's going on, Aman? Can what work?" Curtis asks anxiously.

"A plan, man," Aman answers briefly, then swiftly goes to work with his cousin to see if his plan can work.

"What have you got for me, Curtis? We're approaching the Rail Station. Are we good to go?" Rick asks urgently.

Curtis stutters. "Ah, well shit. No. The Rail Station is no good. Take a lap around the city center. Aman is working on a plan. I'll update you soon."

Jin and Becky pull alongside Rick. They exchange worried glances. "Sorry, guys. This whole thing was a risky move. Guess it was foolish to think we could just hop on a high-speed train all the way home. It almost worked once before. Not such a great plan, I guess," Rick says in a conciliatory tone.

"Something unexpected? Who woulda thought? Don't worry, we're not done yet. I have faith in Curtis and Aman. They'll come up with something," Jin says.

The trio speeds down a corridor and enters a huge domed room at the center of New Zion. The city is vast and vibrant. People are walking through gardens with green grass and trees or relaxing at sidewalk cafes. Obviously, they don't know that topsiders have breached their city.

Curtis spots something on his screen. "Hey, guys. Oh, dang! You've got a group of bogies coming up behind you. They went directly to the Rail Station. Now they're heading to the city center. It looks like your cover is blown. You've got to find a place to hide fast!"

"Curtis, check city maps. Can you find us a safe place?" asks Jin.

Rick leads the way, zipping down a small corridor. "Black Guard will come for us. We've got weapons. They don't know we're prepared. We're not hiding."

Rick checks the city map in his VUE. He spots a corridor that splits into a Y just ahead.

Curtis downs a can of BBQ Pringles in less than a minute. He can't help it. Nervous eating. His mouth is dry, so he hefts himself out of his chair in search of soda. When he's back at his desk, he notices Rick, Jin, and Becky have stopped moving. "They stopped? Why did they stop in the middle of a road? That's not a hiding place! Aman, this is getting too real. What's your plan?"

"Curt-tis, we got this, bro. You worry so much. The plan is already underway."

"It started already. What exactly is this plan?"

Curtis sees Aman's cousin in the background, smiling with a mouth full of teeth, wagging his head up and down in sync with everything Aman says.

"Oh yes. Let me explain. We will share our secure tunnel into New Zion systems with the game," Aman says calmly.

"What? They'll be on to us and shut us down! Are you crazy?" Curtis shouts in a frightened tone.

"Maybe. Crazy like a lemur," Aman says, with a tinny laugh. "If we flood the city with people, it will give our gang the chance to get away. We found an exit."

"An exit plan," the smiling cousin adds.

Curtis empties crumbs from the Pringles can into his hand and tosses them to the back of his mouth. "You'd better be right about this."

Rick pulls the 550 Paracord from his backpack and secures it to the collision protection bollard, a yellow-painted steel pole on the left side of the corridor. Jin ties the thin dark rope as tight as he can to the bollard on the right side of the corridor.

"This Paracord is rated for 550 pounds of dead weight. It isn't super strong, but I think it will work well enough," says Rick

"Is the rope high enough?" ask Jin.

"Just the right height to knock the Black Guard off their maglev's if they hit the rope at high speed. I know it's an old trick, but hopefully it will give us a slight advantage."

Becky is on her Maggie, down the narrow corridor past the rope. "I don't like using Becky as bait. Don't you think this rope is obvious? The Black Guard aren't stupid."

Rick tests the tension of the rope. "I hope they aren't stupid at all."

"What? Now I'm confused."

"The Black Guard will see the rope, and Becky, and figure it's a trap, so they'll move down the other corridor toward us. Hopefully, the rope will make them think, slow them down, and bunch them up. That's when we blast them."

Jin nods his head slowly. "I think I'm liking this plan," hefting his machine gun.

"Becky, wait till you see them. Make sure they see you, then get out of there. We'll be hiding in a doorway down this corridor, ready to attack," Rick explains.

Becky spins around on her Maggie, riding backward as she draws her sidearm. "I'm ready!" she says, raising the dart pistol over her head.

Millie's Delight-Frederick Maryland - Near New Arcadia

Twenty CH-53K Sea Stallion troop-carrying helicopters from MCAS Cherry Point, North Carolina land in a large field named Millies Delight at the south end of Christopher's Crossing. The field got its name from a real estate development that went bust. It's the only open field without parked cars close to the business complex that hides New Arcadia below. One thousand Marines launch out of the copters. As the flying beasts touch down, the Marines take up defensive positions, creating a large perimeter.

C-130J transport planes land one after the other six miles away at Fredrick Municipal airport and unload as quickly as possible to make room for the next incoming transport. The planes unload LTVs (Light Tactical Vehicles), LAV-35s (Light Armored Vehicles) and RQ-10B Shadow Hawk drones, twenty-foot shipping containers filled with drone flight control and mission command centers and pallets loaded with equipment, weapons, supplies, and support troops. Trucks move most of the equipment and supplies to Millie's

Delight, but a separate caravan hauls the RQ-10B Shadow Hawk drones and the drone flight control center to Fort Detrick to set up a secondary base specifically for UAS (Unmanned Aircraft Systems).

The Marines are coming in full force. The bulk of heavy equipment, mobile command posts, and support trailers are in a convoy driving from North Carolina.

An Osprey MV-22 lands in the center of Millie's Delight. General Charles Wilcox, commander of the US Marine Expeditionary Force, steps onto the field. He scans the area as LTVs and LAV-35s arrive from the airport.

Three more Ospreys touch down. Marine officers looking serious, carrying large satchels full of operational orders and site plans pile out of the aircraft.

General Wilcox signals to his command staff. The officers quickly assemble around the general in the busy field. "Get the Shadow Hawks airborne. Let's get a look at what we're up against." The general points to Christopher's Crossing. Abandoned vehicles block the road. "I want that road cleared ASAP. Commandeer tow trucks or whatever it takes. That road is our access to New Arcadia."

Becky hovers on her Maggie gliding left and right watching the corridor beyond the rope. She hears them before she sees them. Maglevs float silently, but the sound of rustling gear gives warning of the Black Guard's approach. "They're getting close," Becky whispers into her VUE.

Becky moves closer to the rope, hoping they spot her and give chase. "Ready, ready," Becky says to herself as she hovers dangerously close to the rope.

She spots the Black Guard gliding four abreast down the corridor, moving toward the Y branching of the corridor. "Here they come." She is tempted to whistle and wave but doesn't dare.

The front row of guard spots Becky and picks up speed. She hesitates a moment, pausing longer than is safe. The guards give chase. Becky speeds down the corridor and hears a loud crash behind her. She spins around, riding backward, firing her dart gun wildly.

Two men in the first row of guard hit the paracord and fell off their Maggies. The others stop in time. As Rick predicted, the oldest trick in the book slowed and bunched up the Guard.

Rick and Jin hear the crash and inch out of their hiding spot. The guards are taking scattered fire from Becky, causing them to focus their attention on her. Jin let loose with the machine gun, sweeping the bunched-up Black Guard squad. Rick fires his handgun methodically, making his shots count. Black Guard fall.

The Black Guard of New Zion has never faced a real threat. They wear lightweight tunics skipping the thick, uncomfortable armored skin suits. Jin sprays the Black Guard with his machine gun, sending more guard to the floor. Rick adds cover fire for Jin while he reloads.

Rick takes a dart grenade from his utility belt. He tosses it, aiming with his VUE, at a spot on the floor below the pack of Black Guard maglevs. The grenade bounces along the floor before stopping at the precise spot, then explodes, sending darts through the air that brings down four Black Guard.

Becky takes fire from the guards in response to her wild shots. She's hit in the leg and torso. She winces at the pain of the impacts. The darts hurt, but they don't penetrate her skin suit. She glides backward, taking more controlled shots. She downs the guard who shot her in the torso. "Hey, I got one!" she exclaims happily.

"Great job, Becky, but back off. Get to the meetup point," Rick orders as he puts down a guard who is aiming for Jin.

Kobalt and Astatine follow at a distance behind the two squads of eight men. They hear the crash. The squad has stopped and is taking fire. Kobalt holds back. Astatine advances into the fray.

Kobalt yells out to the lieutenant. "Can't you see it's an ambush? Order your men back." But it's too late. Astatine zooms headlong into battle and falls, put down by Rick's second dart grenade.

Four Black Guard are still standing. Kobalt puts two fingers to his lips, whistles loudly, and orders the men to retreat. The squad disengages from the battle and moves up the corridor to Kobalt.

Rick and Jin watch the guard's retreat to a tall, hulking bald man. Rick gasps. "Captain Kobalt. How did he get here?"

Jin eyes the big man. "Who's Captain Kobalt?"

"He's captain of the Black Guard in New Arcadia. Not a nice guy."

"Do you think he came here looking for you?"

"I don't want to find out, but if we don't put him down, he'll be relentless. Hold still." Rick places the long barrel of his dart gun on Jin's shoulder for stability. He carefully aims and fires. The dart flies directly for Kobalt. A retreating Black Guard moves into the dart's path. The guard goes down with a thud.

"Nice shot," whispers Jin.

"Yeah, wrong guy." Rick fires again but misses. Kobalt is on the attack.

"Oh, no! What's that?" Jin asks as two Buzz-Bees fly directly toward them. Kobalt directs the Bees through his VUE.

Rick quickly checks his utility belt inventory. He sees an item listed as dart net.

"Dart net, fire!" He uses voice control to launch the net from his utility belt. The net shoots into the air, covering one of the Buzz-Bees, pulling it to the floor.

The second Buzz-Bee increases speed and closes on Rick and Jin's position. The Black Guard squad fires. Rick pushes Jin behind the door for cover.

"Check your utility belt," Rick says urgently.

"I, I don't have a dart net," Jin says frantically.

"You must have something. Try anything," Rick says as he fires shots at the Buzz-Bee, each shot missing the small flittering target.

Jin scrolls through the defensive tools list in his VUE. "I have a sticky wall. Not sure what—"

"Use it," Rick calls out as the Buzz-Bee fires. A dart hits Rick in the shoulder, but it doesn't penetrate his suit.

Jin moves in front of Rick, juts his left hip forward as if to aim and shouts, "Sticky wall," while pointing at the Buzz-Bee.

A rubber ball launches from Jin's utility belt and bounces off the floor. The ball expands instantly, creating a strong sticky barrier that stretches wall to wall, floor to ceiling. The Buzz-Bee fires its remaining shots, all sticking in the gum-like wall.

The Black Guard fire repeatedly at the sticky substance. Kobalt cries out. "I'll end you, Munday. You won't get out of New Zion alive."

As Kobalt screams his vengeance at the gummy wall, Rick and Jin run in rapid retreat down the corridor, then speed away on their Maggies.

"Let's get to Becky. Check with Curtis for an update," Rick says as they move to the meetup point.

Kobalt watches the two men move down the corridor through the translucent gummy wall. "Interesting tactic, Munday. I doubt you learned that in astrophysics class."

Kobalt turns to his surviving men. "You men are a disgrace to the Black Guard. Outsmarted by a wimpy college professor. You don't deserve to be Elite Guard."

Kobalt glides slowly to the fallen men and hovers over the relaxed body of Lieutenant Astatine. He speaks to the unconscious lieutenant while aiming his weapon at the limp body.

"Lieutenant Astatine, which Black Guard training exercise taught you to run into an ambush? You allowed a civilian to drop you in less than five seconds. What a fool." Kobalt fires four darts into Astatine's body.

The remaining Black Guard recoil. One guard speaks up. "That much relaxant venom will kill him, sir."

"Lieutenant Astatine is already dead. Killed by his own incompetence and the criminal, Dr. Richard Munday. You witnessed it. We have three invaders disguised as Black Guard, causing mayhem and murder in New Zion. You will take them dead or alive and bring order to New Zion. Do you understand me?"

"Yes, sir!" the guard bark in response.

Rick and Jin speed along the corridor to the meeting point. Becky is waiting for them. "That was fun. Scary, but fun," Becky says, rubbing the spot on her abdomen where the dart hit.

"Is everyone all right?" Rick asks, giving Jin and Becky a look over. He doesn't mention that a dart hit him in the shoulder.

"I'll have a couple bruises, but otherwise I'm fine. I'm glad you made us wear the skin suits," says Becky.

"That was wild. My heart is still pumping, and my hands are vibrating from the machine gun," says Jin.

"Good shooting, Jin, but we're not home free. Not with Kobalt in the city. Becky, what's the update from Curtis?"

"Curtis says Aman has a plan. We need to get to an older part of the city on the east." The trio views the location in their VUE lens. "He says there's an old unused express rail. I'm not sure where it goes, but it's our exit from the city."

"Let's get moving. Kobalt won't be far behind," says Rick.

Rick speaks the location setting the Maggies' destination and they whisk their way through a maze of corridors, hopefully to their freedom.

Chapter 49: Slingeren

Washington DC–DUCC–Deep Underground Command Center

President Baker receives continuous updates and briefings in the Command Center. The large room is a beehive of activity. Military, Homeland, congressional staff responsible for various committees move in and out of the large room. There is so much information to manage; the president has given instructions that verbal briefings be short and to the point.

Sheryl sets a briefing book in front of President Baker. "Here you are, sir. These are the last briefs before we move to Camp David. We are ready to start whenever you give the word, sir."

"No time to waste. What have we got?" Cliff Baker points to a Marine captain standing at the end of the large conference table. Major Anthony Cortez sits at a table in front of the conference table. Next to him are two analysts wearing VUE lenses. Major Cortez has come prepared.

The captain looks to Major Cortez, nods, and reads the briefing notes projected from a small round puck on the table in front of him. Screens on the wall of the Command Center display the presentation.

"The press is reporting that the White House endorses the Governor's messages directing citizens to the Arcadian cities. Millions of people are moving to the cities."

"That's wonderful. With support from the Marines and Air Force, it should be a bad day for that bastard Cruikshank. Please continue," says President Baker.

"We located the Harpoon launch facility in the country of Suriname. Because of the urgency of the situation, we dispatched an expeditionary force to the launch complex. In an early morning raid, our forces secured the launch site and the Harpoon mission team. The launch complex suffered eight casualties, all local security personnel. Our forces suffered only minor injuries, with no casualties. We now have control of the complex. We have apprised the President of Suriname on the situation and the reason for our presence in the country. He has pledged his support. The Arcadians recruited and controlled the Harpoon mission team, but they agreed to work with us. Apparently, it didn't take much to convince them. Several members of the mission team reported that the Arcadians kidnapped or coerced them to work on the project. Dr. Simmons and his team are at the site now." The captain pauses for reaction.

"Suriname? Where the hell is that? Jerome?" asks President Baker.

The captain doesn't wait for Jerome's finger twitching. "The Republic of Suriname is on the northeastern Atlantic coast of South America. Suriname is the smallest country in South America, remote and relatively obscure. I'm sure that's one reason the Arcadians selected this location. However, the location of the Slingeren Launch Facility is optimal for space launches. It's near the equator and on the Atlantic coast. You might call it Cape Canaveral south."

"Slingeren? The name sounds rather creepy, something Cruikshank thought up, I suppose," remarks Mitch.

"It's a Dutch word meaning to hurtle, hurl or launch, so not creepy if you're Dutch. The Arcadians spared no expense building the launch facility. Apparently, they understood the need for planetary defense against asteroids," explains the captain.

"What is the state of the Harpoon Mission? Will we be able to pull this off?" asks the president.

"The Harpoon team were targeting a different object for their test. However, it seems most of the work is complete. Re-targeting for the Beast, or 2039 JZ966, appears to be relatively straightforward, but there are many factors to consider," the captain reports in a snappy tone.

The captain receives a message on his band. "Sir, the Marines have landed at New Arcadia. They are setting up a staging area in a nearby field. We should have an update from General Wilcox shortly."

"Good! Let's give that old bastard Cruikshank some company. We can save thousands more souls today. Do we have an update from Dr. Simmons?" asks President Baker.

The captain nods the affirmative and swipes his hand over the puck on the desk.

"Dr. Simmons, President Baker, is ready for your briefing."

The call startles Dr. Simmons. "Hello, President Baker. Just in time. I have prepared a mockup of the impactor assembly for a demonstration." Dr. Simmons points to a long metal boom mounted on a four-foot metal box.

"Dr. Simmons, before you get into the nuts and bolts of this asteroid blaster, what are the chances this thing will work? What's the situation there?" asks the president.

"The facilities and staff are amazing. It's as if they spent every dollar siphoned away from NASA and JPL to build this modern launch complex. They have three Harpoon systems fully assembled with ten-megaton nuclear devices. The devices are highly advanced and equipped with extremely efficient lightweight nuclear devices, armed with advanced high-speed triggering systems. They have four launch pads and six SLS rockets in inventory. It's remarkable. The team they've assembled is top-notch. We're working with the harpoon team to re-target for the Beast."

"You said it might take forty atom bombs to blow up this asteroid. They only have three harpoons. Will that be enough to save the world?"

"Can you launch in time?" asks Mitch.

"Patience, gentlemen. We understand the urgency and I know you have many questions. The team is assessing the target object now. The initial assessment indicates that we can disrupt the Beast with the three Harpoons. However, the team is working through that analysis as we speak. I think it's best to brief you on how this will work."

"Please proceed," says President Baker.

Dr. Simmons waves his hand over a drawing of a rocket ship. "I present the Harpoon, otherwise known as a Hypervelocity Asteroid Intercept Vehicle or HAIV. The payload fairing of a NASA SLS rocket will house a single Harpoon. Without getting overly technical, we will launch the SLS in the asteroid's direction. During the Earth departure trajectory, we will continually adjust and correct for the target intercept. Harpoon will impact the asteroid five hours after launch."

President Baker seems pleased. "So, that's the contraption that will blow the asteroid to smithereens?"

Dr. Simmons smiles. "It is one of the three devices that will simultaneously impact the asteroid. Each high-velocity kinetic impactor will target a specific location. The impactors will create craters of sufficient depth to mimic a subsurface nuclear explosion. This increases the energy coupling, at least by an order of magnitude. What we count on is the transmission of shock waves being sent through the rocky body to break up or disrupt the asteroid into smaller pieces. Think of a hammer shattering a rock. It's exciting, don't you think?"

"You're saying you can blow this thing up. That's what you're saying, right?" asks the president, looking slightly confused.

Dr. Simmons turns to the camera. "We are studying the simulations to determine if we can achieve full disruption, but yes. I believe we can blow this thing up, sir."

"However," says Jerome.

"However, what Jerome?" asks President Baker.

"I'll let Dr. Simmons explain," Jerome says while poking and swiping in front of his VUE.

"Well sir, the simulation shows several large pieces will survive disruption. You must understand this is quite a large target, even when pounded with 10-megaton nuclear device disruption may not be absolute. I mentioned this in our first discussion about Harpoon. We are still working to determine if we can achieve a more complete disruption, but time is short," Dr. Simmons reports.

Mitch stands. "You said it could leave some fragments that would go out into space. Now, you are saying large chunks of this asteroid could still hit Earth?"

"If there are residual fragments remaining after disruption of the main body, these fragments will cause much less damage than if the Beast were to remain intact," explains Dr. Simmons.

"Dr. Simmons, are you sure about the course of this asteroid? You're positive it will crash into Earth? We're planning to detonate several nuclear devices in space and you're giving me no assurance it will blow this asteroid into a million pieces," President Baker says in a disturbed tone.

Dr. Simmons stands erect. "The asteroid is on a collision course with Earth. There is no doubt. If the asteroid strikes Earth, our simulations project ninety-five percent of all life on the planet will be dead within five weeks. The impact winter that follows will probably kill off the remaining five percent. We have one shot at destroying it. We're lucky to have that shot."

"OK, so what can we do about these large fragments, as you call them? Won't they be dangerous if they hit Earth?" asks Tug.

"Any large fragments are dangerous if they hit populated areas. We classify objects over one hundred meters in diameter as city-killers."

"We may save Earth but cause horrific destruction if this doesn't work. Is there something we can do about these fragments?" asks President Baker.

"Dr. Simmons, what are the alternatives? What other tools can we use for planetary defense?" asks Tug.

Jerome raises his hand and speaks without looking from his VUE. "Blast the big chunks with Minuteman Threes," he says.

There is a gasp in Command Center. "Secretary Hargrove! You're suggesting we use nuclear missiles to shoot down the large fragments?" asks Senator Campbell.

Dr. Simmons thinks for a moment. "Secretary Hargrove is correct. Suborbital intercepts may be the best solution for incoming fragments. We can launch Minuteman Three ICBMs from silos at Vandenberg, Minot, in North Dakota, and Cape Canaveral. Once launched, the ICBMs would intercept target objects at altitudes, allowing us to create a dome of coverage protecting North America from larger objects."

Major Cortez knows something about this topic. "Dr. Simmons is correct. ICBMs have long been a proposed method for suborbital interception of NEOs, for planetary defense. If our goal is to protect North America, ICBMs may be our best choice." Everyone around the table seems to accept what the major says.

"Anything to add, Jerome?" asks President Baker. Jerome seems distracted but gives the president a thumbs up while focusing on his VUE.

Cliff turns to Tug and the Secretary of the Air Force, who sit across the conference table. "You'd better have those ICBMs ready in case any large fragments head our way."

Tug faces everyone around the conference table. "I hope Harpoon works. I'm not comfortable launching ICBMs at space rocks like it was a damned skeet shoot. There's the risk of EMP effects that could knock out every electronic device on the planet, not to mention the potential for radioactive fallout. I'm worried the cure could be worse than the threat."

Dr. Simmons speaks up. "Harpoon is ready. Let me make it crystal clear. Harpoon is the best and only chance of saving Earth. We will do our best to attain the highest level of disruption. However, we must plan to target large residual fragments with intercepts at altitudes above two thousand kilometers. At this altitude, we will be relatively safe from EMPs and radiation. Everything is moving extraordinarily fast, but we're on track for a successful launch of the Harpoon fleet. The power to save Earth is in our hands."

The room is silent as everyone considers the risks to Earth. Doing nothing means all life on Earth will perish.

"Should we proceed as planned, sir?" asks Dr. Simmons.

"We must proceed. When are you ready to launch?"

"We will launch early tomorrow morning. Harpoon will be ready to fly," says Dr. Simmons.

Cliff nods approval. "Thank you, Simmons. I know you will do your best. Send my regards to your team. Splendid work."

Chapter 50: Stampede

Kobalt speaks to his VUE. "City Command, do you have an update on our three renegade murderers?"

"We heard what happened, sir. An ambush? That's awful. The renegade murderers are moving to the east side of the city. Maybe they're planning another attack, sir. There's nothing over there but the remnants of an old military base, built long before the new city."

Kobalt thinks out loud. "What is Munday up to? We will not fall into another trap. I want all Black Guard moving to the old military base. Munday will not survive an overwhelming force no matter what he has planned." He signals his men to move.

Alarms sound in City Command. The room becomes frantic with activity. "Captain Kobalt, the airport is being attacked! They're shooting down our aircraft. They've knocked out our anti-aircraft guns. Damage is severe. Air Force intruders are taking Army personnel prisoner in the airport terminals."

"Is the city still locked down?" asks Kobalt.

"Yes, sir. We have complete control of city systems."

"Good. The Army is General Mahon's problem. Call the colonel and update him. I'm after the murdering renegades."

An advertisement plays on the Tweaknet stream. The halt in game play has Ceylon Junglefoul worried. How many game recaps and sponsor messages can he broadcast? The views are dropping. It seems like hours since the city AI's halted game. Torpedo can say them boys be cracklin' only so many times. The AI blocked access to all the colonies and the AI at New Arcadia has green ants blocking access to building entrances. The game is frustrating.

The advertisement ends, followed by a roar of excitement. Ceylon thinks viewers are cheering because the commercial has ended.

"Them's cheeky bastards, they is," says Torpedo excitedly. It takes Ceylon a few seconds to figure out what's happening.

"Did they do it?" asks Ceylon with excited caution.

"Team Lucid-Gaze has nabbed control of the New Zion Colony. Doors are poppin' open. Ants are streaming into the stairwells. The lifts are liftin.' This game just kicked into high gear!" screams Torpedo.

Ceylon checks his screens. Team Lucid-Gaze appears to have broken the code at New Zion while other teams struggle to crack the codes of other colonies. All the excitement is focused on New Zion, at least for the moment.

"Tens o' thousands of ants are skedaddling for ev'ry colony entrance. It's an ant stampede, it is," cries Torpedo.

The entire Command Center watches the stream, as the US Air Force attacks Army placements at the Denver airport. The action is swift and decisive. The small fleet of Army aircraft and anti-aircraft emplacements are no match for the ferocity of the Air Force attack.

President Baker watches excitedly. "Congratulations, gentlemen. America prevails. Damn the Arcadians. That was spectacular. Based on what I've seen, we have complete control of the airport. When can we move people into the city?"

The captain conducting the briefing speaks. "You're correct, Mr. President. We have control of the airport and the airspace. Army personnel are being held as prisoners. We've stationed Air Force Academy cadets in the terminals and at other city entrances, ready to assist. However, New Zion is locked down. We have no control of the elevators and stairwell doors remain locked."

"Dammit. Didn't you people plan for this? Blast open the damn stairwell doors if you must. We need people protected in the city," shouts Baker.

Strange sounds come from Jerome Hargrove. People in the Command Center assume he may have some helpful information. Everyone looks at Jerome. He's focused on his VUE.

"YES! Here we go!" Jerome's excitement confuses everyone in the Command Center. "The game is on! Zion colony will fall!"

President Baker leans over the conference table. "Jerome! What in the hell are you talking about? Are you playing a game?"

Jerome waves his hand to stop the stream. "I apologize. I wasn't playing a game. It's the stream of a new game my son told me about. It just launched this morning. Ants are fighting an evil force trying to regain access to their colonies, and they just broke through. I got excited. I apologize." Jerome says, sneaking a look at his VUE to check the game stream.

Mitch looks disgusted. "Jerome, if you think childish games are more important than handling the crisis before us, I think you should excuse yourself."

President Baker holds up a hand, motioning to slow down. "Hold on. Wait. You said Zion, Jerome. What does the game have to do with Zion?"

"Oh, it's one of the colonies. You fight the bad guys to get all your ants in the colony. They were doing great until the AI blocked access. Just now all the entrances to Zion opened...." Jerome pauses, looking like he realized something.

The major swipes his hand before him and pokes at the air. "Sir, we're getting reports of movement at New Zion. The elevators are moving, and stairwell doors have opened. Thousands of people are streaming in through every entrance."

"Oh dear. The game. The ants. The ants are people," Jerome says, grasping that the game stream is not a game.

President Baker looks at Tug. "Could this be our friends, the ones behind the messages? Now what? They've created a game to get people into the cities. If it's the same group, it seems clear, they are with us, against the Arcadians."

Tug isn't sure how to respond. "It would appear so, sir. We are working on identifying this group. I'm still waiting on a response from Homeland."

President Baker raises his voice several decibels. "Who the hell are these people? They're more effective than our military and intelligence departments combined. We can assist them. Hell, they can help us. Find them!"

The bulk of the Black Guard forces are on the north side of the city conducting a final sweep for topsiders who entered through stairwells and elevators before the lockdown. When ordered to the east side of the city, they leave their artillery and heavy weapons behind moving in formation to meet Captain Kobalt, as quickly as possible.

The Black Guard formation speeds past Heavy One and Heavy Two. The area has returned to order with no evidence of the earlier tragedies. A moment after the last Black Guard passes, the huge elevator doors slide open and one thousand souls rush into New Zion. Elevators and stairwells all over New Zion fill with people. People flow into the city flooding the corridors from dozens of entrances.

The new arrivals wander through the corridors. Hundreds of people make their way to the city center in awe of the size and beauty of New Zion. The sight of new people in the city startles New Arcadian citizens.

The sight of topsiders swarming into the city stuns the Black Guard forces.

A platoon leader reports in. "Captain Kobalt! We're being invaded. The corridors are filling with people. They're slowing our progress, sir. What should we do?"

As the platoon leader reports, the corridor Kobalt and his men are traveling down fills with people. "Damn it. Curse you, Munday. Relax them, run over them. Do whatever is necessary. Get to the east side of the city!"

Kobalt hits a young man who steps in front of his maglev. He pulls his weapon from its holster and shoots two others in his way.

"Keep moving, men. Fire at will. Out of the way. Make way," Kobalt yells as he fires.

The three guards with Kobalt also fire, dropping bodies as they cut their way through the mass of people. The shocked invaders slowly clear a path for Kobalt and his men, but progress is sluggish navigating through the confused people.

Kobalt calls City Command. "What the hell is happening? You are supposed to be locked down."

"We're trying to figure it out, sir. They haven't cracked our encryption codes. They've found a different way to gain control of our systems."

Rick, Jin, and Becky arrive in the oldest part of the city. Ahead of them is an old, dark tunnel. The orange tiles end, and the floor becomes aged, cracked cement. Without electromagnetic floor tiles, the Maggies are useless. Rick speaks to the Maggies. "Go to the Rail Station." The maglevs zip away.

Jin peers down the dark, narrow tunnel ahead of them. The walls are rough gray cement, and the ceiling is low.

"This looks kinda spooky," Jin says, reaching for Becky's hand.

Rick calls Curtis and Aman. "Curtis, what's next? We need to keep moving. Kobalt will be right behind us."

Curtis takes a swig of his Gulp cup and smiles. "I hate to tell you, but I told you so. An old, abandoned underground base. Ha!"

"Curtis, we have a situation here. You can gloat some other time," Jin says angrily.

Aman jumps in to explain the rest of the plan. "Hey, guys. Good shooting. That was like the shootout at the OK Corral. Oh, oh, did you see that movie, The Magnificent Seven? Not the second version. It wasn't so good, but the original or the third remake. The third remake is awesome, one of my favorites you know when that guy shoots—"

"Aman, there's a big angry bald man chasing us. Let's have movie talk another time, OK?" Rick says hastily.

"Right, Oh yes. Good times. Ha-ha. OK. Not to worry, we are slowing down the Black Guard, but keep moving. All you need to do is run down the tunnel in front of you for fifty yards, turn left, and go another hundred yards until you pass through the double doors, and you will come to a small subway station. No one has used it for decades, but we are attempting to transfer power to it now. It should be ready to go by the time you get there."

"Should be?" Jin asks.

Becky hears a noise and taps Jin's arm. Jin and Rick hear the noise, too. "Let's move," Rick says as the trio runs into the dark tunnel, disappearing into darkness.

After shooting and pushing his way through corridors thick with topsiders, Kobalt and his men arrive at the old base. He looks down a dark tunnel while hovering over the edge of electromagnetic tiles. "City Command. You're sure this is where they went?"

"Their maglevs paused at your location then headed to the Rail Station without riders. Probably intended as a diversion. They must have proceeded on foot from your location."

"Nice try, Munday, but we're on to your tricks. Where does this tunnel go?"

"We're checking the old base maps. This base was closed twenty years ago."

"It could lead to the renegade hideout, sir," one of Kobalt's men offers.

Kobalt looks at the guard with an evil eye.

"The tunnel leads to the old base structure. I see a subway station. I bet they will use the subway. It's the only way out." City Command reports.

"Where does the subway lead, Commander?"

"I'm checking. Huh, that's strange. It ends beneath the US Air Force Academy. That's sixty miles south of here," says the commander.

"Strange indeed. Prepare two helicopter gunships. We fly to the Air Force Academy immediately. We'll get ahead of them and wait for Munday's arrival." Kobalt smiles for the second time in a single day.

"Captain, the Air Force destroyed our aircraft and air defenses. We don't have any helicopter gunships and the Air Force has control of the air space," the commander explains in a sober tone.

Kobalt's smile fades. "I don't care what it takes. Get me anything that flies and shoots. We're moving to the maglev launch facility. Have the Scramjets ready for launch."

President Baker and his staff dash across the south lawn of the White House to board Marine One, the Marine Corps Super Sikorsky VH-92 helicopter that will transport the president and his top advisers to Camp David.

As Marine One lifts off from the White House lawn, two identical helicopters join Marine One in the air. The helicopters fly in an interweaving pattern, switching positions in a procedure called "the shell game" to disguise which helicopter carries the president.

This is the first time President Baker has been out of the White House since the meteor impact. Flying over Washington, D.C. he witnesses an incredible sight. Smoke billows from hundreds of buildings. Vehicles are buried under two feet of brown fallout. The Washington Monument, once the world's tallest obelisk, lies broken, with the top half buried in dirt. Snowplows work to clear streets throughout the city. Slowly, Washington is digging out.

Cliff looks out onto the once great city. "Jesus Christ, the city looks dead, and half buried. It's worse than a war zone." He turns to an aide. "We've got FEMA out there with food and water, right?"

The aide nods affirmative. "They're also helping people who can't get out of the city to find shelter in basements and underground parking structures."

"Good. Be sure they have all the resources they need."

"Sir, we will fly over the impact zone south of Baltimore. We won't land. We'll do a flyover, but you will provide a statement to the press once we land at Camp David."

"Very well," President Baker says in a somber tone, unable to take his eyes off the horrific scene below.

As Marine One approaches the impact crater, a science analyst sits next to the president to brief him on the impact crater. The analyst begins his briefing as the crater looms in the distance.

"Sir, we have an updated casualty report on the Baltimore meteor impact. The current estimate is three hundred thousand dead and an untold number of missing and injured. We are still six miles out. As you will see in a few moments, the impact crater is three point seven miles in diameter and at least sixteen hundred feet deep. Luckily, the impact was fifteen miles from Washington, D.C. or the situation would be worse."

Cliff Baker huffs. "From what I saw of D.C. it didn't look very lucky." The president looks out the window of Marine One as it approaches the impact crater.

The scene below is complete and utter destruction. The landscape looks like the surface of a strange, bumpy desert planet. Dirt buried everything. Only a few shattered buildings poke through the rocky dirt.

"My God! It's all gone! There's nothing left. Nothing." Cliff Baker shakes as he mumbles the words.

"Sir, the ejecta or fallout covers everything for several miles from the impact crater. At six miles out, the ejecta is seventeen feet deep. As we approach the edge of the crater, the ejecta is sixty feet deep."

The president's face looks tired and sad. Tears well in his eyes. "And the people? Did they suffer?"

"I am sure no one suffered. Every human and living creature within seven miles of the impact died seconds after impact."

Marine One flies over the edge of the crater. A massive hole in the Earth lies before them, stretching four miles to the far side. The crater is startlingly deep with a raised cone in the center.

Senator Campbell sits behind the president. He leans forward to ask the analyst a question. "How large was the asteroid that caused this damage?"

"We estimate the size was six hundred feet in diameter and composed primarily of iron. Based on the complexity of the crater, we believe the meteor broke up at about fifty thousand feet but held closely together, impacting at a velocity of twelve miles per second. Now you can see why I said Washington is lucky."

"Six hundred feet. That's the length of two football fields. That's not large for a space rock, is it? How large is the asteroid we will harpoon?" asks the Senator.

"Correct. Six hundred feet in diameter is not a large asteroid. In fact, over the past thirty hours, we've received reports of several similar sized impacts across the country. Luckily, none have been in heavily populated areas. JZ966 is larger than one kilometer in diameter. You can imagine the devastation it would cause."

President Baker stares out the window at the horror created by the meteor impact. "We've got to stop that thing. For the sake of humanity, we must stop it," he says with deep emotion.

Marine One passes the far edge of the impact crater and flies over the countryside.

"Sir, we will fly over Fredrick, Maryland and the location of New Arcadia, then continue on to Camp David."

"I hope General Wilcox can bust into New Arcadia and save our citizens from this nightmare."

Mike McCoy

Marine One veers to the northwest and flies parallel to Interstate 70. The long caravan of walkers on the endless highway marching toward New Arcadia stretches like a colorful ribbon to the horizon. The procession of human tragedy trudges onward, propelled by hope.

Cliff looks out the window, viewing the endless line of humans. "So many people. How can they all possibly fit into the city? There are too many. Oh, Lord. What have I done?" He trembles with the awareness of his misguided leadership.

Mitch puts a hand on the president's shoulder. "They have nowhere to go. Nowhere, that will save them. We'll get some into the city. I know Wilcox. He'll get the job done. You'll see. We will save some."

Cliff wears the face of sorrowful shame. "Some? We will save some. The fewer and less fortunate. We're no better than that old bastard."

"I'll call Wilcox. See how he's doing. He'll get people into that city," Mitch says, moving away to make the call.

"It's late. There isn't much time before... before it starts." Cliff Baker whispers solemnly to the window. "The horror of darkness beckons to test the souls of man."

The plan was to fly over New Arcadia, allowing the president to view the site held by his nemesis, Colonel Cruikshank, but after his reaction to the slow march on the highway, his staff decides it's best to fly directly to Camp David. Marine One flies north-northwest, avoiding the town of Fredrick, Maryland.

Chapter 51: Desperate Lives

Munday's Hideaway - Friday

Rob asked everyone to meet in the large main gallery. The room doesn't feel as big with twenty-one people filling it. Rob stands next to his desk.

"Welcome, everyone. Rodrigo and Eddie have built bunk beds in two of the rooms. These will be the boy's and girl's rooms, so everyone has a bed. The population in the hideaway is greater than we planned for during the build out. I hope you will all be comfortable. This is our home until the asteroid storms recede."

Edgar raises his hand. "How long will the storms last?"

Rob scratches his chin. "I expect the storms will continue for a month, maybe two. We are in the beginning stages. I don't believe the full force of the storm has arrived."

"Last night was terrible. You're saying it will get worse than that?" asks Eddie.

"Much worse, I'm afraid."

"Thank god we have this place," says Eddie.

"Yes, thank you, Uncle Rob," everyone echoes in chorus.

"We are very fortunate to have the hideaway. Remember, this is a living, working environment. We must grow and harvest food to ensure we have enough to eat. We must monitor and maintain the water filtration system, so we have drinking water. We must all work together to ensure our survival. Everyone will have daily duties. I have created the first week of work schedules. I've posted the schedule on screens, here in the main gallery, in the galley, and on the barn. Duties will rotate so everyone will learn every job." Rob announces.

George touches his singed eyebrows and asks, "When can we go outside? The asteroids only come in the afternoon and night. Can we go out during the day? It could get claustrophobic in here."

"Nobody goes out. This is a hideaway. That means it's a secret place. That's why Rodrigo, Eddie, and I told no one outside the people in this room about this place."

Selina and Margo give each other anxious looks.

"People are likely to come up the canyon. This area is popular with hikers. Thousands of people know about the old mines in the canyons. If we're spotted outside, it will give away our location. In a few days, people will be starving. You can see we're already tight on space. We can't risk discovery. Nobody goes out and nobody comes in. The only exception will be when my nephew, Courtney's husband Rick, makes it back. Does everyone understand?"

Rob watches heads nod up and down, but then a hand shoots up. Selina has a question.

"Mr. Rob, my brother Hector, went to get his wife, Jean. They would have come with us, but Jean was working. Hector went to get her last night. They're the parents of Junior and Claudia. What about them, Mr. Rob?" Selina pulls Junior and Claudia to her and frowns.

"Eddie mentioned them when you arrived. If they arrive alone with no other people, we will make an exception for them. My greatest concern is to protect the people in this room. I hope you all understand that. The hideaway is a delicate environment. If we don't control the number of people inside, none of us will survive. Do you all understand?"

Everyone seems to accept the rules and agrees. Margot pulls Selina aside. They speak with their heads down in hushed tones. Rob thinks they're talking about Hector and Jean.

"I am glad everyone understands. Okay. Here are your work assignments for today. Alyssa and Claudia, you will attend to the sheep. Ethan and Carlos, composting. Courtney, Selina, Isabella, and Maria, you will prepare the evening meal." Rob continues to read out the assigned duties.

"Ants are flowing like a river of ah, ants into New Zion Colony. It looks like Team Lucid-Gaze might have this game clinched. They are close to winning the fifty million dollars," announces Ceylon Junglefoul.

"Shocks and blows, you just don't know. What will this game bring next? It looked like the nippers were all jammed up with their crypto-cracklin', then dingo-dango, a massive flood of ant's swamped New Zion colony. It's brilliant," says Torpedo, excitedly.

Ceylon checks the other colony maps. Out the corner of his eye, he notices a team jumping and high fiving one another. "Something is going on over there. We may have another. What is the name of that team? It looks like they've busted open a colony that's been out of the action, so far. They've breached Colony Nod."

Torpedo has one of the team members on stream for an interview. "What's the team name, Mate?"

A skinny, pimple-faced, dark-haired teenage boy wearing a black turtleneck shirt with the words "Steve Jobs Lives" printed on it responds excitedly. "Team Elk Bucks"

Torpedo screws up his face questioningly. "What's that you said? Elf Butts?"

The boy blinks twice with a look of horror on his face. "No! Elk Bucks You know the majestic male elk with huge antlers," the boy says in a hurried encyclopedic tone.

Torpedo isn't sure he understands. "OK. Elf Butts it is, mate. Your team just crackled your way into Colony Nod. How did you hack the encryption?"

"We didn't exactly. We used a bot to smurf them. It's like a denial-of-service attack where we swamp their servers with requests. While the bot slammed them, we found a vuln or a vulnerability that allowed us to insert a sniffer and snag a user's credentials. That let us install a RAT and now their systems are at our mercy! They can't even tell we're in the system. We can change the encryption code ourselves and lock them out, giving us complete control of the entire city system," the Steve Jobs wannabe explains with a big smile on his pimpled face.

Torpedo looks stupefied. "Well, OK. Good on ya, then."

"The Elk Bucks are now in the game, but they'd better get their ants moving if they want to catch up with New Zion colony. Once again, this game takes a surprising turn. Keep your streams on. Be sure to catch all the game highlights. You never know what will happen next with Colony-Revolution Coup!" Ceylon screams with excitement. The number of concurrent viewers hits a record high.

Rick leads Jin and Becky with his flashlight as they run through the dark tunnel to the old subway station. When they burst through the double doors of the subway station, they see a dust-covered ancient-looking rectangular subway car with a faded blue stripe on its side, sitting where it's waited decades for passengers. The station is dark and silent. Rick shines the flashlight around the car, the station, and down the dark track.

"OK, Curtis, we're at the station. Let's get moving. Where's Kobalt?" Rick asks, catching his breath.

Curtis has his hand in a box of wheat crackers and talks with his mouth full. "Ah, mm. Good news, there. We have delayed Kobalt and the Black Guard. Aman gave our secure tunnel to the gamers. Twenty thousand people have entered the city, and more are pouring in. Kobalt got caught in rush hour traffic." Curtis laughs.

"That's great news, guys. I don't mean to be unappreciative, but I thought you were powering this station up. Where's the light switch?" Seconds later, Rick hears crinkling sounds as lights in the old station flicker on and the electric motor of the subway car whines.

Aman laughs. "Your wish is my command, Dr. Munday!"

"How do you like that for service, guys?" asks Curtis.

The door of the subway slides open with a gritty, sticking sound. The trio jumps into the car and the door closes as the car moves into the dark tunnel. The subway car steadily gains speed, traveling in darkness.

Jin wraps his arm around Becky, pulling her close. They comfort each other in the calm darkness.

"Aman, where is this car heading? Since your granting wishes, I am hoping to get a ride to Los Angeles, and Jin is looking forward to introducing Becky to Curtis in Las Vegas."

"You'll–then after–." The audio and video flicker, then the VUE lenses go dark. Rick pulls his VUE off. "What happened?" Rick asks.

"We lost signal. All the lenses and bands are down. This tunnel isn't part of New Zion. They have no reason to provide signal coverage out here," Jin explains as he removes his Black Guard VUE and replaces it with his VUE glasses.

"Great. We're traveling down a dark tunnel with no idea where it's going. We've lost all communication. We could run right into a trap or a dead end. What a great plan. I knew entering New Zion was a mistake," Rick says apologetically.

"Rick, if it wasn't for you, we wouldn't have made it out of the aircraft catering building alive. It was a good plan. It just didn't quite go as expected. Not a big surprise under the circumstances. We'll get through this and we will help you get home. Honestly, we need your help to get to Curtis," Jin confides.

Becky kisses Jin on the cheek. "I think we make a good team, if you ask me. We did a lot of good today. The city now protects thousands more people from the asteroid storms."

Jin chuckles. "And we gave the Arcadians some extra stress, didn't we?"

"We sure did," Rick says. "But all we did is piss off Kobalt. Wherever this car is going, we need to keep moving and put as much distance between us and New Zion as possible."

The subway car rolls down the track in darkness, destination unknown. Rick welcomes the dark rail car rocking and vibrating. It gives him a chance to rest and reflect. He hopes his family is with Uncle Rob in his old mine, but knows they could be anywhere. They could be at home, somehow unaffected by the storms. They could have gone with other people. There is one possibility he will not allow himself to consider. He must find them. He won't let Arcadians, Kobalt or asteroid storms get in his way.

Marine Command Center

An RQ-10B Shadow Hawk reconnaissance drone flies over the New Arcadian business complex streaming live video to screens in the Marine Comms Module. General Wilcox watches the video feed while a captain explains what they are viewing.

"The building rooftops have Laser Weapon Systems here, here and here," the captain points to the weapon systems as he speaks. "We aren't sure what's behind the large dark windows on upper floors."

Smoke briefly blocks the view of the video stream before going blank. "That would be their laser weapons systems or LaWS taking out our Shadow Hawk. It's the third one they've burned out of the sky. The New Arcadians don't appear to be the welcoming type," the captain says in a frustrated tone.

General Wilcox stands. "Colonel Cruikshank spent years developing these cities created for his few and fortunate. I didn't expect to walk up and have the doors flung open for us. We are intruders, interlopers. We're here to crash Cruikshank's party. Our mission is to secure shelter for the people out there to save a few more fortunate souls. I suppose we should knock on the door and make a proper introduction. What have you got lined up for a little hello, Captain?"

"They reached out to us with their LaWS. I'd like to respond with a nice drone swarm to take them out."

"Sounds downright neighborly of you, captain. Make it happen."

"We'll give 'em hell, Senator Campbell, you have my word." Wilcox finishes a call and steps out of the Marine Comms Module. "Is that road cleared? We need a clear approach to the Parklands. I want to see this place close up with my own eyes."

A staff officer walks next to the general. "The road is clear. I have an LTV waiting to drive us up to the complex."

The Marines launch MQ-40 Raven smart ordinance drones. These are small, high-speed drones. When deployed, they have a two-foot wingspan and carry an explosive charge. The system can launch one hundred twenty drones in less than twenty seconds. Once in the air, the drones fly as an intelligent swarm to their target.

The drones make a one-way trip. They seek, track and smash into a selected target kamikaze-style, exploding upon impact.

Three drone launching systems release three hundred sixty drones. A dark flock of drones flies toward the business complex. A Marine target the LaWS placements on four of the buildings. An individual drone does not pack enough punch to take out a LaWS, but if ten or twenty drones survive to hit the target, game over.

The general's LTV drives to the top of the grassy berm at the end of Christopher's Crossing, looking out over the Parklands. Two Lav35s flank the general's vehicle and another LTV covers the rear.

General Wilcox steps from the LTV and walks along the ridge of the grassy berm. He looks across the Parklands to see a mass of humanity spread across the campus. If it were another day, the tree and grass covered Parklands would look like a summer festival teeming with people. Today, a drone swarm dives to attack the LaWS placements atop the New Arcadian buildings. The LaWS fire laser beams into the swarm. Crisscrossing beams of light traverse the sky. The lasers take out scores of the small drones with defensive fire, but enough survive to accomplish their aim of destroying several LaWS systems.

The battle in the air sends people fleeing for safety. Wilcox feels fear sweep through the crowd.

General Mahon observes the drone attack. Colonel Cruikshank is pushing him to defend New Arcadia. His forces at New Zion suffered a humiliating defeat in a battle lasting less than five minutes. He knows Cruikshank expects decisive action to repel the Marines.

Screens inside an Army bunker three levels below the New Arcadian building complex display the image of General Wilcox walking on the berm at western edge of the Parklands.

Mahon calls Wilcox. "Jack Mahon, you old bastard. I would have called but didn't think you'd answer. You are AWOL. I believe Sec. Def. Tug Grimes has been looking for you."

"Wilcox, stop this nonsense immediately. You are firing on the government of Arcadia, the legitimate government of the land. You are firing on your government," declares General Mahon.

"The United States of America does not recognize the folly of Arcadia. President Baker has ordered me to breach your city and aid American citizens to enter the underground city."

Steeling himself, Mahon stands at attention. "My orders are to secure New Arcadia at all costs. This is not New Zion. Our superior arsenal will wipe you from the field if you do not immediately withdraw."

Charlie Wilcox is red, white, and blue through and through. "My duty is to our commander-in-chief. Stand down Mahon. Have some compassion. You can save lives today. We are the United States Marines. If you do not allow the people gathered here entrance to your city, we will force our way in. We do not retreat," Wilcox shouts.

As the general shouts his pledge, Two Marine MQ-8C Fire Scouts, unmanned rotary aircraft, swoop in, letting loose a volley of 70 mm laser-guided Hydra Rockets blasting positions on the New Arcadian buildings.

Mahon closes his eyes and nods to his staff. The darkened windows on the third floor of the buildings roll down, exposing artillery placements. Artillery rounds rain down on the Marine positions in Millie's Delight, blasting the defensive positions and mobile Comms Module to pieces.

Two more Fire Scouts circling at eight thousand feet over the New Arcadia business complex dive to the Parklands. The Fire Scouts are thirty-five feet long with a twenty-five-foot rotor span capable of staying aloft for twelve hours or more conducting surveillance, but today they come packed with firepower.

Explosions rock the New Arcadian buildings. Flames and dark smoke roil out the windows of multiple buildings. A surviving LaWS placement fires on the Scouts. Seconds later, Fire Scouts are falling to the Parklands below.

Humans on the ground run as the aircraft fall from the sky. One of the Fire Scouts slams to the ground, severing the rotor and sending it cartwheeling across the parkland, tearing up the ground and slicing through bodies before coming to a stop.

People run to escape the escalating skirmish as another dark flock of raven drone's speed to the buildings.

The sky is hot with laser beams and bullets firing at drones while artillery from the buildings aims for Marine positions. UAS command sends in more Fire Scouts as the smaller Raven drones dive for the rooftops and explode.

A thick cluster of meteors burn across the sky, exploding over the city of Fredrick, sending rocks and melted metal spherules to Earth at 28,000 miles per hour, cutting through machines, buildings, and flesh.

The exploding meteors destroy the drone launchers. Fire Scouts explode and fall to Earth. Meteors blast into buildings, wiping out Army bunkers and Marine positions without discrimination.

Thousands of people in the parklands run for their lives, attempting to hide, desperate to escape the torrent of fire raining from the sky. Hundreds find refuge on the ramp that leads to the underground parking structure. The high cement walls of the descending ramp offer some protection from the battle and the storms. Desperate survivors bang on the tall metal doors, pleading for them to open.

Wilcox does not move from his position on the berm as the battle between men becomes a farce compared to the assault sent from God. He calls Mahon. "You've got to let these people in." Wilcox sees Mahon staring at a screen displaying the horror in the Parklands. "How can you sit in your bunker watching this?" Mahon looks morose and says nothing.

Marines, civilians, and army soldiers defending new Arcadia are being wiped out by exploding meteors. The fast-moving hot spherules pass through the flesh and bone of one person and continue passing through the body of its brother, daughter, or wife. Men, women, and children die before feeling the pain of death.

A member of Mahon's staff urgently reports. "Sir, topsiders have broken through the new perimeter fence. Thousands of survivors are rushing the buildings. We must fire on them now. They will overrun our troops."

Mahon is unmoved as he watches the melee in the Parklands.

"Do you give the order to fire, sir?" General Mahon's staff warily observes their leader.

"Order our troops to fall back. I will not fire on our own citizens." Relief sweeps through the bunker.

Chapter 52: End of the Road

Friday–Early Afternoon - Los Angeles

Louis Robles sits reclining in his automobile, surrounded by white leather and chrome. An electronic console wraps across the front of the car. The car is not moving. Louis repeatedly presses the horn icon. "I've driven every day of my life on this freeway. I've seen traffic jams. But nothing ever like this." He honks again.

"You think that will help? Nothin's moved for an hour. People are leaving their cars and walking," says Gloria.

"No, I don't." Louis lays into the horn, giving it three long blasts before pounding on the leather-trimmed control console. "I know it won't help. I just can't bear the thought of leaving this car parked in the middle of the 210 freeway. If you hadn't taken three hours to get ready, we'd be walking into Edendale now."

"That's right, blame me. The asteroids are my fault, too." Gloria presses a button. The car door glides open. She gingerly steps, stiletto heel first, onto the asphalt roadway. She flings her head as she stands, letting her long hair flow in the soft breeze. She straightens, smoothing her slim dress. "My god. What a mess. There's eight lanes of cars on a four-lane highway."

"They told everyone to go downtown, go to safety. For once, people did what the government told them. All fucking twenty million of them. It's a god-damned zoo," Louis says.

Unable to make progress by car, truck, or AutoCar, movement requires creativity. People resort to any means available. They ride bicycles and skateboards. An old woman dressed like a 1960s hippy zips past Gloria on roller skates. A man pulls a wagon with six small shaggy dogs that ride with their tongues hanging out. People drag rolling suitcases, push baby strollers and grocery carts piled with earthly possessions.

Louis concedes the car is not going anywhere. He stands next to his shiny new Mercedes Turbo-Lectric S-800. "Where did all these weird people come from?" He wears a flowery silk shirt the first three buttons unfastened, exposing a heavy gold chain lying on thick chest hair. Large frame sunglasses rest on his broad nose below slicked-back black hair. He wears black slacks pulled over alligator skin boots. The boots, if real, are surely illegal.

Louis scans the horizon. The city is broken and burning. "Fucking asteroid storm. I can't believe this shit. I'm supposed to leave behind everything I've worked for. I leave my house, my beautiful house, my business and now my car? I told you we should have flown to Hawaii or Buenos Aires." Louis spots several small personal aircraft flying toward the downtown skyline. "Look there," he says, pointing. "I told you we should have bought a Fan-Jet."

"I could never fly in one of those things. How do we get to Edendale now?" Gloria asks.

"Edendale? You think it will be a nice place. You're expecting a luxury hotel? Maybe a private suite? Look around, we'll be squeezing in with these people. We'll be lucky to find ten square feet of cement floor to call our own. We're twenty miles from downtown. We'll never make it. We need to get out of this mess and find someplace safe."

A tinny AM radio message plays from every band and VUE lens, echoing through the air. People stop to listen.

"Access to the city of Edendale is closed. The Army has restricted access. Downtown is extremely congested. Do not come to downtown Los Angeles. Repeat: do not come to downtown Los Angeles. Edendale is closed. Return home or shelter in place."

People stand frozen as the message plays. The message repeats and the tide of humanity shifts. People turn away from the city and walk in the direction whence they came. A cavalcade of defeated, hopeless people pass Louis and Gloria as they stand next to their beautiful car, dressed nicely for their holiday in Edendale.

"That settles it. Screw Edendale. Shelter in place? What the hell is that supposed to mean? Nobody will be safe out here if the storm comes tonight. We need to find a place where there won't be a million people. Someplace where the goddamn rocks won't get us," Louis says, talking to himself out loud.

Gloria watches a large family holding hands in a long chain amble past singing a Bible hymn. "We can go to Eddie's secret cave. The one Selina told us about at dinner the other night," Gloria says.

A small boy at the end of the human chain isn't singing. He's being pulled along innocently as he looks at the beautiful woman standing next to an expensive car. He smiles at the woman. His eyes widen when he hears the words secret cave.

"Secret cave? Eddie's secret cave? That's perfect baby! Where is it? Are you sure it's real?" Louis runs around the car and clutches his wife tightly with both hands. Gloria stands stiffly in Louis's grasp. He shakes her slightly. "Is it real, baby? Is it a real place, this cave?"

Louis releases his grip. Gloria finds her footing, taking a step back. "Selina sent me a VUE Message. They were heading to the cave last night during the storm. I haven't heard from her since."

"So, it is real. Do you remember where it is, baby? We've got to get there. It's our best chance. It's by some bridge, right?"

"She said it's up Azusa Ave., then East Fork, all the way to the end of the road. That's where the bridge is. The—"

"The Bridge to Nowhere!" Louis shouts.

"Remember? Eddie was so angry with her. He said it's a secret."

"Good. Eddie's secret is safe with us, baby!" Louis re-energized, spins around, examining his surroundings. Half a mile in the direction of Los Angeles, he spots an overhead road sign. AZUSA AVE HWY 39–EXIT ½ MILE.

"Hallelujah! There is a God in heaven. Baby, grab your bag. We're walking."

Gloria changes into walking shoes and the couple walks toward Azusa Avenue. Gloria holds her Hermes bag tightly to her chest, afraid that someone might try to steal it. Louis pulls a Louis Vuitton suitcase behind him.

"You're going the wrong way," a woman says. "Didn't ya hear? They closed Edendale. No one's gettin' in," says a young man. Other people just give them strange looks.

"Thank you. Much appreciated," Louis says in a friendly tone, walking with a purpose.

Louis and Gloria are so focused on themselves; they don't notice the people following fifty yards behind.

At first, the boy wasn't sure he had heard correctly, but after hearing the words "secret cave" a few more times, he was certain. He broke himself from the human chain and ran to his daddy.

"Daddy, that man and lady are going to a secret cave," the boy says, pointing. The daddy cautiously walked close enough to overhear Louis and Gloria's excited conversation. When the couple started walking toward downtown, the family followed at a safe distance.

The family strolls along, humming a Bible tune. "Folks, the Army is sending people away. That direction's no good," says an old man resting on the guard-rail.

The young boy is about to tell the old man about the secret cave when his little sister beats him to it. "Those people are going to a secret cave. We're following them," she says, pointing to Louis and Gloria.

The boy adds, "It's real. I heard them. It's at a bridge. And, and they have a lot of food."

Another group of people hear the children telling the old man about the cave and become interested. "You know where there's a cave?" a woman asks.

"They do," the boy says, pointing again to the couple up ahead. "We're following them."

"Do you think there's room for us? I don't want to be on the freeway when the storm comes this evening," asks another.

"It's a big cave," the little sister says, holding her arms out wide.

"I heard about it first. You don't know anything," the boy scolds his sister.

He turns to the group with authority. "It's a huge cave. There's room for all of us. They have food and sleeping bags. It's at a bridge to nowhere," the boy says. He then holds his hand next to his mouth as if telling a secret. "But it's secret. So, don't tell anyone. OK?"

Twenty minutes later, Louis and Gloria are walking north on Azusa Avenue, zigzagging through abandoned cars. "Keep moving Gloria, you're falling behind."

"How far are we walking? My feet hurt. I hope you don't expect me to walk all the way to that cave," Gloria complains.

Louis checks his band. "I'm looking for an AutoCar, but they're all trapped between cars. Maybe there's one up a head. Keep walking."

As they continue walking, the number of stalled cars on the road thins.

"Ha! Got one! We've got a car, baby. Just up the road, come on. Hurry, it's not far. Data sucks here. I'm reserving it now so we can get in and start driving. Hurry." Louis moves quickly up the road, nearly dragging Gloria and her sore feet behind him.

Louis is so excited he doesn't see the growing group of people following.

After three minutes of fast walking, Louis's heart is pumping. Sweat drips down his forehead. Gloria's hair has lost its bounce, looking long and stringy. She limps on a twisted ankle.

"Here it is. Get in, baby. We're home free now," Louis says as he throws the suitcase in the backseat and gets in the car. "A steering wheel?"

"This car is ancient," says Gloria.

"I don't care. I can drive by myself. I still remember how to do that," Louis says as he drives up Azusa Avenue.

When Louis and Gloria started walking faster up the road, the large group following them picked up their pace. When they spot the couple get into a car and speed away, the people split into their groups to hunt for cars of their own. One-by-one cars and trucks move in a spread-out caravan up Highway 39. It is a fourteen-mile drive to the junction where East Fork Road splits off from the highway.

Louis drives the car cautiously up the narrow road. It's been years since he drove himself. The farther they go up East Fork Road, the worse the road becomes. The road follows a small river crossing the shallow stream three times. Louis grips the steering wheel tightly, navigating through deep potholes and around big rocks. Finally, after five miles, the road diverts from the river and goes up a long sloping hill. As they crest the hill, they see the strangest sight. "Am I going crazy or is that a spaceship? We must be in the right place. There are trucks parked—"

Gloria bounces up and down in her seat and screams, "That's Eddie's truck! Selina's here. I told you Louis. I told you! We made it! Oh God, thank you. We made it."

Louis parks next to Eddie's truck, gets out of the car, and walks to the edge of the bridge. It's a surreal scene. At the end of a dirt road, a cement bridge spans the canyon with a river running far below. At the far end of the bridge is a small landing, then the steep rock face of a mountain. It really is a bridge to nowhere.

Louis and Gloria wander out to the middle of the bridge. They are deep in Rattlesnake Canyon surrounded by mountains with the San Gabriel River flowing below. "So, now what? Where is this secret cave?" asks Louis.

"Selina said it's across the bridge. It's dug into the side of the mountain. It must be over there someplace." Gloria points to the far side of the bridge.

"Leave the bags in the car. Let's go check. We need to find this secret cave before it gets dark."

They walk to the far end of the bridge. "Look, there's a trail along the cliff face. The cave's probably over there," says Gloria.

Louis navigates the narrow trail in search of Eddie's cave. Gloria limps behind him, holding on to the waist of his pants, afraid to look down. "Gloria, baby, relax. You're safe," Louis says as he drags his wife along the trail.

As they walk around an outcropping, a car crests the hill and stops in front of the space shuttle. A few moments later, a pickup with several people in the truck bed arrives, followed by three more cars. The gravel-covered area in front of the bridge is filling with cars and people wandering around.

Rob walks up the metal stairs from the lower level, past the sleeping quarters, and stops at the galley. The smells from the kitchen are enticing. "Mmm. Smells great ladies. Can't wait to have a wonderful meal with all of us together."

"We'll let you know when dinner is ready," says Courtney.

"Eddie and Rodrigo are training the others on the mine's environmental systems. I'll call them when you give the word."

As Rob walks to his desk, something in the windows catches his eye.

He'd set the windows to view the bridge outside. Although he has scenes from all around the world, the view of the Bridge and Rattlesnake Canyon is his favorite. The windows cycle through five exterior cameras, providing views of the bridge, the trail approaching the mine, the mine entrance, and the area across the bridge.

"People! I didn't expect people in the canyon this soon." Rob says to himself as the windows cycle through the cameras. Two people are on the trail approaching the cave entrance. "How do they know?" Rob asks himself. "Could this be Hector and his wife? Maybe Eddie told them how to find the entrance."

The windows display the area on the far side of the bridge. Rob sees six extra vehicles parked in the gravel area besides the X-37, Rodrigo's and Eddie's trucks, and another car is cresting the hill. People are walking on the bridge. Children are trying to climb onto the spacecraft.

Rob shudders. He is about to switch the view when Selina walks out of the galley holding a small bowl.

"Mr. Rob, have a taste." Selina freezes when she sees two people on the trail. A second later, the windows change to a tropical island landscape.

Selina clutches the bowl to her breast, startled by the sight. "That was Gloria and Louis. Switch back. Switch it, please." She sets the bowl on the long dining table. "I'm sure. It's them. Change it back," Selina asks, loudly.

Rob looks Selina in the eyes. "Are they the parents of Junior and Claudia?"

Isabella, Maria, and Courtney hear Selina and walk into the main room. Selina turns to the women. "I saw my friends, Gloria and Louis, on the windows."

The women see images of palm trees, blue sky, and soft waves lapping up a white sand beach. Selina points to the windows. "He changed it. They're outside. I'm sure of it."

Rob repeats his question. "Are they the parents of Junior and Claudia?" Selina senses Rob's eyes piercing through her.

"No, but they're my friends. We must let them in. If they stay outside tonight—," Selina's voice trails off. She turns her plea to the women. "Isabella, Maria. If they were your friends, you wouldn't leave them out there."

"We all—," Courtney says something, but stops herself.

Isabella, Rodrigo's wife, puts her hands on her hips and lifts her head. "I did not tell my friends about this place."

Selina looks like she'll explode. "You're always acting so holier than thou. You probably don't have any friends," Selina blurts out. Selina is not known for holding her tongue.

Isabella makes a move toward Selina, but her mother Maria holds her back. "My husband asked me to keep this place a secret for our children, our family. Maybe you would value family over friends if you had children."

Selina screams like an injured animal and runs at Isabella. Isabella raises her hands in defense, but Selina slaps her in the face before Courtney and Maria can move between the women to stop the fight.

"Calm down, women. Stop it!" Rob yells. He touches the intercom icon. It broadcasts his voice over speakers distributed throughout the mine complex. "Eddie and Rodrigo. Come to the main gallery. Your wives are out of control!"

Selina struggles, but quiets after Rob's announcement. Eddie and Rodrigo rush to the main room followed by all the children. When Courtney and Maria see the men running up from the lower level, they release Selina.

Selina runs to Eddie, acting wounded. "Gloria and Louis are outside on the trail. I saw them. We've got to let them in. They'll die if we leave them out there."

Rob switches the windows from the tropical paradise to the exterior view. A large group of men, women, and children—are on the bridge. The view switches to another camera; Louis and Gloria are walking back toward the bridge.

Selina points to the windows. "See! I told you. It's Gloria and Louis. We need to save them," she cries as Eddie holds her.

Rob steps to the center of the room with the twenty occupants of his hideaway surrounding him. "This is the situation I feared. Eddie and Rodrigo; You must have thought I was a crackpot for asking you to keep the hideaway secret. Now, because someone did not heed my warning, we have a problem worse than I ever imagined. I count at least thirty people out there trying to find our hideaway."

The camera cycles to display the gravel-covered area at the far side of the bridge. Carlos, the thirteen-year-old son of Rodrigo, points to the windows. "Look! Two more cars are coming."

"She did it. It's her fault. The bitch slapped me because I kept the secret and she didn't," Isabella calls out, pointing at Selina.

Selina lets loose of Eddie and stands ready to fight. "I didn't slap you for that."

"Ladies, you are causing a dangerous situation for our hideaway. Please calm down." Rob hates this. Now, he is forced to make life and death decisions for people he doesn't know. "Eddie and Rodrigo, you know the capabilities of the hideaway. We built it to sustain the lives of fifteen people for an extended period. We are now at twenty-one people. The asteroid storm is just beginning. I believe it will continue for at least a month, possibly up to three. How long will we survive if we open the mine and allow another twenty, thirty, or fifty people inside? More are sure to come."

Rodrigo and Eddie look at each other. Rodrigo gulps and takes a moment before speaking. "If we let those people in, we won't last more than a week. There isn't enough food in storage, and we can't grow it fast enough to feed everyone. The plan is to use the stored food while the crops and livestock grow."

Eddie nods in agreement, looking very somber. "I'm sorry about this. Selina didn't know it was real, you know, the mine. None of us knew we would live in this place. We owe our lives to Rob."

Rob acknowledges Eddie's words. Before he can speak, Eddie continues. "If we want to get through the asteroid storm alive, we need to take care of one another. We are family. We need to work together and respect each other no matter. We have a tough decision before us. If we agree to let other people in, we must understand, it means none of us will survive. Rodrigo is right. We won't last a week."

"If the mine is full of friends and strangers." Rodrigo pauses, looking at Selina. "We don't know what will happen. Our wives didn't last a single day without fighting. What happens when we add thirty or forty complete strangers? It's too risky."

"There is no fault for what's happening. There is no blame unless we blame God or an angry universe. People will die. No matter what we do, people are dying. We can't help that. If I could have built the hideaway for one hundred people or a million people, I would have. Sometimes you can only save the ones you love. That is what we must do," Rob explains.

The windows switch to a camera placed on the slope above the rocky outcropping. The white cement bridge takes on an orange glow as afternoon becomes dusk. A fireball streaks across the sky, leaving a vapor trail behind. Two more fireballs chase the first. Selina shrieks at the sight of the meteors traversing the sky, scaring the children. Ethan and Alyssa rush to their mother. Carlos and Mary hug their parents, Isabella, and Rodrigo. Rob moves to his desk and switches the windows to the tropical paradise.

"No! Don't switch it. If you leave my friends and the others out there to die, you should have the stomach to watch it," scolds Selina.

Rob looks at her. She returns an intense gaze.

"As you wish." Rob switches the windows to the exterior view.

Chapter 53: Supersonic

Friday Afternoon

Rick sleeps. The rhythmic rocking and creaking of the old subway car traveling through quiet calm was a force too strong to resist. Rick dreams. Courtney stands in a gray fog calling out in search of her husband. Rick looks up in fright. The black sky erupts with fire; bright orange streaks fill the night. Courtney cries out as the gray fog winds around her like a python. The dense fog encapsulates her body as the snaking cloud turns to granite, trapping her in solid rock. Rick tries to run to his wife. He runs and runs but does not move. Meteors explode in the sky, raining fiery hell around him as he runs. A wet tear drips from Courtney's eye, streaming clumsily down her rocky cheek. Rick struggles to escape the firestorm and rescue Courtney. A meteor hits the ground and explodes, throwing Rick through the air. He lands with a hard thump.

The subway car jolts to a stop. Rick wakes to a shock. Jin and Becky locked in an intimate kiss. He shudders, the embarrassed observer. Their eyes open. Their lips reluctantly separate.

"Come on, love birds. Looks like this is the end of the line. Let's find out where Aman sent us." The subway door opens with a gritty sound. As the images of his dream fade, he thinks of Courtney.

The trio exits the boxy subway car and stands in a small station. A faded blue-winged insignia adorns the wall next to a metal door with an exit sign above it.

"This looks like our way out," Jin says, walking to the door.

Rick hesitates.

Becky senses Rick's caution. "This is the end of the subway. There's only one exit. I don't think Curtis and Aman would send us here if it wasn't safe." Becky pushes the metal bar on the door and walks through to a stairwell.

Five flights up the stairs and the trio finds another metal door. This time Rick pushes the metal bar, but the door won't open.

"Something is holding it closed. Help me push it," Rick says to Jin. They push the stubborn door together. "It's opening, but there's a metal shelf blocking the door," says Jin.

"Push harder." The feet of the shelf scrape loudly on the floor as it moves. The push until the opening is wide enough to squeeze through, stepping into a brightly lit convenience store.

"The store looks open, but nobody's here," says Jin.

"Hello. Hello!" Becky calls out as she walks through the store.

Rick looks around. "No staff. No customers. It's snack time!" He grabs a bag of potato crisps and munches on salty chips as he wanders through the store. He notices a sign above the entrance. "Fairchild Express. I wonder if anyone knows there's an express train below the store."

"Where are we? The place is deserted," says Becky.

"I don't like to shoplift, but I'm starving and since no one is here, oh well," Jin says as he stuffs his pockets with pastries and packages of nuts. Becky searches for healthier snack choices.

Rick takes a deep breath. "Fresh Air." The air is fresh and clear. "Guess I don't need this anymore." He pulls on the D-Nox ring to remove it from his nose. The ring is lodged deeper in his nostrils than he expected and hurts when he pulls it. He tugs harder and twists to pull it out.

"Hey Jin, Becky. You don't need this anymore," he says, holding the ring for them to see before tossing it to the floor. The ring wiggles on the floor until Rick crushes it under his boot.

Jin carefully pulls the ring from his nose. The ring pops out with a snap. He lets out a long "Ooouch," then continues his shopping spree.

Becky pulls on her D-Nox ring, but it doesn't want to come out. She strains, crossing her eyes as she pulls and wiggles the ring. "Mine doesn't want to come out." She gives a long, steady pull. The fleshy appendages have extended deep into her nostrils. "It's stretching. It won't let go. Ah!" Becky pulls the ring an inch away from her nose, but the tentacle-like fleshy arms stretch, holding fast.

Rick notices Becky struggling with the ring. "Give it a good tug."

"They're going back in!" Becky gives Rick a panicked look as she holds the ring away from her nose, the stretched flesh trying to wiggle deeper, unwilling to yield. She gives the ring a strong yank, and the ring snaps out. "Ouch!" Her eyes well with tears from the sharp pain in her sinuses.

Becky looks at the ring. The long wormy arms are speckled with blood. She squeaks, tosses the ring, then wipes a drip of blood from her nose.

Jin looks out a window and spots a familiar building across a grassy promenade. "It's the Air Force Academy," he says to himself, then speaks louder. "We're at the Air Force Academy," he calls out to get Rick's and Becky's attention.

They look across a courtyard and a grassy field. In the distance is the Cadet Chapel with its iconic design of seventeen spires rising one hundred fifty feet into the sky. The building glistens in the afternoon sun.

Antique jets rising from the quad on steel pedestals decorate each corner of the field. Parked at the center of the field is a sleek modern jet with the canopy open. Rick smiles. "Did anyone order an airplane?"

Becky looks around. "It's so quiet. The entire campus is deserted."

"I guess asteroid storms spoil school attendance," Rick says, eyeing the jet.

Jin works with his VUE. "I'll tap into the Academy net."

"That jet could be our ticket home. Let's check it out," Rick says, enthusiastically pulling Becky and Jin out the door leading to the courtyard.

As they run across the courtyard, three sonic booms in quick succession pound the air. Rick stops to look up. He doesn't see any meteors. Three supersonic jets top the mountains west of the chapel and roar as they fly over the Academy grounds at low altitude and great speed. The trio ducks under a tree with a thick canopy to shield themselves.

"It's got to be Kobalt. Let's go," shouts Rick as he runs to the jet and climbs the metal ladder to the cockpit. From the top of the ladder, Rick calls back, "It's a two-seater!"

"Can you fly a jet?" asks Becky.

"I used to fly Cessna's with my uncle. The fundamentals should be the same. How different can this be?" says Rick.

Jin examines the jet on his VUE. The display fills with information and details about the aircraft. "This is a TX-200B, advanced Air Force training aircraft capable of vertical take-off and landing with a top speed of Mach 1.8 or 1,370 miles per hour with a range of 1,200 nautical miles and a climb rate of 45,000 feet per minute. The TX-200 trainer can—"

Rick interrupts Jin. "Hey, buddy, like I said, how different can it be. You're in first. Climb up. Becky will sit on your lap. It might be cozy. Just squeeze in," Rick says as he steps into the pilot's seat and pulls on the helmet.

"It's the only plane we have, so we'll make do," Becky says as she pushes Jin up the ladder.

Jin scrambles into the rear instructor's seat, sitting as low as possible to make room for Becky. Becky sits on his lap. "There isn't enough room for both of us and the helmet. This has to go," Jin says as he tosses the helmet onto the grass.

The instructor's seat sits behind and above the pilot, allowing the instructor to look over the pilot's shoulder. "Wow, nice view from up here. It's like stadium seating," says Becky.

Curtis's image appears in Jins VUE. "Hey, did you guys make it out of the subway? We lost signal."

"Yeah, thanks to you and Aman. We made it out of New Zion," says Jin.

Becky feels cramped, and her foot is twisted. She presses her hands on Jin's thighs to raise up and straighten her foot. The snacks in Jin's pockets squish and crackle. Once Becky's foot is free, she drops on Jin.

"Ah, ouch! You crushed my Twinkie," Jin cries.

"Sorry, I'm just trying to get comfortable," Becky apologizes as she wiggles her hips.

"Sorry, guys. I hope I'm not interrupting something," says Curtis.

"Hang on, Curtis. We're busy," Jin says, breathing hard with the weight of Becky on him.

Curtis hides his eyes. "Oh Jesus. Sorry."

All Jin can see is the back of Becky's head. He looks to the left and right to view out the sides of the canopy. "OK, Rick. We're in. You sure you can fly this thing?" Jin asks.

"Fly? What? Hey, where are you guys?" Curtis asks.

Rick looks at the cockpit. He expected to see a dizzying arrangement of switches, indicators, and dials, but finds a clean flight console equipped with three touch screens encircling the pilot, a flight stick, throttle control, and a few switches. It's like nothing he's seen before.

"I used to fly my uncle's Cessna Skyhawk, but that was years ago. This is different, but I think I can figure it out. I just need a minute," Rick says as he examines the flight controls.

"Good news. We made it to the Air Force Academy. Bad news, the bad guys are here, too. Good news, we found a jet. Bad news, the bad guys have jets too!" Jin recaps.

Curtis leans back in his chair with a stunned look and mouths. "OK."

Rick flips a switch cover open and presses the power button. Screens in the cockpit come to life and a graphical interface appears in his helmet. He touches an icon marked canopy. The canopy closes. Becky wiggles, scrunching lower, allowing the glass cover to lock closed. "Hey, watch the Twinkie," Jin squawks.

Becky's face is five inches from the instructors' screen, which is a duplicate of the pilots' display. A list of training modules appears. Becky presses the TX-200 introduction module. A video plays on Rick's center screen, showing the exterior of the TX-200 narrated by a gruff training instructor's voice.

"Welcome to the TX-200 trainer. As a qualified cadet, you have fulfilled hours of classroom and simulator training. Your training now continues with the TX trainer and the advanced flight training modules. Once in the air, your instructor will select a training module. I am your flight nom. I handle all tasks related to navigation, management of flight computers, and control surfaces. The Fly-by-Wire and Advanced Flight Control Systems take care of the flying, allowing you to focus on your mission objectives. Think of the TX-200 as your office in the sky. I know you want to pilot the aircraft. This is unnecessary. You can trust and rely on the automated flight controls to do the flying. However, you can override the system and take control via the flight stick and throttle if your instructor allows. I will assist and guide you as needed. Training modules include various mission scenarios. You must successfully accomplish all assigned mission objectives before advancing to the next module."

Rick spots the three jets approaching again. "Our friends are back. I think we will skip class today. Becky, can you mute the nom and override the flight system? We need to get out of here." Three Scramjets roar past, buzzing the top of the Cadet Chapel at a blazing speed, heading east.

"Looks like they were expecting us," says Jin, trying to get a good look at the jets as they whiz past. His VUE locks on to the image of the trailing jet and fills with information about the Scramjet. The TX-200 shakes from the wake of the low-flying craft.

Buckley Air Force Base–Aurora, CO

A radar operator spots aircraft making passes over the Air Force Academy. He alerts the officer in command. "Sir, we have three unauthorized aircraft making passes over the Academy flying at low altitude and high velocity. I also have a slow-moving helicopter coming in from the South."

"Where did they come from? We're supposed to have control of this airspace!"

"The three aircraft came out of nowhere, sir. The helicopter appears to be from Fort Carson," a radar operator replies.

"Operators, you cannot just focus on Denver. Keep your eyes open. Get three F-35's over there pronto. Don't engage unless fired on. Let's see what's going on." Three F-35's hightail it to the Air Force Academy.

Rick watches the high-speed aircraft become small dots on the horizon.

"I don't think they spotted us," Becky says in a hopeful tone.

"At the speed they're flying, I doubt they can see much of anything on the ground," says Jin.

Rick flips a switch to start the engines. The TX-200 turbine engines turn with a whining sound.

Jin reads information in his VUE. "They are flying Hypersonic Scramjets capable of speeds up to Mach 6 with a ceiling elevation of eighty thousand feet. Without Scramjets engaged, they travel at up to Mach 3. Wherever we're going, they can get there faster."

"Maybe we can get out of here before they come back. It'll take a couple minutes for them to turn around and make another sweep. Let's vamoose!" says Rick.

Becky notices another aircraft on the TX-200's radar. "There's another aircraft. It's moving slowly, but it's getting close," Becky reports.

They hear the thumping beat of a helicopter rotor. The helicopter hovers over Fairchild Hall, like it's searching for something. It then passes over Mitchell Hall and moves toward the Terrazzo and the TX-200.

Jin watches the helicopter come in for a landing. He examines the copter in his VUE. "It's an old Huey H-1. Looks like an antique, but is armed and dangerous. They're landing. I think they're looking for us." A squad of Black Guard jumps out of the Huey while it's still several feet above the ground and runs toward the TX.

"Like I said, time to vamoose!" Rick exclaims. He punches VTOL on the screen and the turbines roar to life. The TX-200's thrust vectoring nozzles point at the ground. The front turbofan provides stability as Rick increases thrust, pushing the TX-200 off the ground.

The Black Guard sees the TX lifting off and starts shooting. This time they're firing real bullets.

Becky screams. "They're shooting at us!"

Jin skims the specifications of the TX-200 in his VUE. Instead of reading the specifications out loud, Jin says, "Don't worry. We're bulletproof. At least from small-arms fire."

Several bullets hit the aircraft as it skims across the ground. Becky closes her eyes, scrunching lower. "I hope you're right."

Rick moves the throttle forward. The aircraft rises faster in the air as the thrust nozzles rotate, pushing the jet forward, passing over the Fairchild Building. Soon the TX-200 is flying like a jet.

The Huey takes off in chase, leaving the Black Guard behind. It slowly gains altitude attempting to follow the TX. The Huey lines up behind the TX and fires its M240D machine guns. Bullets ping as they hit the TX. Rick punches the throttle and pulls back the flight stick. The TX-200 rockets into the sky, climbing to fifteen thousand feet in thirty seconds, leaving the Huey far behind.

Rick flies as fast as possible. Once they are clear of the Huey, he drops the TX to a low altitude, heading south. "I'm engaging the Terrain-Following Radar. It's like an autopilot that flies the aircraft to fly at very low altitude, hugging the ground. I'm hoping the terrain masking will help us avoid detection from their radar."

Rick can select a hard, medium, or soft ride. The settings vary how closely the aircraft flies to the ground and the forces exerted on the pilot as the aircraft adjusts for changes in the terrain. Rick selects the icon marked hard. "Hang on. The ride could get rough." The TX-200 dips, flying closer to the ground. In less than a minute, they pass the city of Colorado Springs.

"Set destination. Las Vegas," Rick instructs the flight nom. The navigation system routes the flight path for Las Vegas, and the aircraft adjusts course.

The sound of the helicopter firing on the TX jolts Kobalt into action. He calls the Scramjet pilots. "Split up. Cover north, west, and south. If I know Munday, the last direction he will go is east. There aren't many planes in the air. Find that jet!" The Scramjets peel out of formation in search of the TX-200.

Kobalt's jet heads west over the Rocky Mountains. Within a minute, the Scramjet heading south gets a hit. "Captain Kobalt. We have an Air Force TX-200 flying west-south-west at low altitude."

"That's him. Everyone is to join up, heading south. We've got him," Kobalt shouts confidently.

The TX's Auto-Nav and TFR systems hug the ground at high speed, heading for Las Vegas. The jet rapidly rises and falls with the terrain at a constant elevation of ninety feet.

"You sure you can't make this ride any rougher?" Becky asks through her chattering teeth.

"Sorry for the bumps. I'm hoping Kobalt won't spot us at this altitude."

The Scramjets fly in formation high above, and far ahead, of the TX.

"Time to play a game of chicken with Dr. Munday," says Kobalt.

The Scramjets turn and drop elevation, setting a course to meet the TX-200 head on.

Jin shouts over the noise into Becky's ear. "Beck, relax. I think we lost them. Thirty minutes from now, we'll be landing at Curtis's house."

Rick watches the horizon as the landscape races past, keeping an eye out for Kobalt's jets. He sees a black dot. He checks the radar. The screen shows three objects approaching fast.

"Oh shit. Here they come. Hang on!" Rick holds his hands just above the flight controls and switches the ride hardness to "medium." The elevation of the TX rises slightly, reducing the jostling.

"They're heading right for us," cries Becky.

The Scramjets are moving so fast it's difficult to judge distance. "We don't have a lot of options here. We're hugging the surface. If I drop altitude, the wake from the Scramjets could force the TX down. If I turn and the terrain changes, we could hit a wingtip. That leaves only one direction. My uncle always told me to face my fears head on."

At these speeds, jets cover great distances in seconds. The Scramjets are almost on them. Impact is a certainty. Becky clenches Jin's thighs, closing her eyes. "I can't watch."

As the Scramjets bear down on the TX, Jin nervously repeats, "Oh man, oh man, oh man."

Rick grabs the flight stick, pulling it back hard while jamming the throttle to the max. The TX responds instantly, shooting straight into the sky just as the Scramjets pass. Flames from the TX afterburners lick the canopy of Kobalt's jet.

The G-forces of the rocketing TX push Rick deep into his seat, feeling double or triple his body weight. Becky squashes Jin and they both gasp for breath. Rick levels off momentarily before pointing the TX into a dive, aiming for the cover of the surface. Hugging the surface is safer than being a sitting duck at high elevations.

As soon as Becky can breathe, she shouts, "Couldn't you have just shot them or something?"

"This is a trainer. No guns. Sorry. I didn't have time to warn you."

"Nice move, Rick, but how are we going to lose these guys?" Jin asks.

"I'm thinking." Rick pushes the jet to an altitude of two hundred feet, traveling at six hundred miles per hour and reengages the TFR tracking. The TX dips toward Earth and begins its undulating movements as it tracks the terrain.

The Air Force F-35s spot the three Scramjets playing chicken with a TX-200 but keep their distance. The F-35 pilots cheer for the little TX as it suddenly pulls up to avoid a head on collision with the larger Scramjets. They watch the TX dive back to Earth. "Wow, that pilot is a tiger," says one pilot.

"Those guys were moving at the speed of heat. Warp one, man," says the other.

"Request permission to engage the Scramjets. That TX is gonna need some help or he'll end up a smoking hole in no time."

As the TX zips across the San Luis Valley, Rick spots an opening in the mountains ahead. He takes control of the TX and aims for Highway 160, which curves through the mountains. Rick reengages the TFR, setting the ride hardness to "soft." The TX gracefully traverses and swoops through the mountain passes. "This is better," says Becky.

"The mountain scenery is stunning," says Jin. Each turn of the jet displays a new panorama of snowcapped peaks, lakes, and streams. It's a momentary solace from the menace, hunting to kill them.

The OIC calls the base commander requesting permission to engage the Scramjets. The Base Commander sends video streams from the F-35s to the Raven Rock Mountain Complex, an underground facility which serves as the Alternate National Military Command Center, in times of crisis.

Raven Rock patches the video through to nearby Camp David where the stream appears on screens in the underground command center where Tug Grimes and General Casey, Secretary of the Air Force, get briefed on all developments.

The men watch the TX evade the Scramjets and dive for the deck. "Where did those Scramjets come from? We only have ten in our fleet. Last time I checked, they were all in Asia," says the Air Force general.

Tug watches the TX and wonders. Just an hour earlier, he received an e-mail from an analyst at Homeland with the name of the person suspected of broadcasting the Perth News. "Can the F-35s determine who's flying that TX? And who's flying the Scramjets? I'd like to know who's who before the shooting starts."

The Scramjets have turned and are now in pursuit of the TX, which is weaving its way through the mountain passes, hugging the curves of Highway 160.

The F-35s use their CNI (Communications, Navigation, and Identification suite) software programmable radio to interrogate the radio and data transmissions of the TX and the Scramjets. An F-35 transmits the data received to the Base Commander and Camp David.

Military staff interpret the data and report their findings. "Secretary Grimes, the Scramjets are coming back as not registered. They aren't ours. The TX-200 is assigned to the Air Force Academy for a demonstration day. We picked up data from a VUE lens worn by the occupant of the TX. The lens is registered to a civilian named Jin Goldberg." The military staff member looks perplexed.

Tug Grimes stands. "Take out the Scramjets. The TX is friendly."

Kobalt's Scramjet advances until it's flying above and behind the TX as it makes turns through the tight mountain passes. A Scramjet is a larger craft than the TX with enough room for the pilot, copilot, and six passengers. Scramjets are built for speed and high altitude, so they have a shorter wingspan than a conventional jet. Flying low and slow is a challenge for the Scramjet pilots.

Kobalt sits behind the pilot, giving orders. "Blow them out of the sky!"

The pilot fights to hold the Scramjet steady at low speed. "You know we aren't armed. We don't have any way to blow them out of the sky and I can't hold this speed. We'll crash if I don't increase speed." The pilot pushes the thrust forward and pulls back the flight stick. The lead Scramjet shoots into the sky, followed by the other two.

As the Scramjets race high into the atmosphere, Kobalt thinks out loud. "We will crash. We'll drop on top of them, forcing them down. Number Two will swoop down and land on top of the TX, forcing them down or into a mountainside. Number Three will line up behind Number Two in case Number Two fails. We'll line up behind Number Three. Munday won't have a chance."

The pilots of the Scramjets aren't very excited about this plan. They hope the TX will be the one crashing, and not of one of them.

Rick sweats, knowing the Scramjets are bearing down on them. He hopes the zigzagging of the plane following the highway will make it harder to get a lock on the TX when suddenly the Scramjets zoom past them. "I thought for sure they were about to fire a missile and blow us out of the sky," Rick says.

"Where did they go?" asks Becky.

"I thought we were goners. They must have had us in their sights," says Jin.

The mountains fall away behind the TX as they fly over grassy plains.

"I don't know what they're up to, but I'm not waiting around to find out. We'll be easier prey over these meadows," Rick says as he takes control of the TX increasing speed as they fly over Lake Nighthorse.

Jin checks his VUE to read the specifications of the Scramjets again. "I've got it. I know what happened. We were going too slow through the mountains. They designed Scramjets to fly very fast at high altitudes. We need to slow down."

The TX flies over flat farmland at three hundred feet. "That makes no sense. We're exposed out here. If we slow down, we'll be easier to shoot out of the sky."

Becky checks the map on her monitor. "Mesa Verde Canyon is up ahead. If we can get down in the canyon, it might give us some cover."

"Mesa Verde, here we come," Rick says, as he pushes the throttle forward and jets screams across the low hills and farmland.

The Scramjets make a high turn, then dive one after the other, lining up in pursuit of the TX. Number Two leads the way with Number Three lined up behind, leaving a two-mile gap between them. Kobalt's jet hangs farther back to observe the impending crash of the TX and the death of Rick Munday.

The pilot of Scramjet Number Two reports. "I wish we could just heat up this nugget with a winder. He's using all his go-juice burning for that canyon. We're fangs out."

Number Two speeds forward, chasing the supersonic TX-200 across Colorado farmlands. "I'll try to make the TX crash before it gets to the canyon."

"They're after us Rick. We'll never make it to the canyon. Drop your speed. Slow down," Jin urges.

"They'll shoot us. Jin! Are you crazy?" exclaims Becky.

Rick eases up on the throttle and drops to two hundred feet. Becky feels the TX slowing. "You'll get us killed."

"I think Jin's right. Why haven't they shot us? They could have easily launched missiles from miles away and blown us out of the sky before we ever saw them, but they didn't," Rick says as he decreases airspeed.

The Scramjets are chasing the TX-200 flying east to west. The three F-35s come in from the north flying down a mountain canyon toward the town of Mayday, Colorado. They watch the Scramjets swoop down and line up one behind the other after the TX.

"Isn't that sweet? They're lining up so nicely for us," says one pilot.

Scramjet Number Two zooms close until he is just above and behind the TX. "He's above us. He's right on top of us! What's he trying to do?" Becky asks, looking at the bottom of the Scramjet through the glass canopy.

"I've got a lock on the lead Scramjet, but he's too close to the TX," says one of the F-35 pilots.

The Scramjet pilot concentrates on getting directly above the TX while struggling to keep the larger jet stable at the slow speed. Rick looks up through the canopy, watching the plane above. The Scramjet pilot is about to drop his aircraft on the smaller TX. Rick engages the deceleron, creating an airbrake. The TX slows abruptly and slides behind the Scramjet, just as it drops.

The F-35 pilot sees the Scramjet pull ahead of the TX and lets his AIM-9X sidewinder air-to-air missile fly.

Rick disengages the deceleron and pushes the throttle to maneuver above the Scramjet. He pulls back on the flight stick and punches the throttle, hitting the unstable Scramjet with a burst of jet blast. The Scramjet dips to the right, tipping toward Earth. At the low elevation, even at the slow speed, the Scramjet has only seconds to adjust before slamming into the ground.

Becky and Rick watch the Scramjet dip and cheer triumphantly.

Jin wrenches his neck trying to see the Scramjet. "Is he going—?" Before he can finish his question, the sidewinder hits the Scramjet, exploding in a fury of hot metal and fire. Becky screams as a wave of fire and heat envelope the TX.

Shrapnel from the shattered aircraft hits the TX with a ping, ping, ping, punching holes in the fuselage. Jin braces himself as the jet shutters from the blast. He holds Becky tighter. The F-35 pilots watch the Scramjet evaporate as the TX flies out of the eruption of fire.

"Two more lined up like ducks in a row. Let's heat em up. I've got a lock." The second pilot fires. An AIM-9X leaps off his wing, flying directly for Scramjet Number Three. The third F-35 pilot watches the rocket zoom across the sky toward the Scramjet for several seconds. He gets a lock on Scramjet Number One and fires his Sidewinder. Scramjet Number Three turns and speeds up, trying to outrun the guided missile. Death is delayed—for a second. The Scramjet explodes in a ball of fire.

Kobalt watches in horror as a missile fired by an unseen enemy blows the first Scramjet out of the sky. He knows he has only seconds. If someone is targeting the Scramjets, they will not stop at shooting down just one of them. "Engage countermeasures," the pilot yells.

Kobalt leaps from his seat. The aircraft door is two steps away. He lifts a lever to open the door. The door doesn't open all the way, so he kicks it open and jumps out of the aircraft, pulling the ripcord on his chute as soon as he clears the aircraft. He hears the explosion of Number Three being hit. Seconds later he watches Number One, his Scramjet, disintegrate in a ball of flames. Kobalt is the only survivor.

Kobalt hangs below his parachute shaking his fist and yells, "Damn you, Munday! Your luck won't last."

Scramjets are exploding. Rick looks to the east. It's late afternoon. The storms will start soon, but so far, the skies are clear. Becky is screaming hysterically. She stops mid-scream and shouts, "What the hell is happening?" Rick levels off and returns to his original heading flying over Mesa Verde National Park.

The Three F-35s surround the TX. Becky shrieks. "Oh my God!" The lead F-35 flies in front of the TX and tips its wings left and right. "I'm not sure what that means, but at least they aren't shooting at us," says Jin.

"I think the cavalry arrived to save the day," Rick says as he looks over to the F-35 on the left. Rick sees the pilot give a thumbs-up. Rick gives a thumbs-up in reply.

"They saved us. Jin, they saved us," cries Becky.

"Rick was doing a decent job. But I'd say they showed up at the right time," says Jin.

The lead F-35 pilot radios the TX-200. "Good flying, TX. Glad you made it through that. We are to escort you to Buckley Air Force Base."

Rick keys his mic. "Thanks for your help. Much appreciated. Where's Buckley? We're flying to Las Vegas."

"Buckley Air Force Base is near Denver. We are to escort you to Buckley by order of the Secretary of Defense. It seems you've made a friend. It was his order to intercept you."

"I don't know why the Secretary of Defense would be interested. Thanks for the offer, but we really need to get to Vegas."

Gravity pulls six asteroids from space into Earth's atmosphere, transforming them into super-heated meteors.

"I don't ask questions. It's above my pay grade. You're out for a joy ride in a TX-200 being chased by supersonic Scramjets, of unknown origin. If the Secretary of Defense sends for you, you go. You're going to Buckley." The F-35s move in a tight formation surrounding the TX. If Rick tries to break formation, he will surely crash into one of the F-35s.

The air force jets bank in a slow wide turn with the TX at the center of the formation. As they turn the six meteors come into view soaring through the sky. In the distance a dozen more fireballs streak westward.

The lead pilot radios Rick. "Hey, buddy, storms are starting up. Time to hightail it back. You don't want to be up here with those flaming bitches exploding." The F-35s break formation and begin flying at speed to Buckley.

"Roger that," says Rick, giving the pilot a nod. The F-35's accelerate. Rick hesitates, letting the jets fly ahead.

It takes a few seconds for the lead pilot to figure out Rick is not hightailing it for Buckley. "Hey, what are you doing? I'm telling you once the skies heat up, you don't want to be flying through that crap. If we weren't at risk of being slammed by meteors, I'd drag you all the way back to Buckley."

Rick turns west toward Vegas. "Sorry, like I said we've got to get to Vegas."

The pilot doesn't want to disobey orders, but he doesn't want to risk flying through an exploding meteor, either. "All right. You want to stay out here in the middle of a meteor storm; you are no longer my responsibility. Adios, amigo."

Rick resets the course for Las Vegas. "Muchas gracias, Captain. We appreciate your help. You saved the day. Please give our regards to the Secretary of Defense." Rick pushes the throttle forward and jets toward Vegas.

Mike McCoy

Part Four–Bridge to Nowhere

Chapter 54: Defending Arcadia

New Arcadia City Command–Friday Afternoon

"I've added extra filters to block network traffic, but they aren't working," says a panicked blue tunic.

Cruikshank looks over Zsoldos' shoulder anxiously as the man types furiously. "What's happening? Can you hold them off?"

"The hackers are attempting to swamp our systems. They've launched botnets to flood our network with malware. Not to worry, I'm on to their juvenile tactics," says Zsoldos.

"They won't stop until they've overrun us. Look what's happened at New Zion and Nod. They will gain control. You might hold them off for a while, but it's only a matter of time."

"I can maintain control of our systems. I designed the system. I know what they did at Nod. I won't let it happen here," Zsoldos states calmly.

Alarms sound. "Topsiders have broken into the buildings. They're crowding into the ground level of all eight buildings," reports a blue tunic.

Cruikshank immediately makes a call. "Mahon! What are you doing up there? Topsiders are entering the buildings. You are failing to defend the city! The Marines are attacking. You must fight. Repel the rebels. Attack!" the colonel screams, slamming his cane on the control room table.

"We've been attacking. Our artillery has decimated the marine positions. What we started the storm will finish," the general replies sharply.

"Decimated! The Air Force destroyed our aircraft and bunkers at New Zion. Your troops taken prisoner by cadets. US Army forces overtaken by children. It's humiliating. You are failing. You must not allow Marines or topsiders to invade New Arcadia!" screams Colonel Cruikshank.

"Colonel, it is you who has failed. You failed to keep our location secret and have allowed a sea of humanity to flood New Zion, Nod, and the Parklands above New Arcadia. Your negligence set the US

Marines upon us. The storm kills thousands every minute. Topsiders will not invade New Arcadia. Most of them lie dead in the field. Not by my hand, but by the hand of God. New Arcadia is thirty-five levels down. You needn't worry about a few stragglers inside the buildings."

"Push them out of the buildings. I will not allow those miscreants inside any part of New Arcadia. Defend the city," scolds Colonel Cruikshank.

"Many of my men lie dead in the Parklands. I will not order my men to push the topsiders out. There will be no more death by my hand today." Mahon ends the call.

Level Three–Army Bunker–New Arcadia

"General. There are still thousands of people in the Parklands. They won't all fit in the ground level of the buildings," reports a staff member.

"There are hundreds more packed in at the ramp to Level 2; they're desperate, Sir. They're trying to pry the doors open," reports another.

Jack Mahon stands stoically, viewing the screens filled with wretchedness.

New Arcadia–City Command

Colonel Cruikshank looks dubiously at Zsoldos, working frantically to fight off the hackers and save the city. "Nod's City Command could not regain control of their systems. They're being inundated with topsiders. We cannot risk an invasion of New Arcadia. I won't allow anyone to ruin our plans for humanity!" Cruikshank screams.

"Don't worry, Colonel, we are holding them off. I know all their tricks. The hackers are running out of options. We've turned them back on every attempt," Zsoldos reports confidently.

A blue tunic calls out excitedly. "The ramp doors to level two are opening. They have breached level two!"

Screens in City Command display hundreds of desperate people rushing through the metal doors at the bottom of the ramp.

"Stairwell doors are opening in all the buildings. Hundreds of topsiders are filling the stairwells," reports another blue tunic.

"Zsoldos, they have hacked us! Get control of our systems before they overrun us," shouts Cruikshank.

Zsoldos quickly checks city systems and machine control. "We have not been hacked. City systems remain secure."

"Stairwells are open to level two only," reports the blue tunic.

"The metal doors leading to level two opened to a height of eight feet, then stopped," reports the second blue tunic.

"I confirm. The topsiders are not getting beyond level two. Someone must have done this from inside New Arcadia," reports Zsoldos.

"It's that feeble Mahon. It must be him. He lacks the will to defend New Arcadia. He thinks saving a few thousand people can clear his conscience. Stop him! Cut the Army's systems off from New Arcadia," Cruikshank shouts.

Zsoldos directs several blue tunics, calling out orders. "We are disabling the Army's access to city systems."

"Level two is a vast room covering the area below all eight campus buildings. They can get thousands of people in there," reports a blue tunic.

"Close the doors! Close that ramp door. They will have access to our heavy equipment and reintegration supplies," Cruikshank yells.

"We can cut Mahon's access to city systems, but the Level Three bunker retains control of the upper levels," reports the City Commander.

"Zsoldos. You and City Command are very capable. You have done well to hold the hackers at bay, but I've had enough. We cannot rely on computers to protect the future of New Arcadia. Call up every brown tunic. I alone will stop this invasion. No one is entering New Arcadia. I won't let them ruin our future. Round up the browns. I have a job for them," directs the colonel.

Chapter 55: Rough Landing

Friday Afternoon

"Whoo-hoo! If those F-35s hadn't shown up, Kobalt and his Scramjets would have knocked us out of the sky," says Rick.

"Thank God for them," says Becky.

"I'm sure glad they showed up, but why would the Secretary of Defense send them to help us? Do you have friends in high places, Rick?" asks Jin.

"Not that I know of. Maybe the military is fighting the New Arcadians, but how would they know anything about me?"

"Maybe now we can get to Curtis," says Becky.

"That's the idea. Increasing elevation to ten thousand feet. You guys should be good for oxygen. I can't fly too high since you don't have helmets. Let me know if you pass out, ha-ha! Increasing speed to eight hundred miles per hour. Three hundred miles to go. Let's get ahead of the asteroid storm," Rick explains.

The sky fills with clusters of meteors. Becky looks up to watch the fireballs through the glass canopy. "Sorry, not possible. Meteors incoming. Can this thing go faster?"

"Okay. Here we go! We should be in Vegas in fifteen minutes," says Rick.

A flurry of fiery satellites fly past. Many explode in the distant sky as brilliant flashes while others crash to Earth. It feels like the firestorm over the Arizona desert surrounds the small TX. Explosions fill the air like rolling thunder.

"Luckily, they're exploding far away from us. The shock waves would be tough to fly through, not to mention all the asteroid bits," observes Jin.

Another cluster of fireballs burns in a wide band across the evening sky. They make a sound that reminds Rick of sizzling bacon. "Hear that? It's so weird. Reminds me of Courtney cooking bacon in the morning. Damn, I can almost smell it."

"It's been a while since we've had a real meal. I hope Curtis has more than soda and crackers stocked in his shelter," says Becky.

Rapid explosions sounding machine-gun fire replace the sound of sizzling bacon. A powerful blast of wind slams into the TX. The aircraft violently rolls to the left, pushed by the force of the wind. Phit, phit, phit, phit. Hot spherules pass through the aircraft. The TX creaks and pops as the fuselage bends and flexes in the shock wave.

Becky shrieks. "Oh God, meteorites are hitting us!"

"That must have been a close one, ugh," Jin says, feeling a dull thud in his right shoulder. He lets out a deep grunt of pain.

Rick grips the flight stick tighter, working to keep the aircraft stable.

"Rick, the flight nom indicates you're too heavy on the stick. It says the aircraft's digital fly-by-wire system adjusts faster than a human pilot can react. The flight nom will keep the jet stable," says Becky.

"Maybe that's why we're still flying. The TX just took a beating. I think we're OK, but that was close," Rick says excitedly.

"Let's pray that's the worst of it. Most of the meteors are flying over the horizon," Becky says, looking at a sky clouded with black smoke.

"I hope they go a lot farther. Los Angeles is over there," Rick says, checking aircraft indicators. "Hey, Jin. Do you have an address for Curtis? We will have to change course for his location soon."

Jin doesn't answer Rick's question. Becky nudges Jin. "Hey, babe. Where exactly are we supposed to land?"

Jin doesn't respond. Becky twists, trying to look at him.

Becky squeezes Jin's thigh to get his attention. "Jin, honey. What's wrong? Jin? Jin?" she cries louder.

Jin groans. "I think... I... I'm OK," he mouths slowly in a half-conscious whisper.

"Rick. Jin isn't moving. Something's wrong," Becky says, then reaches around to check him, moving her hand across his chest. Then she slides her hand behind his back and feels something damp. She removes her hand; it's covered in blood. "Jin's bleeding. Oh God. Jin, hang in there. We'll get you home."

"I got hit in the shoulder by a piece of that meteor. It went right through the armored seat and the skin suit. I don't have any pain. I think I'm drugged. Does this suit do that?"

"It might. I saw something on the box about a medicated blood-clotting layer. Maybe that's why the suit is thick. Hang in there, buddy. We'll get you home," says Rick.

Jin pats Becky's thigh with his left hand. "I'll be OK, Beck. I don't feel anything. I'm fine… I think."

Rick looks up as if there's a rearview mirror in the cockpit. "We'll be in Vegas in no time. We need Curtis' address."

Jim tries to mouth the address, but the neurons in his brain aren't connecting. Instead, he lifts his left arm tapping Becky. "Band. My band."

Becky grabs Jin's hand, pulling his heavy arm around her to view the band. "Ow!" Jin's squeals.

"Sorry, babe," Becky says as she taps on Jin's band. The projected display appears, and she brings up Curtis's profile.

"I've got it. 237 North Parawan Street, in Henderson. It's near the corner of East Warm Springs Road and Orleans Street," Becky says.

The fire storm roils the surrounding skies. The TX rocks and bounces from shock waves of detonating fireballs.

"The TX's navigation system isn't like an Autocar. I can't enter an address and expect the TX to fly there, but it'll get us close," Rick says, as he adjusts course for Henderson, Nevada.

"Curtis' house. Here we come. Just a few minutes now." Becky says trying to talk over the sound of the rattling aircraft.

A brilliant light erupts next to the TX. A fierce shock flips the TX, hurling the small jet through the air sideways, flipping, turning, and spinning. Alarms sound and indicators in Rick's helmet display flash red. Rick fights to gain control as the jet spins downward to the Mojave dessert. "We're spinning. Trying to get control," Rick says as he struggles with the flight stick.

He expects Becky to be yelling, but the cockpit is eerily silent. The jet makes a gentle whoosh, whoosh, whoosh sound as it spins. All is quiet. The world spins gracefully as they fall to Earth. The strange silence beckons death. "Sorry guys. I think this is it." Rick stops fighting the aircraft, releasing his hands from the flight stick and throttle, accepting his fate as the desert floor swiftly approaches.

As soon as Rick releases the flight stick, the TX-200 flight control nom adjusts and corrects flight control surfaces. A series of messages scroll through the helmet display, noting control adjustments, while the flight nom works to pull itself out of the spin. The aircraft stops spinning and gains altitude. Fifteen seconds later, the TX-200 is flying toward Henderson.

The aircraft amazes Rick. He lets out a deep breath. "That's one hell of a cruise control. You guys still back there?"

Jin pats his hand on Becky's stomach. "Whoa! We're still with you," she says as she uses both hands to pull her hair out of her face.

Jin gathers his strength to speak. "Would you stop playing around and get us home?"

Smoke trails from the TX. The engine makes intermittent sputtering sounds. The jet is fragile, creaking and cracking with every slight turn. The sounds worry Rick. "Sorry, TX. Just hold together long enough to get us home."

The TX begins a jittery descent. Rick looks out the cockpit. There's a body of water below. He checks his screens. "That's part of Lake Mead." Rick checks the screen again. "Ahead is Muddy Peak. Beyond the peak is the city of Henderson. Guys. We're here. We're gonna make it!"

The TX descends to an altitude of five hundred feet, gliding over the slope of Muddy Peak and Lava Butte directly toward Henderson. Rick takes control of the aircraft.

"Becky, check for data reception on Jin's band. Direct me to Curtis's house. I'm not sure how much longer the engine will hold out." The TX is now past Henderson, nearing the town of Enterprise.

"OK, OK. You need to turn back to the south. Back to Henderson."

Rick pushes the flight stick to the right. The stick pushes back. The jet stutters as it attempts to turn. Rick cocks his head to look at the right wing. "I think the right aileron is out of commission."

Rick pushes the flight stick to the left, and the jet turns left. "Looks like it's left turns only for the rest of the trip."

"OK, left turns work for me. We're almost there. Keep going south past the 515 Freeway below," instructs Becky.

Jin slowly raises his injured arm to initialize his VUE and calls Curtis. Curtis answers instantly. "Jin! Where have you guys been?

I've been trying to reach you since you took off from the Air Force Academy. Where are you?" Curtis asks, waving his Gulp cup.

Jin wears a painful grin. "We've been kinda busy. Rick took us for quite a ride. We're almost home. Go outside and wave your hands. Bring us home, Curtis."

Curtis drops his Gulp cup. "I'm coming!"

Curtis has never moved so fast in his life. He runs up the steps of his bunker pushing open the metal door to his garage. Once in the garage, he calls out: "Open garage door." The garage door rolls up. Curtis ducks under the door, stepping outside. He hasn't been out of his house in weeks. "Wow. Outside is big."

The setting sun in the west turns the smoke in the air an odd brownish orange. Meteors explode in the sky. Curtis feels a hot gust of wind from a distant air burst as he scans the sky for an aircraft, waving his arms overhead.

Rick drops the TX to two hundred feet, allowing the jet to slip forward through the air crossing three highways, then gliding over a residential area. Rick scans the houses.

"Becky, where am I going?" Rick asks.

"Jump Curtis. Wave your arms. We can't see you," says Jin.

The dense residential area gives way to individual houses scattered across the brown dry desert. "Follow that double lane road. That's Warm Springs Road," Becky says as she studies the map displayed from Jin's band.

Curtis sees the jet in the distance. "I see you. This way. Here I am!" he exclaims, jumping and waving his arms in exaggerated motions.

Jin calls out to Curtis. "Can't see you, buddy. Are you waving your arms?"

Curtis is losing his breath. "I'm in the street. I'm waving my arms like crazy."

Rick pushes the jet forward. He spots Curtis jumping in the street directly ahead. "I've got him. I see him."

"We can't see you. Are you jumping?" asks Jin.

"I'm jumping and waving my arms. I can see you. I'm right here!"

Jin laughs. "Oh! There you are! Thanks, Curtman."

Curtis almost collapses. He bends over with his hands on his knees, breathing hard. "Just land the damn plane. We can't stay outside in this storm."

"Now we just need to land this thing," Rick says as he touches the console and selects VTOL. Two exhaust panels open on top of the aircraft and two counter-rotating Lift-fans blow twenty thousand pounds of air straight down, producing downward thrust. The TX engine rotates downward, allowing the aircraft to hover. Landing gear alarms sound: bleep, bleep, bleep. "What's wrong. Oh boy. The nose and left side landing gear are jammed!" shouts Rick.

The right landing gear extends, locking into place. The TX makes a wobbly vertical descent. More indicators light up and alarm: chang, chang, chang. "What now? The main engine isn't fully rotated." The TX moves forward as it descends, blowing up dust in a wobbly hover instead of making a steady vertical descent. Curtis follows the jet, stumbling forward and covering his face from the dust.

"Hold on. This is gonna be a rough landing." When the TX is four feet above the ground, Rick cuts the engine. The aircraft drops to the ground with a crash.

Becky cheers. "We made it. Jin, we made it. You're home."

The Lift Fan continues running with a whining sound for several seconds, coughing up dust. The TX disappears in a cloud of brown dirt.

"Whoo-hoo! We landed. If you call that a landing. Whew! Sorry for the rough ride, guys. That ride is on me. No charge," Rick jokes.

"No man, we owe you big time," says Jin with as much excitement as he can manage through his dulled pain.

"We made it! Whoop, whoop," Becky shouts, pumping her arm.

As the dust clears, the dirt-covered aircraft rests at an angle on the ground, nose in the dirt with the right wing pointing to the sky. The right aileron swings by a single wire.

Rick sits silently for a moment. "Thanks, guys. I couldn't have made it without you. We make a great team!"

A meteor explodes low in the sky over the desert south of Henderson, sending fiery rocks and molten spherules speeding across the desert floor.

The canopy grinds open, hinged on the right side like the lid of a tin can. Brown dirt fills the cockpit, causing Becky to cough. She stands, brushing herself off and calling out to Curtis. "Curtis, help! Jin's hurt."

Curtis runs to the jet, sliding and falling in the soft dust next to the cockpit. Becky smiles at Jin's chubby friend. "Careful, Curtis. We didn't travel all this way to have you break a leg."

Spherules and small fragments from the nearby meteor explosion ping and pop as they hit, piercing the wings and fuselage. Becky braces her hands on the open canopy to steady herself as the plane shakes from the impacts. A small spherule traveling at fifteen thousand miles per hour plinks through the canopy's acrylic material, then passes through Becky's skull, entering just in front of her right ear and exiting out her left temple. The cockpit armor protects Rick, Jin, and Curtis from the impacts.

Rick pulls off his helmet and stands at an angle in the lop-sided aircraft. He surveys the damage and sees a fuselage riddled with holes. The right aileron swings in the wind, the left wingtip is in the dirt.

Curtis rises on his knees beside the cockpit. Rick looks at Jin's friend. "You must be Curtis. I'm Rick. I think I broke the plane."

"Who cares about the plane? I'm so happy to see you guys," Curtis says, as he hefts himself up to stand next to the cockpit.

Becky still stands silent with her head bowed. Her right hand grips the edge of the open canopy. Her hair hides the blood trickling out of the wounds on her head. Blood drips from her nose.

Rick jumps out of the cockpit to the ground and stands next to Curtis.

"Becky, I'll help you down first. Jump down. I got you. Curtis and I will get Jin," Rick offers. Becky doesn't move.

Curtis looks up at Becky. "She's bleeding! Becky, your nose is bleeding."

"Sorry for the rough landing, Becky. Did you hit your nose on the flight console? Give me your hand. I'll help you down. Come on. You can do it," Rick encourages Becky.

Becky doesn't answer. Her hand relaxes, losing its grip on the canopy, and Becky's body tumbles out of the lopsided cockpit. Rick does his best to catch her.

"Oh, God! Becky's hurt. Something's wrong with Becky," Curtis cries as Rick struggles with Becky's limp body.

Jin uses his good hand to pull himself out of the instructor's seat. "Becky, babe. What's wrong?" He sees Rick struggling. "What happened? Oh God, Becky. What happened to her?" Jin has difficulty standing in the tilted plane.

"Sit tight, Jin. I'm sure she'll be fine. Wait here. We'll get Becky to the bunker and come back for you. Curtis, lead me to your bunker," Rick instructs as he carries Becky.

Rick and Curtis move swiftly to Curtis's house. When they reach the door of the bunker, Curtis takes Becky's legs while Rick holds her under her arms as they move down the steep metal steps. Once in the bunker, Curtis extends a four-foot dining table to its full six-foot length.

Curtis helps Rick lay Becky on the table. She's unconscious. Rick checks her breathing and pulse. "She's breathing, and she has a weak pulse."

"What's happened to her?" Curtis asks.

"I don't know. We should get Jin. He's out in the storm."

Rick and Curtis hustle up the metal steps to the garage, where they find Jin limping and covered in brown dust.

"Jin!" Curtis shouts in surprise.

"I fell out of the plane. Where's Becky?" Jin asks, his face and Black Guard uniform covered with brown dust, his right arm hangs limp.

Rick and Curtis help Jin down the narrow metal steps, then he pushes past Curtis, rushing to where Becky lies.

Jin forgets his own injury and hugs the weight of Becky's inert body. "Becky, oh, Becky. What happened?" Jin straightens, looking at Rick and Curtis as tears stream down his dirty face. "What's wrong with her?"

Rick checks Becky's vital signs. "She isn't breathing."

"There's blood on the table by her head," Curtis says.

Rick pulls her hair back. "Small wounds on both sides of her head. It looks like something hit her and passed right through."

Rick checks for a pulse again, then looks at Jin with sorrowful eyes. "I'm so sorry, Jin. She's gone."

"No! No," Jin cries, collapsing on Becky's body. "Don't leave me, baby. It's not fair. We're just getting started. We were going to make babies and grow old together. You can't leave me now. Not now. We made it home. Becky, we're home."

Chapter 56: Evil boys with their pointy little knives

Friday Evening

Gymnasium–New Arcadia

Gordon is the only adult who enters Gymnasium. Gymnasium is for the boys. The boys leave Gymnasium for the spa only. A door opens into a hallway. The hallway leads to the spa. Spa attendants are the only adults other than Gordon to see the boys. There is a second door in Gymnasium that opens to the city. None of the boys have ever seen it open.

The boys know a city full of people is beyond the second door. They aren't allowed to see the city or take part in city activities. The boys' sole purpose in New Arcadia is to serve the colonel. Through their dedicated service, they do their small part in moving the Arcadian principles forward so a new humanity can emerge after the storms.

Gymnasium includes a barracks, galley, communal restroom/shower room and the gym. The barracks are a Spartan three-walled room with twelve beds. Four beds neatly arranged along each wall. The galley has tables, chairs, and four food actualizers to create meals. The various menu pods (Menu pods sounds nicer than pouches full of goop containing proteins, carbohydrates, fat, minerals, vitamins, and chemicals for flavoring and texture) are always full. Gordon's private quarters are between the bathroom and the galley. Gymnasium has no city atmosphere. The colonel doesn't want blood contaminated by the atmosphere that could cloud his mind.

The gym is expansive with a lofty ceiling. Tumbling mats and an indoor jungle gym cover the floor area. Climbing walls and a high catwalk ring the gym with Tarzan swinging ropes, rope ladders, and slides to the floor. The room has plastic blocks and rubber balls, large and small, scattered around. There are sitting areas with comfy chairs and couches scattered around the room, and a large video screen covers one wall. The boys watch city news, old TV shows, and Arcadian Public Television, which is primarily Arcadian propaganda.

There is no school, few rules, and plenty of food. Play and imagined adventures fill the boys' days. One might view Gymnasium as a modern-day Neverland, a play-filled island surrounded by a utopian city. The only cost is the spa.

Gordon is of medium height and overweight. He looks like a college athlete turned coach. His round belly pushes his dark blue tunic out of shape. Gordon might have been good at something once, but those days appear to be over. Gordon spends a good deal of time in his private quarters but sometimes leaves Gymnasium. He makes sure they eat and sleep. He breaks up fights and takes them to the spa. Most of the time, Gordon leaves them alone to play, roughhouse, and watch streams.

Nolan likes to hang out in Gordon's quarters. Gordon doesn't encourage it, but he doesn't kick Nolan out either. The other boys ignore Gordon, thinking it's better to stay off his radar, hoping to avoid being selected for the spa.

Something is different this evening. Even though Gymnasium is cut off from city activities, the boys can sense the tension in the air.

Owen sits rocking in his corner. The boys hear an alert for brown tunics to report to stations. There are rushing sounds of many footfalls outside, echoing through the second door.

Zekiel sits on a big couch next to Aidan, watching streams. Zekiel's skin is still thin and gray, but he's getting stronger. An Arcadian patriotic video streams. Zekiel has seen the video a hundred times. It bores him. He gets up from the couch to wander around. Gordon leaves Gymnasium through the spa door, probably to see what's happening in the city.

Zekiel observes Owen. He sits cross-legged in his corner, rocking. Once Gordon leaves Gymnasium, Owen does something Zekiel has never seen him do before. He rolls to his side and crawls close to the base of the city door. There is a gap between the bottom of the door and the floor. Owen looks through the gap to see what's happening outside Gymnasium. Zekiel goes to Owen. Owen pulls back the gym mat covering the floor, revealing a larger gap below the door.

Zekiel gets on his stomach, joining Owen at the base of the door. "What's going on? Can you see anything?" Zekiel asks.

"I can see feet and equipment moving past. It's not what I see, but what I hear," whispers Owen.

"What do you hear?" asks Zekiel in a hushed voice.

"People talking," Owen says while staring at the gap under the door.

"And?"

"You're right. People are trying to invade New Arcadia. Colonel doesn't like that. He's ordered all entrances to the city welded shut to keep them out."

Owen's comment stuns Zekiel.

"If you want to get out of here. Away from him. We need to go now. If there's no way in. There won't be a way out," says Owen.

"We've got to get through this door," Zekiel says, looking up at an access panel next to the door.

"Gordon will open it."

"How are we supposed to get Gordon to open it? He's not even in Gym."

Owen points to the gap under the door. "He's coming back."

"You recognize his shoes?" asks an amazed Zekiel.

Owen nods with a slight smile. "You better go back to the couch," he says as he rises and scoots to his spot, sitting cross-legged with his hands clasped in his lap, rocking.

Zekiel gets up on his knees. "How will we get Gordon to open the door?"

"We'll think of something," Owen says with a curious smirk.

Zekiel joins Aidan on the couch as Gordon returns. Gordon brings the panic of the city into Gymnasium. The boys sense Gordons heightened anxiety.

Owen screams and wails at the top of his lungs, sparking an electric charge in the room. Gordon runs to Owen. No one can tell if Owen is screaming in pain or having a psychotic event.

Eleven boys rush after Gordon to see what's happening.

Owen lies on his side, clutching his hands to his stomach. Gordon bends down and lifts Owen to his feet. Owen looks up at Gordon and screams like a crazy banshee, clutching his hands to his stomach. The boys surround Gordon and Owen in a tight scrum. Aiden and Zekiel are closest to Owen in the tight circle of boys.

"What's the matter? Are you hurt?" asks Gordon. Owen continues to scream.

"Quiet down. What's wrong?" Gordon asks, examining Owen to see if he's injured.

Owen stops screaming and stares into Gordon's eyes. "Open the door. We want out."

Gordon rises, looking relieved that the situation isn't serious. "No one is leaving Gymnasium. You are here to favor the colonel. Everyone has a functional utility in New Arcadia. Spa is your utility. Outside this door, you're worthless."

"Who says we're staying in New Arcadia?" Zekiel asks with a scowl.

"Open the door," says Aidan.

"There is no way I will open that door. Now get back, all of you. Go watch streams or play." Gordon sticks a fat finger in Owen's face. "You're next for the spa. You faker."

Owen rapidly moves his hands from his stomach, exposing something shiny and sharp. He stabs Gordon in the thigh.

Gordon howls. The boys move in a wider circle, allowing Gordon to hop around in pain.

Owen quickly drops to his knees and reaches under a gym mat, pulling out three more daggers. He hands one each to Aidan, Zekiel, and little James.

Aidan examines the shiv. "You made knives out of spoons?"

"No wonder there aren't enough spoons," James says in wonderment.

"That's why you rock. To sharpen knives. I thought you were bat crazy," says Aidan.

"He's crazy enough to get us out of here!" exclaims Zekiel.

Gordon limps to Owen. "You little bastard. You'll bleed out in spa for this."

Owen points to Gordon's wound. "Two inches to the left, I would have sliced your artery. You'd be the one bleeding out. I would have done it, but I didn't want to risk touching your stinky balls."

"He's not going to Spa, open that door," Zekiel says, brandishing his shiny little dagger. James, Aidan, and Owen jab their pointy blades at Gordon.

Zekiel realizes daggers won't convince Gordon to open the door. He moves to Aidan and whispers. Aidan moves outside the circle of boys.

Gordon laughs. "If I bleed out, you'll never escape. You need my voice and handprint to get through that door."

"You will open that door and lead us to an exit before they seal the city," says Zekiel, steeling his strength.

There's a scuffle and a shriek behind the boys. All eyes move to the sound of the disturbance.

The circle of boys opens, revealing Nolan standing with a rope around his neck. Aidan has used a climbing rope to make a noose.

The rope is slung over a beam under the catwalk. Aidan pulls hard on the rope. Another boy jumps on the rope, adding his weight, and Nolan lifts off the ground, making gurgling sounds and kicking his feet.

Gordon tries to move to Nolan, but he's stopped by the steely daggers. "Let him go!" cries Gordon.

Aidan lowers Nolan, allowing his toes to touch the ground. "I told you. I told you they're bad boys," whimpers Nolan.

"All right, stop it! Enough of your little mutiny. All that colonel's blood flowing through your bodies, I expected some evil deeds, but it stops now!" Gordon pushes James and Owen aside, pressing through the group of boys toward Nolan.

Zekiel steps in front of Gordon. Gordon flings him into the group of boys. The boys catch Zekiel and push him back to Gordon. The metal shiv in Zekiel's hand penetrates Gordon's abdomen. Zekiel holds on to Gordon, repeatedly stabbing him in the belly as he tries to reach Nolan.

As Gordon moves, Aidan jerks the rope tight. Two boys jump on the rope, launching Nolan into the air. Nolan's hands go to the rope around his neck, fighting for breath. His body jerks and spasms.

Gordon pushes Owen to the floor. He scrambles across the gym mat and jabs his sharp knife deep into Gordon's right calf.

419

Gordon's leg buckles, sending him to his knees. As he falls, he pulls Zekiel off him, throwing the boy to the gym mats. Gordon's eyes plead for Nolan, swinging at the end of the rope.

Gordon, winded and bloody, gives in. "OK. Stop! Let him down," Gordon yells, pointing to Nolan. "I give up. I'll open the door, let him down!" Gordon cries, his blood spilling on the gym mats.

Aidan and the boys let loose of the rope. Nolan falls limply to the floor, then pulls the rope from his neck, coughing.

Gordon is on his knees clutching his belly as if he's trying to keep his guts from spilling out. Zekiel, Owen, James, and Davey stand over him.

Zekiel flashes his bloodied knife in Gordon's face. "Nolan's down, not dead. Now stand up and open the door."

Gordon struggles to stand, favoring his wounded leg. Four knives follow as Gordon limps to the door.

Gordon stands in front of the access panel. "The colonel will not like this. He won't like it at all."

Owen gives a quick thrust of his knife in Gordon's butt. "Voice and hand recognition. Get on with it."

Gordon wipes his bloodied hand on his tunic and then waves it in front of the access panel. A voice comes from the panel. "State Name," Gordon responds. "Gordon Szarek."

"Confirm with handprint." Gordon places his hand on the access panel. "Exit granted." The door clicks. Gordon removes his hand from the panel, leaving streaks of blood.

Zekiel grabs the handle and pulls the door open. "Let's get out of here," Zekiel calls out.

The boys laugh and cheer as they rush through the door into the corridor.

"You're free. Run away," says Gordon painfully.

"You're not finished until you take us to an exit stairwell," Owen says, twisting his knife in the air. Aiden and James push Gordon through the door to the waiting group of boys.

Zekiel looks around Gymnasium. Nolan is getting to his feet. Will, the skinny eleven-year-old, stands near Nolan.

"Will, come on, we're free. Let's go!" calls Zekiel. Will doesn't move.

"He wants to stay. He likes it," says Owen.

"Come on Will. You too Nolan. Come with us and you'll never have to spa," says Zekiel.

"The colonel needs us. We are here for him. He might die without us," Will says, standing firm.

Gordon turns to Nolan. "Come along now. You don't want to stay in there."

Nolan shakes refusal with his whole body and fear in his eyes.

"Nolan, if you stay, you'll have no choice. You will go to spa. Will can't do it alone."

A tear streams down Nolan's cheek, but he refuses to move.

Gordon looks to Zekiel and Owen. "You'll let me come back if I get you to an exit. That's the deal, right?"

"You come up the stairwell with us till we know we're safe, then you can come back. That's the deal," says Zekiel.

"I'll be back. Stay here with Will. I'll be back soon," Gordon says as the boys push him down the corridor.

The door to Gymnasium closes.

"Let's move. The faster you get us up a stairwell, the sooner you can get back to your Nolan," Owen says, pushing Gordon.

"This way," Gordon says, limping and his right arm holding his belly wounds.

The boys run awkwardly in their white slippers on the cold, bumpy tile floor. Davey jumps tile to tile, missing the cracks. One hundred yards down the corridor is a stairwell door.

Two brown tunics sit on the edge of a levitating welding platform monitoring an autonomous welding system. Their welding helmets are down to protect their eyes from the hot blue light and sparks flashing as an electrode burns a long bead of metal sealing the stairwell door.

"They're sealing the doors. You boys are too late. Might as well go back to Gymnasium," Gordon says in a hopeful tone.

Zekiel prods Gordon with the tip of his blade. "Where's the next stairwell? We're not going back."

Owen pushes the group forward. "Move faster. My feet are freezing!"

Gordon limps along as fast as he's able. He's motivated by pointy jabs in the ass if he moves too slow. Soon the group reaches a stairwell door.

Gordon stands in front of the access panel. "I'm not sure the door will open. The city is on lockdown."

"Try it and you'd better do it right or I'll bleed you out, stinky balls or not," Owen says with a sneer.

"If you want to get back to Gymnasium, you'll make sure that door opens," adds Aidan.

Gordon presses his palm on the scanner, standing still for facial recognition and then voices his name.

The panel beeps. An indicator light changes from red to yellow. Gordon speaks. "Enter maintenance mode, code 42." The panel replies, Code 42 accepted. "Door opening for maintenance." The light on the panel changes from yellow to green. Gears rotate inside the door. The boys step back as the door unlocks, and a motorized sound accompanies the movement of the door.

Gordon smiles. "I was a maintenance supervisor before I got the job in Gymnasium."

"Who woulda guessed? Let's move before anyone sees us in the corridor. I don't think we'll pass as a typical New Arcadian family unit," says Aidan.

The boys scurry through the opening as the heavy door opens slowly.

"Well, I guess that's it. You boys have a good life with all the asteroids crashing to Earth and what not," says Gordon.

"Not so fast, Gordo. Come in and close the door. You're coming up the stairs until we know we're in the clear. That's the deal," Zekiel says, prodding Gordon into the stairwell.

Gordon reluctantly presses his palm to the panel inside the stairwell and the heavy door closes.

The boys run up the stairs. Owen and Aidan take turns poking Gordon in the butt to make him move faster. There's a feeling of elation among the boys. James and Davey take the steps two at a time. They smile at Zekiel as they pass him and arrive on a landing ahead of everyone else.

Davey turns to look down the stairway. "We're free now, right? No spa?" Davey asks Zekiel.

"That's right, buddy. We're free. You'll never go to spa, I promise," Zekiel answers, winded from the climb.

Ten floors up, the boys slow their ascent, quietly chatting as they walk up the endless steps. Gordon moves fast enough to avoid getting jabbed in the butt. Zekiel, still weak from spa falls behind and uses the handrail to pull himself up.

Muffled sounds drift down the stairwell. "There are your asteroids now. You get what you wish for boys!" exclaims Gordon.

The boys listen. Zekiel catches up with Owen and Aidan. "You think it's an asteroid?" asks Zekiel?

Owen listens a few seconds before answering. "I don't know. It doesn't seem loud enough."

"Asteroid or not, I've gone far enough. You boys are in the clear. Nobody's following. I've done more than my part," Gordon states impatiently.

Zekiel, Owen, and Aidan look at each other and nod in agreement. "Go," says Zekiel.

Gordon rushes down the stairs. Zekiel calls out, admonishing the chubby attendant as he disappears into the darkness of the stairwell. "You're not forgiven. We will never forget. You tortured us and robbed our youth for that sick bastard. You're as guilty as him. I pray you pay the price."

"Bye, Gordo!" James calls out playfully. The other boys call after the fat attendant. "Bye, Gordo!" "Won't miss you, Gordo!" "Kiss Nolan for me!"

Gordon rushes down the dimly lit stairwell. His face flushes from exertion and concern about Colonel Cruikshank's reaction when he learns of the boys' escape. Whatever the punishment, it will be better than being topside in an asteroid storm.

"It isn't my fault; the boys gave me no choice. If I didn't let them out, Nolan would hang, and I would bleed out on the gym floor. It's those evil boys with their pointy little knives. Owen the faker. The sly little bastard and Zekiel, the ringleader. It was their doing," Gordon says, as he huffs down the stairs. He needs to have his story straight. It isn't his fault. "Colonel has Will and Nolan. No avoiding it now; Nolan will spa. The colonel will be OK. The two can take turns."

Gordon makes it to city level, laying his hands on the heavy, secured door. He leans against the cool polished metal to catch his breath. He places his right hand on the access panel. The panel lights up. Gordon voices his name. Access denied. He removes his hand and wipes blood off the panel with his sleeve.

Gordon places his hand on the panel. The panel lights up. He voices his name. Access granted! Gordon is excited. He hears the door unlock and the electric motor whine, but the door does not open. Several seconds pass until the electronic sounds quiet. Gordon tries again. Access is granted, but the door doesn't budge. "They've sealed the door!" Gordon cries, realizing the door is welded shut. Gordon tries again, hoping he's wrong. Access granted. The motor whines, then stops. The door doesn't move.

Gordon bangs his head against the steel door repeatedly in frustration and anger. "Stupid, stupid, stupid." He can go up the stairs but doesn't dare. It isn't the storm he fears. The boys will tell their story to the topsiders. Topsiders won't understand the spa and the important service it provides the colonel for the advancement of Arcadia. "They won't understand." He would rather starve where he stands than face retribution for his deeds. He slaps his hand against the panel and shouts his name. "Gordon Szarek," in a panicked shriek. The panel turns green. The door does not move. "It's not my fault." Gordon dashes his head against the cold steel. "It's not..." He cries as he slams his head harder and hears his skull crack. Blood streams down his face. "Yaaa!" He screams. "My fault, my fault, my fault," he mouths with rapid panting breaths. His eyes go wide. He smashes his head again and again against the immovable barrier.

The boys gleefully hustle up the stairwell. Aidan and another boy help Zekiel. Up and up, they go, turning at the top of every flight, then up the next. There are no doors or indications of floor levels, just more stairs.

"We must have climbed a million stairs. Are we almost at the top?" James asks.

"Every step gets us closer," Aiden replies.

"How many more?" asks Davey.

"It won't be much further, you'll see," Zekiel says, looking up the stairwell with a hopeful gaze.

Several minutes and hundreds of steps later, the group of boys has spread out. Some boys are four or five flights ahead while Zekiel and Aidan are at the back of the pack. The lead boys call out, "Level Three. It says Level Three. There's a door. Quick, come. See!"

"Hold up there. Don't go any farther and keep the noise down," Zekiel calls out.

Everyone hustles to the landing at Level Three. "The door is locked," Davey says. The boys are talking excitedly with all kinds of wild speculation.

"Hush up guys. I don't want us walking into a trap worse than the one we just escaped," says Aiden.

The door on Level Two opens above. Light from the open door causes the boys to look up. The boys hear footsteps and voices as the door closes and the light fades. The boys scurry in fright down the stairwell, pushing each other to hurry away.

"Hey! Who's down there?" a man's voice calls out.

The boys keep running down the stairs in panic. Aidan and Zekiel stay calm, looking up the stairwell.

"Don't go down there. You can't get into the city. All survivors are gathering on Level Two," the voice echoes down the stairwell.

"We have food and supplies up here. We're here to assist all civilians," another man says.

The boys stop when they run into Zekiel and Aidan coming up the stairs. "What do we do?" asks James in a frightened tone.

"If they catch us, they'll send us back to Gymnasium," says Davey.

"They said survivors are on Level Two. We're survivors," says Aidan.

"I want to make sure it's safe. Let's find out who they are. Aidan and Owen come with me. The rest of you wait here," orders Zekiel.

The boys separate, making a path for Zekiel, Aidan, and Owen to walk up the stairs.

"Come up here. Everyone from the Parklands is on Level Two," says the man's voice.

Zekiel, Aidan, and Owen meet the two men on the stairs a few levels up.

One man flashes a light from his band on the trio. "They're boys!" he exclaims.

Owen brandishes his blood-stained dagger.

"Hey, relax. No need for weapons. We're here to help you. I'm Sergeant Cheung. This is Corporal Williamson, US Army."

Cheung and Williamson examine the three boys dressed in light blue pajamas wearing white cloth slippers.

"Where did you boys come from?" asks Sargent Cheung.

"Gymnasium," says Owen.

"Gym what?" asks Williamson.

Zekiel eyes the military men, unsure if they are friend or enemy. Aidan and Owen study the men cautiously, waiting for Zekiel to answer. "Gymnasium is in the city below. We're exploring. I think we got lost. What's level two?"

"You came from the city? Access to the city is blocked," says Cheung.

"We are the few and the fortunate. The seeds of humanity. We are the select, chosen to create a new and better human society." Owen repeats the words planted in his mind from the incessant Arcadian video streams.

"What the hell?" asks a stunned Corporal Williamson, unsure how to react to the unusual statement.

James, Davey, and the other boys have slowly crept up the stairwell and crouch on the landing below, watching.

Zekiel wonders if they support Arcadia. "Do you pledge your life and allegiance to Colonel Cruikshank and the Arcadian Council?" asks Zekiel, standing at attention.

Corporal Williamson cocks his head, examining the strange boys. "Honestly, son, I have no idea what you're talking about."

"I hear words, but don't know what they're saying," says Cheung, laughing.

"It's like their little space aliens," says Williamson.

"Small pajama wearing aliens; probably rode in on one a them asteroids," says Cheung in a spooky voice.

Zekiel, Aidan, and Owen look at each other and silently nod agreement. These soldiers don't appear to know anything about New Arcadia. The boys are safe from the colonel.

"We're not aliens, but how about, take us to your leader anyway," Aidan says in a joking voice.

"Come up then. We'll take you to Captain Rogers. I'm sure she'll be very interested to meet you boys," says Williamson.

"And you other boys down there. Come up to Level Two with us," says Cheung.

"It's okay guys," says Zekiel. The boys run up the stairs to join Zekiel and the others.

"There's hot food in the registration area. You boys hungry?" asks Williamson.

The boys cry "YES!" in unison, jumping excitedly.

"Space alien pajama boys get hungry. Who woulda known?" asks Sergeant Cheung with a big smile?

Chapter 57: Bloody Bridge

Friday Dusk–Rattlesnake Canyon

The large gravel area on the south side of the bridge is crowded with cars and trucks. The latest car to arrive speeds through the congested area, weaving through cars and drives to the middle of the bridge, sending people scrambling, before skidding to a stop.

A young man in his early twenties tumbles out of the car. "It's true. This bridge goes nowhere, man," yells the chubby, blond, white boy who holds a can of beer. He takes a deep swig as he staggers a few steps.

His friend lifts himself out of the passenger seat. A tall, thin-faced, beady-eyed young man with a scraggly black beard exhales a huge cloud of smoke that wafts in the light wind. He puts the vaporizer to his lips, inhaling deeply. He exhales and a thick fog veils his head.

"I told you. It's a bridge to nowhere. Now, where's the god-damned cave?" He asks his question slowly, clouded by the fog. The smoke drifts over the bridge as his beady eyes survey the area. "Where the fuck did all these people come from? This is a goddamn secret cave."

The chubby white boy laughs. "Don't look secret to me, Simon."

Beady-Eyes points at a young woman standing on the bridge watching the young men. "Why you here? Who told you?" he asks sharply.

The chubby white boy drunkenly counts people with his fingers. "Lot a people here." Losing count, he pauses, looking at his fingers. "Lot a people man," he says as he falls back against the front fender of the auto.

The woman doesn't answer Beady-Eyes. She steps back, looking at the people she came with. Beady-Eyes walks to a teenage boy who sits on the cement curb of the bridge looking at his shoes. He bends down to face the teenager. "Who told you? How'd you know to come here?"

The boy slowly raises his head with a dull look. "Same as everyone. Some old guy said he knew about a secret cave. People followed him. We followed them."

"Shit, shit, shit," screams Beady-Eyes as he stamps his foot repeatedly.

The boy watches Beady-Eyes and his angry dance. "Who told you?" asks the boy, squinting questioningly.

Beady-Eyes stops his rant. "Not telling you."

The chubby white boy finishes his beer and throws the can at the boy on the curb. "It's a secret. Supposed to be."

Gloria and Louis are at the end of the trail on the far side of the bridge. "We tried your way. We didn't find the cave. The storms are starting. We need to find cover," Louis says.

Louis looks under the bridge to see if it offers protection. He can see people sitting under the bridge. The south side has a steep rocky path leading to a narrow cement ledge under the bridge. Below the ledge is a sheer cliff. The north side slopes gently down to the river. It doesn't offer much protection, but it's better than being in the open. Louis curses. "People have already taken the best spots to hide."

Fireballs appear high above.

Gloria watches the vapor trails, gazing at the beauty of the puffy clouds. Louis grabs Gloria's hand and pulls her onto the bridge. She protests with a small shriek but is too tired to fight.

Beady-Eyes spots two people walking toward him from the far side of the bridge. The woman looks familiar.

The chubby boy turns to see what beady-eyed Simon is looking at. "More people!" he exclaims.

Simon saunters to the bedraggled couple staring at the woman.

"Hey! Where are you going?" asks the chubby guy.

Gloria is walking too slowly. Louis yanks her hand, pulling her forward. She is about to yell at him when she spots a thin young man walking toward them. She has a flash of recognition and is energized. "Simon! You're here? Simon!" Gloria calls out. She breaks her hand free from Louis and rushes toward Simon.

Simon runs to Gloria. She holds out her hands as they greet. She takes his hands in hers and then hugs him. "Simon, it's so good to see you," Gloria says sweetly.

Louis breaks up the reunion. "Who's this?" he asks suspiciously.

"Louis. You know Simon. He's Audrey's boy. Audrey, my best friend," Gloria explains.

Louis gives a grunt of recognition. "I can't keep track of all your friends." His suspicions eased; he focuses on finding a safe place to hide from the storm.

"Simon, where's your mother? Is she in the car?" asks Gloria.

Simon's face twitches. "She won't leave the house. I told her she's gonna die, but she won't leave. You know her, damn stubborn. She told me to come here. Just Jeffery and me." Simon turns his head toward his friend, who is working on another beer. "She told me about the secret cave, but it doesn't look secret. All these people here."

Gloria scans the far side of the bridge with a surprised look, realizing there shouldn't be other people on the bridge.

"We tried to find it. There's no cave. If you want to make it through the night, you'd better find someplace else. Come on Gloria. Move it," Louis says with a scowl.

Beady-eyed, Simon sharpens his glare. "My mom and Aunt Selina talk for hours every day. She told her everything about this place. There's a hidden gate covered in brush. Behind it, there's a wooden door and an altar." Simon looks to the far side of the bridge and the trail winding around a rocky outcropping. "It's just over there around that ridge," Simon says.

Jeffery staggers to the group. "Hey! We going to that cave or what? Some people are heading back down the canyon looking for a better spot."

A group of meteors fly low across the sky. The angle of descent hints they will explode at low altitude.

Simon introduces Jeffery to Gloria and repeats what his mother told him about the cave. Louis isn't listening. He watches the space rocks, then looks across the bridge. Two cars are leaving.

A group of people gather by the old shipping container. He sees a man facing the container and motioning for the others to back up. He holds a gun. He fires. A young woman standing near the container collapses, holding her abdomen. The bullet must have broken the lock and ricocheted, hitting the woman. The container door opens. People push to get inside the rusted metal box. Children jump off the X-37 and run to the safety of the container.

They pull the door shut, leaving several adults and kids outside. A woman pounds on the metal door crying for admittance. No one helps the wounded woman lying on the ground.

Opportunities to find cover are quickly evaporating. Louis grabs Gloria, dragging her across the bridge. "I'm not standing here talking about that damned cave. Find it tomorrow. We need protection now!"

A meteor flying across the western skies breaks up. The mass bursts into a cloud of fragments, rocketing to Earth at over eight miles per second. Two large fragments slam into the rocky mountainside a half mile down Rattlesnake Canyon. The explosion throws rocks and dirt across the canyon. The force of the blast flips the cars driving down the canyon road.

Gloria pulls away. "No! Simon knows how to find it. Selina is my friend. She wouldn't lie to me or Audrey." Gloria walks to Simon and Jeffery.

Louis shakes his finger furiously. "Your friends! It's always about your damned friends. I'm trying to save us."

It takes twenty-six seconds for the air blast from the impact in the canyon to reach the bridge. The air rumbles and vibrates up the canyon wall with the sound of a heavy truck using a Jake brake. The forty-mile-per-hour hot wind buffets people on the bridge. Jeffery staggers, almost getting blown over.

"We've got to get to the cave. Let's go!" Simon yells, steadying Jeffery as they move across the bridge.

Louis moves too. He has his eye on the X-37. Gloria stands alone, momentarily unsure which direction to go. She looks to Louis, then to Simon.

Louis senses her hesitation. "You never believed in me. You never loved me. Not really. You love spending the money I make. You love the trips, the things. You love your friends. Never me," Louis yells in a sorrowful tone. He flings his arms in the air as a symbolic release and turns away.

Gloria shakes her fist. "You were never there. You were always working. You left me locked in that big house alone. All I have is my friends."

Louis ignores his wife. He has a goal. "Go with your friends. Find your cave. I'll find protection," Louis says to himself, heading for the X-37. "The space shuttle has tile shields. It's the best protection from the storm," Louis tells himself as he moves across the bridge.

Gloria runs to Simon and Jeffery. "Aunt Selina will let us in. We'll get to the gate. They'll save us," says Simon.

Gloria turns to look for Louis. He's running across the bridge. She wipes a false tear from her cheek. Simon, Jeffery, and Gloria run to the end of the bridge and traverse the trail along the steep, rocky cliff.

Louis reaches the end of the bridge and walks confidently past cars with people hiding in them. "Good luck with that, suckers," he says to himself, knowing cars will offer no protection. The thought enters his mind that he should tell them they will die. "There's no time to help stupid people." The woman who banged on the container door sits on the ground sobbing. A few feet away, the young woman who was shot lies on the ground in a sticky pool of blood. Louis moves to the X-37.

He runs his hand over the tiled exterior. Tiles that will save him. He sees scars of previous impacts. It works! He drops to his knees, looking up under the edge of the spacecraft. Carlos crawls under and stands, then checks the doors of the truck hidden beneath the spacecraft, but they are locked. He puts his hand on the driver's side window, feeling the cool glass. Then he ducks back under the shell and dashes to the edge of the parking area, where he finds a big rock.

He runs back, ducks under the shell, and pounds the rock against the window. There isn't much room, so it's hard to get enough velocity or force to do much damage. He pounds and pounds until the window cracks. He pounds again. The glass does not shatter.

There is a layer of laminated plastic inside the window. He uses his fingers to pull broken pieces of glass away. He pounds and pulls at the pieces of glass. His fingers bleed. Slowly, he breaks through the plastic barrier, pushing through pieces of glass on the other side. He sticks his hand through a tight hole, stretching the plastic to the width of his forearm. His fingers move along the door panel, stretching the broken window, seeking the lock button. He pushes the button and the doors of the truck unlock. He pulls his arm out carefully, opens the door, and climbs into the driver's seat.

Simon leads the way along the trail, followed closely by Gloria. Jeffery stumbles and tosses an empty beer can down the rocky cliff.

Simon rounds the outcropping and approaches the narrow alcove. He calls back to his friend. "Hurry Jeffery. The gate should be over here in these bushes. Help me look!"

Gloria looks at the bushes and small trees in the recess tucked behind the rocky outcropping. "Louis and I walked past this spot."

Simon pushes through the bushes in the fading light, searching for the gate. He fumbles through foliage along the rock face at the rear of the thicket when his fingers meet the weathered galvanized wire mesh of a chain-link fence.

"I've found it. I found the gate!" he cries out excitedly, shaking the wire fence vigorously.

Gloria crosses her chest, whispering a prayer. Jeffery runs up the slope of the alcove, pushing past the bushes to join Simon at the gate. "It's locked. Help me. Maybe we can pull it down," Simon says. Jeffery and Simon push and pull the gate.

Uncle Rob, the kids, the grandmas, and the men sit at the long dining tables. Courtney, Isabella, and Margot place large bowls and platters of food on the tables. Selina stands in front of the windows watching the scene play out on the bridge.

Rob looks at the anxious faces around the table. "I don't say my prayers often, so I might not do this right. I just want to say that I'm very thankful to have all of you here. I wish we could help everyone. I'm sorry, that's not possible. I pray for the souls of those outside. I never expected people to find their way here; not like this. I pray the storms will pass quickly, so our young people can live full and fruitful lives. I pray we live together in harmony, helping and supporting one another through this terrible time. Thanks to the ladies for preparing this food. Amen."

The men, women and children pass platters and bowls of food filling their plates. Selina turns to the table, angrily waving her arms. "Eat. Enjoy. People will die out there. What about them? What about my friends?"

The windows show Gloria and two young men walking up the trail toward the cave entrance. "Gloria. She came back. Where's Louis?" The display cycles to the next camera. Selina waits anxiously. Everyone eats quickly during the calm moment.

"Selina, come and eat. Don't watch. It's upsetting you," Eddie says to his wife.

Selina doesn't answer. Instead, she stands in front of the windows with her hands on her hips. The camera cycles to a view over the mine's entrance. It is getting dark. The camera switches to the infrared mode. The image becomes bright gray. A young man is pushing and pulling the fenced gate.

Selina gasps. "It's Simon. Audrey's boy. She must have told him." Selina smiles proudly as she waits for the cameras to cycle again. "Simon, you helped Gloria."

Selina looks at Eddie. "They made it. They're at the gate. Nobody is with them. It's dark. No one will see if we let them in," Selina pleads. Eddie stares blankly back. "Don't just sit there! We can save them. Open the gate. We have to do something!"

The camera cycles. Simon and another young man are pulling on the gate, trying to force it open. Gloria stands behind them.

Edgar pushes his plate forward, stands and steps away from the table. "I'll cut my portion in half. I'll sleep on the floor. I'll do whatever we need. We can make room for a few more."

"Sit down, Edgar. We already decided. Think of our children," Inez shouts.

"I am thinking of our children. We must set the example and show them what's right. What kind of world will they build after the storms destroy this one? We must open our hearts. It's not about Selina or her friends. It's about being human."

Selina's sister, Margot, stands pulling her husband, George, with her. "Edgar is right. I don't like Selina's friends. Sorry, sweetie." Margot smiles innocently at her sister. "But it's not about this friend or that. We're human. We must sacrifice to help others. It's what we must do."

Courtney stands abruptly. "I agree. I know we talked about this, but we can't leave those people out there. I know we can't save everyone, but I won't leave them out there to die." Courtney clasps her hands in front of her, almost shaking.

Rob moves to his desk, checks his screens, and then turns to the group, looking at each one slowly. "The hideaway is not a democracy. You must not expect a committee or popular vote to make every decision. There will be terrible and difficult times ahead. I will make tough decisions without a vote. However, in this case, I will ask for a show of hands. Everyone's vote counts, even you kids. Your decision affects everyone's life in the hideaway. So, let's vote. Raise a hand if you agree to open the gate and allow these three people to join us."

Many hands shoot up. Isabella and Rodrigo are the last to raise their hands after seeing the decision will be unanimous with their votes.

Rob nods to Eddie. "All right. We'll make it work, somehow. Eddie, let's get the blast door open and welcome our new occupants." Rob presses icons on his screen and Eddie makes his way down the tunnel to the blast door.

The land jolts and shakes from great earthquakes. The rising moon is blood red. Hundreds of asteroids penetrate the atmosphere each minute, causing mountains to shake and tumble. The sky becomes a dark billowy blanket. Humans scramble like cockroaches into every hole, sewer, and culvert. Many people wander in despair, waiting for heaven to fall upon them.

Louis laughs. He uses the light beam on his band to scan the dark interior of the Suburban hidden under the X-37. Incredibly, he has the space to himself. He pounds the steering wheel and laughs. He thinks of Gloria and his pounding slows. He feels the pain of a tear forming, but shakes it off.

"Bitch. If she'd listened, she would be safe here with me. She chose her friends. Her friends, always her friends. If only she believed in me—" A door opens at the rear of the truck, banging against the shell of the spacecraft. Louis shines his light at the sound. A young boy stands in the cargo area. Behind him, a young girl climbs into the truck.

The boy hides his eyes from the light. Louis moves the beam. The interior of the truck is dimly lit by reflected light.

"Hi," says the boy to the man behind the light.

435

"Is that your sister?" Louis asks.

The boy turns to look. "Yeah," the boy replies flatly.

"Just you two? Is anybody else coming? Not much room in here, ya know."

The truck shakes from the force of nearby impacts. The boy steadies himself, shaking his head sideways.

"There's two ladies out there. I think they're dead. People are hiding in cars," the little girl says in a soft voice.

"Where're your parents?"

"I saw them, and our sisters run into that container," says the boy.

"We were playing," the girl adds.

"The door closed, so we hid under the UFO until we heard you open the door," the boy explains.

"Close that door," Louis says sharply, pointing to the rear door. The truck rocks from an air blast. The sound of hundreds of small rocky impacts accompanies the hot wind. The sound is like hundreds of metal ball bearings dropping into a tin bucket. Louis holds on to the truck seat, anxiously listening to the impacts, then chuckles. "Hear that? Ha-ha. This UFO just saved our lives. Get comfortable. It's gonna be a rough night."

Louis and the kids cannot see outside. They can't see blown-out car windows. They can't see autos perforated with vicious holes. They can't see the few survivors scurrying from hiding places and staggering in the darkness. They can't see hundreds of holes puncturing the sides and top of the old container. They can't see blood swelling out from under the container door. A door that does not open.

***

Simon and Jeffery push and pull the cyclone fence as hard as they can. The builders carved the face of the granite mountainside to fit two metal posts buried deep in cement on each side to hold the fence in place. The gate is eight feet wide and ten feet high, covering the entrance to the cave. "The gate is so close to the mountainside, there's less than an inch of clearance on the sides," observes Jeffery.

"It's too strong. We won't shake this gate loose," Simon says, with his fingers wrapped through the cyclone wire. He shakes the gate again in frustration. "Argh! The damn thing won't budge. Goddamnit."

Jeffery examines the chain-link fence. "I would have brought wire cutters if you told me we'd need to break in."

"I'm supposed to think of everything. I got us here. How did I know they'd lock us out?" Simon reaches in his pocket for his vape, puts it to his lips and draws deeply.

The ground shakes violently. Small rocks and dirt cascade down the steep mountain face. Gloria pulls herself close to the fence. "My friend Selina is in there. I'm sure of it." She looks up at the darkness of the mountain crying out, "Selina! Selina! We're here. Let us in."

Simon exhales and a cloud of smoke shrouds Jeffery. "Nothing like an asteroid storm to ruin a guy's buzz." Jeffery waves the smoke away. "Simon, I'll climb to the top and pull the fencing. Maybe I can stretch it and make a gap big enough for your skinny ass to slip through. Once you're in, find the doorbell or whatever and get whoever's inside to let us in."

Jeffery climbs the fence using the holes in the wire mesh as footholds. "I'll boost you up," Simon says as he pushes Jeffery's butt with both hands. Jeffery reaches the top and starts yanking and tugging, trying to bend the wire mesh.

"Use your weight, Jeffery," Simon advises.

"What the fuck you think I'm doing?" Jeffery replies, huffing and pulling.

Gloria watches with anticipation as thunder echoes in the sky and meteor impacts roar. The air is dusty. Gloria coughs on the dry air. "I wish I had my silk scarf to cover my face. It's Hermes's."

Jeffery pulls at the top of the cyclone fence, bending the weaved galvanized wire out of shape. "It's working. I made a gap. I think you can get through," Jeffery says to Simon. "Climb up next to me."

Simon climbs the ten-foot-high fence hanging at the top next to his friend. "Help me yank on this," Jeffery says, and they pull the fencing together a few times, making the gap larger.

"I don't know," says Simon.

"You can make it. I'll tuck my head low. Climb over my shoulders to get at an angle and squirm through."

Rodrigo runs down the tunnel to help Eddie with the blast door. Eddie turns the wheel to release the bolts. Then Eddie pushes the heavy door. Rob stops the camera rotation. The window image stays locked on the scene at the exterior gate. Selina watches with excitement. Jeffery and Simon are on the fence, pulling the wire mesh.

"They're trying to pull the fence down, Uncle Rob," Ethan calls out.

"I don't think that will work. Don't worry. Eddie and Rodrigo will get to them in a minute," Rob says calmly.

Simon gets as high as he can, straddling his bulky friend. "OK. Hang on tight. Here I go," Simon says as he dives headfirst with his arms extended, hoping to glide through the slender gap. His head and shoulders make it through, but he gets stuck at his waist. Simon hangs jackknifed over the gate.

"I'm stuck. Get higher. Help me raise my legs," Simon says, gasping for breath.

Jeffery's fingers are racked with pain from gripping the wire fencing. He wills himself to hold on. He climbs higher, pressing his shoulders up to help Simon slip through the gap in the fence.

"You almost have it! You're almost in!" shouts Gloria.

A meteor explodes high over the canyon, sending millions of bits of molten fragments into the canyon walls and riverbed below. Not one square inch of the canyon is spared from the jabbing invaders. A volley of hot spherules thrusts through Gloria's flesh and zips through Jeffery and Simon, continuing through the wooden door. The statue of Mother Mary, in the altar, shatters. Several of the rocky bits strike the thick metal blast door.

Rodrigo and Eddie hear the plink, plink, plink of the impacts, and pull the door closed. Women and children scream in the main gallery. The blast door closes with a loud metallic thunk. Eddie turns the wheel, setting the bolts. Rodrigo and Eddie rush to the main gallery. Everyone is crying.

They stand viewing the windows. Jeffery's body falls heavily to the ground, landing on Gloria. Simon's body hangs upside down before limply slipping through the hole falling headfirst to the rocky ground inside the gate. Three bodies lay at the gate, displayed in the eerie green-gray light of the night vision camera.

Selina drops to the floor, crying. Rob slumps to his desk chair in shock. He presses an icon to start the camera sequence. Allyssa can't take the horror of the scene outside or the overwhelming grief inside. She runs past the galley, down the mine shaft to the lower level.

It's strangely quiet inside the old Suburban. The constant thunderous rumblings fall silent. Louis flashes his beam at the children. They stare forward mouths open listening for something to hear.

"That last one was a big one. Tonight's storm is worse than last night and it's still early. Enjoy the silence while it lasts. There's more to come for sure. At least we're safe in here," Louis tells the children. "You kids picked the right place to hide. Tiles cover the exterior of this space shuttle to protect it from space rocks. Those tiles will save us."

The tiles on the X-37B are called Whipple shields, invented by Fred Whipple. They are hypervelocity impact shields designed to protect spacecraft from collisions with micrometeoroids. When a shield is hit by space debris, the impacting rock is completely disintegrated on impact, leaving a deep dent in the layered shield. The tiles are not designed to take repetitive impacts. Each impact causes damage to the tiles. The shock of an impact stresses adjacent tiles, loosening them and causing cracks. The shields were not designed protect the shuttle from larger fast-moving meteorites.

A loud snap shocks the air, breaking the silence. Seconds later, the spacecraft-mounted Suburban dips to one side, resisting an air blast. The air blast passes and the craft steadies. Louis takes a breath. The sound of distant rumbling rolls up the canyon.

"You're the man who said there's a secret cave. I heard you talking. I told my dad. That's why we followed you," the young boy says. His sister nods agreement.

Louis nods slightly. "Oh?"

"Why aren't you in the cave?" asks the young girl.

"Cuz, you told too many people. It isn't a secret anymore," the boy scolds his sister.

"I did not! You did!"

"The cave is so secret. I couldn't find it. My wife and her friends are searching for it," Louis explains to quiet the siblings.

A meteor violently explodes above the San Gabriel Mountains less than a mile downstream from the Bridge to Nowhere. The explosion propels large fragments at speeds of seven miles per second.

"I'm glad you let us in here. It's kinda like a cave," the young girl says.

"Yeah. It's like a fort," says the boy.

Hard rain drums as meteor fragments pummel the bridge, autos, the container, and the X-37. "Hang on, kids," Louis shouts over the commotion.

A meteorite three inches in diameter hits a cracked tile and penetrates the X-37. The meteorite passes through the Suburban smashing into the granite bedrock under the truck.

The force shock created by the meteorite passing through the Suburban is instantly followed by the reactive force from the impact with the bedrock. The tremendous energy splits the X-37 in half, killing its occupants.

Ten seconds later, a tremendous air blast rips up the canyon at six hundred miles per hour flipping autos in the parking area and flinging them to the river one hundred feet below. The two halves of the X-37 are tossed high against the mountainside and tumble back to the ground. The hundred-year-old bridge is rocked by the air blast.

The south end of the bridge falls to the cement ledge, crushing the people who found refuge there. One of the bridge supports is severed. The bridge shakes and twists. Simon's auto crashes through the cement guard rail smashing on the rocks below. The bridge holds. It leans to one side, sags in the middle, and the south side rests on the ledge six feet lower than the road, but the tough old bridge stands.

Rob watches the impact rip his trusty old X-37 in half. His knees buckle when he sees autos being flung over the cliff and the sturdy old bridge lose its footing. Rob turns the windows off.

Chapter 58: Curtis' Bunker

Henderson, Nevada - Friday Night

The meteor storm rages fiercely above Curtis' bunker. The sound of rumbling thunder and shaking matches the somber mood.

Jin wouldn't leave Becky's side. Rick and Curtis had to convince him to let them remove the meteorite from his shoulder. Curtis projected streams of bullet removal surgeries and suturing to Rick as he did his best to act like a surgeon. After they stitched up Jin, Curtis gave him a tincture of specially formulated THC oil. A few drops under the tongue once an hour eases his pain.

Jin sits at Becky's side, holding her hand. He can't bear to pull himself away. Curtis sits at his desk in front of a thin screen covered wall in his cushy executive chair. He spins around to face Jin.

"Don't worry about the rumbling. We've got twenty feet of cement reinforced with re-bar above and all around us. We're safe unless we get a direct hit like Baltimore. If that happens, we're all toast."

Jin doesn't respond.

"I feel safe for the first time in days. Thanks, Curtis," Rick says.

Curtis smiles awkwardly.

The Colony-Revolution Coup stream plays in a window on the thin screen. "Can you turn up the audio on the game?" asks Rick. "Let's see how they did."

Ceylon Junglefoul and Torpedo stand in front of several trophies. "We've witnessed incredible game play today, overcoming unexpected obstacles and challenges. The players and teams did a fantastic job," announces Junglefoul.

"That's right! I've never seen a new game live up to the hype, but Colony-Revolution Coup really rocked our socks. There was loads of hackin' a cracklin' all day. An' there were surprises, weren't there? It looked like Lucid Gaze had the upper hand until those Elf butt boys turned the game on its head. They did."

"That's right, Torpedo. It was Team Elk Bucks who set the tone late in the game with a unique strategy to defeat the cities. Other teams followed suit using Elk Buck tactics to gain control of most cities, allowing hundreds of thousands of ants to flood the colonies of Nod, New Zion, Ambrosia, and Empyrean. The strange standoff at Edendale continues," reports Ceylon.

"I reckon nary an ant got into that colony," says Torpedo

"There was strong resistance at New Arcadia, but even there, ten thousand ants accessed the upper levels," Ceylon continues.

"Colonies were defeated, and the count is in. The team that crackled their way to victory with the highest percentage of ants in their colony is Team Elk Bucks! Said it right, didn't I, mate? Always new surprises! Get up here, boys!" shouts Torpedo.

The Steve Jobs wannabe and his teammates run up to accept the grand prize as electronic confetti and recorded applause fill the stream. Ceylon and Torpedo stand on either side of the grinning gamers and hand the team a big check and a huge trophy.

"Congratulations, Elk Bucks! That concludes the first Colony-Revolution Coup tournament. Watch for more exciting game streams right here. I'm Ceylon Junglefoul, your lively host along with—"

"Torpedo, KA-BOOM!"

"We'll see you right here, next time, for more exciting game streams."

Curtis salutes the screen with his Gulp cup. "We made a great team," he says in a sorrowful tone.

Jin lifts his head slowly. "Becky would be pleased. We saved hundreds of thousands of lives today. She'd be happy to know we helped save so many souls."

Aman appears in a window on the screen. He immediately starts talking rapidly. "Hello. I hope it's an OK time for a quick call. Not too late, is it? You can call me any seven days. I am so sorry to hear the news. Such terrible, terrible news. My deepest and most sincere condolences for our dear Becky. So, so sorry. Oh my, it's a tragedy. And Jin, sorry to hear of your injury. I hope you are feeling better already. But Jin, Curtis, and Rick, you are safe. So happy you are safe. And that jet. Oh, wow! What an escape! Oh my! So daring.

Very fortunate indeed. It's like that movie, Wingmen of the Four Wars. Did you see that one?"

No one in the bunker responds to Aman's quick rant. "Oh, maybe too soon for movie talk. My cousins and my entire staff are so sad to hear the news of Becky's passing. So sorry. But you guys are safe. Yes, yes. So happy you're safe."

"We wouldn't have made it without you, Aman. Thanks to you and your team for the help," says Rick.

"Find a safe place and keep your head down till the storms are over," says Curtis.

"We will. We're moving to a sub-basement in my cousin's building. It's a good spot. A good, good spot. The storms are getting worse. It's a worldwide disaster. Terrible, truly terrible. We'll keep in touch as long as the trans-ocean fiber optic network stays up. Call anytime, any seven days, twenty-four-seven."

"If we lose the network, you can try to reach me over ham radio. My call sign is N7CPZ. We can use satellites to link up. I'll be on unless the satellites go down or my antenna gets blasted."

"Great idea Curt-tis. I don't have a radio, but we'll try to get one. Be safe, friends."

"Take care, Aman," Rick and Curtis say in unison. Aman waves. The screen goes blank.

Rick walks to the bunker's kitchen and back. "I hate to say this under the circumstances, but I'll be heading out in the morning. You guys can come with me. My Uncles mine has more room than this bunker."

Curtis looks at Jin. Jin stares at Becky's body and shakes his head.

"Thanks for the offer. Jin and I will stay here," says Curtis.

"We understand. You're so close. You need to get to your family," Jin says.

"I can help you with Becky before I go."

"No, I'll take care of her," says Jin.

"We'll take care of her. You can take the Vette. I prepped it earlier today. It'll get you home fast," says Curtis.

"Thanks, Curtis. Are you sure? That Vette is vintage. It's beautiful."

"I've only driven it a couple of times." Curtis looks at Jin. "I don't need it anymore. It's all yours."

Mike McCoy

"Curtis, where's your toilet?" Jin asks.

"Turn left at the end of the bunker. First door on the right. Are you all right to walk?"

"I'm good."

Jin walks to the end of the bunker, which is a large aluminum tube buried in cement, connected to another long tube. Once in the bathroom, he stares blankly at the mirror, viewing his dismal image before splashing water onto his tear-streaked face. Gritty dust makes tears hard to wash away.

Jin explores his pockets, still stuffed with pastries from the Fairchild Express store. He pulls out the cellophane-wrapped Twinkie. It's nearly flattened, cream filling smears the inside of the wrapping. "Beck, you crushed my Twinkie. Now I'm crushed. Oh, Becky. What will I do without you?" New tears flow.

Chapter 59: Launch

Slingeren Launch Complex-Saturday Morning 4:00 AM

Dr. Simmons stands at a large window in Mission Control sipping coffee as he watches three SLS Block 1B rockets creep out of their protective hangers. The three hundred eighty-four-foot-tall rockets stand vertically on crawler assemblies, moving slowly to their launch pads.

"They're magnificent, aren't they," remarks Jeff Duffy, Harpoon Mission Director. Jeff Duffy is a tall, middle-aged, Midwesterner wearing a blue polo shirt with a Slingeren Launch Facility logo.

"This is a monumental morning. What happens here today determines the future of Earth, Duff," says Dr. Simmons.

"I never imagined Harpoon would become so important."

"I'm just thankful your team did such a good job. You will save the world, Duff. The simulations look good for full disruption. All the pieces have come together nicely. How are we looking for launch?"

"We launch at six A.M."

The SLS rockets are now at their launch pads. Jeff Duffy announces, "Ninety minutes to launch."

Dr. Simmons listens to voices in his VUE as they call out pre-launch procedures. "Loading liquid oxygen." "Start fueling rocket propellent-1." "Pressurant loading." "Commencing system checks."

"The air conditioning system is being connected to the payload fairing. It will maintain environmental control through liftoff, keeping your Harpoons nice and comfy," says Duffy.

Lights mounted on lightning protection towers illuminate the rockets. The tall white rockets gleam brightly in the darkness.

Dr. Simmons studies the control room. This is unlike any control room he's seen before. Historically, mission control centers were huge rooms with several tiers filled with hundreds of computers and personnel arranged in front of wall-sized displays. The early SLS launches were crewed by a team of ninety people in the firing room and another sixty in the support room. Over the past two decades, rocket launches have become commonplace, and systems have become highly integrated. Today, at Slingeren, a handful of personnel will manage the launch.

The control room at Slingeren is a forty by sixty-foot room. It looks like a typical corporate conference room minus the conference table. A thin screen covers one wall, displaying mission and systems status. A black-and-white photograph of Houston Mission Control from 1969 covers the opposite wall.

A team of six mission specialists control each SLS rocket. They sit in high-backed reclining chairs. They wear specialized ultra-wide field of view, VUE lenses. Multiple graphic interfaces and control surfaces appear in their lens.

"Coming up on T minus six minutes, team," announces Duff. The transporter-erector strongback retracts.

Dr. Simmons hears voices in his VUE. "Final pre-launch flight termination status confirmed. C-Band transponder, S-Band receiver, GPS receiver, and telemetry transmitters all activated and confirmed."

Duff checks with each of his mission specialists, then checks in with Dr. Simmons. "Simmons, have you ever been the payload manager on a launch?"

"First time, but my team and I are ready." The payload: three Harpoons, are his team's responsibility.

"Sorry, there's not much for you and your team to do now, but watch. You'll get your turn later."

"I wouldn't miss it. I can see the launch is in good hands."

"Thanks for your confidence. We're 100% green. Good for launch. T minus two minutes thirty to launch," Duff announces.

The room hums with the low murmur of the launch control staff talking to their VUE lenses. Dr. Simmons can see and hear the dialog through his VUE. "Range verification, check. Helium Load terminated. Engine chill-down, Bleeders open. Flight computer up."

The screen on the wall shows the pad decks being flooded with water. "EUS-flight pressure, Interstage-flight pressure, Core stage-flight pressure, all tanks flight pressure, Pyrotechnics armed."

At T minus ten seconds, "Go for Main Engine Start." At T minus six seconds, "RS-25 ignition, LIFTOFF." The four RS-25 engines on each rocket start in a 1-3-4-2 sequence.

Dr. Simmons watches excitedly as the four-liquid fueled RS-25 core stage engines and two solid-fuel rocket boosters fire on each rocket. The rockets are held to Earth momentarily by hydraulic clamps while flight computers evaluate engine ignition and full-power performance. At T minus zero, the hydraulic release system is activated and three SLS rockets rise from their launch pads. There are no cheers of excitement, clapping or back slapping praise as the rocket's speed to the heavens.

Cameras follow the ascent of the rockets. After two minutes of powered flight, the cameras capture the separation of the booster rockets from the core rocket. During the next minutes of flight, spacecraft adapters and the launch abort system are jettisoned. At thirty minutes after lift-off and after several stages of separations and engine firings, each spacecraft has attained the proper height, speed, and attitude to reach JZ966. The Harpoon systems are on their way.

Dr. Simmons sends a message to the president advising him of the successful launches. It is five hours until the Harpoons will impact Asteroid JZ966, Dr. Simmons and the mission team settle in for the long wait.

Chapter 60: Ticket to Ride

Saturday Morning
Henderson Nevada–7:00 AM

Curtis rose early to prepare breakfast in the bunker's kitchenette. Expecting the trio's arrival, he stocked up on food deliveries. Curtis has breakfast plates on his long desk when Rick stumbles into the main room.

"Wow, this looks wonderful, Curtis."

Curtis brushes off the compliment. "I hope it's all right. It's been a long time since I cooked for anyone. It surprised me I could still order fresh eggs, bacon, croissants and orange juice." Curtis doesn't mention he paid triple the normal price.

"Compared to what I've eaten the last few days, this could be the Ritz-Carlton," Rick says ecstatically.

Jin steps into the main room. He brushes his hand slowly over the blanket covering Becky as he passes the dining area.

"Hey buddy. Just in time for breakfast," Rick says.

"Not hungry," Jin mumbles.

Curtis rushes to Jin, leading him to sit in his executive chair. He moves a plate of food in front of Jin.

"Jin. Eat. You've got a nasty wound. You need to get your strength back."

"Thanks for patching me up, Curtman. I'll be fine."

Rick studies Jin. "Your body will heal quickly. It will take more time for the wound to your heart. I can only imagine how I'd feel if…," Rick's voice trails off.

"You need to get to your family. They must be sick with worry," says Jin.

"It's normally a five-hour drive. The Vette will get you there faster. Traffic data is not updating on my map, so I can't tell you what the roads are like," says Curtis.

They finish breakfast, then move to the garage. Curtis moves quickly up the narrow stairs. Rick and Jin follow. Curtis steps through the metal door to find the garage half destroyed. The storm has torn off sizable portions of the roof. Attic insulation, wood, and debris are strewn everywhere.

"I always thought a skylight would be a nice touch. Not quite this big, though." Curtis says, surveying the missing roof.

"It really brightens up the room," Rick says.

Curtis looks to the rear of the garage and instantly grieves. "Oh, damn. My baby." Curtis steps through the mess on the garage floor to check his high-pressure extractor. "Ah geez, the compression chambers are crushed, and the monitor is cracked. Oh man, it's ruined. This is bad." Curtis picks through broken parts, mourning the destruction of his custom designed extractor.

He looks to the glass enclosure containing his inventory of THC extracts. "Everything is smashed" Jars and vials of extracted oils drip to the floor. "My work is ruined. Luckily, I stored a bunch of stock in the bunker."

"Sorry about your equipment and the extracts. The storms are destroying everything," says Rick.

Curtis looks at his broken extractor. "It was giving me problems. I was going to tear it down, anyway. Maybe I can rebuild it."

Jin uses his good arm to pull insulation and wood off the Corvette. "We have another problem here. Meteorites have punctured the hood, ooh, in several places."

Rick kneels to peer under the car. "There's a pool of oil on the floor." Rick stands. "This Vette isn't going anywhere."

"How about the Harley's? Check the bikes. A bike might be better, anyway," says Curtis.

"The bikes have tipped over on each other. I'll get the wood and dry wall off them." Rick says. Once the debris is cleared, he lifts the top bike and sets the kick stand. "This one's dead. There's a hole going through the fuel cell chamber."

Jin tries to lift the second bike but struggles with the weight. Rick helps him. "I can get it," Jin says. As they lift the bike, the damage is obvious. "The handlebar of the other bike crushed the battery compartment and smashed the ultra-capacitor. This bike is finished too," says Jin.

Curtis leans down to examine the damage. "I think I can fix this. We can swap parts from the other bike. Might take a few hours. We can do this."

Rick pushes more debris aside to uncover the antique Indian Motorcycle. He stands the bike up. The clutch is twisted out of position. Rick easily pushes it back. He looks the bike over. "This bike is a classic. It looks to be in decent shape. How about this one?" Rick asks, testing out the handlebars.

Curtis gulps. "That one? That's my dad's. It's a 1950 Indian Scout 440."

Rick gives the bike a once over. "It's old, but it's in great shape. You've really taken great care of it."

Jin lifts his good arm over Curtis's shoulder. "Ole Walter wouldn't mind. He'd want to help Rick get home to his family. Don't you think?"

Curtis steels himself. "Oh, man." Curtis stalls. "I know. It's just, it's the only thing I have of my dad's. It was his favorite. I've kept it in the same condition all these years. It's like he's here, with me—"

"Hey, Curtis, I understand. I wouldn't think of asking you to let go of something that means so much to you. I'll find a car. Heck, if I hadn't broken the TX, I would fly home."

"No! No! Hold on. I've got a container of fresh gasoline in the compressor room." Curtis hustles through the mess in his garage.

Rick and Jin clear debris from around the old Indian motorcycle.

Curtis returns with the fuel. "Jin's right. My dad would have insisted you ride the Scout. Let's fill up the tank and get you on your way."

Curtis opens the fuel canister, then asks, "Rick, can you fill the tank? I need to get something."

"Sure. I really appreciate this, Curtis."

Jin clears debris so he can raise the garage door.

Curtis scurries through the debris as quickly as his big frame allows. He pulls open the door to the house and shouts. "Oh Boy! Another skylight in the kitchen."

"Hopefully, this works. Open Garage." Jin commands the garage to open. The door is bent from wind blasts. It stutters as it rises, causing the motor to grind loudly. Jin uses his good arm to push the door past the rough spots.

Curtis returns to the garage loaded with gear. "You need a helmet. This is a Bell Bullitt Retro with a full-face guard. Looks bad!" Curtis says, handing the helmet to Rick. "I got it for when I was gonna ride. And you need a jacket. It gets colder than you think while riding, even in the desert," Curtis explains as he dumps a jacket into Rick's arms.

"Thanks, Curtis."

Rick pulls the jacket on. "How does it look?"

"It's classic. You look like a European military officer from the Second World War," Jin remarks.

Curtis checks the fit on Rick. "It's called a Duster. It's a hundred percent leather. It fits you just right. I bought it when I was on a diet. I was sure it would fit me one day. Oh well. It's yours now."

Rick pulls the helmet over his head and poses for his friends.

"Wow! You look badass," says Jin.

Curtis disappears into the house again.

A few moments later, he reappears carrying a pistol grip compact shotgun and several bags and boxes. "I know you have that dart gun from New Zion. Take this just in case you need something more powerful in the real world. It could get dangerous out there."

Jin gasps. "What is it?"

"It's a Mossberg 500 Chainsaw six-shot pump-action shotgun. Take it, just in case." The Mossberg 500 has an unusual feature. It has a large handle mounted on the fore end.

"You pull this handle to load a shotgun shell," Curtis says, as he pulls the handle.

Rick eyes the weapon. "I'm not sure I'll need it. What's with the neon green ZMB logo?"

"Oh, it's the Zombie killer edition," Curtis says, with an embarrassed laugh.

Curtis hands the weapon to Rick. "It's got a nice heft to it. Zombies, huh? Well, you never know what I'll find out there. Thanks, Curtis. Are you sure? This is too much."

"It's… it's just stuff. I love my stuff, but stuff means nothing compared to friends and family."

Rick loads the shotgun with slugs and holsters it to the side of the Indian Scout. "I put a box of shells, bottled water, and a first aid kit in the saddlebags for you," says Curtis. Rick pulls his backpack on over the jacket and cinches down the straps.

Jin steps to Rick with his hand extended. "Thanks for getting us to Curtis. We couldn't have made it without you."

Rick pulls Jin close, giving him a big hug, then hugs Curtis. Last-minute goodbyes are said, and tears shed.

Rick mounts the Indian Scout and kick starts the bike, bringing the twin four stroke 440 CC engine roaring to life. He twists the throttle, revving the engine, puts it in gear, and slowly pulls out of the garage. As he rides onto Parawan Street, he holds up his left hand, waving a last goodbye.

Chapter 61: All Broke Up

Saturday Morning

Level Three–Army bunker below New Arcadia 9:00 AM

The pack of pajama boys was a quite a surprise for Captain Rogers. She contacted General Mahon immediately when she learned the boys were from the city below. The hour was late, so army personnel fed the boys, gave them clothes and sleeping accommodations.

Now the ten boys from Gymnasium sit at a large conference table with General Mahon, Captain Rogers, and the general's staff.

"Captain Rogers briefed me on your experience in New Arcadia and your harrowing escape. What Colonel Cruikshank put you boys through is unthinkable. Despicable. I did not know the man was capable of such evil. Let me affirm you are safe here," says General Mahon.

"We couldn't stay there and let that old bastard steal our youth. We had to get out," says Zekiel.

"Cruikshank won't hurt any of you again. We've confirmed your report. Cruikshank has sealed the city. Captain Rogers, do we have any other news from the city?" asks Mahon.

"New Arcadia cut our access city systems yesterday, shortly after we allowed access to Level Two," Rogers reports.

"Zsoldos must have figured it was us and not the hackers that opened Level Two to the survivors. I wonder if the colonel knows you boys are missing. I'm sure it would upset him to learn his fountain of youth left the city. You boys want to have some fun with the old colonel?"

"Yes," the boy's answer.

"OK… shh. Don't say anything. Let's see how old Cruikshank is holding up," says Mahon.

A call is placed to the colonel.

453

"Colonel Cruikshank, I may have some difficulty making it to the council meeting this afternoon. We are busy with survivors from the Parklands," the general says coyly.

Cruikshank huffs. "Your presence is no longer required, Mahon."

"I beg your pardon. I am a founding member of the Arcadian Council. The first meeting of the full council is taking place this afternoon. As a founding member I—"

"I have revoked your position on the council."

"I see. Does this have anything to do with the reports I'm receiving about elevator and stairwell doors being welded shut?"

"You failed to protect New Arcadia. Thousands of topsiders invaded Levels One and Two. I know you gave them access. You are a coward. I cannot risk any of your survivors entering New Arcadia. I ordered the city sealed. We have welded shut every access and entry point. I will not allow your incompetence to pervert the Arcadian ideal and our grand effort to reform humanity."

"Pervert, what an interesting choice of words, Colonel. Now that you've sealed yourself into your farcical idea of a utopian city. I suppose you won't miss your harem of boys, will you?" The general makes a hand gesture. A camera focuses on some boys from Gymnasium.

Colonel Cruikshank reacts with a wide-eyed gasp but recovers, attempting not to display his shock.

Zekiel stands shaking a fist. "Let's see how long you last without us, you wrinkly old creep."

Cruikshank chuckles. "Ah, the feisty one. That makes sense. I allowed myself to believe you would gain an appreciation of your service to Arcadia. It's clear I was mistaken. I should have bled you dry."

"I pledge my life to defeat you and Arcadia. You will become weak as we will grow strong. We're coming for you, old man. I'll fight you myself one day if you survive," Zekiel swears.

Colonel Cruikshank scowls at the image of the feisty boy.

"Colonel Cruikshank, you've made a new enemy today. I renounce the Army's allegiance to Arcadia. My next call will be to President Baker. New Arcadia, your promise for the future is now your prison," the general ends the call.

Slingeren Mission Control-10:00 A.M. EST

Dr. Simmons stands in front of a large screen. He views his reflection and straightens the collar of his sport jacket. His long hair is combed. He is ready to give a mission briefing to President Baker. This is a proud moment for Dr. Simmons. He has almost single-handedly brought JPL back to life. Three Harpoon HAIVs are on course and all systems are nominal. He is confident that Harpoon will be a success. Not only has he saved JPL, but he is also saving the planet.

The image of a large room with President Baker, Tug Grimes, Mitch Campbell, Jerome Hargrove, and several others sitting at a conference table fills the screen. "Simmons. We received news of the successful launch this morning. Based on your attire and that big smile, I trust all is going well," says President Baker.

"Yes, Mr. President. The mission is proceeding as planned. Impact will occur in two hours. The impactor booms are extended, and we have enabled on-board targeting. From this point until impact, the Harpoons are running autonomously. They will self-adjust for any minor changes needed to hit each target site. We are sending images from the tracking simulators to your screens. We have live images of JZ966 from a space-based telescope and we also have monitoring from land-based telescopes. You'll be able to view the disruption of the Beast in real time as the nuclear devices detonate."

Screens in the Camp David conference room display a simulation of the Harpoons moving toward JZ966. Another screen displays a black-and-white image of the oblong gray asteroid.

"This is extraordinary, Dr. Simmons. We'll be able to watch the Harpoons destroy the Beast and save the world. Splendid work, Simmons," exclaims President Baker.

Dr. Simmons beams, absorbing the praise.

Jerome Hargrove rises from the conference table, stepping closer to the large screen displaying the real-time image of the Beast to get a better look. He points to the screen. "Dr. Simmons. Is that an object moving toward 966?"

Dr. Simmons' preening is interrupted. He looks at the image of 966, then looks closer. He is instantly sober. He runs to his computer, zooming in on the object and checking calculations.

One of Dr. Simmons's team reports. "An unknown object is on a direct path to collide with the Beast."

Another of his team adds. "The object is approaching from behind JZ966, is approximately one-third the size of JZ966 and is traveling at forty-six thousand miles per hour."

Dr. Simmons looks up from his screen. "This is… unexpected."

The smaller asteroid crashes into the Beast. Gray rock and dust erupt from the Beast. Everyone in the conference room inhales, unable to breathe as they watch the space collision. The telescope operator switches to a wide view of the debris field. The collision severed a large piece off the top of the Beast. The impact propels the chunk of rock through space.

A buzz of commotion erupts in the mission control room. Duffy moves from mission specialist to mission specialist barking instructions. Dr. Simmons works at his computer screen, touching and swiping through images and calculations.

"An asteroid hit our asteroid!" Jerome shouts.

"We can see that, Jerome," replies Mitch.

"That's a nasty-looking chunk," states Tug.

The conference room erupts with questions. "Will it miss Earth now?" "Did the impact destroy the Beast?" "Where's the broken piece headed?"

President Baker views the image of the Beast now spinning slowly, surrounded by rocks and dust. "Silence," he yells. He waits for the room to quiet. "Stop talking. Silence." He gets silence. "Simmons. What now? How does this affect the mission?"

Dr. Simmons motions with his hand to study calculations and simulations while receiving audible reports from his team. "As you all witnessed, an asteroid struck the Beast. An event that was not anticipated. The trajectory of the Beast has changed somewhat. We need time to calculate this new trajectory, but I assure you, the Beast is still headed toward Earth and extremely dangerous."

Dr. Simmons pauses for a moment, listening to reports. "We will send instructions to adjust the course of the Harpoons, using hydrazine thrusters. The Harpoons are one hundred seven minutes from impact. I believe we have time to adjust for successful disruption of the Beast."

"Dr. Simmons. I don't think anyone could have anticipated what happened. Too bad the other rock wasn't bigger, it could have done the job for us," says President Baker.

"Let's find out where that big chunk is heading," says Tug.

Dr. Simmons nods as he listens to the mission team's discussion.

"We'll let you and the mission crew work this out. Give us an update when you have more information, Simmons," says President Baker.

New Arcadia–10:00 AM

Cruikshank storms angrily around his quarters. He swings his cane at a Chinese vase, sending shattered pieces to the floor, then smacks an antique military helmet, sending it flying across the room. "How could this happen? How did they escape? Is everyone around me incompetent?"

The colonel holds his cane, ready to swing at a Japanese Samurai statue.

Zsoldos stands nearby. "Black Guard have searched Gymnasium. They found two boys," he states calmly.

The report of two boys in Gymnasium stops the colonel mid-swing, saving the statue. "Two? Will two be enough?"

"They can alternate spa treatments. You may have to spa less often to allow them recovery time, but it will work if they remain healthy."

"I've analyzed the video recording of your call with General Mahon. The camera focused on the boy named Zekiel and the boys near him. I could not get a complete count of the boys in the conference room."

Cruikshank places a call to City Guard. "Commander. Have your City Guard search for the boys from Gymnasium? They're crafty urchins. It wouldn't surprise me if you found one or two hiding out."

"There have been no sightings of the missing boys in the city, but City Guard will conduct a search. There have been no attempts to leave the city since the sealing was complete. However, we have reports of several attempted entries. Some attempts have been very persistent. I am happy to report sealing the city has stopped all intruders," the Guard Commander explains.

"Persistent entry attempts? What do you mean?" the colonel inquires, his curiosity peaked.

"Let's see. Yes, this person is stubborn. The access door at stairwell twenty-seven has fourteen entry attempts. The requestor is verified but since we sealed the door, entry was unsuccessful. We understand there was a small risk of locking out some Arcadians. A small price to pay for the safety of the city and the greater good of New Arcadia," answers the Commander.

The colonel wonders out loud. "Could some boys have changed their mind?"

Zsoldos checks the city map on his VUE. "Stairwell twenty-seven is two hundred yards from Gymnasium. There are closer stairwells, but it's in the same corridor. What is the name of the Arcadian requesting entry?"

"Ah yes, I have it. The name is Gordon Szarek," the commander replies cheerfully.

"Gordon, Gordon Szarek! He's the Gymnasium attendant. You idiot! Get that door open! He could have the boys with him!" exclaims the colonel.

Las Vegas–8:30 AM

Rick cruises slowly while he gets used to the Scout. Riding this old bike is a manual operation. All four of his limbs are required to control the cycle. His right hand twists the throttle, controlling speed. His right hand also brakes the front wheel by gripping a lever with his fingers. The toe of his right boot presses a pedal to brake the rear wheel. He moves through the gears by pressing or lifting a pedal with his left foot while simultaneously pulling and releasing the clutch lever with his left hand. All of this requires more dexterity and coordination than he is used to managing.

He longs for an Autocar, but he knows those days are over. He shifts into third gear; gripping the clutch and pressing his foot on the gear pedal. Feeling the gear pedal click, he releases the clutch and increases the throttle. The bike jumps forward with a bolt of speed. He enters HWY 215 and moves to fourth gear, looking east. The Las Vegas strip is a line of smoldering broken buildings. Smoke and wrecked vehicles fill the landscape. The helmet covering his face protects him from the sandy grit in the air, but does little to mask the smell of death.

Rick has made the trip to Las Vegas many times. He remembers the clear blue morning skies, the cool crisp air, and the stunning sight of the Red Rock mountains north of the city. He recalls marveling at the natural beauty of the mountains and desert surrounding the city of sin.

This morning there are no clouds. The sky is brown, and the air is heavy and thick. Dust covers everything and swirls in the wind. Brown muck hides the Red Rock Mountains. Storms have scourged the city. Rick swerves through a tangle of cars and revs the cycle to pick up speed as he takes the ramp from the 215 to the 15; Highway 15 South, the highway to Los Angeles.

Asteroid storms have raged for three nights. They will get worse. Dead wrecks block progress clogging the highway once bustling with people who had somewhere to go and some place to be.

Rick guns the throttle to swerve around a burned-out truck as he passes the state line. He is in California.

Munday's Hideaway–8:30 AM

The mood is somber in Munday's hideaway. Breakfast is prepared and eaten in silence. The occupants' distance themselves from each other. Some stay in their sleeping areas while others make busy work in the mine complex. The deaths of Gloria and the two boys are a horror fresh on everyone's mind.

Carlos, the thirteen-year-old son of Rodrigo, walks through the lower level of the mine. As he passes through the garden, he checks the vegetables and fruit trees. He walks to the farm to check on the piglets when he hears soft music coming from the atrium.

Carlos ducks through the low, rocky passage. When he steps out the other end, he looks in amazement at the sparkling veins of gold running through smoky white granite. Soft music echoes in the chamber. Lights illuminate the high walls, shifting from yellow to blue then purple. In the center of the room, he sees Alyssa sitting on a stone bench holding a fluffy white lamb. She cuddles the soft creature, whispering to it. Carlos stands silent, watching.

Alyssa rubs her cheek on the lambs' soft fleece as she hums with the music. Something alerts her and she looks at the entrance. Her quick movement startles Carlos. He jerks up, hitting his head on the rough ceiling of the passage. He coyly rubs his head, his vision never straying from the girl.

Alyssa smiles as she moves her eyes to the bench and back to the boy. Carlos steps into the Atrium as the lights turn emerald green. He feels tall standing over the young girl, who looks up at him in the sparkling light. Alyssa scoots to make room on the bench. Carlos sits next to her. "Sorry to interrupt you."

"It's okay. I had to get away. It's too weird up there."

"It's horrible. So many people dying. The weird thing is all I can think about is…" Carlos pauses for a moment, as he looks up at the roof of the Atrium. "I was going to be on the basketball team this year. Now, that's never gonna happen. I guess it's selfish to feel sorry for myself."

Carlos examines Alyssa's face, studying every curve of her soft cheeks and the shape of her lips. Her eyes, swollen and tearful. He touches her shoulder softly. "You've been crying."

Alyssa nods, rubbing her cheek on the lambs' soft fur. "I guess I was feeling sorry for myself, too. I wanted to go to the fashion show. This is fashion week. My friend, Charnel, is a model. She'll walk on the runway. She's rich and beautiful with so many friends. Everyone adores her. She's so sweet. She's even nice to me. I was hoping my parents would let me watch her." She pulls the lamb closer, keeping one side of her face buried in the thick fleece. She allows a tear to flow. "But now, everyone is dead."

"What a sorry pair we are. They've lost their lives and we sit here crying for the lives we wish we had," Carlos muses.

"The life we've lost."

"Yeah."

"We should be thankful. We are so lucky to have Uncle Rob and the hideaway." Alyssa says.

"At least we tried to save Aunt Gloria and her friends. My dad tried," Carlos says.

"I miss my dad. He's still out there where everyone is dying," Alyssa trembles, as more tears flow. She leans into the boy.

Carlos comforts the weeping girl. Unsure what to say; he holds her tightly, rocking her slowly in his arms, then whispers, "What a pair we are." He pauses, then adds, "We'll be OK. We'll all be OK."

New Arcadia–11:30 AM–Stairwell 27

Sparks sputter from an automated cutting torch as it slices through the weld seam that seals the door. Black Guard stand watch, ready to rush in and rescue the boys.

When the stairwell door opens the Black Guard finds Gymnasium attendant, Gordon Szarek slumped on the floor in a pool of drying blood. A medical team is called. Minutes later, the medical team is moving Gordon on a maglev medical gurney.

Cruikshank watches the stream as Black Guard report. "It's hard to believe, but he's alive. Half his head is bashed in. It looks like a deflated ball. The med team is transporting him to the infirmary now."

Nolan stands in the open door of Gymnasium. He watches the levitating maglev's and vehicles as they zip past. He spots a medical team and gurney flanked by Black Guard moving up the corridor. As the medical team gets closer, Nolan can see that the body on the gurney is a dark blue tunic.

Nolan rushes to the gurney as it passes Gymnasium. He grabs the edge of the gurney clutching the body, crying, "What did the bad boys do to you?" Gordon's mouth moves but he does not speak. He pats Nolan softly with his blood dried hand.

"I'm coming with you," cries Nolan. A Black Guard pulls Nolan away from the gurney. "I want to go with him, please. He's my dad. He's my dad!"

"You can see him later," the Black Guard says, lifting the boy and placing him inside Gymnasium.

Nolan sits in the doorway, weeping.

Mike McCoy

Slingeren Mission Control 11:57 A.M. EST

Dr. Simmons stands pensively in front of the thin screen to brief the president once again. He's draped his sport jacket over a chair. His shirt sleeves are rolled up and his hair frizzled. The president is at the conference table surrounded by his staff.

"Mr. President. Before I update you on the progress of Harpoon, which is going well under the circumstances. I have unfortunate news regarding the large fragment that broke off from the Beast."

"All right, Simmons. Like I told you, cut it to the bone. What's happening?" President Baker asks brusquely.

"The asteroid that collided with JZ966 continued out into space and is no longer a threat. However, the piece dissected from 966 is heading directly for Earth. It is 560 feet in diameter and 145 feet in height. Basically, it cleaved the top of the Beast off. The collision propelled the fragment at an accelerated rate of speed. The object is traveling at 45,000 miles per hour. We estimate it will enter the Earth's atmosphere over the mid-west of the United States at eleven thirty-seven A.M. and impact somewhere in the Los Angeles basin thirty seconds later. If this fragment impacts the densely populated Los Angeles basin, the death and damage will be multitudes greater than the Baltimore impact."

A shocked gasp fills the room, followed by muffled sobs. President Baker stands with his hands extended. "Stay calm. We've had plenty of bad news and there's surely more to come. This should not be a shock to anyone. We're here to find solutions. Let's solve this problem. Simmons, what is your recommendation?"

"The ICBM installation at Minot AFB in North Dakota should prepare to launch. They have two-and-a-half hours. The teams here will help with targeting calculations. That should give them plenty of time to start the launch sequence."

Tug gives an anxious look at General Casey. Tug, Casey, and several Air Force staff members move to a corner of the conference room to plan for a sub-orbital nuclear intercept.

A staff member speaks up. "We should provide notice to the U.K., Russia, China, New Korea, India and Pakistan of our intent to detonate a nuclear weapon in US air space. We don't want anyone to misinterpret our actions."

"Yes, get word to all nuclear nations, or as many as you can. We must save Los Angeles. However, I believe we still have a huge asteroid aimed at Earth. Simmons by my watch, the Harpoons should be minutes from impact. That is, if we're still on track. Give us your update. You said you have better news."

"Yes sir. We used the thrusters and Harpoons attitude control system and the navigation subsystem cameras to re-center on the asteroid. This allowed us to use the navigation filter to solve for the inertial position and velocity of the spacecrafts with respect to the asteroid. We did this by making use of simulation software that's part of the orbit determination toolbox, which is an advanced mission simulation and analysis tool."

"And once again in English, please, doctor," says Mitch.

"Oh, yes. We have reacquired target locations on the Beast. Impact will occur in two minutes. There are some contingencies. There was no time to re-scan the object. We don't know the extent of damage to the Beast from the collision, so we have not updated the disruption simulation. The other challenge: Beast is now rotating, so it's difficult to ensure each Harpoon will hit its optimal impact location for crater creation, and therefore, difficult to predict the shock propagation from the nuclear detonations."

"That was better. I got the gist of that," says Mitch.

"You and the mission crew have worked very hard under difficult circumstances. I'm pleased to hear you've salvaged the mission. Now all we can do is hope for the best and let the Harpoons do the rest," says President Baker.

Everyone in the room stops working to focus on the large screens displaying real time video of the Beast. A trail of dust and rocks follows the large asteroid. A section of the large wall screen displays still images from the Harpoons. The images stutter in at a rate of ten images per second. The Harpoons are closer to the Beast with each new image. Mission control audio accompanies the images.

"Confirm booms extended and locked." "1 minute to impact." "Impactors 660 clicks out." Seconds pass. "Last image from impactors sent." "Impact–fire command issued to NEDs."

A space-based telescope transmits real-time video of the Harpoon's approach. The time between the impactors striking the asteroid creating craters and the fire command for the nuclear explosives is one millisecond, faster than the blink of an eye.

The nuclear devices detonate at three separate target locations, creating huge explosions of rock and dust. The space telescope switches from camera view to X-ray view, enabling examination of the asteroid through dust and debris. The front face and sides of the asteroid are pulverized and blasted away. The shock from the nuclear blasts reverberates through the one-kilometer wide, space rock.

The Beast slowly breaks up as fragments spread apart. Over the next two minutes, hundreds of rocky chunks of diverse size from one hundred feet to three hundred feet in diameter become visible on the x-ray image. The real-time video image is a cloud of dust with a few large pieces becoming visible. Besides the large pieces, hundreds of smaller bits make up a loose jumble of rocks.

"Oh, no!" exclaims Jerome.

"Dear Lord. What have we done?" cries Mitch

President Baker watches the objects in the X-ray view continue to spread apart. "Simmons, have we made the situation better or worse? Where are those rocks headed? Out to space, I hope."

Dr. Simmons is nervous and upset. "None of our simulations predicted this. The asteroid that hit 966 must have caused multiple fractures throughout the core, increasing the porosity. We should not have so many large pieces. We expected a more complete disruption with smaller fragments."

Dr. Simmons listens to a report in his VUE. He gulps and nods. "The shattered mass appears to be on course for Earth."

"Simmons. Lots of pieces is better than one big rock though, right?" asks Mitch.

Dr. Simmons' mind is racing through all the variables that made things go wrong but does his best to answer the senator. "Well, ah. Yes. A single impact from an intact JZ966 would have guaranteed humanity's destruction. Hundreds of large impacts spread across Earth will be devastating, but Earth and the creatures living upon it will survive. Some of them anyway. This… this shouldn't have happened. Too many variables."

"Earth is seventy percent ocean. Hopefully, most of them will land in the sea," states Jerome.

Dr. Simmons brightens. "Secretary Hargrove is correct. Many of the fragments will probably land in the oceans, resulting in less damage. We will track the largest fragments and determine which one's pose the highest risk to population centers."

"When can we expect this pile of rock to hit our atmosphere?" asks Tug.

Dr. Simmons turns to one of his team, then reports. "The impacts will begin around seven p.m., eastern standard time."

Mike McCoy

Chapter 62: Salvation

Saturday

11:30 AM PST/2:30 PM EST

The ride through the Mojave Desert is tedious. Rick detours around wrecked and burned out AutoCars and trucks, often riding on the shoulder of the highway or on the dirt median separating the North and South lanes to get around vehicles. He pushes through as quickly as possible to get past the flies and smell of the dead. Some wrecks are three days old, while others look fresh from the night before. He chases away a pair of coyotes tugging on a human leg hanging out of a car door. He does not see any survivors. The coyotes look well fed.

He feels guilty. The death and destruction should shock him, but he's unmoved. He has two objectives; stay alive and get home to his family. Nothing else matters.

A big pileup often leads to an open road for several miles before he weaves his way through another tangle of wrecks. He is happy to have the old Scout. Curtis' Corvette would never have made it through the mass of smashed cars.

During a long open stretch of road, Rick gazes at the barren desert landscape. He is not a geologist, but he is certain the desert once was the floor of a great ocean. Today, the sky is a dull reddish brown, making the desert look more like the surface of Mars.

Rick passes the town of Baker. There are no signs of life, but even before the storms, Baker was not much more than a strip of restaurants and gas stations. The buildings look intact, but meteorites have shattered the tall gas station signs. Baker is usually a place for travelers to recharge and fuel up. Today it's a dusty turn in the road.

It's Saturday morning. It seems like ages ago when he gave the lecture for Professor Heinrich, but that was just last Monday. He was focused on his grant. Five days later, he's focused on survival.

Rick spots an overpass ahead. The exit sign says it's Rasor Road. A white sheet hangs from the overpass with the word

Salvation painted with what looks like dried blood. Cars jam the area all around the overpass. Cars jammed under overpasses have been commonplace on Rick's ride down Highway 15. An overpass offers the rare opportunity for protection from the asteroid storms.

The overpass at Rasor road has more cars than usual. Vehicles are parked five and six abreast on the two-lane highway, making the road impassable. Rick slows and turns around. He rides back to the exit ramp. He rides up the ramp and is about to pass through the intersection at the top of the ramp before riding down the 'on' ramp to the highway, when he sees three young girls with flowing white dresses running toward him waving their arms and calling out to him.

The girls are the first living people Rick has seen since leaving Curtis' house. The young girls' white dresses billowing in the wind look dreamlike. As the girls run, dust rises and twists in the breeze behind them.

"Welcome to Salvation," he hears them calling.

Rick rides slowly up a dirt road to meet the girls.

The girls continue to call out, "Welcome to Salvation. Welcome to Salvation."

He stops but remains on the Scout, letting it idle as he meets the young girls. "Welcome to Salvation," they say haltingly, looking the rider over. He notices each girl holds a small palm branch.

Rick must look scary to the girls. They face a strange biker wearing a black leather duster, black boots, and slacks with a face hidden behind the dark glass bubble of the Bullitt Retro helmet, but the girls hold their smiles.

The girl in the middle takes a step forward. She is taller and looks older than the others. "Are you the preacher?" she asks.

The two other girls repeat the question. "Are you? Are you the Preacher?"

Rick lifts the visor of the helmet. "I'm nobody's preacher. I'm just passing through. Do you need help?"

"We need the preacher to open Salvation. He said when tribulation comes to meet him here at Salvation. He alone has the key. But he hasn't arrived," explains the tall girl.

"We watched every stream over and over with Mother. Everyone is here. We're prepared," says the smallest girl.

"You're a church group?" Rick quizzes.

"Tribulation Church. We've come to Salvation," the third girl states, as if Rick should know this.

"You brought your Salvation kit, didn't you?" asks the smallest girl looking at the Scouts' saddle bag.

"What?" asks Rick.

"We all have them. White robes washed in the blood of the lamb made from non-actualized 100% cotton, preserved organic palm branches, tribulation limited edition prayer books and a map to Salvation signed by the preacher," the tallest girl states, plainly.

"Didn't your order arrive before the coming of tribulation?" asks the smallest girl.

Rick shakes his head, trying to take in the information.

"Don't worry. Mother bought extras. Join us," says the third girl.

"Sorry. I'm not your preacher. I don't know where he is. I've never heard of salvation kits. My salvation is in Los Angeles. I'd best keep heading that direction. Get yourselves under that overpass for protection from the storm tonight," Rick says as he turns the Scout to leave.

As he turns, he meets two men in white robes walking up from the highway carrying a stretcher between them. The stretcher holds the body of a young woman dressed in a white robe. Splotches of blood ink the cotton. The men look happy. They smile at Rick as they pass, calling out the now familiar greeting. "Welcome to Salvation."

The young girls look at the body of the dead woman with excitement and joy. "She is blessed. She is blessed. Salvation belongs to our God, who sits on the throne and to the Lamb."

Rick's eyes follow the men as they walk toward a small building up the dirt road. He sees a large group of people dressed in white standing around the building. Next to the building are rows of bodies adorned in white robes, lying in the dirt.

"What is this church? Are you all trying to die out here?" Rick asks.

"The Preacher prepared us. He told us: go to Salvation receive the seal and live on. The Preacher said: Although we are prepared, many will die during tribulation. It's OK. They are blessed. The blessed will sit before the throne of God and serve him day and night in his temple. And God will wipe away every tear from their eyes," the oldest girl repeated her rote learning.

"Join us. Come with us. Come to Salvation. Tribulation will get you out here," the smallest girl says, tearing up.

"If you're not trying to die, what the heck is this Salvation?" asks Rick.

"That building leads to Salvation," the second girl says, pointing to the small structure up the road.

"They say it was part of an underground network built by the old phone company, AT&T a long time ago. It has many underground levels and is built to survive a nuclear blast. The Preacher bought it and prepared it for us," the third girl explains.

"It's a big underground house. It's our Salvation! It can be your salvation, too!" cries the smallest girl.

"Oh great. An underground house. Sorry, sweetheart, like I said, my Salvation is in Los Angeles. My family's there. I need to get home," Rick revs the engine of the old Scout.

The sound of a gunshot echoes across the desert, followed by people cheering.

Rick looks back at the small building. "Sounds like someone isn't waiting for your preacher."

The girls squeal as they run up the road to Salvation.

Rick presses his foot to put the Scout in gear, releases the clutch, and rides down the 'on' ramp. "At least they have a place to keep them safe. I pray it's the Salvation they hoped for," Rick thinks to himself as he rides down the highway.

The girls run up to the small building, which is thirty feet long and ten feet deep. There are no windows, but two doors: one, a normal-sized metal door and the other a roll-up metal garage door. A man rolls the garage up as the girls arrive. The girls push through the crowd of white robes to see what is inside. The excitement and cheers go silent.

"It's a freight elevator," says the man. "There's no power. An elevator's no help," says another.

The leading edge of the crowd moves to the small metal door. "Backup! Give him room. Move back," says a deep male voice in the mass of white robes. The crowd moves away, and a shot is fired. The man with the gun kicks the door open, revealing a dark room with a metal staircase dropping into darkness.

The smallest girl squeezes to the front and stands next to a man holstering his gun. "Is it the stairway to Salvation?" the girl asks, reaching to hold the big man's hand. She grasps one of his fingers.

"Mother says it is. You'd better hope so. There aren't a lot of options out here," says the man as several people rush for the door.

A woman in a white robe with long white hair raises her hands to stop people from entering the small building. Her hair is pure white, but her narrow face is not wrinkled, making it difficult to determine her age.

"Hold on, now. Let the elders check first. Jacob, you go," she says, pointing to one of the older men. The woman is calm yet confident. The crowd follows her command.

"Yes, Mother," is his response before entering the dark building.

The tall man with the gun looks down at the smallest girl, allowing her to get a better grip on his hand. "The newcomer wasn't your preacher?"

The small girl frowns. "No."

"Did you convert him? Is he joining us?"

"No. He didn't have a Salvation Kit. I told him Mother has extras, but he rode away on his motorcycle. He said his salvation is in Los Angeles where his family is," the disappointed girl explains.

"You let one get away. I'm surprised," the big man says.

"I think he's from the same army as you?"

"Same army? What do you mean?"

"The stripe," the young girl says, pointing to the gray stripe down the big man's slacks.

Mother and the girls found the bald, muscular man walking along highway 160, near Four Corners where the borders of Colorado, New Mexico, Utah, and Arizona meet. After several hours in the car, the women convinced the man to join them at Salvation. He became especially close to the youngest girl.

The big man squats down to look the small girl in the face. "You mean he wore black slacks with a gray stripe like mine?"

The girl nods vigorously. "Yes, and the same boots."

"Heading to Los Angeles to be with his family," the man repeats what the young girl stated. She nods. Kobalt removes and folds his white robe neatly before placing it in Mother's hands.

"There's something I need to take care of once and for all. Get yourselves settled in. I'll be back before the storms start up."

Kobalt runs to the highway. While the others were dressing the dead in white robes and looking for the Preacher, Kobalt staged a large sport utility vehicle (SUV) under the overpass and cleared a path through the wrecked cars for a quick departure in case of trouble or if Salvation was a bust. He jumps in the SUV and races down Highway 15.

Rob works at his desk. Data signals are down. There is no news and no streams. He expected at some point they would be cut off from the outside world. He didn't expect it to happen so quickly. The windows in the hideaway are off. He would feel guilty if they displayed a pleasant scene.

Rob hears sounds of a discussion deeper in the mine. Moments later, Eddie and Rodrigo approach Rob's desk. Edgar and George trail behind. This contingent comprises the men of the hideaway.

Eddie speaks first. "Rob, we need to take care of the dead."

"We can't leave them out there, not like that," says Rodrigo.

"We agreed nobody goes outside, but we need to take care of them for health and safety issues," adds Eddie.

"The smell," says George, waving a hand in front of his nose.

"And the dogs. Dead flesh will bring coyotes and wolves," adds Edgar, sounding fearful.

"There are no wolves in the San Gabriel's, only mountain lions," Rob says in a scary voice.

"You're right. We must take care of the dead lest we lose our humanity; what little we have left," Rob adds.

The men move up the mine shaft toward the entrance to undertake the gruesome task. Selina startles the men, calling after them. "Wait. I'm going with you. They were my friends. I must pay my respects to the dead."

Rick curses himself for stopping at Salvation. He could have been at Barstow by now. The people are safe. Weird, but safe. They opened Salvation. They have sanctuary from the storms.

He uses the off ramp/on ramp trick to skirt around the crush of vehicles at the Basin Road overpass. The highway ahead is clear, allowing Rick to ride faster and make up lost time. He is peaceful and free. He has only been riding the old Scout for a couple hours, but he feels relaxed and comfortable bouncing lightly on the wide seat, supported by heavy springs.

The desert somehow looks emptier and more desolate than usual. The vastness of the desert is meditative. He allows his mind to wander to pass the time. Time, that's all he needs, a little more time, and he'll be back with Courtney, Rob, and the kids. This is his mantra. He visualizes his happy reunion while he swerves through a narrow gap between stalled cars, before riding up another exit ramp and roaring back down to the highway.

Kobalt sets the SUV to manual mode, driving the electric vehicle as fast as it will move. He focuses on the road ahead, searching for a motorcycle. He uses the same method as Rick to get around blocked overpasses. At the top of each overpass, he squints, hoping the higher elevation will allow him to see farther. Kobalt sees nothing but empty desert and dead autos. He knows Rick Munday is on this highway and there's only one road to Los Angeles. Kobalt presses the pedal to the floor.

Kobalt may have found Salvation, but he will never find peace, not until Rick Munday is dead. Kobalt recalls when Mother and the girls saw him walking along the highway and offered a ride. The oldest daughter rode shotgun. Kobalt sat in the passenger seat next to the smallest girl. He listened to their story. Mother's confident determination to reach Salvation impressed him.

He thought their religiosity, the white robes, and a place called Salvation were over the top. He never went in for the Bible stuff, but he admired their spirit and honored their quest. He plans to stay with them at Salvation. He might be happy there helping them survive the storms.

Now, Rick Munday passes through and, as usual, ruins everything. Rick's appearance is a tortured reminder of Kobalt's failures. He cannot allow Munday to survive. He will never have peace in Salvation if he allows Munday to live.

He measures his progress with each overpass he crosses. He makes it past Field Road, then Alvord Mountain Road. As he crosses each overpass, he looks ahead in search of Rick Munday.

Rick rides past Harvard Road. As the highway clears of cars, he speeds up. The Scout responds with its familiar deep rumble, steady and sure. Four minutes later, Rick approaches another overpass. The overpass at Hacienda Road does not have an exit ramp. Rick slows to get a lay of the land. Hacienda Road starts five miles back at Harvard Road and runs parallel to Highway 15 before crossing the highway, ending at a failed housing development. Cars and trucks jam the underpass so tightly even the old Scout can't shimmy through.

Rick thinks about heading across the desert to ride around the overpass, but a wire fence lines each side of the highway. He doesn't want to risk damaging the bike or his body trying to crash through the fence. He rides across the center median to check the fence on the other side of the highway. There are no breaks in the fence. He's wasting time. There are roads running parallel to the highway on both sides. The road running along the northbound lanes continues past Hacienda road. He decides his best choice is to ride back to Harvard Road and take that road until he can get back on Highway 15.

Rick curses as he crosses into the northbound lane, steering the bike back toward Harvard Road. He hopes there won't be many more detours.

Kobalt clears the cars at Harvard Road and speeds down Highway 15. He is so focused on the road ahead; He almost misses the motorcycle going the opposite direction on the northbound lanes.

Rick sees an SUV in the south-bound lane. He watches it with curiosity. There have been no autos moving on the highway. He looks at the driver's side window as the SUV passes. "It can't be," he thinks to himself.

The SUV drives onto the center median, throwing up a huge cloud of dust.

"Oh, shit!" Rick shouts as he guns the throttle, hoping to gain extra speed from the Scout.

The SUV hits the highway pavement; As its tires grip the asphalt, Kobalt punches the accelerator. "I've got you now, Munday!" Soon, Kobalt is closing the distance on the motorcycle.

Rick tucks his head low against the wind, eking out extra speed. Harvard Road is coming up quick.

Kobalt's heart is pumping. Sweat forms on his brow. He grips the steering wheel, like a Formula One racer trying to make the 200 mile per hour club.

Rick takes the exit ramp for Harvard Road. At the end of the ramp, he drops from fourth gear to second. He does not hit the brakes; downshifting slows the bike, setting it up for the turn. Once in the turn, he gooses the throttle, punches into third gear, and takes a hard right on Harvard Road. Sixty yards later, he takes another hard right, allowing the rear wheel to drift through the turn onto the road that runs along the highway. The signpost reads Yermo Road. He sees the SUV exit Highway 15 as he speeds up, putting the bike into fourth gear; jetting down the road.

Kobalt watches the bike speed down a side road as he reaches the exit ramp. The SUV is moving too fast for the sharp turn at the end of the ramp and spins through the intersection and into the dirt,

almost hitting the Highway 15 North entrance sign.
Speeding through the dirt, he roars down Harvard Road, then cuts
the corner burning rubber onto Yermo Road.

Rick blasts down the two-lane road, hoping to put some distance
between himself and Kobalt. He spots a dust cloud behind him in
the circular mirror mounted on the handlebars, counting his
blessings for the few seconds lead on the SUV.

Kobalt curses himself for his sloppy driving. "Go ahead. Speed
away, Munday. There's no place to hide. You're not getting away
from me this time."
Munday's capture and kill are inevitable. Kobalt preaches
patience to himself as he speeds down the center of the two-lane
road. He caresses his side arm, running his fingers down the length
of its leather holster.

Rick prays that the electric-powered SUV will run low on charge,
hoping the high-speed chase will drain the battery cells faster. Hopes
and prayers aren't proving effective. Rick spies the mirror; the SUV
is coming up fast.
An animal dashes out from the sagebrush, just after the Scout
passes. Rick watches his mirror. The SUV smacks the animal
without diverting. The jack rabbit is plastered to the front bumper
of the fast-moving truck. The dead rabbit slowly slips off the
bumper tumbling under the SUV on the hot asphalt.

Kobalt removes his Sig Sauer P320 from its holster. The
magazine holds nineteen pieces of lead. Kobalt tucks the Sig
between his legs as he presses the SUV faster, coming within feet of
the Indian Scout's rear wheel.
He lowers his window and grips the Sig as he moves the truck to
the right to get a clear shot. He passes the Stop Ahead sign without
the sign registering in his consciousness.

Munday is even with Kobalt's window. Kobalt aims. The cycle slows abruptly. Kobalt fires. The shot misses. Seconds later, the cycle is behind the SUV.

Kobalt looks forward and sees that Yermo Road is ending. There's a T intersection ahead, and he's approaching fast. Kobalt hits the brakes hard, skidding through the intersection, veering to the road on the left. Munday slowed to set the Scout up for a hard-right turn. He increases speed through the turn and zoomed up the road to cross an overpass. Kobalt watches the cycle head north in his rearview mirror. He does a quick U-turn, once again sending up dust clouds and speeds toward the overpass.

Unknown to Rick, the entrance to the highway from Yermo Road differs from other overpasses. The overpass at Yermo Road crosses Highway 15, then makes a long eastward lopsided loop and merges with the highway a half mile east of the overpass. Instead of bypassing a jammed underpass, he is headed directly for it. As Rick rides down the on-ramp, he sees the underpass is blocked by a semi-trailer lying on its side. Kobalt isn't far behind, but there is no choice. He turns the Scout around and heads back up the overpass.

Kobalt has fired at Rick. Rick doesn't want a gunfight, but he's about to be in one. He pulls the zombie killer from its holster. Cradling the pistol grip at his hip, he pulls the pump handle back to load a slug into the chamber, then rests the shotgun barrel on the handlebars.

Rick hears the high-pitched whine of the electric motor being pushed to the max. The SUV crests the overpass.

Rick spots Kobalt coming at him full bore. He doesn't hesitate; he fires the shotgun. The shot misses.

Kobalt sees the muzzle blast. He isn't surprised that the shot missed. "Great shot, you skinny Astro geek. Watch how a professional does it." In a controlled move, he aims the Sig out the window. He has Munday lined up in the sights. He fires.

Rick rides with no hands momentarily to pump another cartridge into the firing chamber, causing the bike to swerve. Kobalt's bullet whizzes past. The distance between the Scout and the SUV is closing fast. Rick grabs the handlebar to recover, aims lower and fires. The windshield of the SUV cracks. The slug puts a large hole in the glass and continues through the SUV, blowing out the rear window. Kobalt ducks below the dash, firing the Sig repeatedly. The shock of a shotgun slug ripping four inches from his head sends his bullets off target.

The Indian Scout speeds past the SUV across the overpass. At the end of the bridge, Rick jumps the bike off the road landing hard on the sandy scruff, then rides up a dirt embankment and onto the highways north bound lanes. Rick holsters the shotgun and runs through the gears to get as much distance between himself and Kobalt.

"Damn you, Munday!" Kobalt curses loudly as he hits the brakes to make another U-turn. "I've had enough of you, professor." He makes the turn onto the off-ramp, chasing Rick down Highway 15, going south on the northbound lanes.

Rick's heart is pumping. He's never fired a shotgun before. The recoil hurt his hand. He is excited and relieved to be alive, but he knows he missed Kobalt. And Kobalt won't give up.

Rick looks ahead. "What? Another overpass!" This underpass is jammed, like all the other underpasses, but this one has no exit ramps. There is a wire fence on his left. The center median has a steel guard rail running down the middle, so he can't cross over to the south lanes. Abandoned cars and trucks stretch a quarter mile in front of the overpass. Rick zigzags through the mess of autos and tractor trailer rigs, winding a path through the destruction.

Kobalt races down the highway and spots the overpass ahead. Wrecked cars are scattered along the road. Kobalt navigates around the wrecks, but as the mess of autos thickens, he drives on the shoulder of the left side of the road until it is impossible to move forward.

The SUV is blocked. "Damn it," Kobalt shouts as he pounds the steering wheel. He then laughs when he spots Munday under the overpass, struggling to get his motorcycle between two cars. Kobalt steps to the roadway with his Sig Sauer at the ready.

Rick hears Kobalt's boots on the pavement and turns to see the hulking brute. Rick dives for the asphalt, rolling under a car as shots ring out. He eyes the zombie killer holstered on the bike several feet away. He'll be dead if he tries to reach it. Rick scoots further under the car. Lying on his back, Rick calls out, "What's your problem with me?"

Kobalt steps slowly through the maze of cars, sweeping the Sig left and right, scanning for a target. "You ruined it. You destroyed everything we worked for."

Rick reaches for the dart gun holstered at his side. "Because I spoiled your secret? That's why you want to kill me? You only wanted to save yourselves, your few and fortunate; damn the rest of us. You knew the storm was coming. You could have saved millions." He quickly rises, aims, and shoots two darts before shuffling down a row of cars.

A dart hits Kobalt in the forearm. He laughs as he plucks the venom pumping dart from his sleeve and tosses it to the ground. "I always wear a skin suit unlike the Black Guard of New Zion. You were smart to use them," Kobalt shouts as he fires three rounds.

"We designed New Arcadia as an optimal society. A framework for advancing humanity after the storms," Kobalt yells out, advancing through jammed cars.

"Arcadia, the optimal society that drugs people into compliance with every breath. A society that needs someone like you and your Black Guard to keep people in line. Sounds perfect to me!"

"You were to join us; to be one of us." Kobalt sees Rick scurrying through the cars ahead and fires two rounds.

Rick ducks around the front of a truck running directly into the dead driver leaning against the front of his truck. Rick wrestles frightfully with the stiff corpse before he pushes the body away and keeps moving. Rick works his way around the truck, hoping to circle back to the Indian Scout and the Zombie Killer. "You kidnapped, robbed, and drugged me. What a way to make a guy feel welcome.

All I ever wanted was to get home to my family. You kept me from getting to the ones I love. Not very utopian, if you ask me."

Rick makes a mad dash, running low through the cars. Kobalt sees Rick's helmet moving and fires. The bullet grazes Rick's helmet with enough force to whip Rick's head sideways, sending him to the ground. Kobalt ejects the magazine from the Sig and inserts a fresh clip as he calmly strolls, stalking his prey.

The Scout is ten feet away. Rick eyes the shotgun. "If I can just get the gun, I can end this; end Kobalt," Rick says to himself. Then he shouts. "I never asked for this, but if it's a fight, you want." Rick stands and runs.

Kobalt fires hitting Rick in the side. The force of the round slams Rick into a car before falling to the ground. The ballistic resistive suit stopped the bullet from penetrating his body, but the suit does nothing to dampen the kinetic force. Rick rolls on the ground in agonizing pain. "You shot me!" Rick's breaths are shallow. "That's a broken rib for sure," he mumbles to himself.

Kobalt moves through the cars. "If that move is you fighting back, you'd best stay down. I'll finish you quick, then I can get back to Salvation. Don't worry, you won't know what hit you."

Rick looks at the dart gun. The load indicator flashes 0,0,0. "Damn," he says, tossing the gun to the ground. He slips off his backpack and pulls out his machete. Rick uses the door handle of a car to pull himself to his knees, machete in hand. Two cars separate Kobalt and Rick. Rick pops up and throws the machete at Kobalt. The big blade cartwheels swiftly through the air, heading directly for Kobalt. Kobalt reaches out with his left hand and catches the sharp blade. Blood drips from his hand.

"Looks like you're out of options, Professor." Kobalt tosses the machete aside. Ignoring the deep cut in his hand, he advances. "Time to be done with you," he says, aiming the Sig.

Ribbons of light alternating from yellow to green to purple looking like the Aurora Borealis glow in the sky through a tower of tumultuous burning clouds behind Kobalt.

"It's amazing. I've never seen anything like it. Look behind you. Look at the sky."

"You and your old tricks. You must have watched too much TV growing up. I'm not falling for that," says Kobalt as he advances.

"No, I'm serious. The clouds and lights are beautiful. Unusual but beautiful," says Rick.

Kobalt and Rick both hear a thunderous rumbling in the sky.

Kobalt forcibly points the Sig at Rick. "Stay down." Kobalt looks over his shoulder to view the sky. "What the hell? What is it?"

"The only thing that causes a cloud structure like that is a nuclear explosion," Rick says.

Rick feels around inside his backpack. His fingers find the KA-Bar knife. He pulls the knife from the backpack and slips the blade from its sheath. Hundreds of fireballs fly out of the fiery cloud, streaking in all directions. Kobalt turns to face Rick as the KA-Bar knife flies.

"Nuclear? Why would they—?" Kobalt asks as the knife punctures his left eye, the blade driving deep into his skull. Kobalt screams and staggers as he tries to extract the knife.

Rick spots a cluster of fireballs heading toward the overpass. Rick uses the calculus in his mind to estimate the trajectory. He moves quickly, ignoring the pain in his side. He jumps over a cement barricade at the shoulder of the road and scrambles up under the overpass.

Kobalt uses his bloody hand to pull the long knife from his eye socket. Blood gushes from the empty black pit as Kobalt screams holding the knife above his head, firing the Sig recklessly.

"Damn you, Munday. I'm coming for you."

A volley of meteor fragments pepper the cars breaking glass and punching holes through aluminum and steel. A soccer ball sized rock blasts through Kobalt's lower back. Rick can see daylight through the gaping hole in the belly of the big man. Kobalt steps forward haltingly dropping the KA-Bar knife. The knife clinks on the pavement as Kobalt tries to scream. A deep, airy bellow echoes through the overpass. His knees buckle, and the big man falls to the pavement. There is no movement or sound from Kobalt, but Rick waits before moving from the protection of the overpass.

Rick stands over the bloody mess of the man who hunted him across a continent. "All I ever wanted was to get home to my family. You should have stayed at Salvation. Why couldn't you just leave me alone?"

Rick looks to the sky. Clouds churn with glowing bands of light radiating from the eruption in the sky. Rick thinks out loud. "Maybe if there was a large meteor, a city killer or worse, the government might try to blow it up with a nuke." Rick walks to the Indian Scout. "That doesn't explain the timing. It's too early in the day. Maybe this storm isn't following the rules."

Rick struggles to push the bike through a narrow gap between two cars. He turns the handlebars and gives the Scout a hard push. Finally, the bike moves forward. "If these oids aren't following the rules. I really need to get moving." Rick kick starts the Scout and rides down the highway.

Chapter 63: Fast Target

Camp David 5:40 p.m. EST

Cheers fill the underground conference room. "Congratulations, we just saved Los Angeles," declares President Baker.

As the room quiets, an analyst provides a recap. "At 5:35 p.m., an MK21 reentry vehicle launched from a Minuteman III ICBM successfully struck the large meteor fragment heading for Los Angeles. This was a very fast target. Our nuclear arsenal was not designed with the intent to target objects traveling through the atmosphere at over fifty thousand miles per hour. Our friends at Slingeren and JPL calculated the intercept path. It was a risky move, but the nuclear detonation disintegrated the meteor over the Mojave Desert. Small fragments are impacting unpopulated areas of the desert, causing no damage."

"An unmitigated success! Thanks to the quick actions of Tug Grimes, General Casey, and the fine men and women at Minot Air Force Base. You've saved Los Angeles from certain destruction," says President Baker.

"What's the status of the Beast's debris field?" asks Mitch.

The analyst checks the notes floating before him before speaking. "We are working closely with Dr. Simmons and his team to track the asteroid fragments. There are thousands of small pieces that will burn up high in the atmosphere. We've noted three hundred fifty fragments of significant size after detonation. At least seventy-five larger fragments will impact Western Europe or land in the North Atlantic. There is a minor chance of a tidal surge along the eastern seaboard. We will continue to monitor this and get warning messages out, if possible."

Mitch does some quick math. "That leaves two hundred seventy-five pieces of the Beast. What threat do they pose and what are we doing about them?"

The analyst steels himself before stating his grim report. "There is nothing we can do." The people in the conference room absorb the dire news silently. The analyst continues. "Many of the fragments are large but, most of them will land in the ocean. Some will cause severe damage, but we don't believe any are city killers and they are too small to target with ICBMs. The debris field is spreading out. You can see the projected path on the screen starting in the northeast, moving across the country to the southwest. Any place along the path is at risk. The fragments are traveling at high speed. A second or two means the difference between impacting Albuquerque or hitting Los Angeles. We can only hope the fragments stay aloft seconds longer, landing in the Pacific."

President Baker sinks in his chair. "At least we saved Los Angeles."

Chapter 64: Bridge to Nowhere

The Indian Scout roars down the highway. Rick is free of Kobalt, but new worries loom. He adjusts the round rearview mirror on the handlebars to view the magical display of undulating lights in the desert sky.

Rick rides past the town of Barstow and views a huge parking lot surrounded by outlet stores. The parking lot is strewn with clothing and store windows are broken.

Carlos and Alyssa walk together past the garden and up the stairs to the main level. The mood in the main gallery now feels more energetic, as Selina and the men of the hideaway undertake the grisly task of attending to the dead.

The windows in the main gallery display scenes of the bridge and the destruction beyond. One window shows Eddie and George moving the bodies of Gloria and the boys. Rodrigo pushes a wheelbarrow to the entrance.

Isabella distributes gloves to Courtney and Margot as they walk toward the entrance. Ethan follows his mother, pulling the large rubber gloves over his hands. Carlos takes a pair of gloves from his mother and heads down the tunnel. Alyssa follows. Isabella smiles sadly. Alma and Maria, the grandmothers stay in the mine with the younger children, keeping them busy in the galley, preparing lunch for the others.

The men struggle with Jefferies body, laying him heavily in the wheelbarrow. Edgar looks at the bodies on the crooked bridge and beyond. "There are so many. What will we do with them all?"

"The ground is too hard to dig graves," says George.

Selina is tearful, kneeling over the body of her friend. "We can't just move them out of the way. We must take care of them properly."

Rob thinks about the problem as he surveys the area. He looks at the old shipping container punctured with hundreds of holes. "We'll use the shipping container. Put all the bodies inside, then we'll burn them. It will be a crematory, their funeral pyre," Rob says, staring at the metal box.

Selina looks to the container, then says, "It's best."

Rob turns to Eddie. "Find a gas-powered vehicle. Hopefully, you can siphon enough fuel for a fire." Eddie nods.

The occupants of Munday's Hideaway begin the ghastly task of recovering the dead. One by one, they lay the bodies to rest inside the shipping container.

3:30 p.m. PST–Cajon Pass

Rick rides past Victorville and down the Cajon Pass, a steep, curvy portion of Highway 15 that descends from the high desert through the San Gabriel mountains and into the Los Angeles basin.

"Courtney and the kids could be anywhere, but I have faith that Rob took care of them. I'll head to his old mine first. If they aren't there, I'll check the house."

The eastern skies streak with a volley of flaming fireballs. This is not one or two meteors traversing alone across the open sky. This is a barrage of flaming rocks that spreads north to south in a curtain of fire chasing through the atmosphere. Rick catches the light in the sky in his peripheral vision. Turning his head, he views the wall of rocks.

"Dammit, can't you just let me get home!" Rick screams.

Pillars of black smoke billow behind Eddie as he walks up the road carrying a container filled with gas. The smoke rises from cars down the canyon filled with bodies and set ablaze.

Eddie steps inside the shipping container. They stacked the bodies along the sides, leaving a narrow aisle running the length of the container. He walks the length of the metal box, drenching the dead with fuel. Shaking out the last drops, he backs out of the container. Rob steps to the doorway, lights a match, and tosses it, igniting the funeral pyre. George shuts the door and secures the metal latch.

485

The occupants of Munday's Hideaway step away from the container and stand between the bent and punctured vehicles that litter the gravel area. They worked together as a team on the macabre project, helping each other without argument or complaint. Courtney holds Selina as she sobs. Isabella hugs them both. "I'm sorry for your friends, Selina. Sorry for everything." Selina nods acceptance as she cries.

Smoke drifts out of holes on the top and sides of the container. "We should say a few words," Edgar says, looking at Rob.

Rob clears his throat before speaking. "Terrible things are disrupting our lives in unimaginable ways. The storms will change the world forever. These people died horrible deaths. More will join them. We pray for them all; may they be at peace. Never again will they feel hunger or worry. They are blessed with endless slumber. It is the living who pain and struggle through each day. God, I thank you for the people standing with me. Together, we will conquer the trials before us and forge a new future for our children." Rob stands silently watching flames flicker out the of holes in the container.

"Thanks, Rob," says Edgar.

"Real nice," adds George, looking to the sky, blessing himself. He sees fury in the skies. "Hey, look at that. There's a ton of them." A barrage of flaming meteors fills the sky with trails of dark smoke.

Eddie turns to Uncle Rob. "Isn't it too early?"

Rob studies the sky. "Yes, early and intense. Get everybody inside."

Rodrigo sweats from the heat radiating from the burning container. "Carlos and Ethan get the ledge and help others get on to bridge." They set a bench seat from a pickup at the base of the ledge to function as a step, making it easier to transverse the six-foot gap. The boys run to the edge of the bridge and jump down, ready to help the others.

Isabella and Inez run with Selina to the bridge. Rob stands staring at the sky. Courtney grabs his hand, pulling him to move. Alyssa grabs his other hand. The three of them run together. The container and the sky burn behind them. Carlos and Ethan help everyone down the ledge. Once on the cement surface, they run across the tilted bridge to the hideaway. After everyone is down the mine shaft, Eddie locks the gate, locks the chain at the wooden door, and then secures the steel blast door.

Salvation, the Mojave Desert

Three levels down, fifty-three white robes eerily reflect light from a single lamp in the middle of the cement floor. Mother sits on the floor next to the elder Jacob. "I'm a fool," she whispers, trying to share her feelings in confidence, but her voice echoes off the hard cement walls. The others listen silently.

"Cuz the preacher's not coming?" asks Jacob.

"Apparently, we've been duped. The Preacher said Salvation is twelve levels deep, with rooms for three hundred fifty people, food stocked for seven years, a water supply, air filtration and power. The preacher sold it well. We have no power, no food or water. Salvation is a cement floor with a rusty old generator that smells of diesel. He told us everything was prepared. There were photos and videos; it didn't look like this," says Mother, in an exasperated tone.

The building rumbles from the sound of exploding meteors.

"You saved me, and you saved that big fella," Jacob whispers. "The building is strong; it'll hold."

Mother leans close to Jacob. "I'm so ashamed. I believed. With all my heart and soul, I believed. What will we do now?"

"Don't be ashamed. Belief and faith got you here. It's what got us all to Salvation. It saved your life and mine. Don't worry. When the big fella gets back, he'll help us figure out what's next." Jacob says.

"I pray he conquers his demons and comes back to us. To Salvation," Mother whispers.

Rick struggles to hold the old Indian steady as a blast of hot air buffets the cycle. Impacting meteors leave a trail of destruction across the Los Angeles basin. Rick watches the flaming missiles descend, losing sight of them below the foothills before they impact. Rick maneuvers the bike past burning cars, broken pavement, and the belongings of a once hopeful person. The world is burning;

death surrounds him. If anyone were alive, they'd see the silhouette of a faceless rider bathed in orange light, his black leather coat fluttering in the wind riding past death. Azusa Road and the mountain road that led to the hideaway are ahead. He is close, yet danger surrounds him.

President Baker sits in the conference room deep below Camp David. He waits to receive calls from world leaders. The US sent a warning announcing the impacts of fragments from the Beast. There are no calls. After the excitement of the past few days, it's eerily calm.

Cliff knows the crisis is not over. People are dying. The living will grow hungry. With the help of a mysterious group, he battled Colonel Cruikshank and saved hundreds of thousands of souls. Dr. Simmons and his team saved the planet from certain destruction. The result, while not perfect, is still a success. Earth and humanity will survive.

Cliff detects a low rumble, then... whack! It feels like he's inside a bank vault colliding with a jet plane. The room shakes and dust falls from the rafters. People in the conference room scream and run for cover.

Cliff holds on to the conference table, hoping to stop it from shaking. The cement floor buckles, rising and cracking. Cracks etch the walls and ceiling. Men burst into the conference room to drag him some place safer as he screams, "What the hell is happening?"

Thirty seconds later, a hot air blast rips through the beautifully forested Camp David compound at thirteen hundred miles per hour. The iconic wood frame structures collapse. The blast tosses autos in the parking area through the air. The hot wind ignites the buildings and trees. Fragments of the meteor and ejecta cover the ground. Some rocks are thirty feet in diameter crushing autos and smashing the remains of buildings. In minutes, material ejected from a nearby impact buries Camp David under five feet of fallout.

New Arcadia–Colonel Cruikshank's quarters

The old colonel sits at his desk, rubbing the knotted muscle in his leg.

Zsoldos enters. Cruikshank looks at the portly man with a haunted face. "Have you found any of them?"

"We sent Black Guard up the stairwell. There's no sign of the boys. Mahon must have them all."

"I'll send Kobalt to get them and take care of Mahon as well! Where is Kobalt? He isn't answering my calls."

"All three Scramjets were lost over Mesa Verde National Park. We believe the Air Force shot them down in a surprise attack. There has been no further contact from Captain Kobalt."

"Please tell me Kobalt got Munday."

"The Scramjets were attacking Munday's aircraft when they were shot down. The fate of Dr. Munday and his friends is unknown."

"Damn it. More incompetence. Kobalt should have finished him in New Arcadia."

"I've interviewed the two remaining boys. It appears they stayed by choice. They said it is an honor to serve you and New Arcadia."

"They will serve me. They will serve me well. I will live to see humanity reborn and emerge from our humble pod to repopulate Earth."

Rick curses the space rocks pelting Los Angeles as he navigates the bike up the rough road. Smoke fills the sky ahead. He imagines the worst, then pushes the thought from his mind. He passes burning cars and overturned trucks as meteors pound the canyon walls. A meteor strikes Rattlesnake Peak across the river. Seconds later, a hot blast of wind sends him tumbling to the ground. Lying on his stomach, he looks up to see a column of smoke rising upward. Rick pushes fear aside. He will know the fate of his family soon enough.

Incoming meteors fill the sky. He runs up a steady rise past crumpled cars lining the edge of the road. He crests a hill; shattered vehicles litter the widening road. Ahead on the left, a shipping container burns furnace hot with grayish-white smoke roiling out. Rick runs through the wrecks some of them upside down and others on their sides. The bridge ahead looks damaged and tilting.

He runs past the debris of a broken spacecraft, one half resting up against the hillside. A child's blood-stained shoe lies in the dirt. Rick gulps.

He runs to the bridge and jumps off the ledge to the bench seat as a meteor slammed into the road two hundred feet down the canyon. Rick hugs the wall of the cement ledge as the Earth rocks, causing the surface of the bridge to crack and buckle. The air blast sends the flaming container over the canyon wall crashing to the rocks one hundred feet below, bursting into flames.

Ethan and Carlos stand next to each other in the washroom. Ethan vigorously scrubs his hands. "They're clean, Ethan. That's enough," says Carlos. Ethan stops scrubbing, holding his hands in the stream of water. "I washed. I changed clothes. I can't get it off."

"Me too. The smell of the dead lingers in our mind. Maybe it's good, so we don't forget too quickly," Carlos says.

"I'll never forget, never," Ethan says, catching a towel Carlos tosses to him.

The boys walk to the main gallery. Alma and Maria are placing platters stacked with sandwiches on the long dining table. Junior and Princess set out pitchers of water while Claudia and Angel set glasses around the table.

Carlos and Ethan go directly for the food. "You boys wait for the rest," scolds Alma. The boys halt, looking woeful.

The reaction of the boys disturbs her. Their faces have changed. They are no longer boys. "Help yourselves. Save some for the rest," she says.

The other occupants of the hideaway emerge from their quarters and sit at the long table. They eat the sandwiches slowly. Everyone is kind and considerate of each other.

Rick picks his moment. He waits for a pause in the onslaught of meteors and runs across the deformed bridge. As he reaches the end of the bridge, a small meteor crashes into the mountainside high above, showering him with small rocks cascading down the hillside. He runs along the narrow trail to avoid getting caught in a landslide.

He steps around the rocky outcropping carefully as the trail narrows. A few yards past the outcropping, the mountain forms an alcove filled with bushes. A day before, the bushes kept the entrance to the hideaway well-hidden. Today the path is well worn.

Rick runs up the alcove to the chain-link fence. There is no foliage covering the fence, revealing the galvanized wire gate. He examines the locked fence and the dark tunnel beyond. The gate is secure, but the wire mesh along the top is bent out of shape. He steps in something gooey; a puddle of drying blood. Fear shoots through his body. He puts his fingers through the chain link and shakes the gate, yelling as another volley of meteors fill the skies.

The kids play VUE games while the adults linger at the long dining table. There is no urgency or stress. They aren't going anywhere. There is no job, no school, no concerns about rent or bills. The man-made worries of the world have fallen away. Life will continue in the hideaway.

The windows in the hideaway display the tilting bridge. Nobody pays attention to the firestorm raging outside until a meteor strikes the road, sending the flaming shipping container over the cliff.

The sudden movement catches Isabella's attention. She gasps. "It's gone! Dear God! It went over the cliff!" Isabella exclaims. Everyone turns to look at the window. The shipping container is gone.

Rob watches as the camera cycles to the next view. "We'll investigate when it's safe. There's nothing we can do now."

"I'm glad it's gone. Looking at it every day would be a sad reminder," says Rodrigo.

Eddie sees a black bundle at the far end of the bridge. "Carlos. Did you leave something on the bridge?"

"No," Carlos replies without looking away from his game.

The dark object stands. Selina shrieks. Others in the hideaway gasp when they see a scary-looking man wearing a black helmet and a black leather jacket run across the bridge, his face hidden behind a dark visor.

"Will this horror never end?" asks Inez.

"He looks mean," says George.

"Another straggler who found his way up the canyon. He may have been watching us while we were outside," says Rob.

Selina sits with a hand over her mouth, viewing the window as the camera cycles.

"He'll find the entrance. It's easy to find now," says Rodrigo.

"We can't do this again. Whoever it is, let him in. He's looking for safety. We agreed to let the others..." Courtney says as her voice fades, unable to finish the sentence.

The window displays the man in black running along the trail, disappearing around the rocky outcropping.

"He looks like a tough guy. What if he has a gun?" asks Edgar.

"Look at that helmet. He could be from a biker gang. What if he's mean and kills us all?" asks George.

Rick shakes the fence, screaming and pleading for the gate to be unlocked. Meteors explode high above. Rick ducks against the mountainside, trying to protect himself from an air blast and flying debris.

"What luck. I make it all the way home, only to die at the locked gate of Rob's hideaway. Someone has been here. Someone died here. I hope Courtney wasn't locked out," Rick says.

"We have weapons. Eddie and Rodrigo arm the men. We'll keep this guy under guard until we're satisfied he's friendly," orders Rob.

Courtney watches anxiously, waiting for the camera to cycle. The men move down the mine shaft. Rodrigo and Eddie enter the weapons room, grabbing rifles and pistols.

"Once we open the blast door, we're vulnerable. I'll call out some questions. Let's see his reaction. If he's peaceful, I'll unchain the wooden door, but keep your guns at the ready," Rob instructs as Rodrigo and Eddie pass weapons to George and Edgar.

The camera cycles. The scary man has pushed his body against the mountainside, hiding from an air blast. Dirt and dust obstruct the view.

Rick calls out again. Realizing he's screaming into his helmet; he pulls it off and tosses it to the ground. He sees the glint of a camera lens mounted inside the cave. "Uncle Rob! Courtney! Let me in. Let me in!"

When the dust clears. Courtney sees Rick's face and sobs breathlessly, unable to speak.

Alyssa runs to the window calling out, "It's Daddy! It's Daddy!"

Ethan stands at the windows. "It's our dad, don't shoot." He runs down the mine shaft. "Uncle Rob. Don't shoot. It's Dad. It's my dad!"

"You're sure?" asks Rob, his voice echoing through the tunnel.

"Yes. He came back to us," Ethan cries out.

Rodrigo and Eddie push the blast door open. Rob pushes through as soon as the heavy door is wide enough and rushes to the wooden door, unlocking the heavy chain. Ethan and the men follow as Rob moves to the chain-link fence.

Rob spots Rick through the fence. "Ricky, boy! You made it."

Rick's body drained of energy slumps against the rock wall next to the gate. "One gate to go and I'll be home," he says in an exhausted tone.

The lock clicks, Rob pushes the gate open. Rick stands at the entrance and gets hit full force by Ethan running into him, hugging him around the waist. Rob joins the hug. "Welcome home, boy."

Meteors explode above. "Let's get inside," Rob says.

Rick walks to the wooden door and sees Rodrigo, Eddie, George, and Edgar all holding guns. "Is this the Munday's Hideaway posse?"

Ethan grabs Rick's hand. "You looked scary. We didn't know it was you."

Rob leads Rick to the main gallery. Courtney stands frozen in the middle of the room. Alyssa runs to her father. He lifts her and kisses her repeatedly until she squirms in his arms. Rick sets his daughter down and steps to his wife. Courtney rushes to her husband. He sweeps her up in his arms, holding her tightly, and kisses her passionately.

Courtney kisses her husband madly. "I knew you would get back to us. I never lost hope," she sobs.

"I've been trying to get home. I didn't think it would take this long. I had a few detours along the way."

The Martinez family members stand silently watching the reunion.

Courtney pushes Rick back to get a look at him. "You look tough. Where did you get the jacket?" she asks, pulling the duster jacket open. "And the suit looks strange. Are you hurt?"

"Probably," Rick says, putting a hand to his ribs.

"Where have you been Ricky Boy?" asks Rob.

"That's a long story," Rick says as he's surrounded in a group hug.

As the occupants of Munday's Hideaway sit in their cozy home protected by a mountain of granite. The world outside suffers through many nights of intense bombardment.

Humans struggle to survive the terror by scurrying like rats into sewers and culverts. If they live in a city with underground parking garages or buildings with basements, they bargain and compete for protective space. Those unable to find a hole sit at home in the dark, hoping the storm will spare them. Millions die.

The storms intensify night after night with unrelenting aerial explosions and impacts, destroying cities and towns, setting forests and grasslands ablaze.

As each day dawns, survivors slowly emerge from their humble sanctuaries to pick through scraps in stores or search empty houses for food and water. They spend the day preparing for the next night's torment while fending off their most terrifying predator; other humans.

For those not living in the hideaway or in an underground city, it seems the storms will never end. Despair replaces hope. The struggle to exist without sustenance exhausts human energy. Hopelessness leads many to walk through the night, begging for the rocks to fall upon them. A request easily fulfilled.

Ramp to Level Two–New Arcadia

James and Davey stand outside the tall door, looking up the ramp to the Parklands. "Come inside, boy's the storm is fierce. They're coming in hot and heavy tonight. We need to close the door," says Sargent Cheung as the sky brightens from an exploding meteor.

"They're still out there," says James.

"Who's out there? Nobody should be outside."

"Zekiel, Aidan and Owen went out to help, but they haven't come back," cries Davey, as the ground shakes from a nearby impact.

"Sorry, boys. They should have come in with everyone else. They're gone by now. Nobody survives out there. I'm closing the door," says Cheung as he reaches for the button to lower the motorized door.

"No!" Davey cries, pushing Cheung away from the switch box.

"Wait. Please. Just another minute," James pleads as a blast of air rushes through the door, bringing a dusting of white powder.

The thousands of new residents of Level Two, the survivors from the Parklands, look toward the wind and the tall door.

Standing at the top of the ramp are three boys silhouetted by the angry, glowing sky. They walk down the ramp, the occupants of Level Two present as witness.

"They walked through the storm," cries a voice. "They survived the blast," shouts another.

The boys walk three abreast down the ramp. "No one survives the storms," cries a voice in the crowd. "They should be dead," calls another. "Yet they live," a woman shouted.

The boys pass through the ramp door. To the astonishment of everyone, white dust covers the boys from head to toe. The crowd surrounds the boys. People crying out. "It's a miracle." "They came out of the storm." "They are blessed."

One man kneels at the feet of the boys. A woman kneels, followed by another man, causing a cascade of people kneeling before the boys covered in white powder as the metal door rolls down behind them.

"Hey get up. What are you doing? Don't kneel," Aiden calls out.

"We're the same as you. Stand," says Owen.

Mike McCoy

"You're supposed to worship God. Not us," Zekiel calls out.

For the great day of his wrath is come; and who shall be able to
stand?

The Author

Mike McCoy is an international businessman and entrepreneur who has traveled extensively and worked in the consumer electronics industry for over twenty-five years. The company he founded developed a variety of innovative products which sold in retail stores around the world. Mike is also an accomplished athlete  known for long distance events. He completed a full Ironman Triathlon in 2006. He thought running fifty miles would be a wonderful accomplishment, so for his fiftieth birthday, he ran a double Marathon (52.4 miles). In 2018, Mike celebrated his sixtieth birthday with a six-hundred-mile bike ride from Florence, Oregon, to San Francisco, California. Somehow, he found time to write.

Asteroids – Bridge to Nowhere is his first novel.

Check the website for news and updates
www.MikeMcCoy.me

also, on Facebook

www.facebook.com/AuthorMikeMcCoy